THE
TOP OF
THE HILL

THE TOP OF THE HILL

IRWIN SHAW

DELACORTE PRESS/NEW YORK

TO MARIAN

VOLUME
ONE

CHAPTER ONE

It was by chance that he met Dunky Aldridge on Thursday on Fifth Avenue after work. It was an unlucky meeting, although they greeted each other cordially and had had good times together and had drunk considerable beer in each other's company. But on Saturday morning, Aldridge was one of the two men who were killed.

"Where've you been, Mike?" Aldridge asked. "I haven't seen you around the drop zone in months. Sneaking away doing secret jumps?"

"I got married three months ago," Michael said, feeling that was enough reason for any absence.

"Congratulations." Aldridge slapped him on the back. He was a burly, red-faced man who had played football in college. They had both started skydiving at the same time at the field and had made many jumps together. "How's it going?" Aldridge asked.

"Euphoric," Michael said.

"Slippers and fireside time now?" Aldridge asked. He laughed, because they were the same age—thirty. "Keeping away from the old pernicious haunts?"

"More or less."

"Would it be against your marriage vows to have a drink with an old pal?"

Michael looked at his watch. "Half-hour before I have to report for duty in the kitchen," he said.

to New York, with the shadows of the afternoon already streaking the road, at least that. He put out his hand to touch hers. Her hand lay still, her face averted as she stared out the window. "I'm sorry," he said.

"Please don't say anything," she said. "For a long while."

When they got to the apartment, he made himself a drink, but when he asked if she wanted one, she merely shook her head and went into the bedroom and lay down, fully clothed, coat and all, as though her bones, to their marrow, were freezing.

He must have fallen asleep sitting in the easy chair, the empty glass on a table beside it, when she came in. She still had on her coat and scarf. He had never seen her face so pale. "You're not ever going to do anything like that again, are you?"

"I don't know," he said. "Maybe next week. Maybe next year."

"Next week?" she said incredulously. "What sort of man are you?"

"Several kinds."

"Don't you love me?"

"I love you. But I don't want to be a man who loves you and lives scared."

"What're you trying to prove?"

"Nothing. Everything. I'll find out later."

"You didn't tell me all this time."

"The subject didn't come up."

"Well, the subject has come up now."

"I'm sorry, darling, I can't honestly promise anything."

"I thought the man was your friend."

"He was. If it'd happened to me, he'd be up next week."

"Macho idiot," she said contemptuously.

"It isn't even that."

"What is it, then?"

He shrugged. "When I find out, when I really understand, I'll tell you."

She sat down opposite him. There was only one lamp on, at the other end of the room, and her face was in shadow, only her eyes glistening. She had waited to cry. At least she had waited. Strong woman.

"Michael," she said, "I have something to tell you." Her tone was flat and emotionless and troubling.

While he was sleeping in the chair he had dreamt that Tracy had

They went into the Gotham bar and they were there more than thirty minutes and had more than three Scotches.

"You still look in pretty good shape," Aldridge was saying. "In fact, I'd say marriage has leaned you down a bit."

"I do my push-ups."

"Listen, we've got two pretty hot new shots at the field. We're doing a four-man star on Saturday morning. If we find a fourth. Like you, for example."

Michael hesitated. Since he had met Tracy, his wife, he hadn't done any free-falls. Or anything much but think about her and spend as much time as he could with her and get through his chores at the office. The sight of his friend stirred old memories. Aldridge wasn't really his friend, except in the rough comradeship around the DZ and in the nearby saloon—they had never even had dinner together and Michael had not thought of inviting him to the wedding and he didn't know whether Aldridge was a Republican or a Democrat or a Maoist or if he was married or was rich or poor or even why he was called Dunky. But they had always gotten along well with each other and Michael trusted him.

"It sounds like a nice idea," he said.

"Bring the lady. Give her a thrill. Her old man dropping out of the sky like a shining angel."

"Maybe I will. If I can get her out of bed. Saturday mornings're tough."

"Tell her it's her chance to meet some fine, upstanding, red-blooded American boys."

"I'll pass the word along," Michael said. He took Aldridge's office telephone number and promised he'd call him in the morning.

Aldridge insisted upon paying for the drinks, as a wedding present, he said, and they went out and Michael got a cab and went uptown, hoping he didn't smell too strongly of Scotch.

Over dinner, which was laid on a table in front of the fire, he stared entranced at his wife and thought of how Aldridge's eyes and the eyes of the other men at the field would light up when they saw her. He told her about the plan for Saturday morning and she frowned. "Jumping out of airplanes," she said. "Isn't that for kids?"

"They're all men, about my own age."

"What do you do it for?"

"Fun," he said. He had known her for more than five months but he hadn't ever told her what other kinds of fun he had indulged in before they met. Time to begin, he thought. "Haven't you ever had a feeling you'd like to fly?"

"Not that I remember."

"One of the mythical longings of the race," he said. "Remember Icarus."

"Not such a happy example," Tracy said, laughing.

"Anyway, you could try it, too. Not free-fall, at least not at first. Just attached to a line that opens your parachute automatically. The earth never looks quite that beautiful again. A lot of girls do it."

"Not this girl," Tracy said decisively.

"Still, will you come?"

"Why not?" She struggled. "If my husband's crazy I might as well find out what he's crazy about. Anyway, I have nothing else to do on Saturday morning."

It was a bright sunny day as they drove out of New York toward the field in New Jersey. As usual, when he left the city, Michael felt exhilarated. Tracy, beside him in the car, dressed in a loose wool coat with a scarf against the brisk autumn weather, gleamed, fresh and excited, like a coed going to a football game with her best beau and looking forward eagerly to the evening's parties.

"There's a great country restaurant not far from the field," Michael told her as they turned north on the Jersey side of the river, where the trees were fading into muted russets and gold along the road. "For lunch. Wonderful daiquiris and lobster."

"Ummn." She looked across at him curiously. "Aren't you scared?"

"Sure," he said. "I'm scared the other fellas're going to think I married a dog."

She leaned over and kissed him. "Next time, I'll have my hair done."

McCain, who ran the jump center and who had taught Michael how to free-fall, was waiting at the shed with the other two men who were to make the jump, and the plane was warming up on the strip. McCain had laid out the target area on the grass, which had just begun to turn damp after the night's frost. The men were affable and polite and obviously impressed with Tracy. McCain, usually a man with the rough manners of an old top sergeant, even said, "Mrs.

Storrs, if you'd like to come along for the ride, there's room. You can be the jump master."

"I'll just stay planted on the ground where I belong, Mr. McCain, if it's all the same to you," Tracy said. "One bird in the family is enough."

McCain grinned and said there was a pot of coffee on the stove in the shed if she got cold.

As the men walked out toward the plane, Aldridge whispered, "Holy man, Mike."

"I don't know what you're talking about," Michael said innocently.

"That's what I call a fitting audience for our skill and daring is what I mean, you sneaky bastard."

Then McCain was explaining how they were going to do the relative work, as free-fall multiple maneuvers were called—giving them the sequence in which they were to exit, reminding them to break away at 3,500 feet, no matter how well or poorly they made the star, so that they would have the necessary five seconds to get safely away from each other before they opened their chutes at 2,500 feet. It was all old stuff to the four men, but they listened carefully. If McCain suspected that anybody's attention was wandering he was just as lief to call the whole flight off.

They got into the plane, McCain at the controls, with the door stripped off, the doorway open, the wind gusting in, cold and biting. They gained speed and took off. Michael looked out the window and saw the small figure in the blue coat standing waving next to the shed. Maybe, he thought, one day I'll get her to see what it's like.

At 7,200 feet, they jumped, one after the other. They made a good star at 3,500, planing and meeting up and touching hands in a circle, then peeling away from each other. Aldridge was the fourth man out. They had separated as programmed, when, for some reason that nobody would ever discover, the third man opened his chute immediately. Aldridge crashed into it at about one hundred and twenty-five miles an hour, and hit the man as the chute collapsed. The doctor later said they were both killed instantly, so they were spared the terror as they streamed down to earth, while Michael and the other man, swinging safely from their parachutes, and McCain at the controls of the plane, watched helplessly.

At least she didn't cry, Michael thought as they drove slowly back left him and he had searched, first in the empty apartment, then vainly in the darkened streets for her, almost seeing her, a flick of cloth disappearing around a stone corner. "You're not going to tell me you're leaving me, are you?"

"No," she said, still in the flat dead voice. "The opposite of that. What I have to tell you is that from now on, after today, I'm going to stop taking the pill. I want to have a child."

He stood up then and slowly walked, without speaking, to the window and looked down. In the light of a streetlamp down below an old woman with a cane was being helped out of a taxi. It's the wrong thing to be seeing at this moment, Michael thought, the inevitable decay and the approach of death when the start of a new life is the subject of conversation.

"Well?" Tracy said.

He turned and tried to smile at her. "Well, give a man a little time to think." He went over to her and bent and kissed the top of her head. She sat rigidly. "You have to admit, it's pretty sudden."

"What's sudden about it? You may disappear like that." She snapped her fingers, the sound like ice crackling in the quiet room. "I don't want to be left with nothing—nothing. Anyway we've been married three months. I'm twenty-nine years old. You're thirty. As far as I know you may never see thirty-one. How old was your mother when you were born?"

"What's the difference?"

"How old?"

"Twenty-three."

"Well . . . ?"

"Those were different times."

"Every second is a different time. That doesn't stop people from getting born." She moved to the sofa and sat down on it. "Come here and sit by me."

He went over and sat next to her. She was shivering under her coat. I must refuse, he thought, to surrender to her anguish. "I destroyed my mother," he said gravely. "I think the real reason she died so young was me. She never admitted it even to herself, I think, but she knew I hated her."

"Those are the risks you take."

"Not necessarily," he said. "There's no law I know of in America that says, 'Go thou now and procreate.'" He sighed. "And I was the unhappiest and most unappealing little boy anybody had ever seen. At the age of twelve I was contemplating suicide."

"You're not twelve anymore. You're a big grown man with a good job and a bright future and a wife, who as far as I know, loves you."

"Let me tell you something about my job"—if ever there was a time for truth and resolution this was it—"I despise it. If I thought I had to continue in it for the rest of my life I'd be the twelve-year-old boy again, contemplating suicide."

"Melodrama," she said harshly.

"Call it what you will," he said. "With a family I'd be locked in for good. The chains would be permanent."

"I suppose I qualify as one of the chains, too."

"You know I don't think that."

"I don't know what you think." She stood up. "I'm going out for a walk. I don't want to talk about it anymore tonight."

He watched her stride toward the door and click it shut behind her. Then he sat at the table before the fire and poured himself a glass of whiskey.

He was still there at the table, with the bottle of half-finished whiskey in front of him, when she came back. She didn't greet him, but went into the bedroom.

When he went in two hours later, walking unsteadily, the light was out and she was asleep or pretending to be asleep. When he got into bed she did not make her usual move toward him and for the first night since they were married they didn't make love.

He couldn't sleep and he got out of bed and went back to the living room and the second half of the whiskey bottle.

I remember Mama, he thought drunkenly. The title of an old play. He sat staring into the semidarkness.

CHAPTER
TWO

Michael Storrs Jr. stopped being Jr. at the age of five, when his father was killed in a barroom brawl. Lila Storrs, the mother of Michael Jr., a fragile, overeducated, incompetent beauty of twenty-eight, called the death irresponsible. The elder Storrs had been an executive in his father-in-law's bank in Syracuse and as far as anyone knew was not in the habit of patronizing saloons. He had stopped in at the bar on his way home after what had been perhaps an especially wearing day at the bank and while sipping his first glass of bourbon had witnessed an extremely bloody fight between two of the other men at the bar and had stepped between them and tried to get them to quit. One of the contestants, later identified as a man who had been released three days before from the Mattewan Prison for the Criminally Insane, had pulled a knife and killed the young banker with one stroke.

Later in life the son was to come to the conclusion that his mother's description of his father's death was inaccurate. If anything, Michael Storrs Sr. was killed in the praiseworthy attempt to be responsible—to his class, the law of the land and the civil relations one expected to be shown in public places by the citizens of a peaceful democracy.

Certainly the death could have been avoided—Storrs could have stepped quietly down to the other end of the bar or merely paid for his drink and slipped out—but Mrs. Storrs, who loved her husband dearly, held the firm conviction that in moving to the center of violence he had put last things first, had forgotten his wife and only child and risked the entire family's happiness for the sake of an aberrant whim or a mild distaste at being forced to endure the sight of two ruffians disturbing the pleasure of his first drink of the day.

"He was killed for a feather," she said, somewhat obscurely.

◇◇◇◇◇

The effects were momentous, especially for the fatherless son. His mother made a nunnery out of widowhood, vowed never to marry again and to devote her life to the care and upbringing of the boy in such a way that the accidents of life would leave him uninvolved and forever safe. Thus the boy was overindulged, overprotected, overfed on highly nourishing and scientifically chosen foods, kept from the hurly-burly of ordinary childhood, forbidden to climb trees, go out for teams, consort with rough children, play with toy guns or bows and arrows and to go to and from the neighborhood school unescorted. His mother drove him to school in the morning and watched until the students were assembled in the yard and marched off to class, and she was there waiting at the gate, standing, watching anxiously, to drive him home when the children came trooping out of the building in the afternoon. When other boys were playing baseball, young Michael was practicing the piano, for which he had no talent. During the summer vacations, when his classmates sported in swimming pools and on beaches and perilous playgrounds, he was taken, well guarded against sunstroke and offensive foreigners, on extended tours of museums and churches in France, Italy and England, since along with the other burdens the boy had to bear there was the heavy weight of his mother's family's wealth to confound him. In the evenings, along with recapitulations of the wonders they had seen that day, he was treated to loving lectures on proper behavior. Profanity was an evil in the eyes of God, masturbation was the cause of untold disasters in later life, sly little girls and wicked older men would try to lure him into corners where unmentionable temptations would be offered to him, belligerence had led to his father's death and contributed to wars in which beautiful young men like himself were killed in the millions. He was the staff upon which she must lean and she would always expect him to remember her words, even after her death; he had a fine and promising future and his grandfather would be there to help him in every possible way if his grandfather thought he was worth it; he was the only thing she loved in this world and he must never, never disappoint her. If Freud had been at the table his giant groan would have been heard from Vienna to Catalina Island.

The result was to be expected. By the time he was twelve Michael was a fat, secretive, clumsy boy, melancholy and precociously bright in class, a trait that somehow did not gain him the affection of his teachers. When his mother observed even the slightest signs of restiveness on the part of her son—pouting at the piano, embarrassment at being delivered and picked up at school like an infant, raising his voice when excited—there were no overt punishments, no slaps, no deprivations, no going to bed without dinner. His mother, Michael learned early, could exact retribution with a sigh, a tear, a sad look up to heaven. He envied his classmates their tales of a good solid beating by irate parents. Meticulously dressed among his peers, who came to school looking like a last battalion of retreating Confederate troops, he became the natural butt of the wits and the bullies who surrounded him and he learned to dread recess periods, where, in the whirl of games and wrestling and whooping, he would be singled out for torture.

He knew enough to keep his schoolyard agonies to himself. If he mentioned a word of them to his mother she would storm into the office of the principal immediately to complain. In two hours the entire student body would hear about it and what he had endured until then would seem like the most friendly and benign youthful mischief in comparison.

From time to time he regarded the mantelpiece photograph of his father, handsome and negligent in a T-shirt and jeans aboard a small sailboat, and reflected upon how different his own life would have been if his father had not gone on that fatal afternoon into a bar for a drink. He had a dim memory that once or twice he had been taken onto the boat for an afternoon's outing, tied to the mast and in a life jacket. It was almost the only memory he retained of his father, smiling and graceful at the rudder in the sunshine. The boat had been sold a month after his father was buried.

His grandparents, to whose large house he was taken every Sunday for lunch, didn't seem very interested in him. There were the usual routine questions about school and then he was forgotten as the grown-ups talked. He was not encouraged to join the conversations. His mother had explained that her parents, like herself, detested unmannerly children. She had told him often that when she saw how other people allowed their brats to career noisily around at family gatherings she congratulated herself that he was so different.

Once, on a warm Sunday afternoon when he was alone on the porch of the great old house, he overheard his aunt, a young woman whom he thought was the most beautiful creature he had ever seen, saying to his grandmother, ". . . she is *devouring* him. We must find her a lover—or at least a husband, or he'll turn out to be the most doleful fat mess we've ever seen."

He had known instinctively that his aunt was speaking of him and, true to his mother's strictures on eavesdropping, had moved silently away from the window. But he had resolved then and there that one day he would show them all. He knew he was too young to escape, but his dreams were full of himself riding wild horses, fighting wars and carousing among the rouged, lascivious women whose photographs he had glimpsed in the pornographic magazines that were sometimes left behind in the classrooms.

He was rewarded for exemplary behavior with Saturday afternoons at symphony concerts, trips to the zoo, a phonograph of his own on which he was allowed to play his mother's classical records, and by large books with colored reproductions of the same sort of paintings he saw in the summers in Italy and France. And he developed an abhorrence of art that would last for years.

As a gesture in the direction of physical fitness his mother hired a lady tennis pro to give him lessons in the sport, as being one in which he would meet a better class of playmates than in football or baseball. He played three times a week on the overgrown court behind his grandparents' house, watched closely by his mother to see that he didn't overexert himself or neglect to put on his sweater when he had finished. He was clumsy and self-conscious on the court and he knew the lady pro scorned him and was relieved when she received an offer for a job and departed for Florida, leaving him with a distaste for tennis that equalled his loathing for art.

There was no television set in the house to give him unhealthy notions of what the adult world was like, and the only radio on the premises was in his mother's room, which he was allowed to visit only by invitation.

They lived in Syracuse, where the winters were rude and cold, and his mother dressed him in a manly little warm overcoat and a fur hat with earflaps. Among the seasonal diversions at recess was a game in which one of the bigger boys would grab Michael's cap and then pass it around as Michael ran, panting, trying to intercept it as it flew from hand to hand. As the bell rang for the end of recess, the last boy would toss the hat over the wire fence, which meant that he would have to run all the way to the gate and out of the yard to retrieve it, which made him late to get in line to go up to his classroom and earned him disapproving remarks from the teachers in charge, who never appeared in the yard before the bell rang.

What he couldn't know at the time was that similar indignities, equal cruelties, worse repressions, had through the ages formed poets and heroes. All he could do was endure and hope that his mother would die.

The most painful moment of his schoolboy career came when the usual game with his hat was being played and a boy his size, Joseph Ling by name, caught his hat just before it was time for the bell to ring. Ling didn't throw the hat over the fence as usual, but held on to it and said, "If you want it, fight me for it."

There was a sudden hush as the other boys gathered round. Fighting, in Michael's mother's list of prohibitions, was the lowest of vices, lower even than masturbation. Ling had a sneering, monkeylike little snubbed face as though there hadn't been enough stuff in his parents' genes to give their son a full-size human nose or eyes, and Michael trembled with the desire to hit him. But his mother's admonition—"Your father died in a fight, never forget that"—was too firmly graven on his brain for him to move. He just stood there in the iron schoolboy hush and said not a word.

Contemptuously, Ling dropped the pretty fur hat into the dirty snow at his feet and ground it with his boot.

Then the bell rang. Silently Michael walked over and picked up the hat and put it on his head and got into line. As he marched toward the classroom he decided to kill himself, and spent the rest of the school day contemplating the various modes of suicide open to him. Later, through the years, he would dream of the moment and awake, sweating at the memory of it.

The next day, the game was repeated. Only now, even the bare tolerance that the boys had shown of him before was gone. As he ran after his hat, he was tripped and sent sprawling and a chant of "Pansy! Pansy!" echoed mockingly on all sides. Finally, Ling got the hat and, just as he had the day before, stood still with it and said, "If you want it, fight for it."

Michael knew there was no other way out. And suddenly he didn't want any other way out. He walked slowly up to Ling and hit him in the face with all his force. Ling fell back a step, more surprised than hurt, and Michael was all over him, hitting wildly, oblivious of everything but the sneering, unfinished face in front of him, an exaltation he had never known before sweeping over him as he hit, was hit, fell tangled with the boy in the muddied snow, felt his nose begin to bleed, punching, kicking, trying to strangle, being strangled in turn, unconscious that the bell had rung, that a man was bending over him, trying to tear the boys apart.

Finally they were pulled to their feet, the two faces bloodied, the hat a trampled mess, the manly little coat torn at the shoulder and filthy. "You wanted a fight, you motherfucker," Michael said, "you got it." He didn't know where the word came from, or what it really meant, and he certainly had never used it before, but it gave him great satisfaction to say it and he repeated it loudly. "Motherfucking little shit." It was like a stream of pure music and he listened to himself, marveling, ignoring the teacher, who was saying, "Enough of that, Storrs, enough. You're in enough trouble as it is."

"Go fuck yourself, Mr. Folsom," Michael said, high on his personal wave.

"Your mother is going to hear of this, Storrs," Folsom said. He was a bachelor of thirty-five who had made a point of talking archly to his mother from time to time when she came to fetch him.

"Let her hear of it," Michael said, suddenly weary.

"Now, get in line," Mr. Folsom said.

Michael didn't put his hat on but threw it over the fence himself. And he didn't try to brush the dirt off the manly little coat, not on the way up to the classroom or when school was over and he went out of the gate to where his mother was waiting beside her car.

When she saw him she began to weep.

"What's there to cry about, for Christ's sake?" he said.

"Get in the car," she wept.

"I'm walking home." And hatless, carrying his briefcase, the blood caked on his face, he walked steadily away.

◇◇◇◇◇

He never went back to the school that was just five blocks from his home and was considered one of the best public schools in Syracuse. Instead, he was put in a private school a hundred miles from home, where, his mother said, boys were taught to be gentlemen and fighting was not permitted. He bore everything in silence, even the interview with the headmaster, where his mother made it clear to the headmaster that her son was not to be allowed to go out for any of the teams, was to be punished when he used bad language and was on no occasion to be allowed off the school grounds, except in the company of herself or a designated member of her family.

He had said nothing but "Yes, Mother" or "No, Mother" since the fight and he said nothing when she kissed him good-bye after inspecting his room in the dormitory. As she left him, he smiled. Now he knew it was not necessary for her to die. Escape was possible.

He made no more friends at the new school than he had at the old, but it was a small quiet place with a teacher for every ten boys and so rigidly disciplined that there was no fighting or bullying. Students who wished to be left alone were permitted to go their own way as long as they kept their marks up to a respectable standard and broke none of the school rules.

What Michael's mother had not realized was that adjoining the school grounds there was a hill with a tow to which the entire student body was led by the physical education teachers four times a week to ski. For the first time in his life, Michael began to feel the exhilaration of grace and speed and soon became so daring a skier he had to be warned time and time again by his instructors to slow down. When the coach of the ski team suggested that he write a letter to Michael's mother explaining that Michael could become the star of the team, Michael shook his head obdurately and forbade him to communicate with his mother. When she came to visit him on Saturday afternoons, he hid his ski clothes and boots in a locker in the gymnasium basement. His skiing was a secret he guarded for himself. He did not mean to offend his mother or worry her; he merely wished to deceive her.

His deception went further. Having glimpsed on skis the zestful uses of his body, he made a grim resolve to lose weight. He worked out regularly in solitary dedication, on the pulleys, ropes and parallel bars in the school gymnasium, and was rewarded by the newfound tone and strength of his muscles, the leanness of his face, the loose-limbed spring in his step. His mother, when he accompanied her in his gray flannel slacks and blue blazer to a nearby restaurant on Saturday afternoon, was pleased by the improvement in his looks and demeanor and innocently congratulated herself on her choice of the school for her son, without wondering how the change had come about. His manners with her were docile and respectful and it was easy for him to maintain them, since he only saw his mother for a few hours every weekend. She, in her turn, went back to Syracuse to boast to her parents that Michael had suddenly grown into a very handsome tall young man and advised all of her friends with boys around Michael's age to send them to the school.

When the skiing season was over, still obeying his mother's injunction to keep away from team sports, he ran cross-country, a lonely, melancholy, determined figure, four miles every afternoon. When the students from an associated girls' school came over for a dance, he even managed to kiss a chubby pretty little girl of fourteen he had smuggled out of the gymnasium and lured into the shadow of the field house.

By now convinced that he could plan his own life, subterraneously, so to speak, he worked unflaggingly at his studies and led his class, with especially high marks in mathematics, for which he had a special talent. He had set his heart on going to Stanford University—first because it was the farthest he could get from Syracuse and secondly because California, with its benevolent climate and athletic population, would give him the widest choice of the sports that had begun to capture his imagination, such as skiing, surfing and sex. Older than his years, honed by duplicity, he aimed himself like a projectile toward a life that would outrage his mother and serve as a revenge for the first twelve years he had suffered.

Each summer, a few selected boys, accompanied by teachers, made a bicycle tour of France. With the help of a letter from the headmaster, he wheedled his mother into allowing him to go along. With some coaching from Michael, the headmaster in his letter said little about the rough means of travel and the primitive hostels at which the group would be quartered but emphasized the educational advantages of the tour. Michael had told the headmaster about his mother's summer voyages with him on the Continent and the headmaster cleverly suggested that Mrs. Storrs could join the group at certain selected temples of culture. Not without many misgivings,

Mrs. Storrs had finally agreed and had busied herself furnishing a large suitcase with medicines against all varieties of European illnesses that Michael might be likely to contract on the voyage.

Then, just before Mrs. Storrs was due to fly to Paris to join Michael at the group's stop there, her mother had died. Mrs. Storrs had to cancel her trip to care for her father and Michael enjoyed the most glorious summer of his life and, with the help of the smattering of French he had picked up on his travels with his mother, lost his virginity to a waitress in Rheims and became furiously addicted to women from that time on.

Again and again, he blessed the name of Joseph Ling.

He was graduated at the age of seventeen, a handsome, powerful young man, a loner who had won the first prize in mathematics and had been accepted by Harvard, Yale, Columbia and Stanford. Without telling his mother about it, he had made a secret trip to Syracuse to talk to his grandfather, who would have to pay for his years at college. In a long session with the old man, who had gone to Yale, but who had not liked it there, Michael had pointed out that Stanford was preeminent in the country in the fields of mathematics and the sciences and that his future would most certainly be brighter if he attended there. His grandfather, who was pleasantly surprised by the intelligent, persuasive and good-looking young man who, he thought, resembled himself at that age and who had developed so unexpectedly from the most unlikely material, agreed with Michael's choice and told him that he would make his mother see the light, although she had decided on Harvard for her son, since Cambridge was easily accessible from Syracuse. But the grandfather had made one proviso. He had known other brilliant students who had fallen in love with the academic life, had gone on to years of M.A.'s and Ph.D.'s and had wound up teaching in piddling, unheard-of colleges, and he wanted Michael to promise that when he got his degree from Stanford he would go to a business school, either Harvard or Wharton, at the University of Pennsylvania, and thereafter devote himself to a sensible career in the business world.

Michael promised and went back gaily to the graduation exercises at the school.

His mother wept as she drove him back to Syracuse and accused

her father of never having loved her enough and of preferring her
younger sister and of having no respect for family ties and of having
kept a mistress through the last ten years of her mother's life and of
having an unreasonable hatred of the Ivy League because he had
graduated at the bottom of his class and never had made Skull and
Bones. But Michael had bribed her by agreeing to go with her to
Venice and Yugoslavia that summer and in the end, faced with a *fait
accompli,* still doubtful of her son's love, she had allowed that perhaps Stanford was a good idea and she had friends in San Francisco
who were constantly inviting her to visit them and it wouldn't be as
though she would lose him entirely for four years.

When he left Stanford three and a half years later it was with a degree granted summa cum laude. While he was at the college he had
earned a pilot's license for single-engine planes, had had it suspended
for buzzing the stadium during a football game, had become a dazzling skier on weekends and winter holidays, had taken up skydiving
and had made twenty-five free-falls, had surfed up and down the
California coast in all sorts of weather and tried some scuba diving,
had talked his way out of having his driving license revoked for
repeated speeding, had grown to be six feet tall and weighed 180
pounds, had paid no attention to his male classmates and a great deal
of attention to his female ones, had made no friends, had attended a
symphony concert in San Francisco with his mother and had made a
plausible pretense of enjoyment and given her great pride, she said,
in the way he had turned out. He had paid for his expensive pleasures by winning at high stakes at backgammon, where he had a considerable edge on his opponents because of his mathematical bent
and training. To the men who knew him on the campus he seemed
lonely and somewhat mournful. To the men with whom he skied or
dove both in the air and under the sea and to the boys he met casually on the surfing beaches, he seemed dangerously reckless and
coldly gay. To the girls and women he slept with he seemed charming, irresistibly handsome in a dark, brooding way, insatiable and
fickle. When he broke three ribs surfing and was in the hospital for a
couple of weeks, he successfully kept the fact from his mother, who
worried that he was threatening his health by overdoing his studies
and advised in her letters that he take walks in the fresh air to bal-

ance the long hours he spent at his books. To one of the girls he particularly liked he spoke a little about his mother and said, "I could write a book about what she doesn't know about me."

To appease his mother, at least geographically, he took the winter off, after he got out of Stanford and before entering the Wharton School of Business, to go back East, to a small ski resort called Green Hollow, in Vermont, where his mother visited him often, although she lamented the fact that he had chosen to spend his last free holiday, before the duties of adulthood engulfed him, in the hazardous and to her eyes demeaning occupation of ski instructor. She was pleased, however, that he was seen out so often with so many different girls and women and not the same one, as she knew he was too young to be married.

She and her father died that summer within two weeks of each other and between them left a surprisingly small trust fund that they had prudently arranged in such a way that nothing but the interest would go to him until he had reached the sober and fiscally dependable age of thirty-five.

At his mother's funeral—where he sobbed, to his surprise, at the graveside—he was distracted by the dark beauty of a girl whose mother had been a classmate of his mother at Vassar. He found out her name—Tracy Lawrence—but did not meet her until eight years later, when he was working in New York for a management consulting concern called Cornwall and Wallace.

CHAPTER
THREE

He was in a theatre lobby between acts when he saw her again, the dark thick hair, the small white pointed face and blue eyes. She was talking to an older woman, her eyes lively and smiling. He was alone. One of the men at the office, a man he rather liked, had asked him to have dinner with him, but he hadn't wanted to talk about work and had declined. When he had begun at the firm and while he was moving up in the hierarchy and learning the politics and intricacies of the trade, he had gladly associated with his colleagues. But now he had to drive himself to the desk and it was only with an effort of will that he could make himself plunge into the work that was being sent his way, in greater amounts, each month.

He had been invited to two parties that evening, but New York parties, like the sessions at the office, had begun to pall on him. After years of foraging among them, always invited as an extra man, that most precious of a hostess's commodities, hearing himself talk, sounding, he now realized, like everybody else, he was bored with himself as well as with the repetitive inconsequential babble. He could not count the times that he had gone home from those parties with women he had not known when he had entered the room and hardly knew two weeks later.

In the theatre lobby he remembered the funeral, the dark blue coat she wore, his quick feeling of guilt as he felt her attraction, with his mother's coffin before the altar, receptacle of so many confusing memories for him. He remembered her name—Tracy Lawrence. In the lobby of the theatre she happened to look his way and, after a hard glance at him, smiled. He made his way across to her and said, "How do you do, Miss Lawrence?" hoping it wasn't Mrs. Somebody by now.

She didn't correct him, so it probably wasn't Mrs. Somebody. "We didn't meet at the funeral," she said. "How do you happen to know my name?"

"I asked." He grinned. The death was far enough in the past so that it could be relegated to the status of just another ordinary occasion of everyday life, a wedding, a christening, an anniversary, with no marked connotations.

The girl—woman—looked momentarily amused, complimented.

"This is my aunt, Mrs. Grenier," Tracy Lawrence said. "Mr. Storrs."

He greeted the aunt. She was fashionably dressed, her hair groomed over a gentle weary face.

"How do you like it?" Tracy Lawrence asked. "The play, I mean?"

"Good for an evening. I'm going back for the second act. And you?"

"We, too," she said. "Better than bed."

"Perhaps we all could go out for a drink after it's over."

The girl glanced quickly at her aunt.

"I'm tired," the aunt said. "I'll just take a cab home. You young folks go have your drink."

The buzzer rang for the curtain and he followed the women into the theatre. She walked erect, her shoulders squared, lovely legs, no coquetry as she moved, a simple, nonrevealing dress, dark green in color.

She sat three rows in front of him and he could see the dark head, distinguish her laugh, full and unconstricted, from the other laughter. He paid very little attention to the play, thinking about her, knowing that he was attracted, not in the generic male way in which he had been attracted often enough by other women, but in a specific stab of feeling, a message across the darkness from her to him, as though he heard a voice whispering, "That one." A look, a smile, the memory of a glance across a mourning congregation. He wondered why he hadn't searched for her before. It would have been easy to find out how to reach her. Guilt before the coffin, probably. Mother, on the subject of decorum.

After the play was over they bundled the aunt into a taxi and she took his arm lightly and they walked over to Sardi's because neither of them had had dinner and when he said that he was hungry, she said, "So am I."

In the restaurant as they were escorted to a table by the head-waiter, he saw that the men along their passage turned their heads and stared at her. She must be used to it. Well, women always looked at him too, and he was used to it. He resolved not to be daunted by her beauty. Or at least not to show it. He had long since given up trying to impress women. There was no need. With his spare good looks, his athlete's body, his increasingly important position in the business world with its accompanying easy money, he had become accustomed to women trying to impress him. That, too, had begun to pall on him.

He ordered a bottle of Chianti and spaghetti for both of them. They discussed the play. "A lot of talent," Tracy Lawrence said, as she ate with gusto, "and not enough thought. The blight of our age. What did you think?"

"I wasn't paying much attention. I was thinking of other things."

She lifted her head quickly and glanced at him, her eyes on his. "Were you?" But she didn't ask what the other things were.

"Business," he lied. "I should have stayed in the office tonight. I have some things on my desk I'll have to report on Monday morning. But by Friday night I get tired of business." He laughed, low. "The fact is, I'm beginning to get tired of business quite early in the week these days. Like Monday morning at ten o'clock."

"What sort of business?"

"Managerial consultant."

"What do managerial consultants do?"

"They consult with managers in the managerial society which enslaves us all," he said.

"More specifically?"

"We go into factories, we examine books, we roam through offices, we interview employees and we strike terror in hearts wherever we go." He realized he had never talked like that to anybody he had met before. Somehow he felt free to say whatever came to his mind with this woman whom he had just encountered.

"Why terror?"

"Because we are trained ferrets, armed with computers, statistics, expertise, coldness of heart. We ferret out incompetence, waste, lar-

He stared at the closed door for a moment, then went back down the steps and into the cab and gave the driver his own address. As the driver started the car, he turned around and said, in an Irish brogue, "I hope you don't mind, friend, but that there was a really beautiful woman."

"I don't mind," Storrs said.

By the time the cab had turned the corner and drawn up at his own apartment building, Michael knew that he was going to ask her to marry him. Probably at lunch the next day.

ceny, nepotism, tax evasion, incompetent bookkeeping, sickly correlations between profit and loss, lack of attention to important aspects of the consumer society such as relations with Washington and unrewarding advertising campaigns. We advise changes, Draconian measures. We are the church militant of efficiency. In some cases on which we have worked, companies have looked like a battlefield after we have passed—with bodies strewn everywhere, factories closed down and left to rot, presidents and chairmen deposed, men who have grown too old for their jobs out on the street."

"Are you good at all this?"

"A rising star." This was no lie. Old man Cornwall had told him the month before that he was pleased, deeply pleased with Storrs' performance, that he was the best man the firm had and had virtually promised him a junior partnership the next time somebody resigned or was fired.

"You don't make it sound very attractive," Tracy Lawrence said.

"It is not the business of business to be attractive. Whatever attractiveness we can muster we save for evenings and weekends."

"I suppose in today's world it's necessary," she said thoughtfully, "but knowing that you're responsible for putting people out of work. . . ."

He shrugged. "It's a living. I do what I'm hired to do. That's what they come to us for—our glorious, rock-bottom neutrality. We're managerial consultants, not the Salvation Army. We leave our hearts at home every morning at nine and pick them up at six in the evening."

"You're putting on an act. I don't believe you're as hard as nails at all. I think you must hate what you're doing."

"Hate it or not, it's what I do," he said soberly. Then more brightly, "Now that I have told you the worst about me, my dear Miss Tracy Lawrence, what have *you* to confess?"

"First of all," she said, sipping at her wine, "it isn't really Miss Lawrence."

"Oh." He felt a dull ache somewhere in his body.

"I'm still married. Mrs. Albert Richards." She laughed. "Don't look so woebegone. I'm in the process of getting divorced."

"How many years?"

"Two. Years of error for both of us."

"What does the man do?"

"He's a theatre director. Like tonight—a lot of talent and no thought. Also, overequipped with ego. Necessary in his profession, he's told me, but not so hot for marriage."

"Where is he?"

"Safely out of the way. Running a repertory company out in the Midwest. He sends me the good reviews. He's a hero in the Midwest. We're good friends when we're a thousand miles apart." She said it carelessly and he found it unpleasant, too much New York, too much like some of the career women he had met who were making it big in the professions in the town and wanted to prove they could be as hard as any man. She was too beautiful, he thought, and too warm, to sound unpleasant, even for an instant.

"And how do *you* earn your daily bread?"

"I'm a designer. I do patterns for fabrics, wallpaper, things like that."

"Good?"

"Not so bad." She shrugged. "I earn my way. People seek me out. You have probably sat on dozens of chairs and sofas upholstered with cloth that I've designed."

"Happy in your work?"

"More than you, I'd think," she said challengingly. "Actually, I love it. The joy of creation and all that jazz." She smiled. She had an enchanting smile, childlike, crinkled around the eyes, without affectation, and she didn't smile too often or merely to ingratiate herself.

"Now," he said, "the preliminaries are over."

"What preliminaries?" She suddenly looked stern.

"The exchange of biographies. Now we go on from there."

"Where?" Her tone was hard.

It was his turn to shrug. "Anywhere we choose."

"You seem too practiced," she said.

"Why do you say that?"

"You're too expert in talking to women. Everything falls into place too quickly. A little night music, a well-rehearsed aria before falling cosily into bed."

"Maybe you're right," he said thoughtfully. "I apologize. The truth is, I haven't talked to anyone else in the whole world the way I've talked to you tonight. And for the life of me, I can't figure out why I have. I hope you believe me."

"That sounds rehearsed, too," she said stubbornly.

"I have a feeling you're too tough for me."

"Maybe I am." She set down her glass. "And now I'm ready to go home. I have to get up early in the morning."

"On Saturday morning?"

"I'm invited out to the country."

"Naturally," he said. "I'm invited out to the country tomorrow, too."

"Naturally," she said.

He laughed. "But I'm not going."

"Well, then, I'm not going either."

He shook his head wonderingly. "Your moves are too fast for me, Tracy, darling. You could make any team in the National Hockey League. I'm dazzled."

"I'm free for lunch tomorrow."

"By a happy coincidence . . ." he began.

"Come up to my place at one o'clock. I'll give you a drink. There's a nice little restaurant down the street. Now, shall we leave?"

He paid the bill and they got up and walked toward the door, the other men in the restaurant staring at her and the women staring at him.

They got into the cab and she gave Storrs an address on East Sixty-seventh Street. He repeated it to the driver.

"I live on East Sixty-sixth Street," he said. "It's a sign."

"A sign of what?"

"I don't know. Just a sign."

They sat apart from each other on the way uptown, not touching. When the cab reached the converted brownstone house in which she had her apartment and studio, he told the cabbie to wait and went up the steps with her to the front door of the building.

After she had unlocked the door, she turned to him. "Thanks for the spaghetti and the wine. I'm glad my aunt was tired."

"Goodnight," he said formally. "Until tomorrow."

She frowned. "Aren't you going to kiss me goodnight?"

"I didn't know matters had progressed that far," he said stiffly. She had put him off balance and he didn't want to give her any more advantage than she had already acquired in the restaurant.

"Oh, don't be a goof," she said and leaned forward and kissed him on the lips. Her lips were soft and sweet-smelling. He didn't put his arms around her.

" 'Night," she said casually and opened the door wide and went through it.

CHAPTER
FOUR

They were married three months later, at the home of her parents, who had a house in the Hamptons, where Tracy had grown up. It was a small wedding and except for old Mr. Cornwall, whom Michael had invited to be his best man, all the guests were friends and relatives of the bride. Mrs. Lawrence had looked surprised when she had asked Michael for the names of the guests he wished to be invited to the ceremony and he had only come up with one. "I know a lot of people in New York," he had said, "but except for Cornwall I don't think any of them gives a damn whether I get married or not." He had grown to like Mrs. Lawrence and Tracy's father, a tall, scholarly man who had retired comfortably from the presidency of a small pharmaceutical company and spent his time reading, bird watching and sailing a twenty-five foot boat on the sound in the summer.

Tracy had two younger sisters, ebullient and pretty, but not with the touch of formal old-fashioned beauty that distinguished Tracy. All the family approved of him and the wedding was a festive affair, although Mrs. Lawrence, when she kissed Michael after the ceremony, wept a little when she said, "It's a pity your poor dear mother couldn't be here for this."

Michael made no comment.

While waiting for the last two months for Tracy's divorce papers to come through, he and Tracy had been sleeping with each other, sometimes at her place and sometimes at his. He was never allowed to keep any of his clothes at her place and she refused to leave any of hers. She didn't explain why she was so adamant about the matter and he didn't press her. He was completely in love and absorbed in the deliciousness of her body and was secretly amused with himself because now he never even glanced at another woman, no matter how pretty she was.

They followed no routine. Some nights, Tracy would call him and say she was busy. She never said what she was busy with and her tone made it clear any questions would be unwelcome. When he had to spend the night alone he went to the movies or watched television or caught up on his reading. For a little while some of the other women he had known would call him to invite him to a party or to the theatre, but he invariably said that he was working that night and after a few weeks there were no more calls.

While Tracy had a regular job at an office in the East Fifties, she often worked at home, too, and Michael had seen some of her designs, flower patterns, abstract designs, some of them in muted colors, others in bold splashes, but all of them delicate and controlled. When he went into a strange room he always looked around to see if he could pick out any of her creations and he was delighted when he found them. His own taste, he knew, ran to undergraduate monotony and disorder and he had the comfortable feeling that when he and Tracy finally moved into their own home, it would be a cheerful and comfortable place. Tracy started to overcome his mother-inspired loathing for works of art, and he happily allowed her to tow him to galleries and even to the opera. "Thanks to you," he told Tracy, "the Philistine in me is in full retreat."

"Give me ten more years," she had replied.

"Now, how can I change *you?*"

"You can't, friend."

"Good," he said, "I don't want you changed."

"Liar," she said, but kissed his cheek.

At the office he found himself daydreaming at his desk and remembering, in the middle of conferences, a certain expression in Tracy's eyes, an impatient twist of her head, her erect, straight carriage, the slender but voluptuous body, the satin feel of her skin, the excited but graceful gesture of a hand as she talked, the abandonment of her lovemaking. After the conversation the first night about her husband in the Midwest, they never talked about him again, although on a walk with Mr. Lawrence along the beach one day, the old man had said, abruptly, "By God, you're an improvement over the other one."

The toasts were in champagne and Mr. Cornwall shook his hand warmly and said, "You've done yourself proud, my boy. Now I know why you seemed on a private leave of absence the last few months at the office." He had laughed heartily, but forgivingly. "Now," he said, "you can stop racing around like a rooster in a henhouse and settle down and do the work you're really capable of." What Cornwall didn't know was that since Michael had met Tracy, his work had seemed all the more unreal, misted over, remote, to him. Once, when he had been away on a field trip for a few days and returned to New York, he had just hurried to put his bags away in his own apartment and gone over to Tracy's place, even though he knew she wouldn't get back from her job for more than an hour. He had started a fire in the fireplace and without putting on the lights had sat staring at the flames, lost in reverie he could not have described. Tracy had let herself in quietly and while he hadn't known she was there had watched him. Then she had gone over to him and kissed him softly on the back of the neck. He had pulled her around onto his lap and just held her, the both of them not moving. "Darling," she said softly, "I'm worried about you."

"Worried?" He was surprised. "Why?"

"When you're alone—like just now—you look—well—I guess the word is melancholy."

"What've I got to be melancholy about?"

"You'll have to tell me."

"I couldn't," he said, "because as far as I know I don't *feel* melancholy."

"Sometime," she said, "you'll have to tell me about your past."

"I don't have a past."

She ignored that. "Your other women, how you grew up, so I'll know why you're like you are now, why I love you."

"You love me because I adore you."

"Nonsense." She got up from his lap. "I need a drink. And you look as though you do, too."

She went into the kitchen to get some ice and he sat staring into the fire. His past—the almost demented mother, her maternal instinct gone rank because of a random death; the clumsy, fat, unpleasant child; the inability or unwillingness to make friends, the loneliness; the recklessness on ski slopes, in the surf, in the air; and then all that behind him as though it never existed and his falling into the false mold of the proper young executive, the meaningless, crowded company of easy unloved debutantes, actresses, divorcées, other men's wives, the wariness with women that had kept him from falling in love until the age of thirty—tell her all that? Never, he thought. It would weigh on her, on both of them, would darken their lives, crop up at bad moments. If he was putting on a show of being the lighthearted, careless, humorous young lover, it was for both their sakes, and if it kept their love unshadowed, the deception was valuable. He had become an expert at deception at the age of twelve and it was too great an asset to lose.

They had had their drinks and had made love all evening after that and then had gone for a late supper to a little place Michael frequented, where a young hawkfaced Frenchman named Antoine Ferré played the piano marvelously and sang sad songs in French, Italian and English, which made Tracy's eyes glisten with unshed tears, although she prided herself on being a hardheaded woman who was miserly with her emotions.

As they drove into New York after the wedding, Tracy said, "Well, it's over."

"On the contrary, it's just begun."

Tracy laughed. "Shall we consider this our first marital disagreement?"

"Agreed," he said. And he laughed, too.

They flew out to Aspen for the honeymoon. Tracy didn't ski and had no intention of learning, but she knew that Michael had skied when he was younger and yearned for the snow and she said that she loved mountains and cold weather and besides she was friendly with a couple who had a small house there who had offered to lend it to them for two weeks.

The snow was good, the weather perfect for a mountain honeymoon and he skied blithely all day, with the old exaltation that he had thought he had forgotten. He left for the slopes early each morning, leaving Tracy lying cuddled lazily in bed. During the day she took long walks in the bulky fur coat he had bought her for a wedding present, and when he saw her in the early evening in the bar they had chosen for their own after the last run down the hill, she was rosy from the cold and looked, he thought, like a glorious eighteen-year-old girl.

He had been stopped on the slopes and warned by a patrolman that his lift ticket would be taken away from him if he was caught speeding down the hills again, endangering not only his life but that of the other skiers on the slope. "I'm on my honeymoon, pal," Michael had explained, "and I'm celebrating and I sure don't want to kill anybody, especially myself."

The patrolman had grinned and said, "Okay, partner. Just make sure my head is turned the other way when you go past. And if you can't restrain yourself, there's a downhill race on Friday and nobody'll try to slow you down. You're pretty old for that sort of thing, but you look as if you won't disgrace yourself. And give my regards to the bride." After that, they had skied down together, fast, but careful to stay on the edge of the run just at the rim of the trees, where there was nobody in their way. Michael invited the patrolman, who was perhaps twenty-two years old, to have a drink with him and his wife and the patrolman had kept staring dumbly at Tracy over his hot wine and stuttered when he answered her questions. "Man," he said, after telling her how he had come to meet Michael, "I wouldn't take any chances with my neck if I was married to *you.*"

Tracy had chuckled at that and patted the young man's hand. "You don't know how hard I had to work to get him," she said.

"I bet," the patrolman said.

Michael ordered another round of drinks and the young man asked where he'd learned to ski the way he did. "Back East, then out in California," Michael said. "Then I was an instructor for a season when I was your age."

"How come you didn't keep it up?"

"I went to New York to make my fortune and wait until Tracy Lawrence came along."

"Maybe I ought to try New York myself, before I get too old," the patrolman said. He finished his drink and stood up. "Got to go now. And Mr. Storrs, anytime you want to ski the way you were going this afternoon, remember you got a wife at home waiting for you."

"Will do," Michael said.

The young man waved stiffly, took one more hungry look at Tracy and clumped off in his boots past the noisy skiers at the bar.

"Nice young man," Tracy said.

"He looked as though he wanted to grab you and take you home under his arm."

Tracy chuckled. "You don't mind if your bride gets a little attention, do you?"

"A little, okay. He was dealing it out in wagonloads."

"I see how the girls keep looking at you. By the way, what do you do with them up on the mountain all day long?" she said teasingly.

"It's ten below zero up there, darling. There's very little fucking over ten thousand feet in altitude in the winter in the Rockies."

"You mean I have to worry about the summers—at sea level." She was still teasing him.

"I want you to remember one thing," he said, more seriously. "For the first time in my life I have discovered the ultimate sexual pleasure—monogamy. I invite you to join me."

"Will do, as you put it," she said.

For a moment they just sat in silence, soberly, looking into each other's eyes.

"You're a different man up here," she said.

"Than where?"

"New York. This seems to be your climate, your ambiance."

"Am I better for it or worse?"

"Better, I think. I haven't caught you looking melancholy since we drove up from Denver. And you seem ten years younger."

He laughed. "That's just what I was thinking about you when you walked in tonight."

"Maybe we ought to set up housekeeping in a place like this and never go down off the hill." There was a note of wistfulness in her voice. "Maybe I'm a mountain woman, myself."

"I have some money," Michael said, "and there's more coming to me when I reach thirty-five, but if I want to continue eating I'm afraid I have to stay in New York."

"Ah, New York," she said ambiguously. "You hate it and love it at the same time. Everything presses on you—the good things as well as the bad things. You always seem to be behind schedule there. Here you go fast on skis—*there* it's your soul that's racing. Here, hardly anybody seems to read the newspapers. You forget there's a war on, people killing each other in the jungle, Americans. In New York, when you read the *Times* you feel it's intolerable, that your own security, your good meals, your warm bed is unbearably selfish. You look at the faces of the people in the street and you wonder how they can take it day after day. Don't you ever feel that way?"

"I know what you mean about the other people but I can't do anything about it, so I try not to think about it."

"Are they liable to take you?"

"I'm too old. I'm safe." What he didn't tell her was that when he was twenty-four, in his last semester at Wharton, when the war in Vietnam was accelerating, he had, after a particularly boring class in statistics, almost without thinking about it, gone down to a recruiting office and said he wanted to enlist. The sergeant at the desk had looked at him dubiously, as though he were drunk or on dope, but had helped him fill out the form and sent him on for his physical examination. The doctor who examined him was a weary, slow-moving captain who looked too old to be just a captain and who kept humming tunelessly to himself as though the whole business bored him. But when he put the stethoscope above Michael's chest he became more interested. After a minute or so he stepped back and took the stethoscope plugs from his ears and said, "Sorry, son."

"What does that mean?"

"It means the Army can't use you. You've got a heart murmur. Maybe you'll die young and maybe you'll live to be a hundred, but either way it won't be in uniform. You can put on your shirt now."

Michael was stunned. The last time he had been to a doctor had been in Green Hollow when he had had a bout with pneumonia, but that had been more than a year before and the doctor hadn't said anything about a heart murmur then.

He had kept the news to himself. He hadn't told anyone that he was going to enlist and now he wasn't going to let anyone know that he had been rejected. But he brooded over it and finally went to see the doctor at the University Hospital for a checkup. He told the doctor about the heart murmur and the doctor ran a series of tests on him. "Mr. Storrs," the doctor said, "either that Army doctor is the least competent man in the history of military medicine or he's running a one man campaign against our being in Vietnam. Your heart is as normal as could be. My advice is to forget the whole thing."

Michael couldn't forget it, but he didn't try to enlist again. From time to time he couldn't help but wonder what his life would have been like if he had run up against another doctor in the Army hospital that morning.

"Safe," he repeated to Tracy. He could have said, saved, and told her the story, but it wasn't the sort of thing you wanted to talk about on your honeymoon.

"I'm married to a safe old man," Tracy said. "Thank God."

On Friday, he ran the downhill race. He had scouted the course the day before and memorized the points where he would have to check if he didn't want to wipe out. It was a tough course, long, with difficult sneaky turns and a couple of places where you were in the air for twenty feet or so and some hidden, sharp drops. He had borrowed a helmet, but had neglected to get himself long racing skis and now, looking at the course, he regretted it. He knew he would regret it even more later. He had a late starting number and he watched intently as the men before him made their descent and noticed that the good ones hardly checked at all, taking everything full out. When his turn came and he skated off he knew he wasn't going to check anywhere, either. He had never gone so fast and even with his goggles his eyes began to tear and he nearly made it to the finish line, where he knew Tracy was standing, watching for him. But just before the last schuss there was a bump that sent him into the air unexpectedly and he came down in a pinwheel, his ski tips digging into the snow. Luckily, the skis came off and he rolled downhill another fifty feet of snow, head over heels, before he came to a stop. He stood up quickly to show Tracy that he was unhurt, but he had to limp down the rest of the way because his knee had twisted in the fall.

As he approached where Tracy was standing next to the patrolman, the young man said, "Your husband is out of his ever-loving mind. I should never have let him talk me out of taking away his lift ticket."

But Michael was grinning as he came up to her. "A marvelous run," he said.

"But not for old men," the patrolman said, his voice unfriendly, and turned away.

Michael looked after the man puzzledly. "What's wrong with him?" he asked Tracy.

"By the time you were in the middle of the course," Tracy said, "he said you didn't know the difference between skiing and Russian roulette."

Michael shrugged. "Kids. They think they know everything. I'm a safe old man. Now let's go to a doctor and have him tape up my knee."

He limped off, Tracy holding his arm, without watching the rest of the race. For the rest of the honeymoon he didn't put on a pair of skis again and they had a fine time spending all day and all night together.

When they got to New York Michael finally moved into Tracy's apartment. Except for an old leather chair that Michael liked to read in, he sold his furniture to a junkman. "Ten years too late," Tracy said.

She turned out to be a good cook, and smugly satisfied with the place they were living in, with themselves and each other, they felt no need for anybody else and rushed home immediately after work to help each other in the small kitchen, eat on a table before the fire with a bottle of wine, spend the evening reading and comparing notes on what they had done during the day. When Michael was sent out of town on a job he tried to cut his trips as short as possible and called home every evening for long talks with Tracy over the telephone.

The euphoria of their honeymoon lasted until the day Aldridge was killed and she told him she wanted a child.

CHAPTER FIVE

The following Saturday morning he woke early. Tracy was still asleep and he dressed quietly in a pair of old corduroy pants and a windbreaker. But before he could get out of the room, Tracy woke and said, "Good morning." He was on the other side of the bed and he could see her looking at him, observing how he was dressed.

"Good morning, darling," he said and went over and kissed her. She moved her head quickly so that he just brushed her cheek. She smelled of sleep and faintly of perfume. "I'll be back by the middle of the afternoon," he said.

"Where're you going?"

"It's just . . ." he began.

"Don't tell me," she said. "I know." She turned so that her back was toward him, and covered her head with an upthrown arm.

"You have to understand," he said, "I . . ."

"Don't try to explain. I'll see you later."

He shrugged and went out of the room.

When he got to the field in New Jersey, the wind was gusting and the wind sock blowing, first in one direction and then another. McCain and his assistant, a lanky blond boy, were in the shed, drinking coffee. McCain looked up at him, without surprise, as he entered the shed. "Early today, aren't you, Mr. Storrs?" McCain said. They had seen each other twice during the week, at the two funerals, but had said nothing to each other.

"I have things to do in New York this afternoon," Michael said.

"I thought I'd just take a couple of nice little mediocre jumps and get back. Am I the only one this morning?"

McCain nodded. "The only one," he said. "Trade's been slow this week. And the weather's not so hot. You sure you want to go?"

"Sure."

McCain got up slowly and after Michael had put on the jump suit and boots which he kept in a locker in the shed, and the lanky blond boy had helped him strap on the main parachute and the flat back-up belly parachute, they all went out to where the plane was still tied down next to the strip. "The wind's tricky this morning," McCain said, as he started the engine. "Stay well north of the field." There was a stand of tall pines that bordered the southern end of the field and it was a standard warning each time McCain took anybody up. "It's not a day to do anything fancy. Pull it at no less than three thousand. Understand?"

"Okay."

McCain gunned the motor and they took off. The plane shuddered and bucked in the wind. Michael had felt sleepy and slow-moving all the way out from New York but now the cold slap of the wind coming through the open door woke him completely and he felt the old expectation, an electric sense, total alertness, the tingle of mindless, ecstatic, primitive pleasure, as the adrenaline started pumping.

At 7,500 feet, McCain gave him the signal and he went out. There was the great feeling first of immense, unguided abandonment to gravity, then of soaring exaltation as he hurtled through space, planing, swerving, supported by the rushing air, purposeful as a bird. His hand was on the rip-cord handle and he didn't bother to look at the altimeter on his wrist and the stand of pines was getting closer and closer, now seeming to be rushing up at him, dark in the windy morning sunlight. It was with regret that he pulled and felt the jerk as the parachute opened above him and he pulled at the toggles to keep away from the stand of pines. He landed hard, with the wind throwing him over at the last moment, not twenty yards from the edge of the woods. He snapped out of the parachute harness and stood up, breathing deeply, sorry it was over, his mind and spirit drowned, overwhelmed, full only of flight.

Gathering the parachute together he walked toward the shed while McCain circled the plane down for a landing. He was in the shed, pouring himself a cup of coffee, when McCain came in. McCain was frowning, biting his lips.

"Mr. Storrs," McCain said, "I told you stay away from the north side."

"The wind . . ."

"I know all about the wind," McCain said harshly. "Tell me, Mr. Storrs, at what altitude did you pull?"

"I would say, twenty-five hundred, twenty . . ."

"I would say more like a thousand, Mr. Storrs. If anything had gone wrong, you'd be lucky to have the time to say, Mother, Mother and we'd probably be scraping you off the ground right now," McCain said, his voice like granite. "I told you three thousand, as always, didn't I?"

"I just felt everything was going fine, and gave it an extra few seconds. It's a beautiful morning."

"So it is, Mr. Storrs," McCain said. "And it's the last time you jump from this field. Two men died here last Saturday and I don't want to make it a weekly habit."

"Whatever you say, Mac." Michael shrugged. "What do I owe you?"

"Nothing," McCain said. "The last two jumps, today and last week, are on the house."

"As you like it," Michael said. He was still feeling too high from the jump to be angry or even annoyed. "Thanks for everything." He put out his hand but McCain turned away without shaking it and poured himself a cup of coffee.

"Listen, Mac," Michael said, "I didn't kill anybody and I didn't kill myself, what's the big deal?"

"Not this time." McCain sipped noisily at the hot coffee. "I had my doubts about you all along. I don't have any doubts about you anymore. With your leave, I'm going to call your charming wife and tell her she'd better take care of you."

"Call anybody you want," Michael said testily.

"I'm going to suggest sending you to a priest or an analyst or your family doctor or a rabbi or a guru or whoever, who could persuade you that it's better to live than to die, Mr. Storrs."

"That's bullshit, Mac."

McCain smiled faintly. "Take your gear," he said, and watched while Michael rolled up the jump suit and took off the jump boots.

"Now drive carefully," he said. "The highways're full of cops on Saturday."

The apartment was empty when he got home. There was a note from Tracy, propped up against the telephone. "Have gone to visit my parents. Will be home late Sunday night or in time for work Monday morning." It was signed "T."

He crumpled up the note and threw it into a wastebasket. "T." Not "Love, T." or "Please call me, Tracy" or "Why don't you get into the car and drive out, too, darling?" In time for work Monday morning—not in time for love. And how did she get out to the Hamptons when he had used the car to drive to New Jersey? Probably one of her old friends hanging around, hanging on, hoping for the best or in this case the worst.

Not even sure which day she was going to get back. Sleep alone, my dear, one night, two nights, what does it matter?

And no little homely note of domesticity—no message that there was a steak in the icebox for him or that they were running short on Scotch, why didn't he go out and buy a bottle for the weekend?

You go your way, the note said, I will go mine. The rebuke was clear. He wondered if McCain had actually called her, as he had threatened, with his talk of psychoanalysts, priests and rabbis, and that was why she had left.

After the beauty of the morning, the freedom of the sky, the cozy little apartment, all neatly tidied up, was like a prison. *They* were getting to him, they were enclosing him. The *they* was not specific in his mind.

Angrily, he picked up the phone and dialed her parents' house. Might as well have it out here and now. Your husband arrived on your scene equipped with certain needs, tastes, aberrations, if that's what you want to call them. He is devoted to challenge, the illusion of escape. The equation is simple—ten minutes of flight, of conquering danger, equals five days from Monday to Friday. It concerns you only peripherally, except that it permits me to live joyously with you. I will not be trapped with female caution. You are not my mother forbidding me to climb trees. This is not Syracuse.

The telephone kept ringing. There was no answer. He let it ring ten times then hung up. *They* were all punishing him. He imagined Tracy standing guard over the telephone in the house within sound of the ocean, not allowing anyone to pick it up, saying, I am married to a madman, guarding the telephone. He is a young man but is already mourning his youth, is proving to himself that he will never grow old. On weekends and holidays he reverts to childhood. On our honey-

moon he could easily have made me a widow. Let him make his
choice. My absence shows him that I have made mine. I will not be
treated as though my life is of no importance. Marriage is a double
compromise and the sooner he learns it the better.

Michael slammed down the telephone. Be reasonable, he thought,
maybe they are all out taking a walk along the beach and in ten minutes they'll come back and she'll pick up the phone and call and ask
him how it was and if he wouldn't like to come out in time for
dinner.

He went into the small room off the living room that she used as a
studio. A piece of paper with a half-finished design in water colors
was pinned to the drawing board. Flowers, in bright, childish colors.
It was impossible that a woman who could paint so gaily, such fragile, perishable things, could be adamantly determined to curb him to
her will. His mother, too, had seemed frail and perishable. But she,
he remembered, had perished.

He went back into the neat, bright living room. Suddenly it seemed
to him that nobody had ever lived in it, that it was like those make-
believe rooms, adroitly lit, cleverly arranged and tempting, that appeared in the show windows of furniture stores and vanished overnight, to be replaced by another, equally attractive make-believe one
the next day.

The telephone didn't ring.

Wifeless, he thought, wifeless. Those nights before they were married, when she had said that she couldn't see him and had offered no
explanations, where had she gone, whom had she seen, what had she
done? I am nobody's jailer, he had once told her. But had he meant
it? And she, who had not volunteered an answer, what was the secret
meaning in her silence?

He had a small desk in the corner of the room where he went over
the reports he brought back in the evening and where he wrote his
letters and kept his checkbooks. On it there was a photograph of her
—it was in color and had been taken on the lawn of her parents'
house on a bright summer day. She was sitting on a garden chair, a
book on her lap, her hands folded loosely over it, her shoulder-
length hair, which she usually wore up in the city, free and almost
blue-black in the sunlight. She was wearing a pale blue blouse with
short sleeves and a long blue skirt and her arms were tanned and
rounded, her face rose, the expression on her face serious, almost
questioning. Not for her the new unisex style. Her femininity was

grave, the heritage of centuries, somehow challenging, demanding homage and protection. He was overcome by longing as he looked at the photograph. It had been taken before they had met that night at the theatre. By whom—her ex-husband? Whoever it had been, the photographer had fully appreciated her qualities. Lady in a garden. In full bloom. Floral, fragrant metaphor. From an earlier, gentler time. "Will be home Sunday night or in time for work Monday morning. T." Contradictions. The centuries moved on. Customs changed.

He tried the telephone again. Still no answer. Saturday afternoon, Saturday night, urban revelry, stretched before him—a desert. He could not bear the empty show window apartment, full of silent reproach. He dialed again, but this time a number he knew well, from before his marriage.

"Josey speaking." A light eager voice, a particular familiar way of answering the ringing at the bedside instrument.

"Michael," he said.

"Ah, the lost bridegroom."

"Lunch?" he asked.

"Why not?" Without hesitation. How many dates, with how many other men, had she broken, without hesitation, for him?

"One o'clock?" he said.

"Will do." She had picked up the phrase from him. "Promptly."

"The old place," he said.

"Of course."

"You're a reliable lady."

"My vice," Josey said. "I'll wear a red rose in my hair so you'll recognize me."

"No need."

"It's been a long time, bridegroom."

"Not so long."

"I'll be lightly clothed."

He laughed. "I'm not thinking beyond lunch," he said.

"I am," she said. "I'm on champagne these days."

"What else is new? I'll have it ready in a bucket."

It was her turn to laugh. Her laugh was a curious giggle, low and girlish. He had been charmed and amused with it for a long time, because it was in such contrast to the way she looked—tall and haughty and disdainful. She had been a fixture in his life for years, off and on, if any woman could be said to have been a fixture in his life before

Tracy. There were no grappling irons between them. When he called, after a month or so of silence, she would say, "Ah, you're convoking me again," but with no complaint in her voice. She had been a simple but stunning young girl when she had come to New York from Alabama, had had a brief but dazzling success as a photographic model, had married rich and divorced rich and had enjoyed every minute of everything, as she sometimes said when people tried to talk seriously to her. "I am the net," she had once told him, giggling girlishly, "under the tightrope of numerous marriages."

So much for Saturday afternoon. He stared at the phone as he put it down, felt a pang of doubt, wondered if he oughtn't to call her back and say he was sorry, it had just been a random impulse, it would be better if they did not meet, better for the both of them. He did not call the familiar number and although he didn't know it then, he was dooming his marriage.

"Ah," she said, with a contented sigh, stroking him with soft fingers after they had made love in her shadowed, alimonied bedroom, "ah, well-known, well-beloved territory. I'm glad you put off breaking your neck at least until next Saturday." He had told her of his jump that morning. She had watched him often and had even jumped twice, to amuse him, although never free-falling, and had gone surfing with him on rough days out at Montauk, although she professed to be a coward and afraid of planes and the sea. "I am just one of those female idiots," she said, "who is that male cliché—a darn good sport. Loads of fun, the boys tell me. If ever I find a man as rich as my ex-husband and one I like as much as I like you, I'll stop being loads of fun so fast it'll be like the sonic boom. Glad to have you aboard, bridegroom, even if it's only on furlough."

"Stop calling me bridegroom."

"Is your wife loads of fun, too?"

"Not in the way you say it."

"Is this the way you usually spend your Saturday afternoons or do I detect a rift?"

"I have no usual way of spending Saturday afternoons."

"How's it going?"

"So-so," he said.

CHAPTER
SIX

"And now," Josey said, "we bid a fond farewell to tender childhood toys, for I am to be well and truly wed tomorrow morning." She patted his cock gently. They were in bed in his room at the Bel-Air Hotel in Los Angeles. Cornwall and Wallace did not stint on the accommodations for their representatives. Now, business over, presentations presented, plans sent on to New York, he lay luxuriously, not alone, with the drapes drawn against the afternoon California sunlight. He had received the invitation to the wedding in the mail in New York and had volunteered to go on a job to a company in downtown Los Angeles so as to be able to attend. After such a long time it was, he thought, the least he could do for a friend.

In the last two years he had volunteered more and more often to go on the out-of-town trips. New York was becoming increasingly unbearable to him and after a week there—the noise, the constant insensate pushing, the unceasing, subterranean jockeying for power in the office, the look of manic effort on everybody's face, the drunken forgetfulness at the end of the day—he found himself with his nerves scraped raw, insomniac, waking fretfully at all hours of the night, listening to sirens, going through the motions of work and marriage with a bone-deep weariness. Living in the same small apartment, he and Tracy had grown steadily apart and the good moments between them had become briefer and rarer.

When he went on his trips—to Chicago, to Denver, to Monte Carlo, Zurich—he no longer called home every night. To avoid hurt-

"Tempered steel," she said. "I haven't had the pleasure of meeting the lady but I have gotten reports from acquaintances."

"Let's not talk about my wife," he said. "Is that all right with you?"

"Everything is all right with me," she said, putting her long, lean-muscled leg over his in the soft bed. "Can I expect further Saturday calls?"

"Time will tell."

"Praise Saturdays," she said, giggling. "Do you think you'll ever work yourself free to take me skiing or surfing again?"

She was an athletic girl, in and out of bed, and was willing to try anything, although after her second jump she had forsworn parachuting. "I've got the idea," she said, "and that's enough. And each time I had the feeling my tits were going to come up and choke me." But it was the only thing she had complained about in the way of sport and she was always available at the last moment for any kind of holiday. At least for him. She had never said she loved him and she didn't make him feel guilty and he was grateful to her for that.

"I asked you a question," she said, whispering, her tongue licking his throat. "Are you working yourself loose from the shackles?"

"As I said, time will tell."

She pulled away from him a little and looked at him soberly. "In some ways, you're such a reckless man—but in others . . ." She shook her head. "Did you ever find yourself crazily, head-over-heels in love?"

"Once."

"With whom?"

"My wife."

"Oh, Christ," she said, "who would have expected a dreary old answer like that? And how long have you been married now?"

"Three months."

"And here you are on a Saturday afternoon in the sack with your good old round-heeled pal, Josey."

"Here I am," he said. "Marriage isn't as simple as some people think."

"You're telling me. If I told you some of the things my husband wanted me to go in for . . ."

"Don't tell me. I want to keep the pure image of you I have always cherished in my heart."

"Boy, you *are* a cold sonofabitch, aren't you?"

"I wish I was," he said sadly. "I wish I was."

"Tell me—did you ever *not* get a girl you wanted?"

"By the thousand."

"The truth."

It was almost the truth. He did not pursue women, but he had gone out many times with girls and women he would gladly have gone to bed with, but had never tried because he knew instinctively he would be rebuffed if he made any advances. He knew he had a strong appeal to the opposite sex and he was not above admiring himself in a mirror, but there was a certain kind of woman, the cheerleader types in college, the show girls and pretty and desirable receptionists in outer offices, the dumb or placid or silly ones, whom he did not allow himself to be interested in for more than an hour or two since in their turn they quickly showed that they were not interested in him and were bored with his conversation. With smart girls and women, although by no means with all of them, he knew he was on a shared psychic wavelength and he felt it when they were attracted to him and at just what moment, without any overt moves on either his part or theirs, the decision to become lovers was tacitly made. It had been that way with Josey. She was frivolous, but she was far from stupid. She used her brain for inconsequential things like the most difficult crossword puzzles and playing charades brilliantly at parties, but her intelligence was evident at all times. It was not only a question of sex with her. When, as had happened from time to time, he had become involved with someone else, he and Josey still saw each other often, for lunch or dinner or merely a stroll in the park. As she had said early in their affair, "The rule here is that there are no rules—everybody is allowed to come and go on his or her own schedule. Nobody is going to break my heart."

Now she was repeating, "The truth? If not by the thousand, by how much?"

"By the dozen."

"I'm curious—what do you *really* think of women? Not me in particular, but women in general?"

"About like men."

"What do you mean by that?"

"They come in all grades. Categories A, B, C, D and so on."

"You tell me how you grade me," she said playfully, "and I'll tell you how I grade you."

"That's not a game I'm disposed to play right now," he said. pulled her to him and kissed her to keep her quiet.

They made love for the rest of the afternoon and after that, wh they were dressing and discussing where they would go for dinr Josey said, "You ought to jump out of airplanes every day. It mal you marvelously horny." She chose a noisy, crowded restaura where she seemed to know everybody and men kept coming over the table and kissing her and saying wasn't it a great party last nig or last weekend or where have you been, darling, while Michael s quietly, drinking a little too much wine and wondering what Tra was doing while he was sitting there. By the end of the evening Jos was wandering from table to table and Michael paid the check ar slipped out and went home, where he sat looking at the silent tel phone for an hour before he went to bed.

ing Tracy more than was necessary he saved his free-falling, his surfing, his scuba diving and skiing for the times when he was away from New York. And when he slept with other women it was also in other cities. Quite often, Josey had flown out to wherever he was to join him but he had not repeated their Saturday afternoon perform-ance of the day in New York when Tracy had left him to go to her parents' home on Long Island.

When he came home from his trips, Tracy asked only the most perfunctory of questions. She was becoming more and more success-ful in her work and had started a small business of her own, with two other women, which involved entertaining clients in the evenings two or three times a week. At first, she had invited Michael to accompany her, but he invariably said those things weren't for him and finally she had stopped inviting him. He went on his holidays alone because if she had any free time she said the only place she wanted to be was her parents' house in the Hamptons, where she could relax and not do anything but lie in the sun.

He was making considerably more money than before and so was Tracy and he had suggested that they move to a bigger apartment where each could have a room of his own, but Tracy had been firm about staying where they were and they still slept together in the same oversized bed. She no longer made advances to him when they lay side by side, but was as warm and ardent as ever when he moved toward her. At those moments he would feel that he would never grow tired of that lovely, familiar body, but when he was away from her he hardly ever thought about her and it did not interfere with his pleasure with other women.

They knew that they were approaching some sort of breaking point, but out of timidity, politeness, memory of happier times, they both postponed the moment.

"Now," Josey was saying, "I am going to get dressed and I am going to walk out of your room and through the garden as though I just dropped in for a cup of tea and from tomorrow morning on I am going to devote the rest of my life to making my gorgeous, rich young husband the happiest man in Southern California. You will be invited to family dinners and the christening of children and you will be asked to cruise with us on our yacht and you will not tempt my husband to jump out of airplanes with you or dive for treasure or whatever it is you do underwater or to follow you down a ski slope. Understood?"

Michael laughed. "Understood."

He watched her get out of bed, stretch the magnificent long body like a giant cat, then quickly, with businesslike efficiency, get into her clothes, whip a comb through her lustrous dark red hair. Gone, gone, he thought, self-pityingly.

Dressed, she gestured toward the bucket, with the half-drunk bottle of champagne in it. "One last, sneaky, delicious stirrup cup?"

"Of course." He got out of bed.

She watched him critically as he put on a robe. "It's a test of character," she said.

"What's a test of character?" He pulled the sash of the robe tight around his middle.

"Giving you up," she said soberly.

"Have you passed it?"

"Alas, yes," she said. She held out her glass and he filled it, then filled his own. They clinked glasses, drank. Surprised, he saw that she was crying.

"What's the matter?" he said, then knew he shouldn't have said it, that it was a stupid thing to have said.

She put her glass down on a table. "Why the fuck couldn't you have fallen in love with *me?*" she cried. Then she turned abruptly and fled from the room, a final dark silhouette against the brilliant sunlight and the green foliage of the hotel gardens as the door swung open, then slammed shut.

It's a lucky thing, he thought numbly, we didn't indulge in one last kiss.

He went to the service in the morning and recognized many of the faces from the movies and television. Josey's husband-to-be was in the oil business, but he lived in Beverly Hills and was popular with the more affluent natives. He was a tall, thickset, open-faced, ruddy man who looked as though he had played football. If Michael didn't think he was gorgeous, it was probably because he used a different vocabulary from Josey's.

Josey came down the aisle on the arm of an elderly gentleman Michael didn't recognize. She looked splendid, disdainful and untouchable, in her best *Vogue* cover manner and gave only the briefest of smiles to the groom, who was looking at her adoringly. But she winked at Michael, the barest flicker of an eyelid, as she passed him.

Michael didn't go to the wedding lunch, but got into his car with his surfboard and drove out to Malibu. This is one afternoon, he thought, that I want to be alone.

He parked his car across from the cove and got into his bathing trunks and walked barefoot, carrying his board, to the beach, where a fine mist made blurred shapes out of the buildings to the north. The sea was rough, whitecaps out beyond the long rolling breakers. It was a cold day and there was nobody else riding a board that afternoon. So much the better, he thought. He disliked it when he was surrounded by dozens of superb young boys and girls fighting for position around him as the waves formed out to sea and looking at him as though he were an escapee from an old peoples' home.

Gingerly, because the water was brutally cold and he hadn't brought along a wet suit, he slipped into the foam, then plunged, lying on the board, and started to paddle out. It wasn't easy. The waves came one after another, in short chopping series, and he was knocked around as he submarined with the board under the curl. After the stiffness and formality of the morning and the confusion of memories in the church, the tingle and roughness of the cold water and the single combat with the waves was delicious.

Finally, he was out beyond the breakers, sitting on his board, resting, still breathing deeply after the struggle to get out, at the point where, he judged, he could start in when he saw the right wave sweeping in behind him. The shore seemed far away in the gray mist and the ocean was his as he rose and fell on the swells. He was warmed by the paddle out and he was in no hurry—no one was waiting for him, his week's work was done, his plane to New York was not taking off till Monday morning. He was blessedly alone, his life afloat, his world wind, water, waves and salt, and he embraced it all. He took a deep, tonic breath, saw the wave he wanted massing up in the mist, started paddling, felt the gigantic power of the Pacific under him, knew that he had caught it right, stood up and sure-footed and triumphant rode the giant diagonally, just in the cup, the crest of the wave foaming high above his head. Then, suddenly, it was too much for him. The wave was breaking more sharply than he had thought it would. He held on for a moment and then the board went shooting out from under him and he was tumbled, deep, over and over in tons of black sea water. He held his breath, fought, came up, was swept under again after just one short breath of air, came up in a turmoil of chopping swirling water.

The board was gone, but he could breathe now, careful to duck when the waves broke on him and hurled him toward the bottom. Calmly, knowing that if he worked too hard he would exhaust himself quickly and never make it, he began swimming, feeling the pull of the undertow, catching a wave when he could to take him a few yards inland, then going along with the current, parallel with the shore, not resisting the ebb tide, until another wave pushed him a little closer toward the rim of beach. If there had been anyone in sight he would have waved for help, but the beach was deserted. He swam, thinking, What luck I didn't stay for the lunch and the champagne, I'd have sunk like lead by now if I had.

It took him a full half hour to get in and as he crawled onto the beach he was sure that he couldn't have lasted another two minutes. He stood up, tottering, then steadied himself. Then he did something that he knew was crazy even as he did it. He threw his arms up into the wide air above his head and with his fists clenched, shouted hoarsely, wordlessly, into the gray, empty mist, shouted with joy.

Then he walked, breathing deeply, along the edge of the sea, his feet in the sucking plaques of foam, until he found his board, careened on the sand. He picked it up, inspected it. It had not been harmed. He patted it, as though it were a horse that had won a race for him, and carried it back to his car. He toweled himself off, taking off his trunks, which were full of wet sand, not caring if anyone who might be passing could see the naked bruised man carefully tending to his body in the cold mist sweeping toward the mountains behind him, off the cold sea.

His clothes felt soft and warm against his skin and he got into his car and drove a little way down the Pacific Coast Highway until he reached a bar. He went in and ordered a whiskey and looked at himself in the mirror behind the bar. His face was scratched from the sand and a little bloody and his sun-streaked hair, now darker than ever with salt water, was tangled and thick with seaweed and sand. Neptune's lucky child, he told himself, grinning at his frightening reflection, what a marvelous day. Where were all the superb young cowards, all those sweet-limbed California boys and girls, this overcast afternoon? Another day, another death, challenged and overcome. Mother, dear, if only you could see me now.

When he got back to the hotel, he washed the traces of blood off his face and showered, to get the sand and the salt out of his hair and off his skin. It was late and he was hungry, but today he didn't want to lunch alone. He knew some girls in Los Angeles but the chances were slim that any of them would be home in the middle of a beautiful Saturday afternoon. The men he knew were all business acquaintances and he'd had enough of business for the week. Then he remembered that there was a nice woman whom he had met a few nights before at a party given by the chairman of the board of the company he had been working with. Her name was Florence Gardner and she was an actress who had come out from New York for a part in a movie. He had seen her once or twice on the stage in New York and had been impressed by her cool good looks and her talent as a comedienne. She had shown that she was clearly interested in him and when he had said that he was staying at the Bel-Air, she had said, "So am I. Maybe we can have a drink sometime."

The sometime might just as well be now, he thought. He asked for her room on the phone and was surprised at how pleased he was to hear the sound of her voice. "I apologize for calling at such short notice," he said, "and I know it's late for lunch, but I just got back to the hotel and if you haven't eaten yet why don't you join me in the restaurant?"

"Well . . ." she hesitated, "I've been studying my lines for Monday. But now that you mention lunch, I remember I haven't eaten yet. What the hell, a lady has to eat. Can you give me fifteen minutes? I was out on my patio in the sun and I'm something of a mess and I have to take a shower and generally pretty up for any kind of public appearance."

"Fifteen minutes it is," he said. "I'll be waiting for you at the bar."

He walked through the gardens toward the bar, to the pleasant tinkling of the sprinklers watering the lawns and the fragrant banks of flowers. The bar was dark and peaceful and he ordered a daiquiri, because he was in California. The rum and lime of the drink was an enormous improvement over the taste of the Pacific.

When she came in, crisp as a stalk of iced celery, dressed in pressed jeans and a light pink sweater, he saw that the sun had put color into her small oval face, color that was brought out nicely by the pink sweater. The jeans showed off her slender but well-rounded hips and behind admirably. She wasn't wearing lipstick but her lips, so flat they almost gave her the look of an Oriental statue, were a natural coral pink, a little darker than her sweater. She had soft, bright blond hair and green eyes that changed color, he noticed, in different lights.

She perched on the stool beside him and ordered a daiquiri too, while he asked for his second one.

"What a nice idea," she said as she drank. "Your calling me. When I'm working I have a tendency to forget to eat or drink."

"What are you working on?"

"Eating money." She waved her hand airily. "I will win no Oscars with this part. To tell you the truth, I'm waiting for the director to tell me why the part's in the picture at all." She shrugged. "Hollywood. Still, it has its uses. And this hotel is a splendid creation after the hole I live in in New York. Nibbling on the lotus from time to time can be nourishing." She had a clipped manner of talking, her voice low and musical. It suddenly reminded Michael of Tracy's way of talking and the tone of her voice. She was about Tracy's age too, he guessed, and her figure was like a slightly smaller version of Tracy's.

Stop thinking about Tracy, he thought, and asked the barman to have a waiter come in and take their order for lunch. When he came they both ordered salads and Michael asked for a bottle of white wine. After the waiter had gone, he noticed Florence examining his face closely.

"I don't like to sound curious," she said, "but what have you been up to? You look as though you've tangled with a kitten."

"Oh, these." He put his hand up to the scratches on his forehead and the bridge of his nose. "I'm afraid I tangled with something a little larger than a kitten."

"A lady?"

He laughed, shook his head. "The Pacific Ocean. I went surfing around noon and the ocean won this round. Does it mar my beauty?"

She chuckled. "Not beyond repair," she said. "Surfing? Are you a Californian?"

"Actually I started it out at Montauk."

"I have some friends out there," she said, "whom I visit from time to time in the summer. But they don't surf. All they do is sit around and drink and adulterize."

"Everyone to his own amusements," he said. "What do *you* do on your holidays?"

He was relieved when she didn't say that she adulterized, too. "Me?" she said. "I catch up on my reading. For some reason it's almost impossible to read in New York. Haven't you noticed that?"

"Now that you mention it—yes."

"A publisher friend of mine tells me that more than fifty percent of all the books sold in the United States are bought in New York. There must be more unread books on the shelves in New York apartments than in the Library of Congress."

"What sort of stuff do you read?"

"I'm a Civil War buff," she said, smiling. "Isn't it absurd? My father was a career officer in the Army and the way he talked about it, you'd think he was at every battle from Bull Run to Appomattox. I'm sorry I wasn't around to meet Robert E. Lee and J.E.B. Stuart. Well, you can't be everywhere."

The waiter came in to tell them their table was ready and after a little grave consultation they decided it was a nice afternoon for another daiquiri and the barman said he'd bring the drinks in to the restaurant.

By the time they finished their lunch they knew a great deal about each other and they were more than slightly tipsy on the daiquiris and what had turned out to be two bottles of wine. It was clear to Michael, too, that the signals he had sensed in her manner the night he met her were not merely standard party flirtatiousness. It was also plain that she was lonely so far from home and grateful to him for having called her.

When they left the restaurant, they hesitated a moment in the shade of a big eucalyptus tree that smelled of pepper. "Do you know what?" she said. "I was going to go over my lines this afternoon. Only I'm not going to. I have a nice bottle of cognac in my room . . ." Her voice trailed off.

"Just the thing after a lunch like that," he said.

So they went to her room. But they never bothered even pouring the cognac.

Exquisitely made and amorously gluttonous, she turned out to be just what was needed after an old girl's wedding and nearly drowning in the Pacific Ocean.

"Is this adulterizing?" she asked. They were both dressed by now and finally she had poured the cognac and they were having just one little nip before going out to dinner and he was very fond of her and wished that he could be more than that and knew that he never could be.

"What do you think?"

"No." She shook her head, her short soft blond hair fluffing around her small, oval face. "It is pleasure given and pleasure taken. The sweet and sensible fruit of the sexual revolution. Did you fight in that war, Mister Storrs?"

He grinned. "I happened to be away at the time. "

"Anyway," she said, "I'm not married. You can't be a woman taken in adultery if you're not married, can you?"

"I don't think so."

"Are you married? I suppose I should have asked that question at the bar, when I was making up my mind, shouldn't I?"

"You were making up your mind *that* soon?"

"I'm famous as a quick decision maker. *Are* you married?"

"Yes."

She shrugged. "*Tant pis.* I studied in France for a year. We're not going to let it spoil our glorious Saturday, are we?"

"No." He took her in his arms and kissed her.

"Signed, sealed and delivered," she said. "Although I don't know exactly what I mean by that. Now, you've promised me dinner."

They ate in a small French restaurant, by candlelight. The food was good and they had the third bottle of wine of the day and they looked at each other with affection, untroubled for the moment by desire. His body felt light and floating, making every moment particular and lasting.

"And tomorrow?" she said.

"Tomorrow we continue as before."

She grinned at him. "You sure know how to talk to girls, don't you? What are the plans?"

"I'll drive you down to the beach and we'll eat abalone and sand dabs and maybe have some fish soup and listen to the roar of the ocean."

"I should work . . ." she began.

"I know. And you're not going to."

She grinned again. "I guess that's what I was going to say." Then she saw a man and a woman being seated across the room and waved and said to Michael, "Oh, there's an old friend of mine from New

York. I had no idea she was out here. Do you mind if I go over and say hello?"

"Will I have to be introduced?"

"No."

"Then go."

She patted his hand and stood up and crossed the room, her blond hair gleaming in the flickering light of the candles on the tables. He was through eating and he sat bent over a little, his elbows on the table, his hands supporting his chin. What a dear, bright, straightforward woman, he thought. He hoped that later on she would not regret the day. He remembered Josey's departing cry, "Why the fuck couldn't you have fallen in love with *me?*" What would Florence cry when *she* departed or when he did? Christ, he thought despairingly, any other man sitting here after a day like this would at least wonder if he was going to fall in love this time. I can't even wonder. I *know.* I go through the motions of love, but love is out of my reach, except for one woman, and she is disappearing farther and farther into the distance. I don't even have the gallantry to try to lie or pretend. And with somebody like Florence it isn't just two bodies senselessly coming together. There's so much more to it than that, but finally not enough, and eventually she'll know it, too, and then how will she take it? There again, it won't be like Josey. He could not imagine Florence ever saying, "No hearts will be broken."

When I leave on Monday, he thought, I must make it clear that it's over, that when we're back in New York we will not see each other. One lovely, perfect weekend and then *finito, basta.* Josey had said, "There are no rules here." That might do for Josey, although he no longer was so sure about that after her parting outburst, but it would not do for him, not with somebody like the woman whose small blond head shone in the candlelight across the room.

He sat back, closed his eyes, rubbed them for a moment, then sat staring straight ahead of him. When she came back to the table and sat down opposite him he blinked his eyes and shook his head as though he were waking himself up. He tried to smile at her, but he wasn't quite sure how it came out.

"Michael," she said, "has anything happened?"

"Why?"

"You look so—melancholy."

The word shocked him. He remembered Tracy telling him the

same thing. "It's just a trick of the light," he said airily. "I'm not at my best in candlelight."

"What were you thinking?" she asked seriously.

"Nothing. If I was thinking anything I imagine I was saying to my-self, Boy, have you lucked out today!"

She smiled, reassured. "Why don't you put it in the plural? I'd like it better that way. Like, for example—Boy, have *we* lucked out today!"

"In this case," he said, glad to have the conversation light again, "the singular is more modest."

"I don't believe in modesty. I'm a good actress and I know it and I let everybody know it."

"I'm not really good at anything, Florence darling," he said, "and I guess I think if I don't brag about myself I'll get the benefit of the doubt and people will believe I'm hiding some great talent or virtue behind my mask of modesty." He reached over and took her hand. "Now, that's enough of talk like that. We're on our own private big glorious holiday—let's save soul-searching for the five-day working week."

They slept together that night in Florence's room and had a sunny day at the beach. As he had promised, Michael did not take along his board. It wasn't a good day for surfing anyway. The sea was calm and the few boys and girls out on boards sat disconsolately on the gently rippling water waiting for waves that never arrived. Where were you yesterday, friends? he thought, feeling superior as he watched the distant figures bobbing listlessly up and down, merely getting sunburned.

They didn't talk about anything serious and Michael didn't ask her when she was likely to be back in New York and she didn't ask him if it was possible that he would be sent back to the Coast in the next month or two, and she entertained him by reciting monologues from Shakespeare and long sections of *The Waste Land* and singing, in a low voice, "The Battle Hymn of the Republic," which, she said, was one of the first songs her father had taught her.

They slept together again that night, reveling in each other and not thinking about the morning. They both had to get up early, she to go to the studio and he to catch his plane, and there was no time to make any plans or deliver warnings. They kissed good-bye hastily and went their separate ways, already at a distance from each other.

When he signed for his bill at the desk, he told the clerk he was leaving his surfboard at the hotel and would let them know where to send it when he needed it.

When he got back to New York he went directly to the office to report in and old man Cornwall teased him about being so tan and asked him if his job in California involved lying on the beach for eight hours a day. He got out of the office as soon as he could. It seemed airless, aseptic, like a hospital, with people hurrying through corridors to tend to terminal cases and other people waiting fearfully to hear mortal pronouncements.

Tracy was sitting looking at the news on television when he got home and kissed him reservedly without getting up when he came into the room.

"Anything important tonight?" he asked after he had told her his trip had been successful.

"Nothing much," she said. "The world is crumbling, as it does every evening at seven. Nothing to worry about except whether we'll all be alive next week. I was too busy to make dinner. I thought it might be nice to go out your first night home."

"That's a good idea," he said, although he was tired and looking forward to a quiet evening.

They did not have much to say to each other during dinner and it was only while they were having their coffee that Tracy said, "I tried to call you Saturday night." She looked at him squarely, without emotion. "Several times."

"Did you have anything special to say?"

"No." She shrugged. "Just that I missed you. There was no answer."

"I was invited out to the beach for the weekend. I should have left the number at the hotel."

"Yes," she said, "you should have."

He was sure she knew he was lying.

It isn't going to last much longer now, he thought. He wanted to get up and fold her in his arms and hold her tight, but it wasn't something you could do in a restaurant, so he merely ordered another coffee.

CHAPTER
SEVEN

He sat in his office, going over the report he was preparing for a textile company with plants in South Carolina and Kentucky but with its headquarters in New York. He had stopped volunteering for trips out of town and since the time in California he had not been out of the city on business for more than a year. In his report on the textile company's intricate dealings, he saw that he had tentatively scrawled, in ink—"Over a period of five years, it can be confidently predicted, a sum in excess of a million dollars could be saved by moving all offices to a central location in the South." He stared at what he could recognize was his own handwriting, but he could not remember how he had arrived at that conclusion or when he had written it. The lapses of memory had started some six months ago and he had thought nothing of it, but now they were coming more frequently and closer together. My mind, he thought, is in the process of absconding.

He wiped his brow with his handkerchief. The air-conditioning was on, but he was sweating in his shirtsleeves. He had complained several times about the air-conditioning in his office and the engineer of the building had come up to test it and told him everything was in order. He couldn't bring himself to tell the engineer what he privately believed—that the machinery that cooled the hot summer air from outside also malevolently extracted most of the oxygen from the cold blasts it blew into his office and that he was having increasing difficulty in breathing. He had suggested to the engineer that it would be better to close off the machinery in his office completely and open the windows, but the engineer had patiently told him that there was no way of opening the windows in the building.

His secretary came in with a pile of letters. "What are those?" he asked. The woman, stern-faced, efficient and forty, had worked for him for five years but for the moment he couldn't remember her name.

She looked at him curiously as she placed the pile of letters on his desk. "You dictated these this morning," she said. She shivered. She was wearing a dark brown cardigan sweater.

"Thank you very much," he said. He didn't remember dictating any letters that morning.

She left the room and he stared at the door after she had closed it behind her. B, he thought, I'm sure her name begins with B. It was 90 degrees outside. Imagine wearing a sweater.

He pushed the pile of letters and the report he was working on toward the back of the desk and stood up and went to a window. It was divided in half horizontally and there was a metal strip that he could reach just above head height. He put both his hands on it and pushed, but of course it didn't budge. He knew it was useless because he had tried it many times before. One day, he thought, it might suddenly, magically open. Still, the men who had designed the building might have very sound reasons for closing out the sound and the fumes of the city from him. His office was on the thirty-sixth floor and if the window was open what would there be to stop him from throwing himself out?

He stared out at the towers that surrounded him, an infinity of windows. Behind each one there were men and women like him, insulated from the climate, the uproar of the city muted, all of them like him dealing in money, money which they never saw, money that was merely figures in books, money that was, as far as they knew, as much a fiction as anything in a child's fairy tale, money for which they sacrificed all their working lives. Are they all serious? he thought. Did they ever say, like him, waste, waste? What was it to him if whoever it was who owned the textile company saved or didn't save a million dollars in five years? What was it, even to *them?*

He stared out the window, looking downtown. He could see the tower of the Empire State Building on Thirty-fourth Street. He had received a note from Florence some months ago and the address on the envelope had been on Thirty-fifth Street. He wondered if one of the windows gleaming in the hot sunlight within his line of vision was hers. Was she at home that afternoon, did she have air-conditioning, was she taking a shower, sipping a cup of tea, learning new lines, thinking of him? He had not answered her letter, and some time later he had received a note from her. "I get the message," the note read. It was signed "F.G." In what book of etiquette had women read that it was elegant to sign only by their initials?

It had been a year since he had seen her in California and while he had not been courageous enough to tell her why he couldn't see her, he had kept his promise to himself. He hadn't called any other women, either. It was no hardship for him. He had no desire to touch a woman. Including, unfortunately, his wife.

He had done his best, he thought, to repair their marriage. He had not gone out of town, except to the Hamptons on weekends with Tracy; he had been chaste, celibate, rather, which was no way to solidify a marriage, but he couldn't help himself. God knew what Tracy thought about it. Probably that he had an affair going that sated him. Better that than the truth.

He admired Tracy for her patience with him, her stoic acceptance of his behavior, her evident quiet love for him, her forbearance of his increasingly forgetful behavior, her gratitude for the fact that he did not slip away to jump out of airplanes or to ski or to hang-glide or surf. The surfboard was still lying somewhere in the storeroom of the hotel in California.

He went back to his desk, signed all the letters Miss Burwell—ah, Burwell, that was it—had laid on his desk. How long, he thought, before I blow?

◇◇◇◇◇

That weekend he drove out to the Hamptons with Tracy. It was raining and it had turned cool and when he was out of the office he could breathe normally and he knew the city would be empty and bearable for two days, but Tracy was intent on getting away and he said he'd love to accompany her. He just hoped her parents weren't giving a party, one of those parties at which he didn't know anybody or had forgotten the names of the people he had met two weeks before and where there was always a drunk who owned a company or was the chairman of some board who cornered him and wanted to talk to him about the state of the economy and the confusion in Washington.

He now let Tracy drive because in the spring he had lost his way, although he had driven out dozens of times and the car could have practically made the trip on its own. They had wound up completely lost, and the trip that usually took only two hours had taken them almost five. He had lost control of himself and had cursed himself in an almost endless stream of gutter profanity as they wandered through the bleak tangle of the streets of Queens, had called himself all kinds of an idiot, using words that he had never used before. He was not a man who ordinarily lapsed into profanity and Tracy had sat white and silent as he twisted the wheel violently around corners, suddenly backed up, grinding the gears, heedlessly slammed into parked cars as he suddenly recognized that twice he had been on the same street before.

At one moment, she had said quietly, "Michael, why don't you let me take the wheel for a while?"

"Will you for Christ's sake shut your goddamn mouth," he had shouted at her and she had relapsed into silence. When they finally got to her parents' house, his hands were shaking and the sweat was pouring from him and he had slumped over the wheel. He didn't say anything for a moment and Tracy didn't make a move to get out of the car. "Forgive me," he whispered, "forgive me."

"Of course," she said quietly and leaned over and kissed his cheek and when they went into the house she made him take a hot bath and brought him a martini to drink while he was soaking in the steaming water.

"Maybe," he said, trying to make a weak joke, "I ought to curse more often. It seems to pay great dividends in husband-pampering."

"Drink it slowly," she said. "You're only going to get one. And from now on I drive."

"With good reason," he said. "This is the best goddamn martini I've ever tasted."

"Why the goddamn?"

"I retract the goddamn." Small favors, he thought. Not enough.

She sat down on a low stool next to the bathtub where he lay, his skin caressed by a froth of opaque rainbow bubbles from a preparation Tracy had put into the water. "Michael," she said, as he sipped at the martini, "I think it might be a good idea if you went and talked to a psychoanalyst."

"Oh," Michael said. "McCain did call you that Saturday morning."

"He did," she said. "He sounded like a thoughtful man. I don't go along with priests or rabbis or gurus, but the analyst is a sensible idea. I don't suppose I have to tell you, but you've been acting awfully strangely for a long time, you haven't been yourself at all."

"And a few hours on the couch, and I'll be back to the carefree, happy-go-lucky young fellow you married."

"You were never a carefree, happy-go-lucky young fellow," Tracy said evenly. "And I didn't think so when we got married. I think you need help and it's worth the chance."

"Help," he said. "My dear Mr. Storrs"—he put on a slight accent that he believed sounded faintly Viennese—"you hated your mother, you felt rejected by your father because he died when you were a child, you are subconsciously equating your wife with your mother, your success as a student raised expectations of success in later life that are not satisfied in the job you hold, your jumping out of airplanes etcetera is an unconscious attempt, a symbolic attempt at escape from restrictions and resentments that are rooted deep in your childhood. A textbook case. You must understand these things and, understanding them, adapt yourself to them. Fifty dollars, please? Or maybe the price has gone up. Inflation."

Tracy sighed. "As usual, you're half again too smart for your own good."

"I've read the same books they have," Michael said. He finished the martini with a long gulp and leaned over and put the glass down on the floor next to the bathtub.

Tracy automatically picked up the glass and twirled it absently between her fingers. "Michael, maybe he'll go further than that. Maybe he'll make you discover why you want to die. Dinner is in fifteen minutes." She stood up abruptly and went out of the bathroom, carrying the glass.

Oh, darling, darling, he thought, the voodoo men will not fix anything. There are no textbook cases.

◇◇◇◇◇

The next day was raw and windy, but Michael and Mr. Lawrence had planned to go sailing in the morning and they got into the car and drove down to Three Mile Harbor, where the twenty-five foot sloop, named after Tracy, was berthed. All the rest of the Lawrence family detested sailing, so, after they had promised to be back at one o'clock for lunch, the two men went alone, wearing heavy sweaters and wet-weather slickers. Even the long, protected, ordinarily placid harbor was ruffled with small whitecaps. Michael looked across the water doubtfully. "Don't you think it's a little rough, Phil?" he said.

"Been out in stuff a lot worse than this," Lawrence said. "I've been looking forward all week to getting out of reach of the sound of female voices." He was an ardent and skillful sailor and he was always hunting for people to help him crew the boat.

"If you say," Michael said, still doubtful.

They cast off and Lawrence deftly got the boat away from the dock and into the harbor proper, using the outboard motor. Once they were in the channel leading out to the wide reaches of the sound, Lawrence cut the motor and they raised the mainsail and then Michael put up the jib. The boat heeled over sharply and sped toward the mouth of the harbor. It looked rough out in the sound and Michael said, "Maybe we just ought to cruise around a bit inside the harbor, Phil."

"Nonsense," Lawrence said. "This boat has handled seas five times as bad as this." He was not by nature a vain man, but he was touchy when matters of seamanship came up. "I'm not a fair weather sailor. If all you did was go out and flap around when the sea is as flat as a pancake, there'd be no sense in owning a boat."

"You're the skipper," Michael said. He could see that the old man, his long gray hair streaming in the wind and his face highly colored and wet with spray, was enjoying himself hugely.

Let him have his fun, Michael thought. He, himself, was a good sailor and had never been seasick in his life. He had sailed perhaps a dozen times with his father-in-law and had been bored when there were only little puffs of wind and they had moved slowly and erratically, trying to catch the light airs.

Out on the sound, the wind caught hold and the sails were taut and straining and the boat, heeled over more steeply now, with the rail in the water, bounced sturdily through the waves, the curl at their bow impressive because of their speed. Michael sat crouched in the cockpit, leaning to port to balance the starboard heel. Lawrence sat next to him, bent over, putting his full weight on the helm to keep them on course.

"This is the life, Mike, isn't it?" Lawrence grinned at him. "Better than bird-watching. And there isn't another damn fool out today." It was the closest Michael had ever heard the old man come to gloating. "Go down into the cabin and if you're lucky you'll find a little locker on the port side. If you open the door you'll find a bottle of fine bourbon there that might sharpen the crew's senses mightily. Don't fall overboard on the way, though." He laughed into the wind.

Michael made his way forward and stooped to get into the little cabin, which was full of sail bags and lines and had a primitive head. He got out the bottle of bourbon and climbed over a life jacket on the way back, noting that it was the only one in the cabin.

"Open it," Lawrence commanded. "And take a swig. The damned steward forgot to put out the glasses." There was a sudden stronger gust of wind and Lawrence said, "Whoops" and fought the helm. "Don't spill any of it, sailor," Lawrence said. "It's twelve-year-old life-giving nectar."

Michael lifted the bottle to his lips and took a good mouthful. He felt a sharp burning sensation in his throat and then a warmth in his gut.

"How do you like it?" Lawrence asked.

"Just the thing for morning tea on the high seas," Michael said, wiping the rim of the bottle and handing it to Lawrence.

Lawrence took a long gulp, snorting as it went down. "Takes twenty years off a man," he said, as he handed the bottle to Michael, who screwed the top back on again. "Hold on to it. I think we'll be making several visits to the bar."

They bounced on in silence for a while, the mainsail cracking like pistol shots at irregular intervals.

"Michael," Lawrence said, his tone changed, "there's something I've been wanting to talk to you about and there's no way of getting you alone in the house."

"What is it?" Michael said, bracing himself for what he expected was coming.

"It's about you and Tracy." The old man took a long breath, as though he would need fresh oxygen for what he was going to say. "You're not getting along very well together, are you?"

"Well enough."

"We'd better have another drink," Lawrence said. "Truth serum." They each drank again.

"I like you, Michael. You know that."

"I know."

"And I love Tracy. The best of the three. She's a tremendous girl."

"Tremendous."

"You're both putting on an act for the old folks," Lawrence said somberly. "The loving smart young couple, living the glamorous New York life. Only you're not the loving smart young couple and you're not living the glamorous life, are you?"

"Not completely," Michael admitted. "No."

"You treat each other as though you're both made of glass. As though if either of you made one wrong move one or the other would crack into a thousand pieces. She's a sad girl now, Michael, and she wasn't made to be a sad girl."

"I know."

"What is it? You got somebody else?"

"No." Go back as far as a year and this was no lie.

"She have another fella?"

"Not that I know of."

"Can I do anything to help?" The old man was appealing directly to him.

"I don't think so. We'll have to work it out ourselves."

"Do you think you'll be able to do it?" Lawrence's tone was anxious.

"I'm not sure," Michael said. "Has she said anything to you or to her mother?"

"Not a word." Lawrence shook his head dejectedly. "She's always been like that. She only brings good news into the house, never anything that she's worried about. Well, there hasn't been any good news for a long time. Daughters're mysterious territory. Let's have the bottle."

He took a long swig. Then Michael took another drink and recapped the bottle.

"You travel too goddamned much, Michael," Lawrence said harshly.

"Not anymore."

"Not anymore." Lawrence nodded, his long wet hair swinging over his eyes, like a shaggy old English sheepdog. "In the past, though?"

"Perhaps."

"You don't mean perhaps," Lawrence said belligerently. "You mean yes."

"I mean perhaps. It goes deeper than that." He could have said that it went back to a downhill ski race, two men colliding and dying in mid-air, himself nearly being drowned a couple of times while surfing, almost being killed because he was driving too fast, going berserk because he was lost in the suburbs of Queens. But he didn't offer anything more. He would not complain to his wife's father about her, would not say that if they both had known about themselves and each other before they were married they would never have been married. All he said was, "There are certain things on which we don't see eye to eye." Like his screaming distaste for his work, his abhorrence of the city, like their not making love for months on end, like his refusal to have children. None of this was the sort of thing you could say to your wife's father while you were sharing a bottle of bourbon with him and he was straining all his old muscles to keep the boat from heeling over completely. "If it's any comfort to you, if anything's gone wrong, it's my fault, not hers."

"One year after I was married," Lawrence said, "I was ready to leave her mother. It was my fault, too. Luckily, it turned out she was pregnant. How is it you haven't had any children?"

"That's a question you'd better ask Tracy."

"She wouldn't tell me, either," Lawrence said sadly.

There was another, stronger gust of wind and the boat shuddered and dipped its bowsprit into a wave.

"The wind's freshening a bit, Michael," Lawrence said. "You'd better put the bottle where no harm can come to it and then get down the mainsail. It's getting a little rough, so you better remember the old maxim—one hand for the boat and one for yourself."

"I've heard it."

"And while you're in the cabin," Lawrence said, almost casually, "you'd better bring out the life jackets. I do believe we're in for something of a squall."

Michael went forward to the cabin and came out with the life jacket. "There's only this one," he said, putting it at Lawrence's feet. Before Lawrence could say anything Michael went forward, holding on with difficulty as the deck bucked beneath him. It took him a long time and all the strength he could muster to take down the mainsail and furl it with the wind snapping at the sail like a pack of malicious dogs.

"Well done," Lawrence said when he got back to the cockpit.

"I've sailed before."

"I know. I'm grateful for it. I've sailed with men who couldn't drop an anchor without going in after it." He looked up, squinting at the darkening, violent gray and black sky. "I guess I misread the weather. *Hubris*. We're going back. Get over to the other side fast when we swing around. Ready?"

"Ready."

Lawrence put all his weight onto the helm and the boat swung around, groaning and creaking, every plank protesting, the wind screeching through the stays. Both of them scrambled, the old man surprisingly agile as he switched his position. Now they were heeling over more than ever even with only the jib up—and Lawrence was whistling through his teeth a tuneless, abstracted sound.

"We're in trouble," Michael said.

"A person might say that." Lawrence kept up the same tuneless whistling, slacking off as much as he dared. "Sorry about that."

"Put on the life jacket," Michael said.

"I told you to bring out the two of them."

"I know what you said. There's only one."

"The cabin's a mess. I always mean to straighten it out," Lawrence said. "You didn't look closely enough."

"There's only one."

"Do you think you can hold her on course while I go and look?"

"I'll hold her," Michael said. "But you're wasting your time."

"Here, take it."

Michael slid over and grabbed the tiller. It nearly pulled out of his hand and he had to lean his full weight on it. The old man must be a lot stronger than he looks, he thought, as he watched Lawrence go crablike forward to the cabin. He wished he had kept the bottle of bourbon up on deck.

In a little while Lawrence came skittering back. "Those goddamn kids," Lawrence said, as he took the helm. "Little wharf rats. They steal everything they can lay their hands on."

"I told you there was only one."

"So you did. Somewhat disappointing, isn't it? Put it on."

"Not me," Michael said. "It's for you."

"It's my fault. I should have looked before we took off. Put it on," Lawrence said sternly.

Michael stared landward. The low bluffs that bordered the eastern side to the entrance of the harbor were at least two miles away. "If it comes to the sticking point, I can swim for it. Christ, I could swim from here to Connecticut if I had to."

"I'm not in the mood for youthful boasting. Put the goddamn thing on. This is an order from the captain of the vessel."

"If you don't put it on, I'm going to throw it overboard. I have no desire to float into shore and tell your family that I left you to drown."

"Nobody's drowning," Lawrence snapped.

"Will you put that in writing?"

Lawrence looked stern for a moment, then smiled, a thin-lipped Yankee old man's smile. "I didn't think I could convince you," he said.

Michael held the helm while Lawrence struggled into the jacket. The wind was howling now and the waves were breaking completely over the craft, the water sluicing through the cockpit. "Have you got a radio on board?" he asked.

"No. Never needed it before. I'm rarely out of sight of land."

"We're in sight of land now," Michael said, "and we could use a radio."

"You should have been around when I outfitted the *Tracy*. You're a few years too late with your excellent suggestions."

Michael stared at the old man, struggling with the helm, his lips bared in a crazy grin. By God, Michael thought, the old lunatic is enjoying it.

Then the jib split, with a noise like a cannon going off. In a few seconds it was in shreds and the boat broached. Hastily, Michael tore off his tennis shoes and threw off his foul-weather gear and sweater, then his pants. If he was going to have to swim for it, he wasn't going to do it dressed as though for a winter in the Alps.

A few seconds later the *Tracy* capsized and they were both in the water. The boat lay on its side, heaving up and down wildly. Lawrence was a few feet away from him, appearing and disappearing in the waves. Michael grabbed him by the life jacket and, both of them swimming furiously, reached the boat. As it swept down upon them, they both grabbed on to the rail.

"Can you hold on?" Michael gasped.

"I'd better," Lawrence said. He swallowed a lot of water, but he held on. From then on he didn't say anything as, side by side, they wallowed in the turmoil of the sea.

Good old America, Michael thought, almost laughing, you can drown on both sides of it. From sea to shining sea.

After a while he could see that Lawrence's grip on the rail was getting weaker and he decided that if the old man let go he would let go too and take a chance that he could keep them both afloat.

Then, as suddenly as the squall had come up, it passed over them, howling westward. The sea calmed magically and it was a lot easier to hang on. But a mist thickened around them and soon Michael couldn't see land and knew that if he had to swim for it, he'd have to guess in which direction to go.

There was no way of telling how long they had been in the water. Both their watches had stopped when they had been hurled overboard and there was no sun to indicate how late it was getting. Lawrence was getting blue from the cold and his hands were becoming a numb, frozen white on the rail. What seemed like many hours later, they heard the sound of a helicopter overhead. Lawrence finally spoke. "They must have phoned the coast guard at Montauk," he said.

But the mist was too thick for anyone to see them from a helicopter and they listened as the sound of the engines dwindled in the distance.

One of Lawrence's hands slipped and Michael put an arm around him to hold him steady. Lawrence grinned weakly at him. "I thought you'd be in Connecticut by now," he said.

Then they heard the sound of powerful motors approaching them. The men in the helicopter must have seen them after all. A shadow loomed in the mist, grew closer, darker, as Michael waved and shouted. The engines slowed and a moment later the coast guard vessel glided up to them and figures on board were throwing ropes down to them. Stiff-fingered, Michael tied one of the ropes under Lawrence's armpits and he was hoisted aboard. Then, with his ultimate effort, he tied a sling for himself and was pulled up to the boat's deck.

As the coast guardsmen were putting a line on the *Tracy* to tow her behind the cutter, they were hustled down below decks and toweled off and given blankets and hot coffee. "What time is it?" Michael asked the captain of the ship, who had come down to see how the two men he had rescued were doing.

"Four-ten," the captain said. "What time did you go into the drink?"

"About eleven A.M."

The captain whistled. "Five hours in the water." He looked with admiration at Lawrence, whose hands were trembling as they held the steaming mug of coffee. "You have a tough old friend."

"You can say that again."

Lawrence seemed too stunned to understand that they were talking about him, shivering and holding onto the mug with his two hands as though that, too, might be in danger of sliding away from him.

"You were lucky, pal," the captain said to Michael. "We got messages that two other boats foundered and we haven't found any survivors yet. You're also lucky that we've had a hot spell these last ten days and the Sound is a lot warmer than it usually is this early in the season. Water sports." He shook his head. "May I suggest that from now on when you want to go sailing on the bounding main you call us and ask for the weather forecast? We were sending out small-craft warnings all morning."

"Talk to the old man," Michael said. "He's the skipper."

Lawrence looked up at the captain and smiled slyly. "Ulysses never called the coast guard before setting out for Troy."

The captain laughed and patted Lawrence on the shoulder. "Okay, Skipper, have it your way," he said and left them to go topside.

"Nice fella," Lawrence said, finally putting the mug down. "A little young to be running a ship this size, don't you think?"

"Old enough for us, Phil," Michael said.

"I guess so." Lawrence stretched out on a bunk and pulled the blanket tight around him. "You don't mind if I take a little snooze, do you? I want to be fresh for dinner." He was snoring in ten seconds.

Dressed in a sailor's pants and sweater that had been loaned him, Michael was on deck as they came alongside the dock at Three Mile Harbor. Tracy and her mother and her sisters were on the dock. They were dressed in sweaters and they were all wearing scarves that twisted in the wind and to Michael they looked like the womenfolk of fishermen, waiting to see which of their men were safe and which ones had been lost on the last voyage. He waved to them, and Tracy's sisters and her mother waved back, but Tracy kept her hands at her sides, plunged into the pockets of her sweater.

So be it, he thought and went down to wake the old man and help him get into a pair of dungarees and a pea coat. There was no comb in the cabin and there was nothing Michael could do about Lawrence's hair, which hung stiffly in all directions and gave him a wild and baleful appearance, like a malevolent, senile pirate. When they climbed to the deck Lawrence waved once to his family, then went aft to look at the *Tracy* lying on its beam, its sail tattered, low in the water. He shook his head sadly. "Poor betrayed *Tracy*."

Michael wished he had given the boat another name.

They debarked, with a sailor carrying Lawrence's soaked clothes and life jacket in a duffel bag. All the women kissed and hugged the old man, and Mrs. Lawrence and Tracy's sisters hugged Michael, too. Tracy stood off to one side watching, expressionlessly. Mrs. Lawrence bundled her husband into the station wagon with the two girls, and Tracy and Michael walked to where the sedan was parked and got in, Tracy behind the wheel, all in silence.

Tracy turned the ignition key and the motor started up, but she didn't put it in gear immediately. "What can we ever do to thank those men?" she said.

Michael shrugged. "Thank them. That's all."

"When I called the coast guard station and told them you were supposed to be home by one o'clock and you were already an hour late, I could hear him say to somebody in the room, 'Two more goddamn idiots.'"

Michael didn't say anything and she put the car into gear and they moved off and followed the station wagon. Michael glanced over at his wife. Her hands were so tight on the wheel that her knuckles showed white and her face was rigid, her mouth set in a grim line, her eyes narrowed and glowering. Finally, she let it out. "It's not enough that you don't give a damn whether your wife becomes a widow or not, you have to drag my father along with you."

"I tried to insist . . ." he began.

"I can just imagine how you tried to insist."

"You ask your father . . ."

"He admires you, he's told me he wished he had a son like you, he'd like to pretend he's almost the same age as you. I know you. Without even saying a word, you shamed him into it. He's a careful, peaceful man, a sensible sailor, it's the first time in his life he's ever done anything as suicidal as this. I wish I'd never brought you into the house."

"Let's continue this when you've calmed down a bit, shall we?" he said placatingly.

"I'm calm right now. And there's nothing to continue."

The rest of the drive they rode in silence until they reached the house.

Lawrence was coughing and looked feverish when he got out of the car and Mrs. Lawrence called a doctor and put her husband to bed, where he fell into a troubled sleep. When the doctor came he said Mr. Lawrence would have to remain in bed for a few days and stay quiet. The atmosphere in the house was mournful and Michael felt that all four women kept looking at him accusingly and he excused himself from dinner and took the car and went into Bridgehampton, where he had a hamburger at a bar and drank too much both before and after the meal.

Tracy was waiting for him when he got home. Except for the light in their bedroom and in the second floor hall, all the lights in the house were out. He felt deathly tired as he went up the steps and stumbled, knocking against a painting on the wall that fell off its hook with a shattering noise. Cursing under his breath, he tried to put the picture back but failed, and carried it the rest of the way up the steps. The door to his and Tracy's room opened and he stood revealed, swaying a little, feeling ludicrous with the picture under his arm, as Tracy came out into the hall, lit by the shaft of light behind her.

"You don't have to wake up the whole house to applaud your entrance," she whispered, but the whisper was frigid and grating.

"No lights," he said with dignity. "And what sort of an idea is it to hang pictures on a staircase?"

"I think we can discuss your ideas on interior decoration in the privacy of our bedroom," Tracy said and pushed the door open wider so that he could go in.

He placed the picture carefully against the wall and went into the room. Tracy closed the door behind her and stood against it, looking at him as he sat down on a straight wooden chair, his body stiffly erect. The pallid rigidity of her face was in contrast to the soft, pretty wool robe she was wearing.

"For your own good, Michael," she said, "I suggest that when you're as drunk as you obviously are now, you leave the car outside the bar or wherever else you happen to drink yourself senseless and take a taxi home. I know you don't mind killing yourself, but I doubt that you'd like to do it crashing unheroically into a tree."

"I'm not drunk." He knew his speech was a little thick and that he had had some trouble climbing the stairs, but his mind felt clear, ready to make sensible decisions.

"In the last year or so, Michael," Tracy went on steadily, "you've become a drunkard. A solitary, pitiful drunkard."

"I won't argue with you."

"I don't intend to argue," Tracy said. "Waiting here tonight I realized it was all over, Michael. It's too bad, but there it is. Today was the end."

"I told you I insisted . . ." he said, feeling misused. "I know I've been guilty a lot of times before for many things . . ."

She laughed, without amusement.

"But today," he continued doggedly, "it wasn't my fault. You have to believe that."

"I don't have to believe anything. It's been coming on for a long time and I kept hoping that one day you'd wake up and see what you were doing to yourself, to me. I can't live anymore being afraid that every time you go out of the house the telephone will ring and somebody will tell me my husband is dead. If you can't bear even to touch me for over a year and you have to whore all over the country—don't think I haven't heard, I have good friends or not-so-good friends who are more than anxious to let me know what my husband is doing— and if you detest me so much you'd rather die than stand the sight of me, why in the name of God do you want to hang on?"

"I love you," he said, staring down at his hands.

Again she laughed, the same mirthless half-sob. "Maybe, in your own crazy way, you do. But if it is love, it's love that's destroying me. And just for your information, you're not the only one who's found consolation in other beds."

"What do you mean by that?" He looked up, genuinely surprised. Somehow, it had never occurred to him that she . . . There had been no signs. Womanly deceit, he thought, hurt.

"You know what I mean," Tracy said. "What did you expect?"

He considered this for a moment. "I should have expected it," he said humbly. "I don't blame you."

"If it's of any use to your ego," she said, "it was never any good, it changed what I thought of myself, it erased me."

"Oh, darling," he mumbled sadly.

"It's too late for darlings."

"Do you want a divorce?"

Standing, tense and accusing, her back against the door, a prosecuting attorney nearing the bitter end of a long trial, she sighed. "I don't know what I want except that tomorrow I want you to take the car—it's your car, anyway, and . . ."

"Our car," he said.

"There is no more our. There's only yours and mine from now on. And tomorrow you take your car and drive in to the city and take every last thing of yours out of my apartment."

He looked at the big double bed. He knew that he couldn't lie side by side with her for one last time for the rest of the night. Finally, he stood up. "In that case," he said, taking great trouble to speak clearly and intelligently, "in that case, there's no sense in waiting till morning. I'll pack my bag and get out right now."

"You can't drive in your condition. You'll wake up in jail."

"Let me worry about my condition," he said and went to the closet and got out his overnight bag and started throwing things into it.

Tracy shrugged. "Have it your own way," she said. She watched silently as he packed his bag and locked it. He picked the bag up and started for the door. She stood there, blocking his way. He felt the tears coming to his eyes as he looked at the lovely grim face that he had adored in so many different moods and was furious for his tears. "What're you going to tell your mother and father?" he asked.

"Something. Anything. That you got a telephone call on business and had to be in town in the morning. Later on I'll figure how to break it to them. I'll take my share of the blame. They like you and there's no need to change that. Incompatibility, how's that for a bright new excuse?" She laughed again. "You really want to go now —tonight?"

"Nothing could make me stay."

She shrugged, moved away from the door. "Drive carefully."

"Will do." He opened the door and stood there for a moment.

"Here," she said, suddenly moving past him through the doorway, "let me put the light on again so you can see where you're going." She snapped on the staircase light, and carrying the bag, he walked slowly down the steps, holding securely to the banister.

He went across the living room, where he and Philip Lawrence had played chess so many evenings while the women chatted in the background, and opened the front door and stepped out into the damp and foggy Atlantic night. Behind him the light went out.

He threw the bag into the back of the car and got in and started the engine. He looked up at the second story where the one light shone. Then that light went out and the house was dark. He drove out through the front gate and onto the road, the fog swirling low on the glistening road in the diffused glare of the headlights. Tears clouded his vision again and again, and he drove slowly and with care, but even so he was alarmed when he saw the flashing lights of a police car speeding out of the mist behind him. But the police car swept past him, the officers not interested in a weeping drunk going forty miles an hour, hugging the edge of the highway, the armed men hurrying to an accident, a murder, a fire, to any one of a thousand disasters that could happen in the middle of the night one hundred miles from the city of New York.

CHAPTER
EIGHT

He was seated at his desk in the office, going over a thick sheaf of reports and occasionally looking out the window at the icy autumnal rain that was beating down on the streets of New York. The heat was on and as usual he was sweating, because there was no way to regulate it in the individual offices and whoever *did* regulate it in the bowels of the skyscraper must have had blood that had been thinned to the consistency of water by generations of pellagra-stricken ancestors who had never been north of Georgia.

Wearily, Michael went back ten pages and laboriously read the columns of figures for the third time. They made no more sense to him than they had made the first time.

The ring of the telephone was welcome. *"Allô—Michel?"* the voice said.

"Antoine," Michael said, because the pianist was the only one he knew who used the French version of his name, "where have you been all this time?" He hadn't seen the Frenchman in more than two years. He had inquired about him at the bar where he had played, but the manager had said that he had just dropped out of sight in the middle of his engagement.

"I've been in Paris," Antoine said. "A foolish romantic impulse. A certain lady suddenly decided she wanted to live in Paris and I knew that if I gave her a two week headstart it would be *au revoir,* Antoine."

Michael laughed. Antoine was by turns overly susceptible and overly cynical in his pursuit of the ladies. He also was overly candid in reciting the most intimate details of his shifting liaisons. "I'm delighted to hear your voice," Michael said. "You're brightening a gloomy day. How did it go in Paris?"

"Calamity," Antoine said. "Absolute Waterloo. Nobody wants to listen to piano players in Paris and the lady married a Japanese tycoon and the next lady . . . But I'll tell you about it when I see you."

"Where can you be found these days?"

"I've been playing at a little place in the Sixties, The Golden Hoop, but do not be deceived by the name, it's a joint. We have a little *réclame,* though, and I am lifting the level of the ambiance considerably, and occasionally a few people come in who look as though they eat with knives and forks." There was a little pause and then he said, "Your wife came in last night."

"Oh."

"She told me you were still working at the same place. That's how I knew where to find you. She looked *exquise,* as usual. She was with two men."

"Two?"

"Two. But both of them older and uglier than you."

"Thank you."

"When I asked how you were she was rather vague," Antoine said. "There has been a rupture?"

"We're not living together for the time being," Michael said, "if that's what you mean by a rupture."

"I commiserate with you, *mon vieux.*" Antoine sighed. "It is the sort of thing that I have become accustomed to in my life, but I didn't think it could happen in yours."

"Everything is possible in everybody's life. Especially in New York. That's why everybody comes here."

"I am happy to see that you are taking your tragedy philosophically."

"Stop sounding like an opera," Michael said testily. "It isn't a tragedy."

"It would be for me."

"Go fuck yourself."

"I expect to see you tonight," Antoine said calmly. "I am at my best between eleven and midnight. I will introduce you to the woman who has swept the memories of all other women I have ever known away from my brain like a wind from the Sahara. Promise me, out of our old friendship, you will reject any advances she makes to you."

"Have no fear," Michael said. "I have given up girls for this year."

"I will believe it when I see it, *mon vieux*. I will see you at eleven," Antoine said and hung up.

Michael smiled. He sat for a moment staring out at the rain, remembering the times he had sat in the shadowed bar late at night with Tracy, listening to Antoine as he loomed over the piano like some dark bird, a cigarette perpetually dangling from his lower lip except when he sang, his deep brown eyes always sad and squinting from the cigarette smoke, his face, marked with what must have been one of the worst cases of adolescent acne in France, intent over the keyboard, his slightly hoarse voice singing a song that Tracy had requested, because it was one of her favorites, *"C'est triste, Venise."*

C'est also *triste,* New York, Michael thought, looking out at the rain. Two men, he remembered. But older and uglier than you. Then he turned back to work.

He stayed late at the office and dined alone and at eleven o'clock went up to The Golden Hoop. The room wasn't crowded and he sat by himself at the bar, nursing a whiskey and trying not to overhear the conversation of the couple next to him, a fat man of about fifty who was talking about various sexual adventures in his past which he obviously thought was preparing the overblown blonde with him for conquest. Antoine had waved to Michael when he came in but the pianist was in the middle of a set and kept on playing. Tracy was not in the room. After all, Michael told himself, if she had been in the night before, it was unlikely she'd come in tonight. But knowing that hadn't prevented him from peering in the semidarkness for her face. There was no evidence, either, that any of the ladies present was the one who had succeeded in sweeping the memories of all the other women Antoine had known from his brain like a wind from the Sahara.

Antoine was playing as well as ever, softly, cleverly improvising changes on the melodies, but never straying far enough from them to falsify them. How satisfactory it must be, Michael thought, to be able to do something as well as that, something that gave yourself and so many others so much pleasure. He remembered the gloomy hours he had spent practicing and grinned across the years at the leaden child who had banged so unharmoniously and with such hatred at the keyboard.

Antoine finished his version of the theme from *The Sting* with a little flourish and came over to the bar and embraced Michael. *"Enfin,"* he said, "it is about time." He stood back and examined Michael. "Let me see how you look," he said. "Ah. Aging. You are not taking care of yourself, *mon vieux.*"

"What the hell happened to *you?*" There was a long scar from the ear down to the mouth on Antoine's left cheek.

"Oh, this." Antoine touched the scar. "A memento of Paris. A lady . . ."

"Don't tell me you're going around these days with ladies who carry straight-edged razors."

"Not the lady," Antoine said. "The gentleman-friend of the lady. A monsieur from Marseilles, well known in the milieu for having a hasty temper. Only until he pulled out the knife he was not well known to me." He shrugged. "It's not really so bad. Cosmetically not appealing, perhaps, but I am no beauty at the best of times, anyway." He swung up on the stool next to Michael's and ordered a Perrier. He didn't drink when he performed.

"Where's the beautiful lady you promised me I'd meet?"

"She is, what shall we say, undependable." Antoine sighed. "She comes and goes as the mood seizes her. She tells me she likes to see me when she has the *cafard.* I guess she is feeling jolly tonight. She has a great many admirers she likes to see when she is jolly. So far, my dear friend, I have had no great success with her although I have laid my heart at her feet—repeatedly."

Michael laughed. "You're laying it on thick tonight, Antoine," he said. He had always been amused when Antoine went into one of his elaborate speeches on the subject of women and he appreciated it when Antoine purposely delivered an extra-florid oration for him.

Antoine studied his face keenly. "You look as though you might have a touch of the *cafard* yourself tonight, Michael."

"I worked late."

"Ah, then you are not mourning the absence of the glorious Madame Storrs?"

"Let it lie, please," Michael said shortly.

"She did not look jolly either, last night. I detected an inner sorrow."

"In the light in this bar, you're lucky to be able to detect the location of the piano."

"The soul sees into the darkest corners," Antoine said pontifically.
"Remember, I am an artist."

"You're a piano player in a bar, and a damn good one. Be
satisfied with that and don't go snooping into darkest corners."

"Not all artists play at Carnegie Hall," Antoine said with dignity.
"Is there anything particular you'd like to hear?"

"Anything but 'C'est triste, Venise.' "

"I understand." Antoine shook his head despondently. "It is sad,
seeing you here alone. And seeing Mrs. Storrs come in with two ugly
old men. You made a brilliant pair. Two shining animals. All eyes
were drawn to you together. Whosever fault it is, you are both making a mistake."

"Go play the goddamn piano, will you?"

"What I said had to be said."

"Go play the piano."

Antoine hopped off the stool and glided over to the piano. When
he moved it was as though to some inner syncopated music. He sat
down at the piano and lit a cigarette and stared down at the keyboard in silence as though he were almost afraid to touch the sacred
object.

Next to Michael, the overblown blond woman was staring at him
and Michael became conscious that the droning, grasping voice of
the fat man she had been with had stopped. He turned and looked
frankly at the woman. She was alone. She smiled at him coquettishly.
Actually, she was quite pretty, gaudy but pretty, and the full, well-
rounded bosom was temptingly displayed, a considerable length of
cleavage showing.

"Good evening," the woman said. "My boyfriend got discouraged
and went home. Would you like to buy me a drink? I've been looking
at you ever since you got here."

Michael bought her a drink and had another himself and after a
half-hour of conversation with her during which he learned that she
was a physiotherapist and came from Seattle and that her name was
Roberta Munson, he thought, Why not, after all this time? and left
the bar with her, sketching a farewell wave to Antoine, wreathed in
cigarette smoke at the piano, looking deserted. They got into a taxi
and he kissed Roberta Munson politely because he knew that was
expected of him and couldn't honestly tell whether he enjoyed it or
not.

Roberta's flesh was fragrant and tasty, firm, as befitted the body of a physiotherapist, and she was as enthusiastic as a man could wish, but after a half-hour of useless effort in bed, he said, "I'm awfully sorry, but I guess tonight is not the night," and got up and began to dress.

"Ah, what a pity. A beautiful young man like you. New York is a terrible town for men. Maybe another night?"

"Maybe another night," he said, knowing there wasn't going to be another night with her, or perhaps with anyone else. He leaned over and kissed her forehead apologetically and then went out of the bedroom and let himself out of the apartment.

As an experiment, he tried once more, the following week, with a girl he had particularly liked in the days before he met Tracy, a girl who was sunny and serene and uncomplicated and who had been among the most persistent of the women who had kept calling him after, as he ironically put it to himself, he had dropped out of the circuit to spend all the time he could with Tracy. It had been years, but when he telephoned her, her voice was as fresh and eager as it had always been, and wonder of wonders, she had not gotten married or moved out of town or turned Lesbian or taken up Zen or dope or had a nervous breakdown. He had a pleasant dinner with her and took her to hear Antoine play and sing and Antoine had arched his eyebrows in approval when he saw her, but when he took her to her apartment and she began to shed her clothes in her frank, uncomplicated way, he knew that it was going to go wrong and it did.

As he got dressed, he tried to avoid her eyes. She lay naked on the bed, young, distressed and appetizing, looking at him worriedly. "Something's happened to you, hasn't it?" she asked. "The well gone dry temporarily?"

"Poisoned," he said. "I hope temporarily."

"God be with you, baby," she said. "And thanks for the dinner and the music."

One more try, he thought as he descended the stairs from her apartment, and it will be all over town. He wondered what Tracy would think if she heard.

◇◇◇◇◇

He met Antoine's undependable love, a girl by the name of Susan Hartley, with a tiny lively face and long hair that seemed too heavy for that small head to bear up under and dark eyes that would have been described as flashing if she had been Spanish or a character in a novel about the South before the Civil War. But she was just a nice American girl from New Jersey who worked as a laboratory assistant in the research department of a big cosmetics firm and tried out the company's products on herself constantly, so that you never could guess in advance what color her hair would be when you saw her next or what outlandish shade she'd be wearing around her eyes or using on her fingernails. She seemed to like him and treated Antoine with amused sisterly affection and was pert and delicate in her movements and obviously attractive to men, with her hearty laugh and deep voice, surprising coming from the small fragile body. She did not look as though she would sweep the memories of anybody from a man's mind, but Antoine's tastes had always been erratic.

She came into the bar quite often and did not seem to be noticeably suffering from the *cafard* on any of the occasions Michael saw her.

"Praise me to her," Antoine said on a night when they were sitting together at the bar, Susan between the two men. "She has no notion of my true qualities and my profound talent for affection. Perhaps a kind word from an old friend like you will soften her heart."

"Oh, Antoine," Susan said, laughing, "why do you have to go public with everything—even your failures?"

"I have an open and sincere nature," Antoine said. "I am not an American, but a warm, emotional Latin. What I feel I tell. I repress nothing and that is why the whole world loves me. Except you."

"I love you," Susan said.

"There is love and love," Antoine said darkly. "I will now go back to the piano and sing sad songs that will make you regret the way you are treating me." He rose from the bar. "Michael, be convincing."

Michael laughed. "Call me Cyrano."

"Don't be too eloquent. She has a deplorable weakness for eloquent men."

"I will describe you to her in plain but forceful language."

"I trust nobody," Antoine said, and went over to the piano.

"I'll say one thing for him," Susan said. "He never gives up. Do you think he'd change if he became an American citizen?"

"For the worse."

"Does he do well with girls?"

"So-so," Michael said. "You can never be certain how much of what he tells you he's making up."

"You can say that again," Susan said. "I like him, but—" She made a little moue. "That acne and that scar. Time will tell. Now, be eloquent." She looked at him fixedly and he became uneasy.

"That's not my strong point," Michael said. "Let's listen to the sad songs." Now there was no question that she was flirting with him. He hoped it was only an ingrained habit begun when she was in the sixth grade in grammar school. Besides, it was probably all in fun and not to be taken seriously, a more modern version of the debutante's old-fashioned divertissement of collecting names of beaux for a waltz on a dance card at a formal ball. But from then on he was careful not to do or say anything that might disturb Antoine and for the most part managed to confine their conversation to the subject of skiing, which she was so passionate about that she took all her vacations in winter so that she could ski in Zermatt or Davos or Kitzbühel or Vermont. They innocently, he hoped, compared runs they had made in Europe and America. She professed to be amazed that she always saw him in The Golden Hoop alone and offered to introduce him to one or all of her girlfriends, tall, petite, smart, stupid, blond, brunette, married or not married, but Michael put him off as good-naturedly as possible and finally she stopped, saying, "I know what it is—you're having a dark secret romance with somebody famous and you can't be seen in public with her or it would be all over the papers and her career or her marriage would be finished and each night after you leave here you rush to her luxurious town house and it would never do if one night she caught you with lipstick on your collar."

He laughed at that and said, "Now you've got it, Susan," and they left it at that. He had no desire to tell her the simple fact that he was impotent.

Although he dropped in to The Golden Hoop for at least a few minutes almost every night, Tracy never came back again.

⟡⟡⟡⟡⟡

He celebrated his thirty-fifth birthday by going down to the office earlier than usual, although he was aware of the fact that by the terms of the wills of his mother and grandfather he was somewhat wealthier than he had been the day before. There was a meeting scheduled with the president of an electronics concern in Pennsylvania for the afternoon and he wanted to go over the report he had prepared. Nobody in the office knew that it was his birthday, so he was spared all congratulations. Tracy had always celebrated the occasion by coming to the breakfast table with a gift and a bottle of champagne, but if she remembered this day she had neglected to call or perhaps had called, but too late, because he was out of his room at the hotel by eight o'clock. He had not seen or heard from her for more than a year, but as he sat at his desk with the small pile of neatly typed folios on it, it took a conscious effort not to call the hotel and ask if there were any messages.

When Mr. Lewis, the president of the electronics concern, came into his office at three o'clock, Michael was sweating as usual, as the heat was full on, although it was a mild, golden day and New York was glittering like a box of jewels in the Indian summer sun. The president of the electronics concern was a small, portly, fussy man with a worried look on his face. Michael knew that Mr. Lewis was enormously rich and he guessed that the worried look came because Lewis went through his days and nights certain that everybody was conspiring to get his money away from him.

"There it is, sir," Michael said after they had shaken hands. He pointed to the folders on his desk. "It's all there. The bottom line. Chapter and verse. Costs, income, capital flow and investments, taxes, personnel, profit, research and development, the lot. In black and white. Do you want to read it here or take it home and have some time to digest it?"

"I'll read it here." Lewis had a gruff, suspicious voice. "I don't want anybody in my office or even in my home to know what's in it until I've made up my mind what I want to do."

"It will take some time," Michael said. "I have some things to do outside the office for about an hour or so. Make yourself comfortable."

"Thank you, sir," Lewis said. He sat down behind Michael's desk, put on a pair of gold-rimmed glasses, then took out a monocle which he held next to his right eye and opened the top folder and glared at it.

Leaving Mr. Lewis to cope with his myopia and the problem of how to conserve and multiply the millions of dollars he had stored up in his far-flung business, Michael went out of the office. He had nothing to do away from the building, but he wanted some fresh air.

He hadn't bothered to put on his topcoat and the little nip he felt from the wind off the river was welcome after the sealed cloying warmth of his office.

He walked toward Fifth Avenue and went into the St. Regis Hotel, with the idea of having a drink, then thought better of it because he had promised himself that he wouldn't drink before sundown anymore and went downstairs to the row of telephone booths and dialed the number of Tracy's office. He didn't know what he wanted to say to her and they hadn't spoken since the morning he had cleaned his things out of the apartment and he had to catch his breath when he heard the familiar low voice saying "Tracy Lawrence" over the wire.

"Michael," he said.

"Michael." He could hear the sharp intake of breath over the phone. "Happy birthday."

"Time marches on," he said. She had remembered.

"I'm glad you called. There are some things I must talk to you about."

"Today's as good a day as any. Dinner tonight?"

She hesitated for a fraction of a second. "All right."

"Shall we meet at the bar of the Oak Room and then go on someplace for dinner?" One thing was certain—he wasn't going to pick her up at her apartment. Birthday or no birthday, the apartment was one place he was not going to visit.

"Fine," she said briskly.

"Seven-thirty."

"Seven-thirty it is." She hung up.

He walked slowly back to his office, wondering what she wanted to talk to him about and dreading what it might be.

Mr. Lewis was pacing back and forth in his office when he got there. He had taken off his glasses and put away his monocle and looked more worried than ever. "You guys cut pretty deep," he said to Michael as soon as Michael had closed the door behind him. "You're asking me to fire thirty-five men who've worked with me for twenty years or more."

Michael sat down behind his desk while Mr. Lewis kept pacing the floor, looking, Michael thought, like a nervous, pouting, fat little bird. "We guarantee that the efficiency of your firm will be improved by at least thirty percent in every department, Mr. Lewis." His tone was neutral, nonargumentative. "But if you don't want to take our advice it's up to you." *Our* advice. Spread the responsibility around, although he had done all the work on this particular assignment. "We made it clear from the beginning that we would merely suggest."

Mr. Lewis sighed, the little bird confronted with the problem of flying or not flying, with the necessity of choosing whether he would have ten worms a day or fifteen worms a day. "Yes, you did," Mr. Lewis said unhappily. "You were admirably frank." He sighed again. "You were highly recommended to me. Highly. With good reason." He blinked, as though the light coming through the windows was suddenly too bright for him. "The bottom line, as you said. Well, I suppose business is business. Yours and mine." He began to stuff the folders into the attaché case he had brought with him. "Still, I'll have to sleep on it."

"By all means, Mr. Lewis."

Mr. Lewis clicked the attaché case shut. Michael stood up and they shook hands and Michael escorted the man to the door and opened it. "Good luck, sir," he said.

"I'll need it," Lewis said bitterly. Michael watched the little plump man, with the lives of hundreds of other men in his hands, pigeon-strut down the corridor, already pondering what he would say to the thirty-five men who had worked for him for twenty years or more.

Michael closed the door and took off his jacket and loosened his collar now that he was alone, annoyed with the sweat marks on his shirt from the goddamn steam heat. He went over to the cabinet where he kept some bottles and a silver Thermos ice bucket. This was one day he couldn't wait until evening. Anyway, it was his birthday. He took out a bottle of Scotch and a bottle of soda. When he opened the soda bottle it fizzed over and splashed over his shirt. He brushed at the wet spots. Who would have thought the old man had so much blood? he thought ironically, as he poured the soda over the whiskey and the ice. Then, holding the drink in one hand and the soda bottle in the other, he went over to the window and stared out at sunlit New York in its harvest season. He drank slowly, but it didn't do any good. "Shit!" he said aloud and suddenly threw the soda bottle with all his strength at the window that could not be opened in winter or summer. The bottle shattered in a hundred pieces against the window, strewing shards of glass over the carpet. There was no mark on the window. I've got to take a shower, he thought, ice-cold. Business is over for the day. He put on his jacket and, carrying his topcoat, went home. The shower helped, but not much, and the hotel room seemed dingy and unwelcoming and he decided that next week he would look for an apartment for himself where he wouldn't feel like a transient whose life or death was of no interest to any living soul in the city.

She came into the bar of the Oak Room, cool and splendid, in control of the city, the men, as usual, staring at her as she made her way to the table near the window where he was sitting. She was wearing a new dark fur coat, not the one he had bought her as a wedding gift. Whose gift was this? he thought as he stood to greet her. Unworthy thought. A girl who looked like Tracy had a right to as many fur coats as she could lay her hands on.

She didn't make a move to kiss him as they said hello and they stood facing each other awkwardly for a moment and then shook hands, which made Michael feel absurd, especially since they both moved in circles in which people kissed each other on the cheek at the most casual meetings.

Over their drinks the conversation was impersonal. Tracy was tanned and had been in the Bahamas for ten days and it had been warm and the weather perfect in the Bahamas. Her father and mother were well. Her father had sold the *Tracy* some time ago. Her middle sister was living in California and had married a newspaperman in San Francisco without warning. Her own business was doing well and they had had to move to larger quarters on upper Madison Avenue, which was convenient for her because she could walk to work in five minutes. They had both seen two of the same plays, on different evenings, and they disagreed politely on their merits. No, he had not had the time last year to do any skiing, but he had taken up hang-gliding last summer and liked it. She looked at him coldly after he told her that and abruptly changed the subject and asked him how he was doing at the office. He was doing fine, he said, but no one at Cornwall and Wallace had resigned or been fired and Mr. Cornwall's promise that Michael was going to be made a partner had not been realized so far. Still, he couldn't complain. He had even bought himself a Porsche last year with a big Christmas bonus. Yes, Antoine was playing and singing even better than ever. Yes, Antoine had told her about his new dazzling girl, but Michael didn't think she was as dazzling as all that.

There was no mention of the fact that she had said over the phone that afternoon that there were some things she had to talk to him about.

When they finished their drinks Michael said he was taking her to a new, very good Italian restaurant on Sixty-first Street. He had carefully chosen it because they had never been there together.

The small talk continued over dinner. Let her tell me what is on her mind, he thought; he would not ask. Then, over coffee, she said, abruptly, "Michael, I think it's time we got a divorce. I can't go on hanging in limbo like this forever."

"Whatever you say," he said. Unreasonably, he was shocked. Living together or living apart, he still thought of her as his wife. A wife was a permanent fixture. "If that's what you want."

"That's what I want," she said. "There's a man I've met and I like him and he wants children, too. I'm getting too old to wait much longer."

"You look eighteen."

"Look." Her tone was bitter.

"What sort of man is he?" he asked. "What does he do?"

"He's forty," she said. "A widower."

Older and uglier than you, he remembered Antoine's description. "He manufactures fabrics. He's very well off."

"Your parents will be pleased."

She ignored that. "Naturally I won't ask for alimony or anything like that and there's nothing we have to divide," she said, crisply businesslike. "But we'll both have to get lawyers."

"Of course," he said. "There's a law firm that does the work for our office. I'll put them on notice."

"It shouldn't be too much trouble," she said. "Thank God we don't live in Italy or Spain where they make such a fuss."

"Thank God."

She looked at him harshly. "Don't be ironic."

"This is my first divorce. I don't know what the proper reaction should be."

"Not irony."

"I'm just trying to be civilized and modern," he protested, willing to hurt her now, because he was hurt. "I don't suppose I met your friend jumping out of airplanes or sailing or hang-gliding or anything like that, have I?"

"No, you have not. Now you're turning ugly. It isn't like you." Her voice was trembling as she spoke.

"Give me time to get used to the whole thing and I promise to improve. I may even turn out to be the perfect divorced husband as matters progress."

"I'm taking my maiden name," she said, "and I'll keep it after I'm married."

"Go with the times," he said.

"It's my firm's name, anyway," she said. "Why not?"

"I shall introduce you from now on as Ms. Lawrence."

"Introduce me as anything you wish," she said. "Are we finished here?"

"Finished," he said, and waved for the waiter and the bill.

Outside the restaurant she surprised him. Just as he was about to hail a taxi to take her home, she said, "It's early yet. I'd love to hear some music. And Antoine's place is just around the corner."

He looked at her speculatively. Was she trying to punish him, taking him to where Antoine's playing and singing would remind him painfully of all the good times they had had together and how much he had loved her then and what he had given up? But all he said was, "I'm sure Antoine will be most pleased to see you again." He took her arm and they walked down the street, arm-in-arm, like a sedate married couple.

Antoine kissed her when she came in and made them sit at a table next to the piano, so that, as he said, he could feast his eyes on her while he was performing. Susan came in with a man soon after they were seated and stopped at the table and Michael introduced Tracy as his wife. Tracy did not correct him and Susan and the man she was with went back to the bar, where three large men were speaking loudly in what Michael guessed were the accents of Texas.

"You're wrong," Tracy said in a low voice.

"About what? Saying you're my wife? You still are, legally, you know."

She shook her head impatiently. "No. About her. The girl. She *is* dazzling. Have you kept your hands off her?"

"That's a question I don't have to answer," he said. "But if you're curious, I haven't touched her. She's Antoine's girl."

"Since when has that ever stopped you?" There was a steely edge to her voice.

"Let's not bring up happy old memories," he said lightly.

Then Antoine began to play *"C'est triste, Venise"* in Tracy's honor and made a small bow to her from the piano. Tracy smiled widely, like a little girl who had just received a present.

Then Antoine began to sing the words. Sentimental French bastard, Michael thought, displeased with the way Tracy was leaning forward, intent, singing softly, in her nice American French, along with Antoine.

The loud men came away from the bar, marching three abreast toward the piano. "Hey, listen to that, will ya," one of the men said, "he's singing frog."

"I do believe he is. Frog," one of the other men said.

They were standing at the piano now. "Hey, lissen, pal," said the first man, his voice booming, "you're in the good old U. S. of A., taking our money in dollar bills, the least you could do is learn the language."

Somewhere in the room, a woman hissed. The three men ignored her. Michael could feel his body tensing and Tracy, almost instinctively, put out her hand and touched his arm.

"Venice," said the third man, who had not spoken yet, "he's singing about Venice. I was there once and it smelled like a sewer."

"Come on, pal," said the first man to Antoine, who was bravely smiling as he sang, "give us a little 'Yankee Doodle Dandy.'"

"Sit still," Tracy said, gripping Michael's arm because she could see his fists clenching.

"Well, then," said the first man, who was the largest of the three of them, "if you won't we will." He started bawling, "The eyes of Texas are upon you . . ." and the other two men joined him, drowning out Antoine's faltering voice completely.

"All the livelong day," they sang.

Michael jumped up, tearing away from Tracy's grip on his arm. "Shut up, you fucking shit-kicking drunks," he shouted.

Grinning, the three men sang on. "Join in," the first man said to Michael. "We'll make it a quartet. You sing soprano." He put his arm around Michael's shoulders, the feel of his hand on Michael's arm not at all friendly.

Roughly, Michael pushed the man's arm away. The man swiveled and pushed Michael, hard, under the chin, with the heel of his hand. Michael hit him on the jaw, with a wild, intense pleasure as he saw the man's eyes go momentarily blank, Joseph Ling in the schoolyard all over again.

"Okay, pal," the second man said, "you asked for it." He hit Michael in the stomach and Michael doubled over. Then while the first man, who had recovered by now, held Michael's arms from behind, the other two hammered at his face, his ribs. Michael dropped to the floor. Dimly, from somewhere in the room, he could hear a woman screaming. Then he went out, as the first man kneeled over him and clubbed him with the side of his clenched fist twice more. The man stood up and looked around the hushed room. "Anybody else here don't like our choice of music, just step up here and voice your objections." Only Tracy moved. Sobbing uncontrollably, shouting, "Animals! Animals!" she sprang up, holding her glass, and threw her drink in the man's face. The man grinned. "Sit down, you New York whore," he said and pushed her violently back onto the piano. Then the three men marched abreast, deliberately, toward the exit, with everyone between them and the door getting silently out of their way.

◇◇◇◇◇

He woke up in the hospital.

Tracy was sitting on a chair by the side of his bed. He tried to smile at her.

"How do you feel?" she asked, tremulously.

"Someone is exploding giant firecrackers inside my head," he said in a voice that he couldn't be sure was his own. "And it is no great pleasure to breathe. Otherwise I'm in tip-top shape." He began to feel himself sliding under again and he fought to remain conscious.

"You've been out for two and a half hours," Tracy said, "and you've got three broken ribs and a beautiful concussion. Otherwise, as you said, you're in tip-top shape."

Michael chuckled, then gasped as the ribs moved.

A nurse came in and said, "Oh, you've come to." She laid a cool hand on his head. "A little fever. Not too bad, considering. Here, this will help you sleep." She gave him an injection in the arm and he tried not to scream because his arm was so sore.

"Are you going to stay with him, Mrs. Storrs?" she said. "It's awfully late."

"I know. But I'll stay," Tracy said.

"Well, if he needs anything, push the buzzer. I'm just down the hall at the desk." She went out, footsteps noiseless.

"Now sleep," Tracy said, taking his hand.

"Well, it was to be expected, winding up in a hospital, it being my birthday and all." He smiled brokenly. "I'm sorry," he whispered.

"Ssh. Sleep."

He closed his eyes and slept, clutching his wife's hand.

CHAPTER NINE

He had a week's growth of beard because his face was too sore and swollen to shave. The nurses refused to let him see himself in a mirror. The one he was fondest of, a robust Irish girl, said, "No, my lad, you don't want to see it. If *my* face was in that condition and I saw it, it would send me into a shivering shock for a month of Sundays." Her theory of convalescence was obviously that the ill were not to be pampered.

Tracy came in to visit him every day, but she saw that it was hard for him to talk, and she only stayed a few minutes and didn't say anything of importance and seemed in a hurry to get out of the room.

He was told that Antoine had also come to the hospital, but Michael had been sleeping, which he did most of the time, and the nurse sent him away.

By the end of the week he felt ready to leave the hospital. The firecrackers had stopped going off in his head and he could eat solid food again and his ribs only bothered him if he laughed or happened to cough. He got the hospital barber to shave him and when he looked into the mirror afterwards he chuckled grimly at his reflection. The swelling had gone down, but the left side of his face, or faces—there seemed to be two Michael Storrs in the mirror, with the ghost of a third—was streaked with a variety of colors, going from purple through yellow and a selection of sickly greens. The doctor assured him that his face would return to its normal color in due time but refused to discharge him. "You had a massive concussion, Mr.

Storrs," he said, "and you have to remain under observation for at least ten days before we know for sure that something nasty won't kick up in your brain."

Michael didn't tell the doctor that when he looked at him he saw two or sometimes three doctors. If he had mentioned this interesting phenomenon, God knew how much longer they'd keep him in the hospital. He was grateful to the barber. If he had tried to shave himself, he would have had to guess which of the two or three faces to lather.

Antoine, too, when he finally was allowed to visit, appeared in a multiple version, but he was glad to see the Frenchman just the same. He was tired of his own company and Antoine always cheered him up.

"How is it, *mon vieux?*" Antoine said.

"I'm bored. Otherwise splendid."

"You do not look splendid. Those barbarians."

"Did anyone ever find out who they were?"

Antoine shook his head. "The police came with the ambulance, but they said if nobody knew their names or where they were staying, there was very little the police could do. They were very insouciant about the matter. *Les flics.* Scum of society. What could be a question of life or death to a civilian is merely routine to a policeman. However—they were not insouciant about me."

"What do you mean?"

"They saw that I was French and they asked me for my passport."

"Well, you have a passport, don't you?"

"Of course. Only it's French."

"What's wrong with that?"

"Nothing. The center of culture and science. Marianne, the mother of every civilized person everywhere. Only they then asked me for my permit to work in the United States."

"And you don't have one?"

Antoine shook his head sadly. "It is very difficult for a pianist. There are many unemployed *American* pianists, the man at the immigration office told me when I applied. He was barely polite."

"Ah, they'll forget it," Michael said, more because he wanted to reassure Antoine than because he believed it.

"I'm afraid they won't forget it," Antoine said morosely. "The policeman took down my name and address in one of those fat notebooks they carry."

"Did he say anything?"

"No. But he *looked*. The look was not sympathetic. There will be repercussions. In fact, there *has* been a repercussion. The boss fired me. If you go to The Golden Hoop, you will hear a fat blond lady playing the piano like a cow."

"I'm sorry."

"You have nothing to be sorry about. You behaved magnificently. Which is more than I can say about anybody else who was there that night, including me. And excepting Tracy. They hit her, too."

"They did?" Michael could feel something buzzing furiously in his head. "Why?"

"She called them animals and she threw a glass of whiskey into the face of their leader. Didn't you know?"

"Tracy didn't tell me anything."

"A noble woman. I believe you were on the floor and unconscious when she did it. What a fatal evening." Antoine sighed mournfully. "I should have stopped singing when they came up to the piano and gotten up and walked with dignity to the men's room and locked the door. I always do the wrong thing in a crisis and my friends suffer because of it. I offer you my most abject apologies for my idiotic behavior."

"Cut it," Michael said curtly. "It was just one of those things. There must be at least a hundred fights a night in the bars of New York. A lot of them not as harmless as that one."

"Harmless." Antoine laughed bitterly. "More than a week in the hospital and with your face the color of the flag of a small African country. They could have killed you."

"Well, they didn't. Stop talking about it. You're supposed to cheer up people when you visit them in hospitals."

"I am not very cheery these days," Antoine said. "Forgive me. I am out of work and I have had to move—"

"Why? You afraid those three guys're looking for you? That's foolish."

"Not them," Antoine said. "They're probably back in Texas pumping oil at exorbitant prices by now. The Immigration."

"Oh. Have you heard from them yet?"

"Not yet. But they will come. I feel it in my bones. I can already hear the engines of the airplane warming up to take me to France. They will not dance in the streets to celebrate my arrival in Paris. The man from Marseilles was most explicit about what he would do to me if he ever saw me again. My life has turned into a sordid mess."

"Your bones don't know anything about the Immigration," Michael said. "Don't be such an old lady."

"*You* can say that. You don't have to have a work permit. I have moved in the utmost secrecy to a small hotel on the West Side. A perfectly horrid small hotel, which is used almost wholly to house pimps, whores, dope pushers and women who scream all night as though their throats are being cut. It has one advantage. The police do not dare approach it. I will give you its telephone number if you promise not to give it to anyone else—not even Tracy. And if you ask for me, my name is now René Fernoz."

"It's a nice name," Michael said, smiling. "Write it down for me. There's a pad and pencil on the table here." He watched Antoine scratch the name of the hotel and his new name and telephone number on the pad.

"There," Antoine said, laying down the pencil. "The new false Frenchman."

"Is there anything I can do to help you? A little thing like money, perhaps?"

"You have helped me enough and have suffered enough." Antoine put on his noble face, diminished in effect somewhat by the scar and his acne.

"Yes, I helped you to get fired and maybe deported. Why don't you get down on your knees and thank me? Do you need any money?"

"Not for the moment," Antoine said. "If there arrives another moment I will take advantage of your foolish generosity. It may be very soon. Thank you, my friend."

"Forget it. You'll pay me back."

"I never have paid anybody back in my whole life," Antoine said glumly. "It is an aspect of my character that I deplore."

Michael laughed. "All right. Then don't pay me back. I've just come into some money and I'll be able to eat no matter how deplorable your character is."

"And you?" Antoine asked. "When you leave the hospital what are you going to do?"

"I'm going to quit my job and get out of the city," Michael said, surprising himself as the words came out of his mouth, because he hadn't thought of anything but fleeing the hospital since they had stopped sedating him.

"*Mon Dieu!*" Antoine looked shocked. "Why would you want to do that? You are a prince in this city."

"The price is too high."

"Where will you go? What will you do?"

"I haven't thought about it yet. Someplace, anyplace."

"Please, don't do anything hasty. Just because of an incident in a bar over a foolish little pianist. The chances are a thousand to one you will never have another fight in your life."

"That has nothing to do with it. That just triggered it off. Something else—maybe a little less showy—would have triggered it off one time or another. I was getting ready for it a long time before that night, only I didn't realize it."

"Why don't you consult with Tracy before you . . ."

"It's none of Tracy's business," Michael said brutally.

"If you do go—and I implore you to think it over carefully, you are in no condition now to make grave decisions—if you do go, will you let me know where I can find you? I have too few friends to see my best one disappear into the wilderness of America."

"Of course I'll let you know," Michael said gently. "I couldn't bear not hearing you play the piano from time to time."

"You are my tower of strength and goodness, Mike," Antoine said emotionally.

"Will you for Christ's sake stop sounding like a literal translation from Racine?" Michael said roughly, to hide how deeply Antoine had touched him. "And now get out of here because the doctor said for my head's sake I should talk as little as possible."

Antoine stood up. "I've brought a small present for you." He fished in the pocket of his overcoat and brought out a pint bottle of Scotch. "I have been in hospitals a few times myself," he said, "and I know the dark moments when a little alcohol lifts the clouds. Do they frown on drinking here?"

"I imagine they do. I haven't put the question to them yet but my impression is that the motto for the organization is 'There shall be no pleasure within these walls.'"

"In that case, it would be wise to keep it from prying eyes." He stuffed the bottle under Michael's pillow. "Now I must go. Please come out of this place soon—and unchanged."

"*Au revoir,* Monsieur Fernoz," Michael said.

He watched Antoine walk to the door and noticed that his walk was different, slower, less jaunty, as though he no longer heard the interior syncopated music to which he used to move.

Michael lay back wearily, but contentedly. Antoine's visit had cheered him immensely, but not in the way he had expected. Actually he had cheered himself. Antoine's questioning had brought him to a decision that he had too long postponed. "I'm going to quit my job and get out of the city," he repeated, whispering to himself, establishing it as a fact as he lay back on the pillow, feeling the comforting hard outline of the bottle under it, thinking, elatedly, Better times ahead.

He lay back luxuriously, his arms beneath his head, starting slowly, and with pleasure, to think of all the places he might want to go after he had told old man Cornwall they would have to find another man for his job.

There was a little gust of wind which stirred the curtains around the window that Michael had insisted upon leaving partially open. He turned his head and looked out at the weather. It was beginning to snow, large, wet, deliberate flakes. He smiled. Of course, he thought. That part of his decision was being made for him. Snow country. There was a lot of snow country in the world and he was in no hurry to decide which mountains he would favor with his presence.

Soothed, confident now that his life would sort itself out, a devotee of winter, he slept.

◇◇◇◇◇

By the time Tracy came to take him back to his hotel three days later, he had decided. Looking back upon his past, it seemed to him the calmest and healthiest period of his life had been the months after graduation from Stanford which he had spent as a ski instructor at the little town of Green Hollow in Vermont. Of course, it might have changed and probably had, as had he, but as a possible starting point on a new existence it attracted him. For some reason he had never gone back—fearing perhaps that his memories of a particularly pleasant segment of his young manhood would be spoiled by a later examination. Also, once he had started working for Cornwall and Wallace, he had been sent out often to the West, where the skiing was much more challenging and spectacular than in Vermont. Now, he told himself, hoping it was true, he was no longer interested in that kind of challenge, at least for the time being, and a winter in

Vermont, in a place where there still might be comfortable old friends, might just be the thing to help him recover from New York.

In the taxi with Tracy he told her he was quitting his job and leaving the city. She nodded, almost as though she had expected it. "I was ground down to the bone," he said and she nodded again. "It took the ten days in the hospital to make me think it all out. I don't want to make a career of fighting in bars just because my nerves have given way."

"It was maniacal," she said softly. "When you got up and started with those men I swear I could hardly recognize you—you looked crazed, and in a terrible way, overjoyed. You know, I think that even if they all pulled out guns and knives you wouldn't have stopped. I have never been as frightened in my whole life. I think at that moment I understood you better than I ever had before. You really don't care whether you live or die. It's not a pleasant thing to know about a man you've loved for such a long time." Then she fell silent. There was nothing he could say that would make her change her mind or alleviate her sorrow. She was probably right. Even if the men had whipped out guns he wouldn't have been able to stop himself from throwing himself at them. So he said nothing.

The silence in the cab endured through two red lights. Then Tracy said, her voice calm, "Have a nice, peaceful winter. You can use it. And call me if you need anything."

"Thanks. When I settle in I'll give you my address, if you have to talk to me about—well," he said lamely, "well—about the divorce or something."

"I'm not going through with the divorce," she said, "unless you want to."

He shook his head.

"I can't live with another man," she said, almost whispering in the back of the cab. "At least, not for the time being. I can't live with *you,* either." She smiled wanly. "That makes everything just hunky-dory, doesn't it?"

He took her hand and put it to his lips and kissed it.

"Don't say anything now," she said, "you're in a weakened condition. And so am I. Better to keep quiet and both go our separate wonderful ways. And remember, the doctor said no undue exertion—physical, mental or emotional."

"Doctors give me a pain in the ass."

She chuckled. "I suppose you have your reasons. Well, if you won't listen to them, I'll try to."

The taxi drove up to the hotel and she looked at its front door with distaste. "Is that the best you could find?"

"It was close to the office," he said. "Want to come in for a drink?"

She hesitated for a moment. "No," she said, "I think that would come under the heading of undue exertion."

He closed the door of the cab and went to the desk to get his key. There was a pile of mail waiting for him, but he told the clerk to throw it all away. There was no one in the world he wanted to hear from.

"I heard what happened to you, Mr. Storrs," the clerk said. "What a terrible thing."

"The best thing that ever happened to me in my life," Michael said jauntily.

The clerk was looking at him puzzledly as he went across the lobby and rang for the elevator.

When he got to his room, it smelled, he thought, like a crypt. He threw open a window and stood in front of it, breathing deeply, as the cold blast blew around him. When he turned around, the furniture, which had seemed to him to be trembling when he came in, was now steady and solid. He went into the bathroom and turned on the light and stared at his face. Only one face stared back. I beat it, he thought, I beat it.

Two days later, with most of his belongings packed into a trunk in the hotel basement, he got into the Porsche and started north. It was a windy, clear day. As he sped into the foothills of the mountains, there were patches of snow on the fields.

VOLUME TWO

CHAPTER
TEN

He stopped for lunch just as he crossed the border to Vermont, at a place he remembered from the trips he had made from Syracuse to Green Hollow—what was it—fourteen years ago? It was an old Colonial inn that smelled of wood smoke and lemon furniture polish, glitteringly clean, its dining room shining in the frosty sunlight which cast spidery shadows from the bare trees outside the window. There were only a few people having lunch, an elderly couple and three young men whom he overheard talking about real estate and who were, he guessed, local businessmen from the nearby town. Because, at least for the day and probably for a long time to come, he would not have to attend any business lunches, Michael ordered a martini and sipped it slowly before his meal came, feeling like a boy playing truant on a particularly fine afternoon.

The scene with Cornwall had gone better than he had expected. Cornwall had been saddened but understanding when Michael told the old man he had to escape the city of New York. "Everybody wants to escape from something," Cornwall had said. "Very few people manage it, but God be with you. How long have you been with us?"

"Twelve years."

"I've been here for thirty," Cornwall said, "and I haven't escaped yet. They do it better in the universities. Every seven years, they give a man twelve months off. Recharge the batteries. Tell you what—let's consider this your sabbatical year. With no salary." He smiled frostily. "But when it's over, you can come back and no questions asked. Your place will be held for you."

"I doubt that I'll be back."

"Call me in twelve months," Cornwall had said and fished out a bottle of whiskey and poured drinks for both of them. It was the first time Michael had had a drink in the office with the old man. "Here's to you"—Cornwall had lifted his glass—"and mind you, keep out of fights in bars."

The climate in Cornwall's office had been the same as in his own, too warm and lacking in oxygen. Boss or no boss, Cornwall couldn't open the windows either. Michael was glad when the interview was over and he could go out into the frigid late-autumn air.

Sitting alone, looking out at the shadows of the trees on the scanty cover of snow on the lawn and eating the New England boiled dinner for which, he remembered, the inn was justly famous, Michael wondered how Cornwall had remained so lively and human after thirty years of taking the elevator up to the thirty-sixth floor five days a week.

It was almost dark, the Porsche humming along like a jeweled clock, when he reached what he recognized as the approach to Green Hollow. The car radio was turned on and a symphony orchestra from somewhere in New England was playing "The Ride of the Valkyries." He pressed down on the accelerator, smiling. Good old Wagner, he thought, he wrote automobile music before they ever invented the automobile.

He was going eighty-five miles an hour when he saw the flashing lights of a police car far behind him. He knew he could outspeed the police car, but then he would have to go right through the town of Green Hollow and not come back, so he slowed down, like a respectable citizen. When the police car came up close, its siren wailing, he pulled over to the side of the road.

The cops got out slowly and strode to the car, one on each side. The one on Michael's side was very young, with a bushy red moustache obviously grown to age him into policeman's authority. The effect was somewhat weakened by a wall eye that was focused on a point well above Michael's head. Michael smiled ingenuously at him, then stared. Despite the moustache, he recognized the man. Fourteen years ago, when Michael had spent the winter in Green Hollow, Michael had chased a ten-year-old redheaded boy with a wall eye and spanked him for throwing iced snowballs at his car. Michael grinned up at him. He even remembered the boy's name, Norman Brewster. His father had run a gas station in town.

"Where the hell do you think you were going?" Norman Brewster asked, trying to sound at least thirty years old and a pillar of the law.

"I was escaping," Michael said politely, thinking, I will tease my way into the town. He saw Norman Brewster's hand move toward his pistol holster, while he looked significantly across Michael at his partner, an older man with a bored expression on his face, leaning against the window on the passenger's side of the Porsche.

"Escaping from what?" Norman Brewster said.

"The old ennui," Michael said, relishing the moment when he would disclose to Norman Brewster that he had once whipped his ass.

"No jokes, mister," Norman Brewster said belligerently.

"Actually, from New York. New York City, New York, Area Code 212, Fun City, the Big Apple, etcetera. We're a fast group down there."

The older cop had the other door open by now and the window down, so he could be heard. "You were hitting eighty-five, you know."

"I didn't know, really," Michael said. "I guess I wasn't looking. Wagner was pushing me on."

"What do you mean, Wagner?" Norman Brewster peered suspiciously into the car. "Where is he?"

Michael pointed to the radio. "The music. Richard. He races the blood."

"Turn that goddamn thing off," Norman Brewster said.

Michael turned the radio off.

"And let's see your license."

Michael took out his license and handed it to Norman Brewster. He had the impression that the older cop was letting Brewster do the talking to see how he handled himself. Brewster peered at the license, using a flashlight. "No points on it," he said, sounding disappointed. "Lucky for you. This your first offense?"

"I didn't mean to be offensive, Officer," Michael said mildly. "I was just responding to the lure of the open road. It was a kind of special day for me. Don't you ever have a special kind of day?"

"Have you been drinking, mister?" Brewster asked, shining his light into Michael's eyes.

"Copiously."

"Ahah," Brewster said triumphantly, sensing an important arrest. "Driving while impaired."

"Almost everybody I know is impaired in one way or another," Michael said, pleased that Brewster was beginning to seem flustered. This is better than spanking, he thought. "Don't you feel that about the people you know?"

"I ask the questions, mister," Brewster said heatedly, "and you answer them."

"The truth is, Officer," Michael said, "I had one drink before lunch four hours ago and two cups of coffee. By the way, whom have I the pleasure of addressing?"

"Officer Brewster. And we can't stand here all night arguing with you."

"Norman," the older cop said, boredly, "don't make a Federal manhunt of this."

"Fred," Brewster said plaintively, "you said this time it was going to be my case."

"Okay, okay," the older cop said.

"Let's see your car registration," Brewster said.

Michael searched in the glove compartment but didn't find it. "Sorry," he said, "I must have left it in New York."

"Where were you heading for?" Brewster said menacingly, as though he expected Michael at any moment to make a break for the Canadian border.

"Green Hollow," Michael said. "I heard it was a charming place, with clean, unpolluted air and an upright police force."

"I don't like your attitude, mister," Brewster said. His throat seemed to be swelling above his collar. "Is anybody expecting you in Green Hollow, somebody who can identify you?"

For a moment, Michael was tempted to say that Norman Brewster might, but decided to prolong the comedy for a few minutes more. "Not that I know of," he said.

"Are you willing to submit to a blood test?" Brewster said in a voice that they must have taught him in police training school.

"I get faint at the sight of blood," Michael said.

The older cop sighed. "Norman," he said, "our tour ends in ten minutes."

"You said I could handle it, Fred," Brewster said, "and that's what I'm doing. By the book."

"The book takes too fucking long," Fred said, "but go ahead."

Brewster took out a balloon. "Would you agree to take a Breath-aletor test, mister?" he said, trying to keep calm and glaring at his colleague across Michael's head.

"I stand on my constitutional right not to breathe," Michael said, mischievously.

"Get out of the car," Brewster roared.

"Norman, Norman . . ." the older cop protested gently.

Michael got out of the car.

"Now walk a straight line," Brewster barked.

Michael did so, with small, mincing steps.

Brewster bit his lip, disappointed. "All right. Now let's hear you recite the alphabet backwards."

"I hate parlor games. And even when I was in college, I never had an English professor who could recite the alphabet backward. Can you?"

"That's beside the point," Brewster said, exasperated. "And I'm not interested in your goddamn education."

"Let's hear you," Michael persisted politely. "I'll buy you both a drink if either of you can do it."

"He's some kind of nut," the older cop said. "Write out his ticket and let's get back to the office."

"You heard him, didn't you, Fred?" Brewster said loudly. "Offering us a drink if we let him go. You know how that's going to look on the report. Next thing you know he'll be flashing dough to get off. I don't care how goddamn late it is. If you want my opinion, if he's not drunk, he's on dope or something and I'm going to find out what it is." He turned toward Michael, who was leaning languidly against the roof of the Porsche. "You like to live dangerously, don't you, mister?"

"Funny," Michael said, "that's what my wife says. Ex-wife. Almost ex-wife."

"I'm going to teach you you can't sass an officer of the law. Haven't you ever heard of police brutality?" Now, Michael noted gleefully, Brewster was reduced to sarcasm.

"Not in a ski resort, Officer," Michael said. "I'm that most sacred object of all objects in a resort—a tourist."

"Fred," Brewster said, "I'm going to run him in and take a good look at what he's carrying in this fancy little car."

"Oh, shit," Fred said, lost in the generation gap.

"Gimme your hands," Brewster said and snapped handcuffs on Michael's wrists professionally. "You're under arrest, mister."

"Interesting," Michael said.

"Oh, shit," Fred said again.

"I'll take him with me in the wagon," Brewster said to Fred, "and you follow me in that peewee car."

"Don't grind the gears, please," Michael said to Fred over his shoulder as Brewster pushed him toward the patrol car. "Do you know how to drive a car without an automatic transmission?" Pure childish taunting, he thought with pleasure, remembering his bad days at recess in the schoolyard as he climbed into the back of the squad car, behind the grid that divided it from the front seats. Brewster, breathing heavily and righteously, got behind the wheel.

Brewster started the car and with Fred behind him in the Porsche drove toward town. They passed a sign that read, WELCOME TO GREEN HOLLOW, VT., and Michael said, "I return in triumph."

Brewster grunted at the wheel and tooted the horn angrily at a girl on a bicycle riding in the middle of the road. Michael grinned and gaily waved his manacled hands at the girl.

The police station was new. It had not been there when Michael had been in Green Hollow before. It was a pretty little Colonial building next to the town bank. It had none of the dingy grimness of the precinct houses of New York, which gave architectural proof of the prevalence of manifold crime and harsh and unusual punishment.

Inside, there was an old cop with bifocal glasses seated behind a high desk. As Brewster took the handcuffs off Michael's wrists, he said to the policeman behind the desk, whom Michael didn't recognize, "I'm booking this fella, Henry. Speeding. We clocked him at eighty-five."

"Naughty, naughty," Henry said.

"No jokes, Henry," Brewster said, annoyed. "That isn't all. How do you like disrespect to officers of the law? And suspicion of drunken driving?"

"Naughty, naughty, naughty," Henry said. He looked as though he had been drinking himself all day long. Michael took an immediate liking to him and smiled up at him. Henry winked at him. Obviously young Norman Brewster's zeal was a subject of amusement in the police department of Green Hollow.

"And you can put down in the ledger one more item," Brewster said gravely, "offering a bribe to arresting officers."

Fred, who had been lounging silently against the wall, sighed audibly.

"One drink?" Michael said, as though surprised. "You guys must come cheap."

"You keep your mouth shut, mister," Brewster said loudly. He grabbed Michael's arm. "Come on in here." He led Michael into a back room with lockers in it. Off to one side there was a single cell. The cell was shining clean and looked comfortable.

The front door to the station opened and a burly, outdoor-looking man, dressed in rough woodsman's clothes, came in. "Hi, Henry," he said to the policeman behind the high desk. "Anything new on my truck yet?"

"Sorry, Mr. Ellsworth," Henry said respectfully. "We got fliers all over the state. Nothing yet."

"Kiss one truck good-bye," Ellsworth said. "Damn it, it's the first time in fifty years anything of mine's been stolen. We're getting the wrong element up here, Henry."

Michael, who was sitting at a desk with Brewster and Fred, while they were laboriously filling out forms, recognized the voice, but didn't say anything and waited for Ellsworth to recognize him.

Ellsworth looked curiously through the open door to the back room. He could see only the back of Michael's head.

"Some smart alec New York fella," Henry said. "Brewster's throwing the book at him. Mostly it'll come down to speeding, I reckon, when Brewster cools off."

Then Michael turned around. Ellsworth looked surprised. Then he laughed. "Hello, criminal," he said.

Michael stood up. "Hi, Herb." The two men shook hands and Ellsworth clapped Michael on the shoulder.

The two policemen looked up at the two men, abashed. "Hello, Mr. Ellsworth," Fred said, standing. "You know this fella?"

"Only for how long, Mike?" Ellsworth said.

"Fourteen years."

"That long, is it? Only for fourteen years," Ellsworth said to the policemen. "He saved my life, once."

"Don't exaggerate, Herb," Michael said.

"Saved my life," Ellsworth said emphatically.

"I thought you said you didn't know anybody in Green Hollow," Brewster said peevishly.

"I don't like to boast," Michael said.

"Lord, Mike," Ellsworth said, grinning, "you haven't changed, have you?"

"A bit," Michael said. "This time I got caught."

"You sure did, mister," Brewster said.

"Come on, boys," said Ellsworth, "you're not going to make trouble for an old friend of mine, are you?"

"He was going eighty-five, Mr. Ellsworth . . ." Brewster whined.

"Come on, Norman," Fred said wearily. "Act your age."

"I suppose . . ." Brewster said reluctantly to Ellsworth, "if you vouch for his character."

"It used to be mostly bad," Ellsworth said, "but he must have grown out of it by now. You going to be a good boy now, Mike?"

"I promise," Michael said to the policemen. "I'm sorry if I gave you any trouble."

"Okay," Brewster grumbled. "Just get your registration up here quick."

"Will do," Michael said. "Now will all you three gentlemen join me in a drink to celebrate my arrival in town?"

The two policemen looked at each other questioningly. "Well—" Fred said. "We're knocking off in a couple of minutes, anyway. Why not? The saloon's around the corner. It'll take just a little while to finish up our paper work."

"Okay," Brewster said, but couldn't resist one last parting shot at Michael. "Still—you're lucky Mr. Ellsworth happened in, I tell you . . ."

"This is my lucky day, gentlemen," Michael said.

"Here're the keys to your car, Mr. Storrs." Fred handed him the bunch of keys.

"Thanks," Michael said and went out with Ellsworth, waving airily at the drunken old cop high up behind his desk.

Brewster stared at the retreating backs glumly. "You think he *really* saved Mr. Ellsworth's life?" he asked.

"Herb Ellsworth don't make jokes," Fred said.

"You know," Brewster said reflectively, "I'm beginning to feel that I know that fella from somewhere."

"You can ask him over the drinks," Fred said and sat down and squinted at the report lying on the table.

Outside, Michael said, "Wait a minute, Herb. I want to lock my car. I have stuff all over the back." He locked the doors of the car as Ellsworth looked admiringly at the Porsche.

"You must be doing pretty good for yourself these days," Ellsworth said.

"It's not a bad little car," Michael said, smiling at the modest description of a machine that had cost him over twenty-five thousand dollars. "Pretty good." Then, more soberly, he added, "In a manner of speaking."

They walked around the corner toward the saloon. "How about you?" Michael asked. "How are you doing? You must be a big shot around here—the way they treated you."

"I can't complain. The construction business is swinging along. People from all over New York and New England are building houses here, even from Canada. You have some hills these days and a little snow and you're not too far from one or two big cities and you're a major industry."

They walked in silence for a little while. "I often wondered what happened to you," Ellsworth said.

"A couple of things."

"You married?"

"Sort of. Separated for the time being."

Ellsworth grunted, as though that was a sufficient expression of his sentiments about modern marriage and modern divorce. "You still ski?"

"A bit."

"Crazy as ever?"

"I try not to be."

"Why didn't you come back here from time to time?"

"I don't know," Michael said. "I skied out West—in Europe. Maybe I felt it never could be as good as it was here in the old days and I didn't want to spoil what I remembered. Maybe there were a couple of people I didn't want to run into again . . ."

"Mrs. Harris is still around," Ellsworth said. "Only she's not Mrs. Harris anymore." He looked at Michael obliquely.

"Oh," Michael said, "you knew about her."

"It's a small town, Mike," Ellsworth said. "The word finally gets out. She bought a house a few years ago. Still likes them young."

"That lets me off the hook."

"I wouldn't lay any odds."

"How does she look these days?"

"Pretty good, considering. She keeps in shape, skiing and all."

"Any permanent connection?"

"While the snow lasts. I don't know about after." Ellsworth looked at him quizzically. "You want to know her telephone number?"

"Thanks, no. I play in the veterans' tournaments now."

Ellsworth chuckled.

"You sure raised hell in this town," he said.

"I was twenty-one years old. I gave myself six months before settling down to being a responsible citizen, working in an office, getting ahead . . ."

"You get ahead?"

"I guess you might say that."

"How long you plan to stay up here?"

Michael shrugged. "I don't know. Maybe forever."

Ellsworth stopped walking, surprised. "What about your job?"

"I don't have a job."

"You get canned?"

"Quit. It was that or out the window."

Ellsworth started walking again. "Well, that's one good thing about Green Hollow. Ain't a window high enough in town so a man could do more than sprain an ankle jumping. You got enough money to last you a long while?"

"A while," Michael said. "I thought maybe I could teach skiing this season."

"You won't get rich doing that. What did you get when you did it back then?"

"I guess I averaged about sixty a week."

"You won't average much more now," Ellsworth said. "In real money. What with inflation. You sure you know what you're doing, Mike?"

"Pretty sure," Michael said, as they went into the bar. Pretty sure was about all he could honestly say about anything he thought or felt.

They ordered whiskeys and lifted their glasses to each other. "Herb," Michael said, "it sure is good to see you." He had roomed for a few weeks in the Ellsworth house and even after he left Mrs. Ellsworth had mothered him and had nursed him through a bout with pneumonia that had felled him late in the season and kept him in town for three weeks after the lifts had closed. Mrs. Ellsworth had fed him devotedly and their daughter, Norma, who was then seventeen years old, had silently adored him and he had had some memorable days on the mountain with Ellsworth who, despite his bulk, was a swift and graceful skier. It was the one time in Michael's life that he had felt part of a real family. "Now," Michael said, "what about you? Aside from being prosperous—which proves to me that capitalism has many things to be said for it—what about the family?"

"The wife's fine. And Norma's made me a grandfather. Twice. Two boys."

"Little Norma." Michael shook his head. "Who'd she marry?"

"The same one she was going around with when you stepped in." Ellsworth looked at Michael soberly, waiting for a reaction.

"Old David Stone-Face. The town hero," Michael said.

"Dave Cully. He waited you out. He runs the ski school now. He's a good husband and father."

"Is that enough for Norma?"

"You ask her yourself tonight. She's invited for dinner. And you're invited."

"Thanks."

"Dave can't come," Ellsworth said. "He has some kind of meeting."

Michael hesitated before he spoke again. "You think Norma would want to see me?" He had had a wild, surprising scene with Norma, during which she had wept and told him she loved him and that he was the only man she could ever love. He had tried to be as gentle and friendly as possible with the girl, but after that he had made a point of never finding himself alone with her.

"I haven't discussed the subject with Norma," Ellsworth said. "Yet."

"Listen, Herb," Michael said earnestly. "Maybe you, and for all I know, maybe the whole town thinks I had an affair with your daughter. I didn't. I liked her, I never had a brother or a sister and she filled a place in my emotional life that was good for me—I rooted for her when she was racing . . ." He shook his head. "Ah . . . all right, she had a kind of schoolgirl crush on me."

"She wasn't any schoolgirl," Ellsworth said. "She was seventeen and you were twenty-one. Maybe I blamed you after you left. If I did, it's finished now."

"I was busy in other bedrooms," Michael said. "Among others I was having a thing with a married woman . . ."

"Mrs. Harris," Ellsworth said flatly.

"We thought we kept it a secret and almost the only other girl in town I was ever seen with more than a couple of times was Norma, so naturally—you believe me, don't you, Herb?"

"All I know is that when you pulled out without saying good-bye, she was a very sad girl," Ellsworth said. He was accusing Michael now, but sorrowfully, a father who had an inconsolable child to console, confronting a grown man who, innocently or not, had caused his daughter pain. "It was a long time, Mike, before she pulled out."

"I don't like good-bye scenes now and I didn't then. I'm sorry. What do you think, Herb, do you want me to leave town tonight? Say the word."

Ellsworth played with his glass, brooding, for a moment. "Come to dinner," he said finally.

"You make me feel like a bastard."

"You weren't a bastard," Ellsworth said shortly. "People fall in love with the wrong people. That's all."

Brewster and Fred came into the bar and Michael ordered a round of drinks for them all.

"Say, Mr. Storrs," Brewster said, brushing away the foam of the beer he had ordered from his moustache, "I was just telling Fred here I kind of think I know you."

Michael smiled. "You did, Officer. I gave you a good licking when you were ten years old."

"Oh," Brewster said, laughing, "you're the sonofabitch. I couldn't sit down for a week. Sure I know you. You had a hand like a fucking iron bar. Welcome back." He shook his head. "And to think I had the chance to put you in the clink and muffed it." He grinned. "Wait till I tell my old man. My mother wouldn't let him touch me and he said you did me more good with that whipping than ten years in school. He wanted to send you a bottle of whiskey but I didn't know your name." He put out his hand and Michael shook it. "Welcome to Green Hollow, Mr. Storrs."

They had another round of drinks on that and Fred asked Ellsworth what the story was about Michael's saving his life.

"Well," Ellsworth said, "we used to ski a lot together, days when the ski school let him off, and we were skiing in a blizzard and it was beginning to get dark—one thing you could rely on Mike for was that anything could happen when you were out with him—high, high up—and I took a fall and broke my leg—later on they found out the tibia was snapped in two places. There was nobody else around and if

Mike had left me alone to go down and get the patrol and then come back to try to find me, I'd've frozen to death. It was about twenty below zero and I couldn't move an inch. I weighed two hundred and ten pounds and this little soft college fella picked me up and carried me piggy back down the hill."

"Is that true?" Brewster asked incredulously.

"What Herb doesn't say," Michael said, "was that it was pure self-preservation on my part. I was completely lost. I couldn't pick out anything with the snow coming down the way it was. And Herb'd been skiing here since he was three years old and knew the mountain like his own living room, and besides he was born with a compass in his head. I just picked him up so that he could give me directions. I was ready to kill him for being stupid enough to break his leg in that sort of weather."

"Yeah," Ellsworth said. "Be that as it may, Mike Storrs is a son in my house anytime he shows up."

They ordered another round and drank to the sentiment.

"Well, gentlemen," Michael said to the policemen, "have you got that balloon I can breathe into now?"

"You know something, Mr. Storrs," Brewster said generously, to cement the new friendship, "I believe you could whip my ass even now."

"Just don't throw any snowballs, Norman," Michael said, "and you're safe."

It was a perfect way to end the long trip up from the city, Michael thought as he got into the Porsche and followed Ellsworth's car to a new hotel that Ellsworth said was now the best in town and where he thought Michael might like to stay until he found a place of his own.

CHAPTER ELEVEN

The hotel was called the Alpina and as they walked from their cars toward the entrance Ellsworth explained that it was owned by an Austrian couple, whose own house a few hundred yards farther down the road he had just finished remodeling. The hotel was pleasant looking, architecturally unpretentious, rambling in shape, of white clapboard, rooted in New England, making no claims to be part of a Tyrolean village.

Inside, Michael saw that it was furnished comfortably with Colonial and rustic pieces, everything impeccably polished. Ellsworth introduced the man behind the front desk as Mr. Lennart, the manager. Mr. Lennart was a stout, unflappable-looking man of about fifty-five and seemed friendly as he asked Michael how long he expected to stay.

"A week, maybe," Michael said, as he signed the register. "At least for starters."

"Treat him right, Joe," Ellsworth said. "He's an old friend of mine."

"We're still just about empty," Lennart said, "so we can start by giving him the best room in the house." He rang the bell on the desk and a young man in a checked shirt who looked like a skier appeared, and Michael gave him the keys to the Porsche so he could get the baggage out of it.

"Well, then, you're all set," Ellsworth said. "See you at the house about eight. I imagine you still know how to find it."

"I'll be there."

Just as Ellsworth was about to turn and leave, a woman came down the main staircase into the entrance hall, followed by a big golden retriever. She was a handsome woman somewhere in her thirties, with a mass of ash blond hair done up in a neat, rather severe bun. She had blue eyes set in a long, pointed face and was wearing a light gray fur coat that Michael guessed was lynx.

"Good evening, Mrs. Heggener," Ellsworth said. "May I introduce a friend of mine who's going to be staying with you for a while? Mr. Michael Storrs."

"How do you do, sir?" Mrs. Heggener said. Her voice was reserved, her accent slight but unmistakably foreign. She did not offer to shake hands. "I hope you have a pleasant stay, Mr. Storrs."

"I'm sure I will," Michael said.

"I hope your husband is doing better," Ellsworth said.

Mrs. Heggener shrugged. "As well as can be expected. He's getting the best care possible. At least in America."

"Is he here?" Ellsworth asked. "I haven't seen him around."

"He's still in the hospital. More tests. Ridiculous." Her tone was sharp. Michael was glad that he wasn't the doctor in charge of testing Mr. Heggener.

"I expect he'll be back in a week or so," Mrs. Heggener said. "And I should have the house ready for him when he comes. Now that you've finished *your* job on it, mine begins. I must tell you, I think it's come out very well."

"Thank you," Ellsworth said.

"I have to make sure the new furniture gets here in time and the rugs laid and the curtains hung. Help is so hard to find these days . . ."

"Everybody's busy getting ready for the season," Ellsworth said, "but if I hear of anybody . . ."

"That would be kind." Mrs. Heggener fluffed the collar of her coat up around her face and made a little clicking noise to the dog, which had been sitting beside her making small, impatient sounds. Michael and Ellsworth watched her go out. No nonsense there, Michael thought.

Then the bellboy came in carrying Michael's bags and Michael followed him up one flight of stairs to a large room, with a big double bed, a fireplace, a wide desk, a rocking chair and two deep green corduroy-covered easy chairs. Everything was crisply clean and in order, brass lamps on the desk and tables throwing a subdued and comfortable light.

After the bellboy had left, Michael went over to one of the windows to see what the view was. The room was at the front of the building and in the light of the lamps that lined the driveway he saw Mrs. Heggener, bundled in her coat, with the dog trotting beside her, walking toward where the Porsche was parked. Mrs. Heggener stopped and peered at the car. The dog lifted his leg and peed against the rear wheel. Mrs. Heggener looked up at the window of Michael's room. He knew he was outlined against the light of the lamps and he knew she was staring at him. He had the impression that she was smiling.

He stepped back hastily. I hope the damn dog isn't an omen, he thought. He was sorry Mrs. Heggener had seen him at that moment.

He unpacked, bathed and shaved and put on fresh clothes, then wrote a short note to Antoine giving him the address of the Alpina and asking Antoine to go to the hotel in New York where Michael had left the bulk of his belongings and search for the registration for the Porsche. "All is blessedly peaceful here," he wrote, finishing the letter. "So far there is no snow, but it is balanced by a distinct absence of pianists and Texans. *Au revoir,* Michael." He remembered to scrawl Antoine's alias on the envelope and the address of the loathsome hotel to which Antoine had fled. Then, carrying an old sheepskin coat that he had had since his days in college, he went down to the desk and gave his key to the nightclerk.

Mrs. Heggener, now dressed for the evening in a long black gown, was sitting in a little sitting room visible from the lobby, the retriever lying on the carpet beside her. She was reading a book, but looked up as Michael stood at the desk and nodded at him and he nodded back. As Michael was waiting for the stamp to put on his letter, a tall, slender, exquisite black girl, very young, dressed as a maid in black, with a small white apron, crossed the lobby carrying a tray with a bottle of white wine and a single glass and went into the room where Mrs. Heggener was sitting. He couldn't help but stare.

The girl poured the wine into Mrs. Heggener's glass and Mrs. Heggener raised it in salute to Michael. She was obviously used to the guests of the hotel staring at her beautiful servant. She said something that Michael couldn't hear to the girl and the girl came over to

Michael and said, "Mr. Storrs, Mrs. Heggener asks if you would like to join her for a glass of wine," her voice melodious and shy.

He looked at his watch, decided he could spare five minutes and said, "Thank you very much," as the waitress went off to fetch another glass.

"It's very kind of you, madam," he said, as he threw his coat over the back of a chair.

"Please do sit down," Mrs. Heggener said. "It's good of you to join me. This is the time of the year I like best—before the season really begins and I have the place practically to myself. But there are moments when one is grateful for a little company. You are familiar with the town?"

"I spent a winter here many years ago. This hotel wasn't built then."

"No, my husband and I are comparative newcomers." Her tone was even, the words carefully spaced and clear, giving or taking nothing.

"When I was here before, no one dressed for dinner. I'm afraid I left anything fancy back in New York."

"Oh, this," Mrs. Heggener said, flipping a fold of her skirt slightly. Her hands, Michael saw, were long and pale, with polished, pointed nails. "I dress as the mood moves me. Our guests are encouraged to do the same. Tonight I happened to feel rather formal." She studied him frankly. Almost automatically, his hand went up to the open collar of his flannel shirt. Mrs. Heggener smiled. "Don't worry, you look splendid."

He put his hand in the pocket of his tweed jacket. Nobody had ever told him he looked splendid.

"Do you plan to stay long?" she asked.

"For the season. At least," he said, "if all goes well."

Mrs. Heggener arched her full, unplucked but shadowed eyebrows, as though surprised. "For the season? Well, we shall have to see that all goes well."

The waitress came back with a second glass and Mrs. Heggener poured. She lifted her glass. *"Prost."*

"Prost," he said.

"For the season," Mrs. Heggener repeated. "How fortunate for us. There are very few Americans your age who can tear themselves away from their work for a whole winter."

"I'm one of the lucky ones," Michael said, drinking. "The wine is delicious."

"Austrian," Mrs. Heggener said. "Have you ever been in Austria?"

"I've been in St. Anton, Kitzbühel, a couple of weeks."

"You're a skier, of course."

"I manage to get down the hill," Michael said. He had the feeling his credentials were being examined by this cool critical woman, with every movement measured.

Mrs. Heggener sipped at her glass. She had a wide mouth with full, unrouged lips, somehow, Michael thought, not fitting the same face as the cold blue eyes and the fine-downed almost ascetic lines of her cheeks. "My father grows this wine," she said. "I've drunk it since I was a child. One grows attached to the tastes of childhood. Shall I have Rita leave a bottle for you in your room for a nightcap this evening?"

"That would be very nice. Thank you."

"If you don't mind a rather mournful empty dining room," she hesitated, "perhaps you would like to share your dinner with me."

"That's very good of you, madam, but I'm dining with the Ellsworths."

"Of course," she said. "He's an old friend of yours, I take it."

"Old enough."

"He's a good friend, too—of my husband's. He helped build this hotel. My husband found him most straightforward and companionable. You could not be introduced under better auspices. It's a good breed—mountain men. You're from New York, aren't you?"

"Except on weekends and holidays."

Mrs. Heggener laughed. Michael had the impression that she was a woman who did not laugh often or heartily. It was a pity, he thought, because the cold face softened attractively when she laughed and she had perfect gleaming teeth. "I know what you mean," she said. "One fortnight there and my nerves are ragged. If I may ask, what do you do between weekends and holidays?"

"I struggle along," Michael said evasively. He didn't like being quizzed, judged, categorized by this cool, self-possessed woman.

"The struggle is not without its rewards, I believe," she said. "I saw your car."

"I occasionally pamper myself." Michael put the glass down and stood up. "Thank you for the wine. I'm afraid I must be going."

"If there's anything you need, please don't hesitate to ask. The service will be worse later—when the crowds come. Enjoy your dinner."

"I look forward to it." He took a step toward the door.

"Oh," Mrs. Heggener said, stopping him, "and forgive Bruno here." She patted the dog's great head. "In a way, what he did was a compliment. He . . . ah . . . anoints . . . only the most luxurious of machines."

Michael laughed. "Good old Bruno." He bent and patted the dog's head. The dog panted and wagged his tail lazily.

"He's a snob about people too," Mrs. Heggener said, plainly approving of Bruno's character. "He is very choosy about whom he bestows his friendship on."

"I'm flattered," he said.

"I'm sure you're used to flattery, Mr. Storrs," she said. "Have a pleasant evening."

"Goodnight, madam." She nodded and picked up the book she had been reading and ruffled the pages to find her place.

Glacial, he thought, as he went out of the hotel. Then he shivered and put on his coat and got into the car and drove off.

As he pressed the front door bell of the Ellsworth house, a gray-shingled two-story New England structure to which Ellsworth, Michael noticed, had added a new wing, he remembered the first time he had rung that bell. He had just arrived in town and had seen the sign, ROOM TO RENT, and he had spent the first two nights in a noisy, unkempt small hotel full of roaring college kids who couldn't hold their liquor, and the neat gray house had promised comfort and peace. It had given him that and more—prodigious meals and the friendship of the family, although he had only stayed two weeks then, because by the time two weeks had passed he had become involved with several ladies, including the one who was no longer Mrs. Harris and there was no possibility of entertaining the then Mrs. Harris or any of the other ladies in his small bedroom at the back of the house where the church-going and straitlaced family could hear every move he made through the thin wooden walls.

"Come in, come in," he heard Ellsworth's voice booming from somewhere in the house. He opened the door and went into the familiar hall as Ellsworth came out of the living room carrying a glass. He was coatless, the collar of his shirt open around his bull neck.

"Minna was beginning to worry," Ellsworth said, helping Michael off with his coat. "She remembers you like your roast beef rare and she was afraid you were running late and it would be overdone."

"I was held up by a lady," Michael said as they went into the living room.

"So soon?" Ellsworth said, but did not sound surprised.

"The owner's wife," Michael said. "Madam Heggener."

"Oh," Ellsworth said flatly. "That one."

Michael looked around the living room. It had hardly changed. The same grandfather clock ticking away, the same sofa, with the print a little more faded, the same photograph of Herb and Minna Ellsworth on their wedding day, their faces grave, their bodies rigid, Ellsworth big, but athletically trained down in a lieutenant's uniform.

"I have some great memories of this room," Michael said softly.

"Mostly of me sitting here with my leg up in a cast." Ellsworth waved his glass in his big rough hand. "I'm drinking whiskey," he said. "What's yours?"

"I was drinking white wine. Austrian wine."

"Ah, yes," Ellsworth said. "She tell you her father grows it?"

"Right off."

"She tell you her father was a count or something in the old country?"

"No."

"Wait," said Ellsworth. "She stepped down, marrying a hotelkeeper. Only the hotelkeeper supports the count these days. And his vineyard. I have a bottle of wine in the refrigerator. I'll go get it." He went through the dining room into the kitchen.

He might be a friend of the husband, Michael thought, but he's no friend of the wife. Ellsworth's dogs had never been snobs.

Michael went over to the mantelpiece, where, next to the wedding picture, there was a photograph of Norma Ellsworth, now Cully, with two small children on skis. She had not been a pretty girl, pale and skinny, and age had not made her any prettier. She stared out of the photograph, an uncertain small smile on her lips. The two boys seemed robust and took after their father. Luckily, Michael thought.

Ellsworth came back into the living room with an open bottle and a glass and poured for Michael. "You don't mind if it's not Austrian?"

"Not a bit." He tasted it. "Not bad."

"New York State," Ellsworth said.

Minna Ellsworth bustled into the living room, a plump, hearty, motherly woman in an apron, flushed from the heat in the kitchen.

"Mike," she said, emotionally. She embraced him and kissed his cheek, her arms solid and strong around him. Too bad, Michael thought, the daughter hadn't taken after either of her parents. She stepped back and examined him critically. "It's been too damn long."

"You're absolutely right, Minna," Michael said. "The place is as beautiful as ever. And so are you."

"Still a liar with the ladies, aren't you, Mike?" she said indulgently. She looked around the living room, though. "It's not too bad. Though everything's turning into an antique. Including the television set and me." She laughed, a rumbling, deep laugh. "Well, we can continue at the table. Dinner's ready." She went back to the kitchen, her wide bottom firm and strong under the sensible dark wool skirt.

"She looks great, Herb," Michael said to Ellsworth.

"Put on a little weight," Ellsworth said. "She enjoys her own cooking. Let's sit down."

They went into the dining room. There were only three places set on the big heavy oak table.

"Just the three of us?" Michael asked.

"Just us."

"I thought you said Norma was . . ."

"She said she couldn't come tonight," Ellsworth said, without expression.

They were silent for a moment. Michael finished his glass of wine and put it down on the sideboard. "You told her I was coming," he said, making it a declarative sentence.

"Uhuh."

"I see."

"Women," said Ellsworth. "Let's sit down."

"I saw the picture of her on the mantelpiece, with the two kids on skis," Michael said.

"Good kids."

"Did Norma keep up with her skiing?"

Ellsworth shook his head. "That was another of her disappointments. Just when it looked as though she was going to go on the circuit she tore her knee apart. Now she skis with her kids and that's all."

"Is she happy?"

"She would have been happier, if she'd gotten out of town and made a life for herself somewhere else. I never thought just being a housewife would be enough for her. However—" He shrugged his massive shoulders. "She made her decision. What's past is past."

Minna Ellsworth came in with a platter on which a big roast beef steamed, surrounded by browned potatoes. Tacitly, the two men didn't speak about Norma anymore during the meal.

After dinner, they watched television. There was a professional football game on and the two men watched intently while Minna did some sewing in a rocking chair, looking up occasionally, when the roar of the crowd became louder.

"They sure are wonderful," Ellsworth said. "But I'm glad I'm not playing these days." He had played in high school, but had not gone to college as he had to go to work and then into the Army right after graduation. "It's not a game anymore. It's men fighting for their lives for money."

"We all ought to be ashamed we watch it," Minna said unexpectedly. "Grown men tearing each other apart, their whole futures depending on whether they catch a ball or break their necks. And in skiing, the difference between being rich and famous or poor and a failure is a couple of hundredths of a second. There's enough competition in this world without burdening children with that kind of strain. And what it does to them later . . . It makes you want to cry. Just about every kid in this town who got a picture in the paper because he or she could slide down a hill faster than the other kids has turned out the worse for it. I tell you, I thanked Almighty God when Norma broke her knee."

Ellsworth turned the television off. "Minna," he said crossly, "can't you let us enjoy ourselves for a few minutes?"

She got up out of the rocking chair. "Women're supposed to be a civilizing influence. I'm going to bed. If you want you can turn on that damn tube after I leave, if you keep the noise down." She went over to Michael and kissed his forehead. "Goodnight," she said. "Don't forget where we live, now."

"I won't," said Michael.

She went out and Ellsworth reached toward the television set, then thought better of it and let his arm drop. "The hell with it," he said. "We can find out who won in the papers tomorrow. Want a whiskey?"

"No, thanks."

"Good. Neither do I," Ellsworth said. "They fix you up all right at the hotel?"

"Couldn't be better. Tell me, how come an Austrian couple run a hotel in a place like Green Hollow?"

"The way I got it," Ellsworth said, "Heggener's family were rich and owned a fancy hotel in Vienna, but the old man didn't like Hitler and saw the handwriting on the wall and got the family over here before the *Anschluss*. Heggener must have been ten or eleven, maybe a little older, at the time. They got their money out in time, so they were loaded. The old man put together a string of small hotels in America and Heggener inherited. Did damn well on his own after his father died, too, from all appearances. Met the lady at a reception at the Austrian embassy to the U.N. and reverted to type. She must be at least twenty years younger than Heggener, but it's better than working, I guess."

"What's he in the hospital for?"

"Poor bastard," Ellsworth said. "He came down with tuberculosis. One of those new strains that they can't cure with penicillin. We'll miss him when he's gone," Ellsworth said sadly. "He's very popular in town."

"And she isn't?"

"She doesn't go out of her way to win any popularity contests." Ellsworth yawned.

Michael stood up. "I'd better be going," he said. "It's been a full day. Anyway, thanks to you, I'm not sleeping in the slammer tonight."

Ellsworth chuckled as he walked Michael to the door. He looked up at the sky and sniffed. "Looks like we're going to have snow. Not a day too soon. Sleep well, Mike."

When Michael entered the hotel he saw the nightclerk sleeping with his arms folded on the desk and his head on his arms. Quietly Michael went behind the desk and lifted his key off the hook.

There was a fire going in the fireplace in his room and an opened bottle of wine was in a cooler with two glasses on the table between the two easy chairs. He wondered whom Rita thought he was going to bring back with him for the second glass. He threw off his coat and jacket and put another log on the fire, poured a glass of wine for himself, sat down and leaned back luxuriously, sipping the cold wine, staring into the flames. Snow tomorrow, Ellsworth had predicted. If there was enough coming down between now and morning to make it worthwhile that would make everything perfect. He'd heard that there were some new steep trails cut through the forest and he wanted to explore them.

There was a knock on the door. He looked at his watch. It was nearly midnight. Puzzled, he went to the door and opened it. Mrs. Heggener was standing, still dressed in the long, loosely flowing black gown.

"Oh," Michael said, surprised.

"Good evening," Mrs. Heggener said.

"Good evening," he said, not moving from the door. "Is anything wrong?"

"No. I was coming along the corridor and I happened to see the light under your door and I decided to make sure you were comfortable."

"Couldn't be more so." He noticed that she didn't explain what she was doing prowling around the hotel in the middle of the night.

"You're sure you have everything you need?"

"Everything."

She looked past him into the room. "Do you mind if I come in for a moment and see that everything's all right?"

"Of course." He stepped aside to let her pass him. He was about to close the door, then thought better of it and left it ajar.

Mrs. Heggener crossed the room, inspecting it as she did so. Michael was sorry he had thrown his overcoat and jacket over chairs and that he had left a pile of shirts on a table.

Mrs. Heggener touched the radiator. "Warm enough?"

"Just right."

"The wine cold enough?" she asked. "I could ring down for some ice."

"It's fine, thank you." He was feeling ill at ease. The sight of the handsome woman moving around his room so intimately in the middle of the night began to make him wonder if perhaps with her . . . "Oh," he said, making a sudden resolve, thinking, What have I got to lose? She's over twenty-one. "Would you like to join me in a little wine? There seem to be two glasses."

"So there are. I suppose Rita doesn't approve of solitary drinking." She seated herself across from the chair in which he had been sitting, crossing her legs, showing a very pretty, rounded calf and a fine ankle. Whatever she was, *she* wasn't ill at ease.

He sat down and poured some wine for each of them.

"I was speaking about you this evening," Mrs. Heggener said.

"Oh, you were?" Maybe he ought to stop all this inane small talk and just grab her and see what happened. By now he was sure that it would not be what had happened in New York with the physiotherapist and the old girlfriend. His erection was firm and unmistakable, caught awkwardly in the folds of his shorts and trousers and he had to sit twisted to keep it from being noticeable, like an old-fashioned actor in a drawing room comedy.

"An old acquaintance of yours dropped by. David Cully. He was coming from a meeting and he gave me the schedule of the courses and the events they've planned from Thanksgiving until Christmas. As the head of the ski school he and I often have things to discuss for the benefit of my guests. He's a great favorite in town. I suppose this is the only place people remember that he won all those downhill races out West that year." She sighed. "Fame," she said. "Especially in America. People flicker on, then flicker off. I feel sorry for Mr. Cully, although he seems quite happy himself, with his wife and children. He said you'd been a beau of his wife, Norma, when you were here."

"That isn't exactly true," Michael said, twisting again in the chair.

"He didn't seem to take it too seriously," Mrs. Heggener said. "He said you were the stud of the year, you had all the girls chasing you."

"I was young and exuberant in those days," Michael said lightly, although he disliked the way the conversation was going. The word stud had always annoyed him and it sounded particularly provocative coming, accented, from Mrs. Heggener's lips.

"He said you were a very good ski teacher and that they tried to prevail upon you to come back."

"He said that?"

"You sound surprised."

"I thought we didn't part exactly friends," Michael said. "Anyway, I had other things to do."

"So I gather. Do you plan to teach again this year?"

"I've played with the idea."

"David said he'd like to see you. They're running short on instructors this year. There's a new lift just been put in and they have to expand."

"Maybe I'll look in on him."

"I ski, too," Mrs. Heggener said. "But I'm one of those timid souls who has to follow an instructor at all times."

"I must say, Mrs. Heggener," Michael said, "you don't look like a timid soul to me."

"Eva is the name, Mr. Storrs. And appearances can be deceiving. And remember, I am on my own home ground here in the hotel. No ski slope feels to me like my home ground." She poured some more wine for both of them, leaning forward as she did so, her breasts stretching the cloth of her dress a little. She put the bottle down and leaned back again. "I know all the instructors here well," she said. "Too well. As in Europe, the conversation is limited, to say the least. Country boys who are only beguiling when they are going downhill. In my country—peasants. Only you can't call anyone a peasant in America."

"No," he said. "In America we range only from middle-class to noble."

She looked at him speculatively. "I have a feeling that your conversation would not bore me."

She is getting ready to lay it on the line any minute now, he thought. "You must not flatter me, madam," Michael said ironically.

"Eva," she said.

"Eva," he repeated.

"If I tell David I want you, he will assign you to me as a private instructor. I pay the ski school and the ski school pays you. It is an impersonal arrangement."

"The best kind," he said. He sneaked a look at his watch. Half-past twelve and we're still talking, he thought. But he'd be damned if he'd make the first overt move. "And if you find that my conversation, too, bores you . . . ?"

She shrugged. "I will tell David that we do not hit it off. That you go too slow for me, or too fast, or are too demanding. And ask him to suggest someone else."

Bitch, he thought, but sounded interested as he asked, "Do you ski every day?"

"No. Only sporadically. And in the afternoons mostly. But I like to have the instructor on tap in case I get a sudden urge to go up the hill. When I am in a dark mood, I seem to want to ski more often. It is a way of forgetting." Her speech, he noticed, was beginning to sound a little thick, the accent more marked. He wondered if she had been drinking all evening, alone. "I thank God for winter," she went on, her voice crooning sadly now.

"What do you have to forget?"

"That I am living in a country not my own." She seemed on the verge of tears and Michael wondered if she was one of those women who had to cry a man into bed. "That when I want to see my husband, I must go to clinics, hospitals all over the country, different places, every time my husband hears of a doctor who has developed a new treatment or one who has saved a patient's life. . . . That when he is at home with me, I am a nurse. That when I say, Take me home to Austria, he says, Yes, dear, perhaps next year. He was born there, you know . . ."

"I know," Michael said. "Ellsworth told me."

"But when he goes there, he can't stand it for more than a week at a time. It is a make-believe country, he says, it is no place for him."

Finally, Michael felt moved, although whether it was for the woman who, acting or not, was on the verge of tears, or for the doomed husband he had not yet met, he did not know. He leaned forward and took her hand. It was cool and steady and limp in his own hand. "I hope I will not go too slow for you or too fast for you or be too demanding," he said. Now he didn't know whether it was he who was acting or whether he honestly wanted to console her.

"Do you mean that?" she whispered dramatically, breathing deeply.

"Yes, I do."

"We shall see," she said abruptly. She withdrew her hand, stood up and moved quickly to the door. He watched, stunned, thinking, What in hell was *that* all about?

She stopped at the half-open door, then pulled it shut with a sharp little click and locked it. She turned and faced him, her head high, put her hands up to her hair, pulled something, and the ash blond hair, almost reddish in the firelight, cascaded down over her shoulders to her breasts and to the middle of her back in golden tumult. "Now," she said, staring at him seriously, "please put out the damned light."

Her body was deceptive. Given her height and the narrowness of her face, he had taken it for granted she was thin and angular. Her figure had been hidden in the loose black gown. But now he saw it was full and rounded, nourished on Viennese pastries and pots of rich hot chocolate *mit Schlag* from the best *confiseries* of the old capital of the Austro-Hungarian Empire.

The ascetic face proved also an illusion. There was nothing ascetic about her tastes and no reticence in her performance. She was instructive and demanding and he, reveling in the renascence of his virility, was happily instructed and answered all her demands. In the imperial balls in the old palace it must have been one of her grandmothers who led the waltzes, not the hussar who was her partner. Half-smothered in the fragrant flood of her hair, he could not help but think, in one of the rare moments he thought at all, the physiotherapist should see me now.

He had no idea how much time passed before she finally rolled off him and stretched out beside him, one leg across him. She sighed contentedly. "Another way of forgetting," she said. "Maybe the best."

He noted, a little bitterly, for future reference, that she was categorizing him merely as a teammate in a particularly vigorous sport and he was not pleased with the image. Affection, he guessed, was not in her repertoire.

"And to think," she said, "all Europeans keep saying that Americans don't know how to make love. And I listened to them." She chuckled, rolled a little closer to him and kissed him under the ear. "You said before that you would stay at least for the season. If all went well. Has all gone well?"

"Extremely well."

She chuckled again. *"That's* American, I must say. The laconic Yankee. The Gary Cooper syndrome. An Austrian would be quoting Heine or Schiller to me for a half-hour."

"Unfortunately, I don't know anything from Heine or Schiller. Next time, I'll try Yeats, though. 'When I am old and gray and full of sleep . . .'"

"You're not as old and gray as you think you are."

"Not tonight." If only she knew what he had been through since the day he and Tracy's father had nearly drowned in Long Island Sound.

"Not tonight," she said, musingly. "I take that as a compliment."

"It was meant to be."

"Have you any idea what time it is?"

"A quarter past delirium," he said, and she chuckled once more, complacently. She was, he could tell, used to pleasing men. He

reached over for his watch on the bedside table and peered at the il-
luminated dial. "It's twenty past four."

"Mein Gott. The maids will be moving about soon. It would not
do to see the lady of the house leaving a guest's room at this hour in
what used to be called complete disarray." She got briskly out of bed
and dressed quickly, but left her hair down. Then she came over and
kissed him.

"You're something," he said.

"A lady does her best," she said and kissed him again, then said,
softly, *"Du. Du."*

"What does that mean?"

"You," she said. "You. The familiar second person singular."

Well, he thought, be grateful for the small gifts the night bestows.

Then she was gone, a silent shadow in the last glow from the fireplace.

He stretched hard in the warm bed, appreciating the taut pull of
his muscles. For once, as he closed his eyes, he didn't regret that he
was no longer twenty-one. Snow or no snow, he thought as he
dropped off to sleep, it's a cinch I'm not going to get up early this
morning.

CHAPTER
TWELVE

He ate a late hearty breakfast in the deserted dining room, served by the boy who had brought in his bags. Looking out the window, he saw that it had snowed, but lightly, and what there was on the lawn was already thawing down to the grass in the warm sunshine. No skiing today. No matter.

Mrs. Heggener, as he still thought of her, was nowhere to be seen. He remembered that she had said Dave Cully wanted to talk to him and when he finished breakfast went out to get in the car and into town to the ski school.

There was an old station wagon parked next to the Porsche and as he went between the two cars, he heard a woman's voice say, "Hello, Michael."

It was Norma Cully, sitting at the wheel of the station wagon.

"Hello, Norma," he said. "What're you doing here at this time of the morning?"

"Waiting to see you. Pa told me where you were staying." She was wearing a bright checked scarf over her head and she looked pale and tired with all that color around her face. She kept twisting her hands nervously as she smiled tentatively at him. "There're a couple of things I have to tell you. Have you got the time?"

"Of course."

"Do you want to get into the car? It's a cool morning and I've got the heater on."

"I'm all right here," Michael said.

"You needn't worry about coming close," Norma said, smiling wanly. "This time I won't attack you."

"Why didn't you come to dinner at your parents' house last night?"

Norma shifted uneasily on the driver's seat. "Account of you. I didn't know how I'd act the first time I saw you and I didn't want to make a fool of myself in front of Ma and Pa. I didn't know whether I'd laugh or cry or fall down in a faint or accuse you of ruining my life or throw my arms around your neck and say you're the only man I've ever loved. Anyway, I needed at least one night to think you over."

"Norma, dear," Michael said gently, "you had a schoolgirl crush on an older friend of your parents' fourteen years ago. Now you're married and have two kids and you're a grown, sensible woman, according to your mother, and you wouldn't have done any of those things. You would have said, 'How are you, Michael? We're all glad to see you back again. Have you seen the pictures of my two kids?'"

"Maybe," Norma said doubtfully. "But maybe I'd have said you shouldn't have kissed me goodnight after taking me to the movies that time and you shouldn't have said you liked skiing with me better than with any of the other girls and maybe I'd've said you had no right to tamper with the affections of a simple mountain girl and lead her on so that she had fantasies of making love with you and even marrying you and going to live with you in New York."

"I'm sorry, Norma," Michael said, with a pang of guilt at his thoughtlessness so many years before. "I liked you. I thought you were a nice girl, as indeed you were, and I just was too stupid to guess anything about your fantasies."

"You must have guessed that just about every girl in town, and almost every woman, too, was crazy to get their hands on you."

"You had a higher opinion of my charm," Michael said dryly, "than I ever did."

"You seemed so sure of yourself. As though everything was due you. It was one of the things that attracted women to you, as much as anything else."

Michael laughed ruefully. "Did I seem like that then? Well, I wasn't at all sure of myself then and I'm even less sure of myself now. Anyway, we can be friends now, can't we? The next time I come to dinner at your parents' house, you'll come, won't you?"

She didn't answer his question. "I put on an awful act when you left without even saying good-bye. I wept and I wouldn't leave my room for days and I nearly drove my poor father out of his mind with my goings-on. I guess I'd seen too many movies about great tragic loves, girls left behind while their lovers went off to war or took up with other women." There was a harsh self-mocking tone to her voice as she spoke. "Anyway, I was ashamed of myself. And I did something worse, that I'm even more ashamed of, and that's why I decided I had to talk to you right away, before you settled in here."

"What's that?"

"I boasted."

"About what?"

"About you," she said. "I sort of let it be known to some of my girlfriends and some of the boys, too, that I'd had an affair with you. You were the catch of the year and I wanted to make them jealous and at the same time make myself important. Now you're back you're going to hear some stories and I thought you ought to be prepared."

Michael sighed. "Thank you for telling me. It was foolish, but it's not important. Both you and I will survive."

"I wish it had been true," Norma said defiantly. "Even now, looking at you, I feel very funny."

Michael laughed at the childish word. "I feel funny when I see a lot of people, Norma."

"I heard you were married."

"We're separated."

"I'm going to tell you something awful, Michael," she said. "I'm glad."

"I'm not," he said soberly.

She leaned toward him, through the open window. "Will you kiss me, just once, for old times' sake?"

He pulled back a little. "Old times're not what they used to be, Norma."

"I suppose you're right," she said sadly. "Anyway, I'm happy to see you here and I guarantee I won't make any trouble for you and that's what I came here to say and I've said it."

"You're a dear woman."

"Dear," she said dully. Then she started her car and drove off.

He watched the car wind down the road and disappear, then shook his head and got into the Porsche and headed for town.

He parked the car in front of the store in which the ski school had its headquarters. But he didn't go in immediately. He was more shaken by the scene with Norma than he had realized and he took a few minutes to compose himself before he entered the building.

There was a young girl sitting behind a desk, typing with two fingers, her forehead furrowed in concentration. Behind her was a poster with the schedule of rates for the school and a list of the dates and types of races to be run for the season and an advertisement for a hang-gliding school. The office was big and roomy and businesslike, which it had not been fourteen years before.

"Good morning, miss," Michael said to the girl, who glanced up from her typing. "I'm looking for Dave Cully."

"He's out for the moment," the girl said. "You can find him in the diner across the street. He's having his morning coffee."

Michael crossed the street to the diner and went in. Cully was seated alone at a table in a corner, drinking coffee out of a mug and scowling at a newspaper he had spread in front of him. Cully was a big man, much heavier than when Michael had seen him last, and was beginning to grow bald. He had always looked like a mountain man, sturdy and thick, but now, with age, he looked as though he had been hewn out of the side of the mountain.

"Hello, Dave," Michael said.

Cully looked up. "Hi." He had been a handsome young man, but the years had thickened his face and there was a lost puzzled look in his eyes.

"Mrs. Heggener tells me you'd like to talk to me."

Cully nodded. "Sit down. Coffee?"

"Thanks."

Cully called to the waitress behind the counter, "Sally, another coffee, please. And give me a fresh cup, too." He examined Michael across the table, without saying anything. "You seem to have weathered well," he said finally.

"Careful living."

"I would have given odds you'd be dead by now." Cully's voice was heavy, without timbre or inflections. "Nobody would've taken them."

"I'm still around."

"So I see. Thanks, Sally," he said, as the waitress put the two mugs of coffee on the table. "You fixed up pretty good at the Alpina?"

"Never been in a hotel I liked better," Michael said, without going into details.

"Yeah, they've helped the town, helped us. Nice type of clientele. Don't mind spending money and don't give anybody any trouble." Then, with a glint of humor in his eyes, "You don't feel a little out of place there, Mike?"

"I've slowed down in my old age."

"That's not what I hear. I ran into Norman Brewster last night and he said they pulled you in for going eighty-five and sassing the police."

"It was all a great misunderstanding," Michael said, laughing. "There wasn't any need to be in a hurry to get here—"

"You can say that again. It looks as though it ain't going to snow before Christmas this year," Cully said, looking unhappily up at the blue sky through the big plate glass window of the diner. "There ain't much to do around this town unless you can ski. What'll you do with yourself?"

"I saw a poster on the wall of your office for a hang-gliding school. Deltas. On a nice day I might take a few flights."

Cully looked at him incredulously. "Don't tell me you go in for that sort of thing."

"Occasionally."

"Well, you'll like the kid who runs it. He's crazy, too. I was against letting him set up shop but I was voted down."

"What do you have against it?"

"The nearest hospital is in Newburg and that's twenty miles away. That's what I have against it."

"You ever try it?"

"At my age?" Cully said. "My idiot days're over."

"You're missing some great kicks."

"You mean to say you like it?"

"Why else would I do it?" Michael said.

"Showboating. Look, Ma, how brave I am." Cully looked sharply at him. "Those exhibitions you gave doing double somersaults and twists off cliffs. Almost every kid here could beat you in the downhill, but they wouldn't dare try half the things you did and if they did try they most likely wound up in plaster. Christ, I was the hottest thing in town and I wouldn't think of competing with you in damnfool crap like that."

"I had a peculiar talent," Michael said mildly. "I worked out tumbling for years in gyms. It was fun . . ."

"Maybe," Cully admitted. "Maybe. But maybe you were trying to prove something to yourself that you didn't ever want to admit was bugging you. Is still bugging you. But somersaults on skis isn't hang-gliding. You might crack yourself up, but you don't drop from a thousand feet. Do you do it for money?"

"Come on, Dave," Michael said, "I'm not a professional stunt man." He thought for a moment. "I don't think it's showboating. I don't need an audience. For the rest, maybe you're right, Doctor." He'd had enough of Cully's analysis. His reasons were his own. He only wished he knew what they were. "Anyway, if the wind is right, I'll try it today. It looks as though there ought to be some pretty good hills for it around town."

Cully shook his head. "Remember me in your will."

Michael laughed.

"You really serious about saying you might want to work this year?" Cully asked abruptly, getting down to business. Michael realized that they both had been sparring with each other, feeling each other out. "Mrs. Heggener told me," Cully said, "you might and that if you did, she wanted you assigned to her. I said I'd arrange it if you were serious."

"I guess I am."

"Just don't get Mrs. Heggener hooked on hang-gliding. I'd be run out of town if she crashed."

"Don't worry," Michael said. "She told me she's a timid soul."

Cully merely grunted. "We're hungry for instructors this year," he said. "We're going to stretch the regulations to handle the crowds and we can use a few older guys who know they're being paid for teaching skiing, not for hot-dogging all day and smoking pot and screwing the girls during working hours. Some of the types we get these days, the young ones . . ." Cully shook his head sadly.

"Well, at least I'm an older guy."

"You were a good teacher, I'll say that for you. I won't say yea or nay about your off-time activities." Cully grinned sourly. "You been skiing much? You look in good shape. Better than me," he said glumly.

"I've done my share of skiing. Out West, Europe . . ."

"Don't tell me." Cully scowled. "I haven't been off these hills anywhere since I got this damned job ten years ago." He tapped the newspaper in front of him loudly. "I'll be lucky to get a day off to see the downhill at Placid during the Olympics. It might be the one year, too, when an American took a first place. The miracle year," he said sardonically.

"Aren't there any kids that look as though they could make it in town anymore?" Michael asked curiously.

Cully shook his head. "A lot of kids with talent," he said, "but it's a different breed. They won't do the work, they won't train, they won't make the sacrifices. To tell you the truth, I don't blame them. What have I got to show for it? My legs're so banged up it takes me twenty minutes to get out of bed in the morning. Three operations on the knees." Under the table he moved his legs and there was a loud crackling sound, like bones breaking. "Listen to that, will you? Sometimes I look at the medals and the cups in my house and then look at the scars on my knees and think I'd trade. Give back the medals and give away the scars." He chuckled harshly. "And what am I good for now? Running a two-bit ski school in the winter, occasionally getting some V.I.P. fat cat, like a senator or the president of an oil company, down the slope, making sure he doesn't get his brains knocked out. No good for anything better, because when everybody else was going away to college I was running up and down hills, lifting weights, following the circuits wherever there was snow—yeah, I saw Europe for two months, only all I saw was the same snow as here and a couple of new airports—and thinking I was a big shot because I got my picture in the papers and had my choice of girls for a year or two because I came in first at Sun Valley and then what . . . ? People coming up to me from time to time, saying, I know your face from somewhere. . . . Nah, I'm no shining example for the kids around here. Anyway, they're spoiled. Too much mama and papa, too much money. When I skied we were lucky to get board and lodging."

"Still, even if it was only for a little while, you had a great time, didn't you?"

The massive man looked sullenly at Michael across the table, as though Michael were asking him a delicate and unfortunate question. "Yeah. It wasn't bad for a while," he said.

"Would you do it all over again if you had the chance?" Michael persisted. He, too, had had his great times and had paid for them.

Cully pondered, rinsing his mouth with coffee before he answered. Then he laughed ruefully. "I guess so," he said. "I'm just as dumb now as I was then." He shook his head sadly. "A three-month-a-year career. In the summertime I work in my father-in-law's lumber yard. For vacation I paint the house. If my kids want to go to college when they grow up they'd better be good enough to get scholarships because it's a cinch their old man won't be able to afford the tuition. You're lucky you were never tempted."

"My temptations were different. Maybe worse."

"Tell me about your troubles, friend," Cully said ironically. He closed the newspaper and rolled it up, as though it was offending him. He looked inquisitively at Michael. "You want to say why a man who owns a Porsche . . . ?"

"Oh, you heard about that, too?"

"Norman Brewster," Cully said. "He asked me if you were a bookie or a white collar criminal or something."

"What did you tell him?"

"I said I wouldn't be surprised." Cully grinned again. "Anyway, why does a guy who has dough enough for a car like that want to take a piddling job teaching skiing in a half-ass resort like Green Hollow? You want to say?"

"Actually, no," Michael said.

"Didn't think you would. No matter. If you want the job it's yours and glad to have you back."

"Are you sure?" Michael asked doubtfully. Even after what he had said to Eva Heggener, he still wasn't certain that was how he wanted to spend the winter—teaching. "After . . . well . . . everything?"

Cully took a loud sip from his mug of coffee. "Coffee ain't what it used to be, have you noticed that?"

"I haven't noticed."

"Just ain't," Cully said. He took a deep breath, stared evenly at Michael. "It was a long time ago. Just stay away from Norma and there'll be no trouble."

"Dave," Michael said, hoping that the man would never learn of Norma's visit that morning, "I don't know what Norma's told you but I swear . . ."

Cully put up a big hand to stop him. "I don't want to hear about it," he said harshly. "I didn't go into all the details of my life when I asked Norma to marry me and I ain't interested in what she was up to before she walked up the aisle to the altar. I need a few older men and you fill the bill. Nobody says we have to be bosom buddies or keep on sweating out what happened in the Dark Ages. Anyway, Mrs. Heggener wants you and in this town what Madam wants, we supply. I ain't doing you any favors. She's a hard lady to please. Last year she went through four instructors. The other guys'll vote you skier of the year for taking her off their backs. Just make sure there's no damage to the goods from now to April. You'll earn your pay. Which ain't saying much. If you don't get killed dropping out of the clouds before lunch, come into the office this afternoon and I'll fit you into one of these jackets and a Green Hollow sweater; they're due in by three P.M. And if we ever get any snow, maybe we could do a coupla runs together."

"Thanks," Michael said, standing, glad that the interview was over, recognizing the invitation to ski as a gruff and indirect way of approaching a common ground of friendship.

"See you later," Michael said, as Cully called for another coffee, saying to the waitress, as he waved good-bye, "I'll drink myself to death with all this lousy coffee."

The hang-gliding school was not beautified by any ivied towers. In a narrow valley, with a respectable hill looming above it, there was a battered pickup truck and a mud-spattered small living trailer, each with "Green Eagle Hang-Gliding School" painted on it in irregular large green letters. A ramshackle shed that once had been used for storing hay surrounded what might be described as the campus, a muddy stretch of dead turf about twenty yards square.

Michael looked into the shed and then into the trailer, where an unmade bunk, some unwashed pots and pans, a radio and the pervading smell of pot reassured him that someone actually lived there. There was nobody either in the shed or in the trailer. He went out and looked up at the sky. A hang-glider was slowly circling for a landing.

Michael smiled at the sight and felt the first tingle of excitement. He watched critically as the man in the glider, in a sitting position, landed perfectly only a few feet from the pickup truck. The man unhooked himself and came toward Michael. He was young and gangling and blond, with a swooping, dank moustache, also blond, and a sad, sunburnt, skinny face. He walked loosely, as though his joints were unhinged. His clothes, jeans and a patched old army windbreaker, looked as though he had slept in them for a month.

"Hi," Michael said, as the man approached.

"Hi." The man gave him a languid wave of the hand, hardly lifting his arm.

"That looked pretty good up there," Michael said.

"A piece of cake today. Just enough wind. You lookin' for somebody?"

"I thought I might take a little spin. Who runs this outfit?"

"Me," the man said. "Williams. Jerry Williams. Sole proprietor."

"Michael Storrs."

"Hiya, Mike." They shook hands. Williams's hand was callused, but he applied no strength. He would never make a politician with a handshake like that. "You been up before?"

"A few times."

He had taken up the sport more or less by accident. One of the mechanics who worked in the garage where Michael had his Porsche serviced had shown up one day with his wrist in a cast and out of politeness Michael had asked what had happened.

"Hang-gliding," the mechanic had said. "Nothing much. Hairline fracture. Won't keep me grounded. Fact is, I'm going out again on Saturday."

"What's it like?" Michael asked. "Hang-gliding, I mean."

"The greatest, man." A dreamy look came into the mechanic's eyes. "I tried free-falling and compared to gliding it's like just rolling out of bed. I hear you do some skydiving."

"Some," Michael said.

"Different breed of cat." The mechanic spat as though he were talking of an inferior caste. "Gravity does all the work."

"Where do you go?"

"The Catskills, the Poconos. This weekend it's the Poconos. You interested?" Suddenly there was a note of challenge in the mechanic's voice, the proletarian who worked with his hands offering the elegant gentleman with the absurdly expensive car a chance to prove just how tough he really was.

"I might be interested," Michael said. What the hell, he thought, I've tried just about everything else. "Why not? I haven't got anything on this weekend."

"I guarantee you'll be hooked, man," the mechanic said.

Michael hadn't been as hooked as all that, but the lessons had been fun and the instructor, who looked as though he could have been Jerry Williams's brother, had said he had natural talent for it and he and the mechanic had become weekend friends and the Porsche benefited from it.

"What kind of kite you used to?" Williams was saying now.

"Delta," Michael said. "Like yours."

"Got it with you?" Williams looked doubtfully over at the Porsche, which had hardly enough room to carry an umbrella in it.

"No. I did some housecleaning awhile back and sold it."

Williams looked him over carefully, the first time that there was anything but a dull glaze over his eyes. "Um," he said. "You staying here?"

"New boy in town. I'm an instructor in the ski school."

"Not much instructin' to do so far," Williams said, looking up at the clear sky. "Fucks up my business, too. People just don't come and it ain't even cold enough nights to turn on the artificial snow machines. Keeps up much longer like this, I'll fuckin' well have to go to work. They pay you while you're waitin'?"

"Theoretically, yes."

"I get balls," Williams said, but without anger. "I'm an individual entrepreneur. The backbone of the country. Down to my bare ass. I shouldn't talk like that to a customer, should I?"

"I don't mind."

Williams gestured to where the glider was lying. "You land where you want to land, Mister Storrs," he said, "or where the machine wants to land?"

"Both," Michael said and they both laughed.

"Well," said Williams, "at least you're honest. I'll drive you up to the top of yonder hill"—he pointed to the wooded mountain that cast its shadow over the valley—"there's a road goin' up, the other side. I'll watch you take off. If you can, come down here. If you can't, I'll find you. Please try not to wind up in a tree, trees're hell on kites. If you bust up the machine, you pay. Or your estate pays." He grinned.

"Fair enough."

"Come on into the office and sign the papers. It's a waiver in case of injury. I talked to a lawyer friend of mine and he gave me legal advice when I started the business. So you can't sue me and I can sue you if you wipe out my kite."

"Again," Michael said, "fair enough." He was anxious to be up in the air.

Williams led the way into the shed, where a plank, stretched over two sawhorses, served as a desk. He searched around a bit and came up with a wrinkled sheet of paper with some printing on it. "The lawyer had his girl run it off for me on the machine," Williams said, handing it to Michael, along with a stub of pencil.

Michael signed it without looking at it.

"Don't you want to read it?" Williams asked, surprised.

"No need," said Michael.

"I like your style, man. Let's go."

Outside, Michael helped Williams take down the machine and stow it in the long canvas carrying bag and put it in the back of the pickup truck. Then they both got into the cab and drove off, the engine coughing resentfully. The road was winding and narrow and steep in some places and here and there it looked as though the truck wouldn't make it, but they finally came to a little grassy plateau on the crest of the hill. From there, Michael could look down at the whole town, toylike at that distance. The Alpina was visible, set among lawns and trees and Michael saw a swimming pool behind the hotel that he hadn't known was there.

The two men assembled the machine, Williams nodding with satisfaction as he saw that Michael knew what he was doing. Then he helped Michael buckle into the glider. Sloppy as he might be in his office and the trailer in which he was living, he was meticulous in every move now and the glider itself showed that a great deal of care had been lavished on it.

"You got an updraft on the side of the hill," Williams said, after he had made sure everything was secure, "so you don't need much of a run for takeoff. You ready?"

Michael nodded. If he had tried to speak, he was afraid that he couldn't control whether he would whisper or scream. He could feel his body trembling with impatience.

"Have a nice ride," Williams said. "And don't fly too low over town. The natives're nervous. I should be waiting for you at the shed."

Michael took three deep breaths, then started running. He ran for about fifteen yards, clumsily, with the wings making him feel like a landbound bird, and then he soared off in the updraft, into invisible supporting cold space, everything slow and silent and blue. "Ah," he whispered to himself, as he made the first banking turn, "ah, God."

He thought of making a one hundred and eighty degree turn and going back over the takeoff plateau and saluting Williams, but gaining altitude was chancy business and the updraft wasn't steady. Another time, he thought, as he banked first to the left, then to the right, the controls responding beautifully. He banked down regretfully, everything in dreamy slow motion, time suspended. Despite Williams's warning not to fly too low over the town, he couldn't resist coming down to about five hundred feet above the Alpina, which was on a little knoll and outside the town, anyway. He saw a Mercedes drive up and a woman get out and look up at him. He recognized Eva and made an extra little swoop. She didn't wave, but turned on her heel and stamped into the hotel.

Then he made for the Green Eagle Hang-Gliding School and saw that Williams, who was standing in front of the shed, had beaten him down the mountain.

Moving precisely, Michael made sure to land exactly where Williams had landed on the previous flight.

"I guess you weren't lying," Williams said, as he helped him out of the harness, "when you said you'd been up before. How'd you like it?"

"Like driving a Cadillac," Michael said, regretting already he was back on the ground.

Williams grinned. "That's not what they all say. Want to go up again?"

"I guess I won't press my luck," Michael said. "Maybe tomorrow."

For the first time Williams looked uneasy. "Uh . . ." he said, "you want to pay now or put it on the tab?"

"Which do you prefer?"

"Pay now," Williams said, relieved. "That way I can buy myself lunch. Ten bucks."

Michael paid him. Ten dollars for ten minutes of unalloyed pleasure. Bargain of the age. "You're not doing a rushing business, are you?"

"Waiting for God to start the season with a little snow. He's late this year. Too busy other places with all the shit that's going on. Meanwhile I get a lot of free rides." He walked Michael over to where the Porsche was parked. He ran his hand approvingly over the gleaming metal of the hood. "Nice little heap you got there. I shoulda charged you twenty."

"I was good for twenty," Michael said as he got behind the wheel.

"Chalk up one lost sucker," Williams said good-naturedly. "Say, we're going to have some competitions when the season starts. Tricks, landing in target circles, length and duration of flight, stuff like that. Prizes. I know some hot fellas who already signed up. I got a lotta friends in the sport. You want to sign up?"

"Thanks. If I have the time. Be seeing you."

"See ya, man," Williams said and lounged back to where the pickup truck was parked. He stared gloomily at it for a moment, entrepreneur, backbone of the American system, sole proprietor, then kicked a tire savagely.

As Michael drove back to town, he was humming. One marvelous thing about the morning, he said to himself, I haven't thought about Norma for at least a half-hour.

CHAPTER THIRTEEN

"I suppose you've heard about me," said Annabel Fenstock, whom he'd known as Mrs. Theodore Harris. "I'm notorious as the town bang." She smiled gently over the drinks they were having in the corner of the deserted barroom of the Hotel Monadnock. Mount Monadnock was in New Hampshire, but the owner of the hotel was a native of New Hampshire and it was his way of showing his loyalty to his native state.

Michael had run into her in the town drugstore, where he had gone to buy some magazines and books, as he had just about sampled everything in the small library in the Alpina. There still wasn't any snow and there wasn't much else to do in the afternoons. Not that he minded. He had begun to take long naps, as the nights continued to be lengthy and strenuous. Three times more he had done some hang-gliding, but the weather had turned nasty, with high winds, and he passed the best part of his day in happy, recuperative somnolence.

"I haven't heard anything, Anne," Michael lied.

Annabel smiled sweetly. "You were always a gentleman, Michael. Anybody who's been here ten days has heard about me."

"How do you know I've been here ten days?"

"The drums beat. I got five telephone calls the night you arrived. None from you." But she didn't sound resentful. "Older folk with long memories."

"I've been busy."

"No doubt," she said. It would have been false to say that at forty she was as good looking as she had been when she was twenty-seven, but the snub nose and the merry eyes, although there were lines around them and the sun had done some harsh work on her skin, were still appealing, and her figure, with all the skiing she did in winter and the tennis she played in summer, had remained elegantly youthful in the skintight slacks she had worn then and still wore.

He had been tempted once or twice to call her, but the overwhelming presence of Eva Heggener and the sad memory of Norma Cully had made him decide that the past was the past and that no good would come of digging around among its debris.

"A smart man I once knew told me," Annabel said, "when I was contemplating buying a house here that single women who hang around ski towns turn into withered old spinsters and objects of ridicule. I weighed the pros and cons and bought the house and am enjoying taking the consequences."

"They don't show as yet," Michael said. "The consequences, I mean."

"Dear, gallant Michael." She blew him a little kiss across the table. "When my late dear husband asked for a divorce, at a generous premium I must admit, he called me a loose woman. I don't know what he called himself. He'd screwed everything that moved—especially if it was under twenty—between Newport, Rhode Island, and Sea Island, Georgia. I examined the term for what it meant for myself. I decided that, for better or worse, I am incapable of love but more than capable of lust. You, I'd say, are capable of both. That you're happier for it is something I doubt. As for me—a transient sensualist is what I hit upon as a fitting description, and I'm devoted to youth, which is generally regarded in America as an admirable quality."

"Somebody told me you liked them young."

"I'm sure they did," Annabel said complacently. "And a ski resort is just right for that sort of thing. It's not a sport for the aged—"

"Like me." Michael couldn't help but say it.

"Like you," she said brightly. "And they have to go back to school or work, with an occasional lively weekend thrown in and then a new batch arrives because they stagger their holidays or they get suspended from Harvard for a week or two and all's well. On Sundays I wear my scarlet letter, tastefully set in diamonds by

Tiffany." She frowned slightly, as though trying to remember something. "How old were you when we . . . ?"

"Twenty-one."

"Barely under the limit," she said.

"Annabel, you're incorrigible."

"And I hope to stay that way for some years yet," she said good-naturedly. "After that I'll devote myself to Eastern religions and good works and wallow in old lady's memories of the great hours I've spent in my lifetime."

"Do you ever get invited to parties here?"

"Only kiddies' parties. Thank God. Pot and generalized groping. The others bore me out of my mind. If you have an evening free, give me a ring—I'm in the book—and I'll cook you a dinner. Although," she said, with just the trace of a tiny smile playing around the corners of her lips, "I imagine you're being very well taken care of where you are." Then she looked at him consideringly, soberly. "You look nice and healthy and well groomed, but somehow I get the impression from your face that something bad has happened to you."

"Something bad is happening to everybody in the whole world at this very moment," he said, trying to keep her off the subject of Michael Storrs by launching into generalities.

"When I walked into the drugstore and you were standing in front of the stack of paperbacks, and you didn't see me, I had a queer feeling—I thought you looked desperate."

"Anybody trying to pick out a good book these days is liable to look desperate," he said, trying to put her off.

"No joke, old lover. I was shocked. When I knew you when you were a kid I thought, There's one man who's not going to suffer. First of all, you were one of the best looking things I'd ever seen . . ."

"Annabel, you make me blush for my decay."

"And there was something wild and joyous about you. All right, now I'll be fancy—unconquerable."

"You mean now I look conquered?"

"I'm afraid that's what I mean, Michael."

"Stick to the young, darling," Michael said roughly.

"I didn't mean to hurt you, sweet," she said. "But we're old friends and we used to say what we meant to each other."

"You've become the town bang since then. Your words," he said, cruelly, retaliating. "And I've become something maybe worse, only I don't have your gift of phrasing to describe it. Let's leave sleeping friendships lie."

"You can't insult me, Michael," she said, with dignity. "I liked you too much for that. If there's anything I can do to help you, I'm here."

"I don't need any help," he said, sounding, even in his own ears, like a stubborn child.

"Have it your own way." She stood up and kissed him lightly. "Thanks for the drink. I must be off."

The drums do beat, Michael thought, as he watched her walk off, her slacks tight and brave and revealing, her walk swaying and youthful. The town bang. What price reputation? What price self-knowledge? He wondered if she wept the nights she was alone. At any rate, she was happier than Norma Cully and a lot happier than he, himself.

He ordered another drink and sipped it slowly. The drink calmed him down and he thought, with pain, I behaved like a neurotic shit with a nice woman whom I've remembered fondly for a long time. He paid for his drink, looked up her address in the telephone book and went to the town florist and ordered a dozen roses and had them sent to her with a note saying, "Forgive me. I had a bad afternoon. Love."

It had become a routine, each evening, after dinner which Michael and Eva Heggener ate together in the dining room, for them to go for a walk, with the retriever trotting beside them. Although there was still no snow, there were a few guests, who had booked their rooms in advance and who by the hour kept looking hopefully up at the recalcitrant sky. Michael had avoided becoming friendly with any of them and if they speculated about the relationship between the hotel owner's wife and the ski teacher they kept their thoughts to themselves.

This night the sky was overcast and the moon could not be seen and Michael took along a pocket flashlight to light their way. Eva had been especially silent during dinner and Michael wondered if somehow she had heard that he had been seen drinking at the Monadnock that afternoon with Annabel Fenstock.

Finally, her head bent, her eyes on the little circle of light thrown by the flashlight as they walked up the road, potholed by other frosts, Eva said, "There will be some slight changes tomorrow. My husband is arriving."

"Oh," Michael said. He didn't know how Eva expected him to receive this news.

"We won't be able to move in just yet, but the house is about ready," she said. "I know he'll be pleased. It was his idea to have it redone. He said it was going to be his last house and he wanted it to be perfect." She spoke matter-of-factly, as though arranging for a perfect house in which a man was to die was the most normal of activities. She had not invited Michael to see the house and he was in no hurry to do so. By now he had seen enough of Eva's taste in all things, in the way she dressed herself and the way she had furnished and run the hotel, that he was sure that the house would serve Mr. Heggener's tastes, whatever they were, admirably. He had seen no photographs of the husband and knew no more about him than Eva had told him the first night and he had no mental picture of how the man looked or how he would behave. Probably bent over and coughing and rheumy-eyed and barely able to move.

"Perhaps," he said, uneasily, "I should find another place to live."

"I've been thinking about that," Eva said. "And I want to show you something."

They were approaching a large stone gate, with two heavy iron gratings swung open onto a graveled driveway. "Let's go in here," she said. Just behind and to one side of the gate there was a small brick cottage. Eva took out a key and opened the door of the cottage and flipped on a light inside. "Come in, come in," she said. The heat had been turned on and a little wave of warmth came through the open door. "This is the gatekeeper's cottage, from a time when there still were gatekeepers."

The living room was quite large, with a curved Victorian sofa covered in worn beige silk and a big desk and old oil lamps now wired for electricity. There was a fireplace with the mounted head of a stag with spreading antlers over the mantelpiece. There was a door open through which he could see a small kitchen and another which led to a bedroom. There was even a telephone and a television set.

"How do you like it?" she asked.

"The gatekeeper was lucky."

"How would you like to live here?"

"Don't you have to consult with your husband first?"

"I don't consult with him about domestic affairs," Eva said. Put down, he thought, I am a domestic affair. "The big house is four hundred yards away," Eva went on, "and there are woods in between and you can make all the noise you want without disturbing us or our seeing who comes and goes in and out of here. You can make yourself useful, shoveling snow, keeping the driveway clear, bringing in wood for the fire, driving my husband when he's too tired or I'm too busy to drive, things like that. We have a maid, but she's seventy years old and she's barely strong enough to cook our meals. Naturally, we wouldn't expect you to pay rent."

"I could always sell my Porsche," Michael said, "and live in luxury at the hotel and I wouldn't have to bring in the wood." She was, he felt, talking to him as though she were hiring a servant.

"Once I move into the house," she said coldly, "it will not be possible for me to visit you in the hotel. I hope you understand that. Unless, of course, that is of no importance to you."

He took her in his arms and kissed her. "I'll show you later how little importance it has for me."

She pulled back, smiling, then opened her coat and pressed hard against him. "I would like a demonstration immediately," she said. "Let us inaugurate this dear little house here and now."

He followed her into the bedroom, where she had turned on a lamp next to the big, oversized bed with a patchwork quilt on it. He closed the door to keep the dog in the living room. There were some sights, he believed, that dogs should not be allowed to see.

Eva no longer insisted upon turning out the light. They had made love one rainy afternoon and the light coming in through the drawn curtains had been strong enough so that they could see each other and now she said it was more exciting when they could look at each other when they had their orgasms. She did not take her hair down and the contrast between the wild, ecstatic expression on her face and the primly curved bands of hair wound around her head gave a new dimension to his immersion in her body.

"As you see," he said, "no great importance."

She chuckled. "I didn't really need confirmation," she said, little beads of sweat, that tasted salty when he kissed her, all over her body. "I just didn't feel like waiting."

"I'm going to give you more confirmation," he said, glad finally to share the memory of the fears that now had proved groundless. "For about two years before I came up here I thought I was impotent."

"You?" She got up on one elbow and stared at him.

"Me."

"You owe me a great deal, Mr. Storrs."

"You don't know how much."

"Women are lucky," she said pensively. "They don't have to prove anything. Or do they?"

"They do," he said soberly.

"So they failed you."

"No. I failed myself."

"Do you know why?"

"Not really," he said reflectively. "General despondency. The life force at a low ebb and that sort of thing."

"And now the life force is . . . ?"

"Raging."

"May it continue."

"Have no fear." He put his hand on her breast and caressed it, feeling her nipple starting to stand up, hard. "Again?"

"Why not?" she said.

He wished he could say he loved her or get her to say that she loved him but he was certain neither thing would happen. It was possible that she had said it at other times, but he had said it to only one woman. Capable of love, Annabel, the town bang, had called him, but perhaps he had exhausted that particular capability. Well, then, if that were so, there was a great deal, he thought, running his hand over that generous, severely coiffed, blond, pastry-nourished Viennese body, a great deal to be said for lust.

When she had made the bed in neat, housewifely fashion, so that whatever it had been used for would not be evident, they turned out all the lights in the warm gatekeeper's cottage that they had doubly inaugurated, and closed and locked the door behind them. It was beginning to snow. The snow was wet and cold on their faces and was like a benediction on the evening and Eva said, her bare hand with his in the pocket of his big sheepskin coat, "Snow at last. There will be joy all over town in the morning and visions of thousands of cars discharging skiers this weekend and of mortgages being paid off by spring. We are like the peasants in India, waiting for the monsoon rains. No matter how many gadgets and snow-making machines we have, without our mountain monsoons we face starvation—or at least the banks, which amounts to the same thing. In the old days we would have blood sacrifices at the winter solstice."

Michael wasn't thinking of mortgages or winter solstices, as he strode beside her, with the dog beside them putting out his tongue to catch the snowflakes. "What are you going to tell your husband?"

"My husband?" she said. "Nothing. I guarantee he will like you. You are just the sort of man he is attracted to."

Later on, lying alone in his bed, Michael wasn't sure that he wanted to be the sort of man her husband would be attracted to.

◇◇◇◇◇

He was having a nightmare. He was going down a steep, icy slope on skis, with mean little rocks showing in the bare spots and sparks flying up from his skis as the steel edges hit the rocks and threw him off balance. He was going faster and faster and below him there was a deep dark gully. The wind was screaming past his ears, and his speed became greater and greater as he neared the gully. He tried to stop, but he knew it was impossible on that ice. He screamed, but the wind took the sound out of his mouth. He knew he was going to crash and he knew it was going to be bad and he resigned himself to how bad it was going to be.

Then the telephone rang and he awoke, sweating. He didn't know how long the telephone had been ringing. His hand shook as he reached out for the telephone.

It was Dave Cully. He sounded happy. "Mike," he said, "it's really coming down. There should be over a foot of new powder by morning. I'm opening the lifts at nine. How about making the first run of the season with me?"

"Great," Michael said, trying to keep his voice steady. "I'll be there. What time is it now?"

"Quarter to eleven," Cully said. "Did I wake you?"

"No," Michael said, his voice stronger. "I was doing some research on monsoons."

"What?" Cully asked, puzzled.

"Indian storms," Michael said. "No matter."

"See you at nine," Cully said and hung up.

Another husband who finds me attractive, Michael thought, grateful for the ringing of the telephone that had awakened him. For other reasons, no doubt.

He looked at his watch to see if Cully had had the time right.

Twelve minutes before eleven. It had been a full day. He got out of bed and went to the window and looked out. The snow was coming down heavily, beautifully, evenly glittering in the light of the driveway lampposts in the windless night. Then he saw Eva Heggener walking in the snow in high after-ski boots that came up to the bottom of her thick fur coat, the dog gamboling and rolling deliciously in the new snow. After what happened in the cottage, he thought resentfully, where does she get the energy?

He left the drapes pulled open so he could watch the snow falling and got into bed and tried to sleep again, but the phone rang again. It was Susan Hartley, calling from New York.

"Hey," Susan said. "It's falling like Siberia in New York. How is it up there?"

"There'll be at least a foot of powder in the morning."

"Will the lifts be open?"

"Nine A.M."

"Oh, bliss. I'll take a week off and then there's the Thanksgiving weekend, that'll give me ten days. Antoine's with me now, can you find a room for him, too?"

"How is he?"

"Suicidal."

"Don't tell me," Michael said. "I'm having a good time."

"He says skiing will take his mind off disaster. How's the hotel you're staying in?"

"Bliss," he said, imitating her.

"Get me a room adjoining yours," she said playfully.

"This is Vermont," Michael said sternly. "They frown on such things here. And stop teasing Antoine. And tell him I will make sure that you will get a room in the attic, three floors up from mine and on the other side of the building."

"Ski heil," she said airily. "We'll arrive late Friday night. Stay up for us."

He hung up. He stared at the phone. He didn't know whether he was pleased or not pleased that his friends were coming. Well, he thought, at least Susan would be good for some laughs. Thanksgiving. He had forgotten about Thanksgiving. Did he have anything to be thankful for? He would look into the pros and cons before the holiday and act accordingly.

He sank back into bed, pulling the blankets around him, half-hypnotized by the steady, straight, silent fall of snow outside the window and fell asleep quickly and did not dream.

❖❖❖❖❖

Cully was waiting for him at the chair lift exactly at nine. The word had not yet gone out that the lifts were working and they were alone. The slopes above them shone untracked in the sunlight. Cully had an expression of faraway, almost sensual pleasure on his weathered, tough face as he looked up, but all he said as Michael greeted him was, "It's about time we had it."

As they were putting on their skis, a gray-haired black man of about fifty, his skin almost copper-colored, came out of the shed. He was wearing an old tufted down-lined parka and a peaked corduroy woodman's cap with earflaps. He had a battered old pipe stuck in his mouth and was puffing contentedly.

"Everything ready, Harold?" Cully asked.

"Ready for the thundering herd," the man said. "Enjoy yourself, Dave, this is the last moment of peace you'll have for a long time."

"Harold," Cully said, "this is Mike Storrs. He's working for me this winter. Mike, Harold Jones."

Michael shook the man's hand. It felt like a steel clamp. Jones looked at him closely. "Didn't I see you someplace before, young fella?" His accent was exactly the same as Cully's.

"Maybe. I was here a long time ago for a winter."

Jones nodded. "I thought so. You did all those crazy tricks, like once I saw you somersaulting over a six-foot-high pile of stacked cordwood."

Cully laughed. "The same."

"How many bones you broke since then, Mr. Storrs?" Jones asked.

"None," Michael said. He told himself that the man was referring to skiing and that ribs cracked in barroom brawls didn't count.

"God takes care of fools and drunkards," said Jones. He held the chair that was swinging around on the overhead cable for them and they slipped onto it and started up.

"Who is that old guy?" Michael asked.

"Our chief engineer. Fix anything from a cotter pin to a fractured skull."

"He sounds as if he's from around here."

"He was born here. His great grandfather's got a picture of himself in the town library. He came up from the South on the underground railroad before the Civil War and liked it and stayed, farming a little, doing odd jobs, and some painter who came through town painted his picture. This was a lumbering and farming town until the 1920s. No ski bunnies up from New York and Boston then and no drinking on Sundays, either. The town was dying on the limb during the Depression but the family stayed and then the skiing craze caught on and it turns out Jones owns about a thousand acres he'd been buying up for peanuts all around town. One smart fella. He could retire if he wanted to but you'd have to call an armed guard to get him away from his machinery. His kid works at the Alpina, the waitress. Smart kid, finished high school at the age of fifteen, but she refuses to go to college. Her old man doesn't care one way or the other, he's told me—he's seen the college kids come up here and he says he wouldn't give a broken ski pole for the lot of them."

They rose steadily upward through the swath cut in the forest for the chair lift, the branches of the pines still laden with snow in the below zero sunshine. A deer looked up at them inquiringly but without fear from a spot under a spreading tree where there was still some dried grass showing. There was a slight whirr from the cable but otherwise the silence was absolute and both men understood that to break it would mar that particular moment of the morning of their first ascent of the year to the mountain. Here and there below them, too, there were rabbit tracks and a track that Michael thought was that of a fox. New York, he thought, was continents, ages away.

At the top, they skied down the little slope off the lift and Cully waved to the man who was on duty in the shed in which the great round wheel returned the chairs downhill again.

Without saying anything, Cully skied off on a traverse on the bald top of the mountain. Michael followed him. He had never skied this side of the hill before, because the lift had been installed after his time and new trails cut through the woods. Finally, Cully stopped and they both looked down. A hill as steep as any Michael had skied anywhere before, in America or in Europe, dropped, almost sheer, below them, for a straight hundred yards, then veered sharply to the left, out of sight, into the forest.

"I see," Michael said. "We do the easy ones first and gradually work our way up to the beginners' slopes."

Cully grinned. "They call this run the Black Knight. All the kids do it," he said.

"I'm sure," said Michael. "With parachutes."

"Remember what the man said—fools and drunkards."

"Follow me, you son of a bitch," Michael said and skated off and down, the powder fountaining like foam from the prow of a ship behind him. He whistled tunelessly as he sped straight downhill, to remember to breathe. He had wanted to schuss the whole thing to the turn, but he knew he was out of control halfway down and it wouldn't do to wind up smeared against a tree on the first run of the winter with Cully. As he made his turn to brake his speed, he saw Cully glide past him, his skis together, pointed straight downhill. "Showboat," Michael called and Cully waved a pole debonairly at him. Michael was relieved to see that at least Cully didn't schuss the whole face, but made four turns before stopping and waiting at the place where the run curved into the forest.

"Pretty good for an old fart," Michael said when he stopped beside Cully. Somehow, he could talk to Cully on the hill in a way that he never could on the flat.

Cully grinned again. "After this it becomes more technical."

"I am with you, friend."

"What I mean by that," Cully said jovially, "is that it narrows and becomes a little steeper and there's a boulder about two hundred yards down in the middle of the trail that you don't see until you're right on it, because it's in a little clearing right after you make a sharp turn out of the woods."

"It sounds like fun," Michael said. "*Allez, allez.*"

From then on, Cully was merciless. Comradely, smiling, but merciless. It was impossible to believe that he spent most of his days at a desk. Huge, overweight, paunchy, balding, he never stopped, never looked back, jumped bumps twenty feet in the air, landed lightly as a bird, a bird made out of steel springs that would not reveal any signs of metal fatigue even under x-ray examination after ten thousand flights.

Michael hung on doggedly, sweating through his parka, his city muscles screaming within his legs, fell twice, wanted to just lie there in the cooling snow, abandoning himself to shameless defeat, but made himself scramble up and pound down after the inexorable broad back below him.

It was nearly noon, and they had done every run on the two hills of the ski area, with only the blessed respite of the trips up on the lifts to allow him time to regain his breath, when Cully finally stopped. From two hundred yards above him, Michael saw Cully bend to take off his skis near the lodge which abutted the parking space. He put on one last, groaning burst of speed and stopped flashily, throwing a great spray of snow over Cully.

Cully looked up. "Showboat," he said, smiling. "Have a good morning?"

"Never had a better," Michael gasped, leaning bent forward on his ski poles. "Thanks."

"It was nothing," Cully said. "But I didn't notice you doing any somersaults."

"I like to do things like that when there are girls around."

"There's one." Cully pointed up the hill. "Maybe she'd like a sample."

Michael turned with difficulty, too tired to take off his skis. High up the slope a slender figure in red was making swift, perfect short turns through the powder. "I think I'll leave tricks to later in the season," Michael said.

Cully laughed. "Maybe you ought to get more sleep at night." He patted Michael's shoulder. "You'll do," he said. "I thought I could shake you and I couldn't." Michael knew that he had been put to some private, simple-minded test of Cully's and he had passed it. It was silly, but he was happy. He knew he had done nothing that should make him feel guilty in Cully's presence, but he had still felt uneasy until now. Cully, he saw now, was doing everything he could, in his taciturn, heavy-handed and merciless way, to show him that he liked him and that they could be friends.

Michael wiped the sweat off his face and forehead with a handkerchief and watched the girl in red come swooping down the hill. When she got near enough, he saw that it was Rita, the waitress from the hotel, Harold Jones' daughter. "Holy man," Michael said, "she really can ski."

"She ought to," Cully said. "She's been on skis since the age of three. Hi, Rita," he said, as she came to a neat, modest stop in front of the two men. "Nice morning?"

"Splendiferous," she said, beaming, looking more like ten years old than sixteen. "It makes you sad, too."

"Why?" Michael asked.

"Tomorrow it will be crawling with people. Today I owned the mountain. Except for you two. I saw your tracks wherever I went," she said, stepping out of the bindings of her skis. "Hey, Mr. Storrs," she said, "those were pretty fancy tracks you made."

"They were Dave's," Michael said. "Mine looked as though they were made by a drunken webbed animal."

She laughed. "I can recognize Dave's. He's been signing his name on these hills since before I was born."

"Listen, you two," Michael said, finally recovered enough to bend and get out of his skis, "I'm dying of thirst. Let's go into the lodge and I'll treat you to something cold."

"I'm not thirsty," Cully said.

"You dog," Michael said.

"Anyway, I have to go back to the office. I played hooky long enough. Mike, come in if you have time later. You might as well sign the contract. It will make you a rich man for three or four hours, if you don't do anything extravagant, like buying a sandwich."

"I'll be there," Michael said. "How about you, Rita? You got time for a drink?"

"Fifteen minutes. Then I have to get back to the hotel. I'm on for lunch today."

"I'll drive you," Michael said. "That'll give you more time." He picked up her skis and with his own on the other shoulder started toward the lodge, while Cully went to where his battered station wagon was parked.

"You shouldn't carry my skis, Mr. Storrs," Rita said in a low voice as she walked by his side toward the steps leading up the lodge.

"Why not?"

"Not everybody in this town is like you," Rita said flatly. "And if they told Mrs. Heggener you were seen carrying my skis, she would say it wasn't seemly."

"Nonsense, Rita," he said, sharply. Then, more lightly, "I make a point of always being seemly."

"I don't want you to get any wrong ideas," Rita said hastily. "Mr. Cully is not one of those people. Not in a million years."

"I know," Michael said, still keeping his tone light. "He's most seemly, too—in his own rough way, of course."

He leaned the two pairs of skis against a wall and poked the poles into the snow beside them. "I've been dreaming about a cold beer since nine-thirty this morning," he said. "Following good old Dave Cully down the hill is warm work."

"Isn't that man something?" Rita shook her head admiringly. She had been skiing without a cap and her cropped black hair trembled as she moved and there were still little flakes of snow in it that made gleaming highlights over her forehead. Her skin, Michael noticed, was considerably darker than her father's, and was glistening with youthful health. "Imagine being that old and fat and still skiing like that," she said.

"He's not much older than I am," Michael said with dignity as they mounted the steps.

"Oh, I'm sorry." Rita put up her hand to her mouth, abashed. "I didn't mean to offend you. Anyway, you're not fat." She giggled.

"I will be," Michael said, "if you keep giving me those huge portions at the hotel every meal."

"If you're going to ski with Dave Cully, you better keep your strength up."

At the self-service counter inside, he picked up a cold beer and she took a Coke. They sat at a corner table, after Michael had taken off his parka. His shirt, he saw, embarrassed, was dark with sweat, but Rita didn't say anything about it. She drank slowly, through a straw, while he finished the beer in three voracious gulps, then went back for a second. "Nectar," he said with a sigh, after he had taken the first swallow of the second bottle. "One day I would like to own a brewery and swim in the vats."

"Mr. Heggener likes beer, too. He always has a bottle before dinner."

Michael was tempted to ask about Mr. Heggener, but refrained. Whatever the girl might say, however innocent, she might regret later.

"I want to thank you," Michael said, "for remembering to leave a bottle of wine for me each night." He had gotten into the guilty habit of rinsing out the second glass and drying it and returning it to exactly the same position it had arrived on the tray so that in the morning whoever came in to clean up would suppose that he had drunk the whole bottle himself. Better the reputation of a drunkard than of a lecher.

"With Madam Heggener around, we make sure we don't forget anything."

Michael got off the subject of Mrs. Heggener quickly. "You ski awfully well, you know."

Rita shrugged. "I was born here. I ski like all the kids."

"I know. I met your father this morning."

"He was whistling when he left the house at dawn," Rita said. "At last his lifts were working."

"He remembered me. Not too fondly. He said God protects fools and drunkards."

"That's Daddy." She laughed. "He's an outspoken man." She had unzipped the top of her ski suit and dropped it around her waist. She was wearing a boy's cotton shirt and he noticed that there was no sign of perspiration coming through the thin cloth. She was flat and thin and angular and he saw that he could have put his fingers easily, with something to spare, around her fine-boned wrists. "Rita," he said, "have you ever been hurt? Skiing, I mean?"

She looked surprised. "No. Should I have?"

"I mean, you're so slender and your bones . . ."

"Skinny, you mean." She looked wistful. "My mama swears I'm going to develop. I'm stronger than I look. I have to be. I've been rassling with my brother all my life."

"Have you ever raced?"

Rita laughed, something surprisingly condescending in the sound, as you might laugh at a child who had amused you with a silly question. In a moment she was an adult. "Have you ever heard of a black downhill racer?"

"Not really," Michael said, sensitive to what was behind the question. "Still, before Jackie Robinson, there never was a black second baseman in the National League, either."

"I've talked about it with my daddy," she said seriously. "Give it another fifty years, my daddy says. In fifty years I'll be sixty-six. How many sixty-six-year-old girls, black or white, do you know of in the Olympics? And I'm not even the good one in the family. You ought to see my brother . . ."

"How old is he?"

"Eighteen."

"What does he do?"

"He works with my father."

"Maybe we can all three of us ski together one day," Michael said.

"He gets Thursdays off." She looked pleased with the invitation. She changed from moment to moment, child to adult, adult to child.

"And you?"

"Mornings, mostly. I usually start work at lunch and go on till ten P.M."

"Maybe we can arrange it for next Thursday," Michael said. "One day a month with Dave Cully does it for me, thank you. And I don't like to ski alone."

"That would be very nice. If you're not busy with Madam."

"Oh," he said, "you know about my being assigned to her?"

"News gets around. A little town . . ."

"How does she ski?"

"Very well," Rita said. Again she sounded condescending, but this time not because of her color. "Considering her age."

Michael laughed. "You know," he said, "I'm older than she is."

Rita giggled, suddenly very childish. "I did it again. I'm sorry."

"That's all right," Michael said, thinking that he had to get used to people Rita's age regarding everyone over thirty as decrepit and on the brink of extinction.

They finished their drinks and went out to where the Porsche was parked, with Michael carrying the two pairs of skis and Rita not objecting now. He put the skis in the rack and the poles in the back of the car and Rita sank luxuriously into the passenger seat. "Mr. Storrs," she said, "do me a favor, please."

"Of course."

"Drive slowly through town. I want everybody to see me in this car."

Michael drove sedately along the main street of the town. There were two people on the street whom she knew and she waved, grandly, all the time babbling excitedly. Skiing didn't interest her all that much, she said, what she really wanted to be was a singer. She sang in the church choir and was one of its soloists, but that wasn't what she meant. "What I want," she said, "is to go out dressed in a crazy costume, all feathers and spangles and long stockings, red is my favorite color, maybe after purple, and see twenty thousand people out there screaming 'Rita, Rita!' at me and pick up a microphone and belt out one song after another and have them go crazy and rip out the chairs and travel with my own band—New York, San Francisco, London, Paris . . . with the money coming in so fast I'd have to hire three college graduates just to count it."

Michael laughed at the girl's dreadful vision of the good life and hoped, for her sake, that her ambition would never be fulfilled. But he didn't have the heart to remind her of the many popular singers whose admirers had staged riots in their honor and who had wound up suicides or dead from drugs before the age of thirty. Instead he said, "There's a friend of mine, a Frenchman, who plays the piano and sings in bars and who's very good indeed. He's coming up here in a few days and he's very nice and I'm sure I can arrange to let him listen to you and give you some useful pointers."

"You're kidding . . ." She gasped at the grandeur of what he was offering as she said it.

"No. Honestly."

"Mr. Storrs," she said emotionally, "you're just the nicest man I ever met."

"I hope," he said, embarrassed by her intensity, "I hope later you'll find someone, lots of someones, a good deal nicer, Rita."

She leaned her head back against the leather bucket seat and closed her eyes, a dreamy smile on her face as he drove the last few hundred yards to the hotel.

When he took her skis off the rack, she said, "Better take yours off, too. They steal skis around here if they're left unlocked. Up to now it looks like heaven in Green Hollow, but when there's snow on the ground we get some real uglies up here."

Obediently, as Rita hurried in to begin her working day, Michael took his skis off the rack and put them and his poles in the hotel ski room. Then he went to the front desk and asked if there were any messages for him from Mrs. Heggener. There was a message. Mrs. Heggener wished to ski at two-thirty this afternoon. He hoped she wouldn't be as active on the slopes as she was in bed.

CHAPTER
FOURTEEN

He had his lunch, alone, with Rita serving him silently and decorously, the dining room now alive with the first thin wave of skiers, most of them dressed in garish colors with outlandish stripes that reminded him of professional football uniforms.

At two-thirty, promptly, Eva Heggener came down into the lobby, where Michael was waiting for her. She was wearing a navy blue ski outfit, tucked in at the waist, that showed off her figure and a fur hat that made her delicately colored, sharply cut face look like that of a court beauty in an old Dutch painting. She glanced up at the clock over the front desk and nodded approvingly at Michael's promptness. He got their skis out of the ski room and put them on his car.

"We should really take my car," she said. "The bill for gasoline can mount up over a winter."

He didn't know whether or not she wished to annoy him with her offer, but she had. All peasants, he remembered. "I'll make it up in tips, perhaps," he said, meanly.

She laughed. "My," she said, mildly, "aren't we touchy."

"I fold like a flower at the slightest touch of wind," he said, as they got into the Porsche.

"Anemones," she said. "Famous for it. My American anemone." She patted his hand soothingly.

At the bottom of the lift he bent and put on her skis. "Service with a smile," he said, to get even with her.

On the way up, she asked, "How was the skiing this morning?"

"Vigorous."

"Did Cully approve of you?"

"In a way. He's not what you call a demonstrative man."

"By the way," she said, as they mounted in the crystalline silent air, "do you know how to play backgammon?"

"I've played. Why?"

"My husband is always looking for partners. If you play with him be careful. No high stakes. He's terribly wily."

"I've been wily in my time."

"I'll warn him. By the way, I talked to him on the phone this morning and I spoke to him about you and he'd like us all to have dinner together tonight if he's not too tired."

"Wouldn't you rather have dinner alone, his first night back?"

"There are so many first nights back with him, I think he looks forward to a change. We have said just about everything there is to be said between us."

"I'd be delighted," Michael said formally.

She was quiet for a moment. Then she said, "Rita told me you'd watched her ski this morning. She was all excited about what you told her—about the possibility of her taking up racing and then the thing about your friend the pianist. By the way, the manager told me he's arranged about the two rooms. It was a squeeze, we expect a crowd this weekend. Do they really need two rooms or are they just being proper?"

"They're just friends. At least, that's what they tell me."

"You never can tell about Americans."

"He's not American, he's French."

"Then I suppose they *are* only friends. We'll manage." She slapped her gloved hands together as if she were cold. "I'd be careful about what you say to the girl—Rita, I mean. It would be tragic if she turned from a charming first-rate servant into a second-rate ski bum and a third-rate singer."

"I don't know about the ski bum and the singer," he said, consciously restraining his anger, "but I'm sure no matter what I say or you say, she's not going to remain a servant."

"Men are naive," Eva said flatly. "They think a pretty face is a universal passport."

What about your face and your passport, he thought, but didn't say it.

They were at the top now and Michael saw that she slipped out of the chair deftly and made the little descent holding her poles under one arm and swinging down gracefully.

"Do you know the slopes by now?" she asked, as she ran her wrists into the thongs of the pole handles.

"Cully had me all over the place, and I've looked at the maps of the runs. Do you have any preferences?"

"Any run but the Black Knight," she said. "Steep places give me vertigo. Go ahead now, I'll follow you. I'll tell you if you're going too fast for me." She was all business now.

Michael set off on the easiest of the slopes, looking back from time to time to see how Eva was doing. She skied confidently and with grace and had obviously had a great deal of expert instruction. He put on speed and she followed on the heels of his skis. Vertigo, my ass, he thought, what is she trying to prove? But he stayed away from the Black Knight.

It was getting dark when they made their last descent, this time with Michael going at about three-quarter speed and Eva having no trouble keeping up with him. When they stopped near the lodge, her face was glowing as she looked up at the mountain and said, her voice tinkling in the frozen twilight, "That's what it's all about, isn't it?" and he wanted to kiss her there and then.

"Satisfied with your instructor?" he asked.

She nodded. "More than," she said. "Satisfied with your pupil?"

"Some pupil," he said. He hadn't said a word about her skiing all afternoon, although there were moves she made that were unnecessary with the new equipment and the more modern refinements that were now being taught. "Maybe tomorrow," he said, "I'll say a word or two about how to improve your style." Lean back a little more, use your knees, not your ankles, flatten your skis on the turns, the usual, ever-changing, profitable mumbo jumbo.

"I will listen to teacher with bated breath," she said mockingly. "Maybe by the end of winter I'll ski as well as your new friend, Rita, and you'll advise me about taking up a new career."

He no longer wanted to kiss her as he knelt to get her out of her skis.

◈◈◈◈◈

Mr. Heggener turned out to be neither bent over, coughing, rheumy-eyed or barely able to move. He was a slender, gentle-looking man, perhaps fifty-five years old, his skin translucent, with a full head of white hair, and a small, neat white beard. His narrow face and dark, sad eyes looked like those of an eighteenth-century Spanish grandee and his manners were exquisitely polite and formally friendly. He was wearing a beautiful dark green pressed wool loden jacket, with elaborate black embroidery around the buttonholes and a gleaming white shirt and dark silk tie. Although the table at which they were seated was in front of the fireplace in which piled logs flamed brightly, he had a Scotch-plaid lightweight blanket over his shoulders. A little nervously, Michael had dressed for the occasion, too, and wore a collar and tie and a blue blazer. Eva was wearing the same loose long black gown she had worn the night Michael had arrived, but she had on jewelry tonight, a rope of pearls and a gold brooch high on her shoulder. They had started dinner late and by the time Rita was serving the dessert they were alone in the dining room.

Mr. Heggener was a perfect host and the conversation, Michael was relieved to discover, flowed easily—mostly about the lucky downfall of snow, the condition of the runs, the difficulty in finding teachers of acceptable caliber for the ski school, the inevitable growth of the town since Michael had been there before and the accompanying changes, the necessity of laying out courses for the new craze of cross-country skiing, the difficulty of finding good films for the new movie house of which Mr. Heggener was the principal owner. Mr. Heggener had a light, pleasing voice and spoke without an accent and was careful at first not to monopolize the conversation, bringing his wife and Michael into all the discussions. Mr. Heggener, Michael noticed, was interested in a rather Olympian way in his fellow townsmen and their peculiarities, but when he mentioned the names of any of them with whom he had to deal, it was always with some phrase of approval. During the meal he never touched his wife's hand, but Michael could see that he was deeply attached to her and listened intently when she spoke, which was not often. She seemed content to listen most of the time to the two men and sat back relaxed in her chair. She ate with a good appetite and smiled when her husband complimented her on how well prepared the meal was and told Michael that the present chef had arrived after a long line of dismally incompetent journeymen cooks, who had come to them highly recommended but who, he suspected, had come straight out of diners and hamburger stands.

Over dessert, he said, "I suppose, my dear Mr. Storrs, that you, like so many of our guests, wonder how I came to be here. My settling here, if it could be called settling, might be considered . . . ah . . . fortuitous. There is a clinic outside town that somebody told me was run by a professor who had performed miracles. Perhaps he had" —Mr. Heggener laughed lightly—"with others. Unfortunately, he was not in his magic phase when I visited him. But I fell in love with the town. . . . Thank you, Rita," he said to the girl, who was putting a demitasse of coffee in front of him. He looked at it with amused distaste. "Sanka, unhappily. I am not permitted real coffee. However, yours is real, am I right, Rita?"

"Yes, sir," she said.

Mr. Heggener turned to Michael and his wife. "Shall we have a cognac?"

"Andreas . . ." Eva said warningly.

"My dear," Mr. Heggener said, "after such a superb meal, after hospital fare. . . . There is always a choice," he explained to Michael. "What your soul says is good for you and what some man in a white coat, who knows nothing of souls, since they have not yet described them in medical literature, although I am sure one day they will get around to it, as they undoubtedly will to everything else . . ." Michael could see that the man relished his qualifying clauses and had worked on them as a personal style. "What some man in a white coat, as I was saying, told you is bad for you. On balance, tonight, homecoming night, my soul has the better arguments. Mr. Storrs—a cognac?"

"Thank you," Michael said. He was feeling expansive, too, his fears of the meeting dissipated with the good food and the wine.

"Three glasses, please," Mr. Heggener said to Rita. "The Blue Ribbon." Then, to Michael, "Would you like a cigar?"

"No, thank you," Michael said. "Among the things the doctors and my soul agree on is that I should give up smoking."

"Have you managed it?" Mr. Heggener asked.

"Almost," Michael said. "I only smoked one cigarette today." It had been in the lodge with Rita at noon, after the workout with Cully.

"Abstinence has its own pleasures. No cigars, thank you, Rita. As I was saying"—Michael noticed that Mr. Heggener had a habit of using the phrase, like a composer going back to a series of notes he had used previously, to bring back the listener to a motif he had not yet exhausted—"as I was saying, the town pleased me, the gentle mountains. The majesty of the Alps dwindles men who live in its valleys. I come from a hotelkeeping family. Generations. We have old ledgers with the names of those noble young Englishmen who made the Grand Tour in the eighteenth century. If I were of an unscientific turn of mind I would be inclined to say that I have hotelkeeping in my blood. When I see a place that has a certain intangible, attractive atmosphere, a combination of geography, population, beauty . . . and . . ." he chuckled, "I must say, the lure of profit, about it, my thoughts immediately run to building, buying, landscaping, personnel, length of season, etcetera. So with Green Hollow. Do you have some similar obsession, Mr. Storrs?"

"I'm afraid not." After a meal like the one he had eaten he would cast a pall over the table with a detailed account of the obsessions that ruled his life.

"A pity," Mr. Heggener said.

"I envy you," Michael said. "You have a fine place here."

"So they tell me," Mr. Heggener said. "My accountants, I am happy to say, also reassure me. Hotelkeeping, if one keeps a proper distance from the inevitable daily annoyances, can be a very satisfactory profession. It is a little like being the captain of a ship. One is the master, one charts the course, as it were, one can pick the most pleasant ports of call. One can invite the most interesting of the passengers to one's table to entertain you, as we have had the good fortune to invite you . . ."

Michael laughed. "I'm afraid it's the other way around. You've been entertaining me."

"Ah," Mr. Heggener said, sighing with mock theatricality, "I do like an active listener, I must confess, and I impose myself when I have one captive." Having satisfied himself with this apology, he went on sonorously, his neat white beard moving rhythmically, "As I was saying, one meets a great variety of people, all of them finally astounding in their various views of life, one hears all the gossip, which is dear to an old Viennese's heart . . ."

"You haven't been back to Vienna in two years," Eva said sullenly, as though the mention of the city had touched some old wound within her.

"True." Mr. Heggener waved his hand airily. "Which is why I can be sentimental about it after a good dinner. Despite its bustle and the stability of the schilling, if one is in Vienna for any length of time, there is no avoiding the feeling that you are visiting a crumbling museum, making glorious statements about the past and keeping a glum silence about the future. But enough of Vienna. I was speaking of the métier I was lucky enough to inherit. As I was saying, one must keep a proper distance to enjoy it. I am lucky there, too. I live almost half a mile away and I have an excellent manager here, whom, rightly or wrongly, I believe to be honest, to listen to the complaints about mistaken bookings or cold meals or leaky pipes or crying children. And I can contrive to be absent when cooks leave on holiday evenings and when chambermaids discover they are pregnant."

Rita had come up silently behind him with a tray holding a bottle of cognac and three small glasses and was waiting until Mr. Heggener stopped talking for a moment so that she could put the tray down on the table before him. If she had heard his words about pregnant chambermaids, her face didn't show it. "Ah, thank you, Rita," Mr. Heggener said, slightly embarrassed when he realized she was there. "Just put everything down here on the table." He watched while the girl placed the bottle and the three glasses in front of him. "And Rita," he said, "you must go off to sleep now. Since there was nobody to talk to in the hospital I am liable to talk all night here and I mustn't allow my garrulousness to deprive you of the rest your youth demands. Go, go, child, and sleep well."

"Thank you," Rita said and slipped off silently.

Heggener poured the cognac carefully, but with relish. He raised his glass. "To the best of all possible winters."

They drank to the best of all possible winters, although Eva barely touched the glass to her lips.

"Ah," said Heggener, sniffing the brandy, "my soul was correct, and the doctors, as usual, in error." He turned his head and looked at the door through which Rita had disappeared into the kitchen. "Eva," he said to Michael, "has told me about the interesting conversation you had with our charming Rita this morning."

"She's a lovely skier," Michael said. "With some coaching, she might amount to something, even race."

"And why not?" Heggener said. "In the field of athletics, the blacks of this country—by the way, I am an American citizen, Mr. Storrs, if that is of any importance to you—the blacks are a great natural resource. One has only to look at a game of football or baseball on the television to see how many of them there are, how beautifully they play, with what skill and ferocity and determination, how they excel. Perhaps if we could persuade enough of them to put on skis, we would finally do better than a place or two in the first ten in every other Olympics."

"Your broad-mindedness does credit to you, Andreas," Eva said, with a touch of sarcasm in her voice, "but you forget, the blacks have never congregated in the mountains in America."

"Perhaps we should invite them to altitude," Mr. Heggener said. "Perhaps in my will I shall leave a fund for that express purpose. One of my disappointments as a young man was that I never could win a race. Maybe after I'm gone my money will win one for me." He laughed, and white, even young man's teeth, his own, showed above the trim white beard. "It's an intriguing idea. Maybe from wherever I am I will be able to lean down and shout, soundlessly, of course, 'More wax, more wax!' to one of my dark protégés."

"You've skied, Mr. Heggener?" Michael asked. Somehow, it was hard to imagine the frail figure in the chair opposite him, with the plaid blanket thrown over his shoulders, as ever having been robust enough to cope with snow.

"After all, my dear Mr. Storrs," Mr. Heggener said, "I was born in Austria. Yes, I skied. And I have a limp to prove it." He laughed, then looked at Michael seriously. "Skiing, I take it, is not your profession?"

"No," Michael said, but added nothing more.

"I didn't think so. I mean nothing disparaging by that, I assure you."

"He also hang-glides," Eva said. The disapproval was plain in her voice.

"Oh," Michael said, "you recognized me." She had not spoken about it before, nor had he to her.

"I certainly did," Eva said. "I hope you've had your flight for the winter. The ski school is shorthanded enough as it is. At least wait until spring before you kill yourself."

"It looks more dashing than it is," Michael said.

"I've read the stories," Eva said. "I saw the picture of one of the champions hanging dead on a high-tension wire in California."

"He overrated himself."

"You don't overrate yourself?" By now she was frankly hostile, baiting him, and Michael wondered what her husband was thinking about this argumentative familiarity.

"I try not to," Michael said mildly.

"Hang-gliding," Mr. Heggener said, musingly, as though he had absented himself momentarily from the conversation. "Kin to the birds." He made a swooping graceful motion with his pale hand. "Every generation finds a new way to risk its neck. A new adventure. To say nothing of that old, permanent adventure. War." He poured some more cognac in the pause that followed the ominous word. He swished the brandy around in his glass and sniffed it. "Luckily," he said, "I was too young. And nobody was quite sure what side I was on. Adventure. And you, Mr. Storrs—have you had your war?"

"No, thank you," Michael said, uneasy with the question and not prepared to answer it honestly. "I was offered Vietnam, but luckily I was deprived of it. Anyway, I don't consider war an adventure. I don't mind risking my neck, I suppose, but not if it means killing anybody."

"An admirable sentiment," Mr. Heggener said. "Not widespread enough, I'm afraid." He made a brisk motion of his hands. "We were talking about professions. Mrs. Heggener has told me certain things about you, but she has been vague about that. If you don't mind my asking, what is yours?"

"I suppose you could call it business," Michael said uncomfortably.

"A wide field," Mr. Heggener said. "More explicitly . . . ?" He sounded apologetic. "I don't like to be inquisitive, but it seems as though we are going to be rather closely . . . ah . . . connected . . . this season. . . . Eva has told me she's offered you the cottage and I am delighted . . . and it might make it more comfortable if a certain exchange of information takes place. You must realize that you are not the ordinary type of young man one picks out of the ski school. . . ."

"My business?" Michael said. "It used to be dollars and cents. No more. As you said about doctors, my accountants said no, but my soul said otherwise."

"Ah, well," Mr. Heggener said, "leave it for another time."

The manager came into the room, treading softly. "I'm sorry to disturb you," he said in a low voice to Eva, "but there's a call in the office for you."

"Thank you," Eva said to the manager and got up and Michael stood, as did Mr. Heggener, although with difficulty.

Mr. Heggener looked after his wife, his eyes sad, as though he never expected her to return. "Another cognac?" He put his hand on the bottle.

"No, thank you."

Mr. Heggener played idly with the bottle, twisting it on the table. "I suppose," he said, "you've heard that I'm dying?"

"I've heard."

"I'm a medical rarity," Mr. Heggener said, almost with relish at the distinction. "I have tuberculosis. Nowadays almost instantly curable by antibiotics. But I seem to have the honor of being afflicted by a new, clever, resistant strain. The hazards of progress. No matter. I have had a good life, I am no longer young and I am for the moment in a state of remission, as the doctors call it, that I am enjoying these days, when all things again seem possible to me. If it weren't for Eva, I'd gladly just turn my head to the wall and go. But she means a great deal to me. More than I show to anyone. Maybe more than I show to her."

He must have been drinking before he came downstairs, Michael thought, talking to me like that.

"She has her seasonal young men," Mr. Heggener went on matter-of-factly. "You, I would say, are infinitely more acceptable than the ones who have gone before you . . ."

"Mr. Heggener . . ." Michael began.

"Please don't protest, Mr. Storrs. I have gone through too much and have worn too thin to indulge in that worst of passions—jealousy. She is more like a beloved daughter to me than a wife, if you, at your age, can understand that. However, let me say . . ." He stopped, then spoke after another pause. "By the way, do you hunt, Mr. Storrs?"

"What has that got to do with it?" Michael asked, bewildered.

"I have hunted a great deal in my life. That stag whose head is over the fireplace in the cottage which Mrs. Heggener has offered you was shot by me. It is one of the passions of my life. I have no patience with the pseudo-humanitarians who eat steak and deplore the killing of game. Which would you rather be—a stag shot down with one shot on a green hillside, or a poor castrated steer dragged squealing into a slaughterhouse? Well, I won't argue the case. However, as I was saying, I am a hunter and I killed a man. An accident, naturally, such as happens every hunting season. One of my best friends. Unfortunately, he had degraded my wife. We both attended his funeral. This was in Austria, some time ago. The deer are plentiful in Vermont. Perhaps we can hunt together when the season opens. Eva says you are considering staying here permanently. I'm sure you would not regret it if you decide in our favor. The autumns here are magnificent."

Eva Heggener came back into the dining room, her black gown swishing around her legs, the pearls and the gold brooch shining in the firelight.

"Anything wrong, dear?" Mr. Heggener asked.

"Nothing," Eva said. "An old friend of mine from Boston. She wanted to know if she could have rooms for her family over the holiday. You know them—the Hortons."

"Charming family," Mr. Heggener said. "Charming. And now, dear, if you don't mind, I'd appreciate it if you helped me upstairs and turned on a little Brahms while we prepare for bed. Ah—Eva has told me you play backgammon. Perhaps we can have a game or two tomorrow evening. And now goodnight, and thank you for a most enjoyable evening."

"I thank you," Michael said stiffly. "Goodnight, madam. Goodnight, sir."

"Goodnight, Michael," Eva said. With her husband leaning on her for support, the blanket floating loosely around his shoulders, she led him slowly out of the dining room.

Michael sat stiffly for a moment. "Whew!" he said to himself.

There were footsteps behind him and he turned. Rita came toward him from the kitchen. "Is there anything more you need, Mr. Storrs?"

"I thought you'd gone to bed."

"I don't like to leave while there's anybody in the dining room. Is there anything . . . ?"

"Nothing, thank you, Rita."

Rita began to clear the table. "You look disturbed, Mr. Storrs," she said.

"Me?" he said. "What would I have to be disturbed about?"

"Then goodnight, Mr. Storrs. Sleep well." Carrying glasses and the bottle of cognac on a tray, she went out, turning out the lights as she went.

Michael didn't move, then rubbed his eyes wearily. From above he heard the opening strains of the Brahms *Variations on a Theme by Haydn*. He looked up at the ceiling and smiled wryly, then dropped his head on his chest and sat staring into the fire, listening to the faint music from the room two floors above him.

VOLUME THREE

CHAPTER
FIFTEEN

"You cost me a good hour's sleep," Cully grumbled as Michael came out of the hotel. It was just a little past dawn. The tops of the mountains were rosy, but the valley was still in shadow. The slalom poles were stowed in back of the ski school pickup truck. Michael had prevailed upon Cully to put them up so that they could see how well Rita could handle a descent with gates set close together. Michael had skied again with Rita, a whole morning, and now it was time to find out how she would do on a real course. Skiing, even very good skiing, was one thing, but running gates was another. So Cully had arranged with Harold Jones for the lift to start an hour earlier than usual so that they would have a clear slope for the test.

Michael had gone to bed early, to be fresh for the morning. He had not been disturbed. The Heggeners still were in their rooms on the third floor of the lodge because Mr. Heggener was waiting for an antique chair he had picked out himself to be reupholstered, saying crankily, playing the invalid, "I want everything to be in place so when I walk in I'll feel completely at home."

So there had been no nighttime visits from Eva. And the Heggeners had dined in their rooms, so Michael had eaten alone and spent the evenings reading. He had seen Mr. Heggener, at a distance, walking, with his cane, once or twice, but they had not spoken to each other since their dinner together. They had not as yet played backgammon.

Michael had skied twice more with Eva, but she hadn't said anything about her husband's conversation over the dinner table and Michael had not brought the matter up, although he thought about it constantly and was both eager and reluctant to know more about the frail Austrian gentleman. In his mind he couldn't quite accept him as an American. No American had ever confided in him that he had shot a very good friend because he had degraded his wife.

Michael had started giving small hints about position on skis and the distribution of weight to Eva, and meticulous and controlled as she was in everything, she had been quick to follow his instructions and after one swift run had said, gaily, "By the end of the season you'll have made me a skier."

"You were a skier before you ever saw me."

"I mean a *skier*," she said.

Cully drove over the rough roads, the old pickup bumping on broken springs, his weather-beaten face wrinkled in a scowl. "I don't know how you talked me into this," he said, sounding surly. "I've never done it for anybody else."

"Come on, now, Dave," Michael said, jolting on the broken passenger's seat, "the kid's in heaven."

"I'm not," Cully said. He was, Michael had found out, unwilling to give the appearance of softness in any way and he always made it seem that any act of generosity on his part surprised him unpleasantly.

When they arrived at the parking lot, Rita was waiting for them, her skis on. She must have walked here in the dark to meet us, Michael thought, as he waved to her.

They pulled out the slalom poles and, with Cully carrying half of them and Michael the other half, started toward the lift, with Rita skating alongside them, her face tense with excitement. Harold Jones saw them approaching and started the lift. "What the hell are you doing here at this hour," he asked his daughter. Obviously, Rita had kept the morning's experiment secret from her father.

"They're going to see how well I do in a slalom, Daddy," Rita said.

"Love of God," Jones grumbled. "What the hell next?" But he held the chair for her. As Michael and Cully stepped into their skis, Rita went up alone.

"Racing now." Harold Jones looked disapprovingly up at his daughter being carried up the mountain. "As though there isn't enough trouble. Sometimes I wish I'd been born on the lone prairie with not a hill within a thousand miles. Now, listen, Dave," he said to Cully, "don't give her any wild ideas about how great she is. If she's lousy I depend upon you to tell her so."

"Don't worry, Harold," Cully said, as he slipped into the chair that Jones held back for him, "the truth will out. And thanks for getting up so early."

"I don't know why I did it," Jones said as he let the chair go. "If I'd known it was for Rita, I'd've stayed in bed. Still no broken bones, young fella?" Jones said to Michael as Michael sat down and adjusted the slalom poles.

"Give me time," Michael said.

"She thinks you're Godalmighty wonderful," Jones said. "My kid. Just don't teach her no somersaults." He gave Michael's chair an extra hard push and the chair swung as it began to climb.

Cully and Rita were already going across the traverse on the top of the hill when Michael arrived at the end of the lift and skied off it. He saw that Cully was heading for the Black Knight. He hurried after them and caught up with Cully. Rita, not encumbered by the slalom poles, was ahead of them. "Dave," Michael said in a low voice, so that Rita couldn't hear him, "why don't you start her on something more mellow?"

"Might as well know the worst right off," Cully said.

Rita helped them place the gates on the clear slope after the glade with the boulder in the middle of it. At least, Michael saw, as she skied surely on the steep face, *she* doesn't suffer from vertigo.

They put in twenty-eight gates. Michael and Cully would mark off the finish line, about fifty yards above a path for pedestrians that a snowcat had made across the slope.

"All right, Rita," Cully said, "now you climb up, it'll warm up your legs, and when I give you the signal, like this"—he raised his arm and then suddenly brought it down—"you start. Got it?"

"Got it," Rita said, in a whisper, her voice trembling just a little bit. She started to climb, herringboning up the slope alongside the course.

"It's good of you, Dave," Michael said, "to take time to watch the kid."

"I'm not doing you any favors," Cully said. "Anything to get out of that damned office." He was watching Rita climb. "Pretty strong for a skinny kid like that. How much you guess she weighs?"

"One five, one seven," Michael said. "Around there."

Cully nodded. "Lucky there's no wind. Blow her right away. I weighed one seventy when I raced. Over two hundred now. Christ!" He stared up at Rita, who was nearing the top of the slope. "My kids're fat already," he said. "And Norma's built more like her. There's no telling about Nature." He gestured toward the figure in red above them. "It's a funny thing," he said reflectively. "I guess I must have seen that girl ski again and again through the years and it never occurred to me that she ought to be racing with the other kids. I guess it takes an outsider, like you, to see things that you just take for granted if you stay in one place. And I've always liked her and her whole family, too." He stared sternly at Michael. "One tip. Don't fool around with her. On or off the hill. Her father'll have your ass."

"Dave," Michael said, protesting, "she's only sixteen years old."

"That never stopped you before."

"I'm a different man these days."

"I'll believe it when I see it," Cully said.

The sun had hit the slope by now and Michael turned to face it, grateful for the warmth. Down below, on the path, he saw Mr. Heggener approaching. He recognized him by the old-fashioned black shiny cloth coat with the mink collar and by the soft green Tyrolean hat. For a man who professed to dislike Austria as much as he, he certainly liked to dress Austrian. Michael waved to him and Mr. Heggener waved back, then stopped walking and leaned on his cane and looked up at where Rita was now nearing the top of the course.

Michael turned back to watch her as she poised herself even with a tree that Cully had designated as the beginning of the run. Cully raised his arm and Rita crouched, ready. Then Cully dropped his arm sharply and the girl took off, skating, into the first gate. She came down fast, snaking expertly through the gates, hitting most of the poles with her shoulder to cut the turns shorter, knocking some of them out of the snow in her passage.

"Not bad, eh?" Michael said, watching the flying red figure.

"Not bad at all," Cully said. He made a little grimace, which showed that he was surprised and impressed.

Rita swept through the last gate and got into the egg position and pumped, her poles tucked straight out behind her, under her armpits, as she crossed between the two men and skidded to a stop.

From below, there came a faint sound of clapping. Mr. Heggener had taken off his gloves and was applauding.

"How did it look from the valley, gentlemen?" Rita asked as she climbed back toward them. She was panting, but not too hard.

"Okay," Cully said. "How did it feel?"

"Like first place in the Kandahar," Rita said, laughing and gasping a little at the same time.

"Well," Cully said, "you have one important thing. Self-confidence. Why'd you say you never've raced before?"

"I haven't. But when they have the poles up I practice. When I have the time."

Cully looked at her severely, his eyebrows lowered, as though she had deliberately deceived him. "There's a race in ten days. There're some good college kids who come for them every weekend. This'll be the first of the season, you may have a little jump on them, being up here all the time and all. I'll put you in it if you want."

Rita looked inquiringly at Michael. "Mr. Storrs, do you think I should . . . ?"

"What've you got to lose?" Michael said.

"My job, for one thing. Mrs. Heggener doesn't like skiing waitresses. Last year two of them broke their legs in the middle of the season and we were shorthanded in the dining room till the end of the year."

"I'll talk to Mrs. Heggener," Cully said. "If you're as good as I think you may be, with some coaching, it might be a nice bit of publicity for the hotel."

"Just promise you won't break your leg," Michael said.

"I promise," Rita said. "Put me in, please, Mr. Cully."

"I'll ask Swanson to take you out a couple of times to show you a few things that might cut your time a second or so. He's the best coach in town."

"I don't want to be a bother," Rita said. "Mr. Storrs has been awfully helpful."

"Leave Mike to the older ladies," Cully said. "The only thing he could teach you'd be how to crash. Everyone going back to town? We can pile into the pickup."

"I'll walk, thanks," Michael said. He had seen that Mr. Heggener hadn't moved and seemed to be waiting for company on the footpath.

"I think I'll give the hill one more workout," Rita said, "while the poles're still up."

"Don't worry about them when you're through," Cully said. "I'll have the patrol pick them up when they come down in the afternoon." He set off down the hill, skiing easily, without poles, as did Michael, since they had both carried the slalom markers up.

"Mr. Storrs," Rita said, "I don't know how to thank you and Mr. Cully . . ."

"Rita," Michael said, "you can do me a favor. You can call Mr. Cully Mr. Cully until you're fifty, but I wish you'd call me Michael. You make me feel ninety years old."

"Okay," Rita said shyly. "Mr. . . . Michael." Embarrassed, she turned and started climbing quickly up the hill toward the top of the slalom course.

Michael watched her for a moment, then skied down to the footpath, where Mr. Heggener was standing.

"Good morning, sir," Michael said, as he came to a stop just above the path.

"It *is* a good morning," Mr. Heggener said. "Best time of the day."

"You're up awfully early."

Heggener shrugged. "Sleeping is not my strong point these days. Oh . . . I have a message for you. Two, to be exact. Eva can't ski today. Too busy, she says. I'm not quite sure at just what. I was to tell you if I happened to run into you. And two—your friends arrived."

"So early?"

"They said they drove all night. A very handsome lady." Heggener looked up to where Rita, now a red dot on the white glare of the snow, was nearing the top of the slope. "Quite a sight on a beautiful morning like this—that pretty little girl drifting like a feather down that hill."

"She was doing some pretty fast drifting."

"I noticed. By the way, how're you getting back to the hotel?"

"On foot, I'm afraid," Michael said. "I came out in Cully's truck."

"Good," Mr. Heggener said. "Then we can walk back together. If you don't mind."

"My pleasure," Michael said politely and got out of his skis and put them over his shoulder. They started walking back toward town, Mr. Heggener moving with surprising briskness, taking deep, satisfying breaths of the cold, thin air. "Ah, the mountains," Mr. Heggener said, sighing. "I'm devoted to everything about them. The crispness of the air, the color of the shadows, the sound the snow makes under your boots. It was the purest luck that I fell in love with a woman who shared my . . . ah . . . dedication . . . to the heights. The happiest days of my life. . . ." He sighed again. "A morning like this makes me nostalgic for my own skiing days. Tell me, Mr. Storrs, have you ever made the run from Zermatt, under the Matterhorn in Switzerland down to Cervinia, in Italy?"

"Twice," Michael said.

"It was my last run," Mr. Heggener said. "The last run of my life. It was a day like this. Blue sky, cloudless, perfect snow, no wind. Just about two years ago. Maybe to the day. I have it jotted down in a diary someplace. I was feeling up to anything, like a young boy. I always made a point of being in good shape to start the season. I respect the mountains, one must not take them lightly. Before the season started, I climbed, did an hour of calisthenics a day, ran. . . . For a man my age—I don't like to boast—but I was considered a formidable skier." But there was no self-pity in his voice. It was a modest statement of fact. "Oh, I had a little cough. Nothing. Maybe a little cold coming on. I had a favorite guide. A small, solid Swiss who'd been born in Zermatt, who read the snow the way you would read a book. A slightly different color, a wind ripple, and he'd know where an avalanche could come down, where a snow bridge might not hold your weight. You could follow him safely anywhere. I was not a daredevil. I loved the mountains, but as I said, I respected them. I never believed that any run was worth a death." He looked keenly over at Michael, as though what he had said had a special message for him. "We went up to the Theodul Pass, the whole world beneath us, except for the great slab of the Matterhorn, with little white wisps of cloud around its crest. As you must remember, the run down is one of the longest in Europe. Great open slopes above the timberline, it seemed that you could ski and ski forever, sailing over the planet, unattached to it, its problems not your problems. Nourishing illusions for a few glorious hours. You've heard of Cousteau, the French underwater explorer . . . ?"

"Yes. I do a little scuba diving myself . . ."

"Then you know his phrase—'the euphoria of the depths.'"

"Yes."

"Trust a Frenchman to come up with a phrase like that." Mr. Heggener smiled. "That day, under the Matterhorn, I felt the euphoria of the heights."

"I know what it's like," Michael said, thoughtfully, engaged with his own memories now, diving through the air, going down to the limit of his oxygen to where sunken ships lay on the bottom of the sea, with multicolored shoals of fish swimming in and out of the broken wrecks. "Hang-gliding, free-falling."

"Euphoria," Mr. Heggener said. "Even the word, the word alone, sends a tingle up your spine. It is a wilderness word—you wouldn't ever think of using it to describe anything that might happen to you in a modern city. Joy, perhaps, ecstasy, but euphoria never. Euphoria is a word that needs silence." As if speaking the word had hushed him, he walked on silently another twenty paces, the only sound the crunch of their boots on the snowy path.

"Cousteau caught something there," Heggener said finally. "The relationship between exaltation and danger. The prerequisite, you might say. The danger of drowning in the depths, the danger of uncontrolled speed, daring the mountain, outrunning avalanches." He laughed lightly. "I'm older now, I no longer can ski, I can speak wisely about a run not being worth a death, but I have ridden avalanches down precipices in my time. I had a friend when I was a young man, a friend my own age, a magnificent skier, and he died that way—going into an avalanche slope. It took twenty-four hours to find the body. Still, when we did find him, I swore there was a smile on his lips. It had been a powder avalanche and he must have died almost instantly, suffocated, almost before he could have realized he was in peril. Well, young men die with less reason. . . ." He had spoken softly, elegiacally. Now his tone shifted abruptly. "As I was saying," he said matter-of-factly, "on that day I had a slight cough. When I got back late in the afternoon, coming down to Zermatt after a marvelous Italian lunch, the cough became more annoying. My wife insisted upon my seeing a doctor. The doctor insisted upon x-raying me. They are neurotic about lungs in the Alps. He diagnosed tuberculosis. Not an advanced case, the doctor assured me, I'd be skiing again the next year. It happened he was wrong. Not the first doctor to make a wrong prognosis." Mr. Heggener shrugged, made a little, uncharacteristic dandyish wave with his cane. "So here I am on foot, plodding along."

Michael stopped walking. "How far is it from the hotel to here?"

Mr. Heggener stopped, too, and looked at him, puzzled. "A mile and a half, maybe a little more. Why?"

"And you walked all the way?"

"It was such a fine morning. I walk slowly, as you see."

"Not as slowly as all that," Michael said. "If you can walk more than a mile, what's to prevent you from skiing? Slowly, of course."

Mr. Heggener laughed. "My doctor would refuse to see me again."

"He's not doing you any good as it is, is he?" Cruelty was to be preferred to manners today.

Mr. Heggener made a balancing, ambiguous movement with his gloved hand. "No," he said.

"Then what have you got to lose? That's what I asked Rita just now when Cully offered to put her in a race."

"Is she going to be in it?"

"Yes," Michael said.

"Good girl," Mr. Heggener said. He stared reflectively down at the beaten snow of the path before him. "It's possible," he said, "that I could do a little mild skiing. As long as there was someone to pick me up when I fell. I'm not strong enough to struggle up by myself."

"Look," Michael said. Although the man had for all intents and purposes just about threatened to shoot him the first night they had met, he could not help but admire the candor and courage and grace with which he was facing his fate. And the stoical finality with which Heggener had described his last run down the mountain touched him. Somewhere in the future there was going to be a last run for him, too, and he knew he would seek for consolation then, just as the man beside him, without asking for it, was seeking consolation now. "Look—I'm being paid for a whole day's work by the ski school," Michael said. "Your wife usually skis only in the afternoon and not every afternoon, at that. I'd be delighted to take you out. You know how skiing is—it takes your mind off everything else."

Heggener nodded. "Yes, it does. Sitting around day after day with a blanket over your shoulders and making sure there are no drafts in a room smelling like a hospital doesn't take your mind off anything but the grave. As you said, What have I got to lose?" He spoke almost gaily. "If it's a nice day tomorrow, I'll take you up on your offer. I still have some skis and a pair of boots somewhere in the basement. I didn't know what I was saving them for, but maybe I was saving them for this." He sighed. "A man my age in my condition is apt to be pessimistic, but one must always remember that unexpected things can happen, unexpected people come into your life— that not *all* hopes are inevitably dashed." He looked up at the sky. "Sun," he said, "shine tomorrow." He laughed, sounding young and full-bodied. "Eva will be in despair."

"Why?"

"If it were up to her she would put me in a hothouse and keep me there. She is desperate about preserving me as long as possible. I am not quite as desperate."

They were in the town now, walking through it to get to the road that led to the hotel. With his cane Heggener saluted the shopkeepers standing out in front of their establishments and tipped his hat to two ladies who were wheeling baby carriages. Everyone seemed to know him and smiled warmly at him and told him they were glad to see him back. "In America," Heggener said, "small towns are the last bastion of civil behavior. The feuds run deep and from generation to generation, but everybody knows he must live with everybody else and people conduct themselves accordingly. They are not strong on art or culture, perhaps, but they are careful about form and manners. One could argue that the village volunteer fire brigade, with its trucks manned by men whose families have not spoken to each other since 1890, is one of the finest institutions of American democracy." He chuckled at his conceit.

They passed the last few houses of the town proper and walked through a tangled forest of second-growth birch and scrub pine. In the sun, the snow was melting off the branches of the trees, falling with soft irregular plops onto the snow beneath.

"Contrary to most people my age," Heggener said, brushing some snow off his mink collar, "I do not applaud the approach of spring. Winter is my season. Luckily, we are far from spring. Which brings up another point, Michael." He used his companion's Christian name naturally, as though the conversation they had had on their walk could only be between friends. "Do you really intend to stay the entire season?"

"As of now, yes."

Heggener nodded. "Eva told me that you had not yet said yes or no about the offer of the little cottage on our property. I sincerely hope you will accept it. I gather that you can afford to stay at the Alpina as long as you like, but living in a hotel, for three months at a time, even one as spectacularly comfortable as mine"—he smiled, deprecatingly—"can finally be dreary. I must admit that Eva and I are not being completely unselfish. I have to go out of town on business, or to Boston to the clinic, sometimes for weeks at a time. I worry about leaving Eva alone, just with our seventy-year-old maid, who is so deaf she would not awaken from sleep if they shot off a cannon

outside her window. To add to her virtues, she does not speak anything but German. During the season, as you may have heard, the
town is visited by some extremely undesirable young people—ski bums
who live by stealing when they can't make money any other way, and
sometimes even if they can—and recently, whole groups of young
people, and some not so young, who smoke marijuana, shoot up on
heroin and indulge in other modern amusements of a similar kind.
There have been some nasty evenings in the last few years and jail
sentences and one case of arson. Has Eva happened to tell you why
we had to have the house redone completely?"

"No."

"Last spring," Heggener said, "we were in New York for a few
days and only the old lady was in the house. A gang of young men
and girls, too, according to the police, broke into the house. The dog
must have been barking, so they shot him. Shot him. Bruno is a re-
placement. Then the gang tore up the house, ripped every cushion,
broke all the china, smashed the doors to the cupboards, sliced the
clothes hanging in the closets, everything. Then, as a final touch, they
shat on the floor. The old lady slept through it all. Incidentally, they
were never apprehended. You can understand that I was reluctant to
move back into the ruins. The house needed remodeling anyway, it
was dark and a little old-fashioned. But now I keep a pistol in a
drawer, a useful Smith and Wesson thirty-eight. Having you nearby
would tend to discourage any further depredations. If you do move
into the cottage I will show you where I keep the pistol. Have you
ever used one?"

"No."

"No matter. You never use it at more than ten feet if you want it
to be effective. At ten feet it's almost impossible to miss."

The idea of using a pistol at ten feet did not make Heggener's offer
of a place to live any more attractive, but Michael felt that it was impossible to refuse. He had been tested by Cully for speed and endur-
ance on the hill and now he was being tested, he felt, for cowardice.

"I'll move in when you tell me it's ready," Michael said, without
hesitation.

"I'm sure you'll be happy there. And it will be convenient when
you want to play a game of backgammon. I assure you, aside from
the backgammon, we will not interfere with your life." Suddenly,
Heggener stopped and began to cough. It was a racking, nerve-rasp-
ing sound. There was a bench in a little clearing off the road and

Heggener sank onto it and, with a handkerchief to his mouth, continued coughing. Slowly, the seizure ended. Heggener looked at the handkerchief. "No blood," he said calmly. "The season is beginning well." With the aid of his cane, he pushed himself to his feet. "Shall we continue?"

Michael wanted to take his arm so the man could lean on it, but knew that Heggener would resent it. They walked, not briskly now, the last few hundred yards to the hotel.

As they neared the front steps, they heard the sound of a piano from within. "My friend," Michael said. "He's a professional. If there's a piano anywhere, he'll find it."

Heggener cocked his head appreciatively, listening. "Schubert. He plays very well."

"Poor bastard. He got into a ruckus in New York in the bar he was playing at and the police came in and they found out he didn't have a work permit in America and the boss fired him and he can't work in New York anymore."

"What times we live in," Heggener said sadly. "You have to have the permission of the government to play the piano."

They went into the hotel together. At the bottom of the staircase, Heggener said, "Thank you for a most pleasant promenade." He smiled wryly. "I, as usual, talked too much. My social opportunities have been limited recently. Until tomorrow morning, if the sun shines . . ." He climbed the stairs with effort.

Michael went down the flight of steps to the bar, which was located in the basement. Antoine was bent over the piano, playing intently, a cigarette hanging from his lower lip, his sad, dark eyes squinting against the smoke. He was wearing baggy green ski pants and a sweater that was at least three sizes too large for him, of an indeterminate color that looked as though it had been lying out on the seashore, with the tide running over it at regular intervals. On his feet he had a pair of low, laced leather ski boots that Michael had seen on no hill for fifteen years.

"Antoine," Michael said, loudly enough to be heard above the music.

Antoine stopped playing and bounded up and embraced Michael, without losing his cigarette.

"*Mon vieux,*" he said, "you look like a god."

"You look like a horse's ass," Michael said. "Where did you get those clothes?"

"I have had many splendid days racing down the Alps in these clothes," Antoine said with dignity, "and I am attached to them. I made a very good impression with them at the ski school office."

"What were you doing at the ski school office?" Michael asked suspiciously.

"I took one look at this town and decided I was going to remain. To remain, I reasoned, would take money. So I went down to the ski school . . ."

"Was the boss there, a big man named Cully?"

"No. Only a charming young girl. I explained to her that I was French and that I was an expert instructor, registered with the French Federation and a friend of yours and did they need any instructors."

"You didn't," Michael said disbelievingly.

"I did."

"Do you know how to ski *at all?*"

"Do not be cynical, *mon ami,*" Antoine looked hurt. "I have played the piano at Mégève, at Courchevel, at Val d'Isère, stations that would make a place like this look like a retreat for rheumatic pensioners."

"Playing the piano is one thing," Michael said. "Skiing is another."

"That reminds me," Antoine said. "This piano is definitely out of tune. I would bring up the subject to the management if I were you."

"Can you *really* ski?"

"That is beside the point at the moment. The charming girl said they get many Canadians here who like to be taught in French, especially children. I said I am a specialist in children, patient and wise. Beginners, I said, especially beginners. They won't be able to tell the difference."

"The first time they see you in those baggy pants and laced boots, they'll bust a gut laughing and then they'll come after me with a club."

"If necessary," Antoine said resignedly, "I will outfit myself in the absurd regalia you seem to find *comme il faut*. As for the skiing, that is where my good friend Michael will come in."

"What do you mean by *that?*"

"There is no need to start immediately," Antoine said. "The charming girl explained that to me. The crowd doesn't start coming here until the Christmas holidays. Between then and now, my good

friend Mike is going to take me to a secluded place, away from prying eyes, myself dressed *à la mode de* Green Hollow, and will brush
up my style and instruct me in just how one teaches children and
grown-ups, if that is unavoidable, who have never been on skis before, so that if anyone puts me to the test and they happen to find
any fault with my pedagogy, I can merely say, 'That is the new
French technique.'"

Michael couldn't keep from laughing. "You know, Antoine," he
said, "you might just get away with it. I'll fit you out after lunch and
then we'll go behind the hotel, there's a little slope there, and we'll
see what we'll see. Remember, a mountain is not a piano. You can't
improvise while you're falling off into space."

"I am convinced that with you as my teacher, everything will be
possible," Antoine said. "I am young." Then he qualified that with a
shrug. "Young enough. I have a sense of rhythm. I do not mind the
cold. I actually have skied from time to time. I have watched good
people, the best in the world. As a musician, for example, there is
nothing original in the way I play, but I am an accomplished mimic.
I can play in the style of Arthur Rubinstein, Fats Waller, Joplin.
After a few lessons with you I'm sure I'll have your style, if not your
speed and reputation. I am sublimely confident. And I have the nerve
of a burglar. And . . ." he said, pathetically, "I need the money.
Mon Dieu, do I need the money. And I have to make it someplace
where the Immigration isn't poking its nose into corners. In New
York I had the feeling they were circling around me, like Indians
around the covered wagons in Western movies. Mike," he said, with
absolute seriousness, "I love it in the States, I love this country. I
can't go back to Paris. . . . I've tried everything in Paris and I've
failed."

"Okay," Michael said, touched, but still reluctant. "We'll give it a
try. I don't guarantee results. I'll finance you till Christmas."

"I knew I could depend upon you," Antoine cried and bounced
down to the piano stool and hit three resounding triumphant major
chords.

"Ah, shut up. I'm going upstairs to take a shower and change for
lunch. By the way, where's Susan? Sleeping off the ride last night?"

"Not a bit of it," Antoine said. "She is a woman of demonic energy. She's skiing. She couldn't wait."

"How is she?"

Antoine sighed. "Elusive."

"I thought you told me you were just friends."

"She may think that," Antoine said darkly. "I am more demented about her than ever. She is a glorious and infuriating woman. I am not like you. One look and here is the key to my room. Ah, there are those that have it, like you, and the ones who do not have it, like me. And the ones that have it think nothing of it and the ones that don't think of nothing else."

"Will she be back for lunch?" Michael asked, refusing to engage in this particular philosophic discussion with Antoine.

"Who knows?" Antoine said. "She never tells me her plans."

"Well, if she comes back," Michael said, "we'll have lunch together. The food here is very good."

"I will never leave here."

"We'll see about that," Michael said and started upstairs as Antoine swung the stool around and began to improvise on the sad theme of "Send In the Clowns."

CHAPTER
SIXTEEN

Michael was drying himself off after the shower when there was a knock on his door. Still dripping, he threw on a terry cloth bathrobe and opened the door. Eva was standing there, looking businesslike in a plain skirt and sweater. "May I come in?" she said.

"I'm not exactly dressed to receive company," Michael said, using the towel on his wet hair.

"It won't take long." She came into the room and Michael closed the door behind him, feeling guilty, as he had the first time she had come to his room, that the room was messed up. His ski clothes were strewn all over the place, with one sock on the bed and the other on the floor.

Eva faced him, unsmiling. "You're doing something unforgivable," she said.

"What are you talking about, Eva?" Having one sock on the bed and one on the floor might be careless, but it could hardly be called unforgivable.

"Tempting my husband to believe he could ski again."

"If he can walk the way he did . . ." Michael began.

"You ought to see him now," she said accusingly. "He's stretched out on the bed as pale as a sheet gasping for breath."

"I'm sorry."

"You should be. I forbid you to mention the subject again."

"Eva . . ." Michael said. "Nobody forbids me anything. Not even you."

"You'll kill him," she said flatly.

"I doubt it. In any case, he's a grown, highly intelligent man and he knows how he feels better than either you or I and it's up to him to make decisions that concern him. I happen to think that a little easy skiing will help him, if not physically then at least psychically."

"Up to now," Eva said sardonically, "you have successfully hidden the fact that you have a degree in psychiatry. You've talked to him twice and you think you know him. I've been married to him for twelve years and I assure you, you don't. You talk about a little easy skiing. That's because of your ignorance. He does nothing easily and never has. At his age he isn't going to change. Are you going to tell him that you've thought about it and he'd best listen to the doctors and his wife or . . . ?"

"Listen," Michael broke in. "Maybe I was wrong to suggest it, but now that he's got the idea, he's going to ski, whether he does it with me or with somebody else. I may not know him as well as you, but I have the impression that when he makes up his mind . . ."

"Foolish man," she said, not speaking of her husband. "Fool. And I thought, after what's happened between us you would feel you owe me something, not much, but something."

"You don't owe me anything," Michael said, angry now, "and I don't owe you anything."

"I'll remember that," Eva said warningly.

There was a soft rap on the door. "You have company. We'll discuss this some other time," Eva said.

Michael went over to the door, leaving Eva standing rigidly in the middle of the room. He opened the door and saw Susan Hartley standing there, in ski clothes, her hair blown from her morning on the mountain.

"Hi, lover," she said and kissed Michael before she saw Eva Heggener behind him. "Oh."

"That's all right," Eva said. "I was just leaving. I hope you had an enjoyable morning on the slopes." She had transformed herself in the flick of an eye to the mistress of the establishment, but her voice was cold. "That's a pretty outfit you're wearing." Susan was in an all white ski suit. "The color becomes you." The manner in which she said it made it plain that she did not think that the color became Susan at all. "I'll leave you two now. I'm sure you have many things to talk about."

She marched stiffly out of the room. Michael closed the door behind her gently.

"Did I interrupt anything?" Susan asked.

"A medical discussion," Michael said. "Nothing."

Susan looked around the room. "What a nice room. Fireplace and all." She stretched luxuriously. "What a shining morning. I feel like a new woman already. Can you see it?"

"The white flower of the hillside."

"Approve?"

"Unreservedly."

"The beautiful lady didn't. Approve I mean." She made a little grimace.

"Don't jump to conclusions."

"I sensed an aura of . . . ownership." Susan looked obliquely at him, half-smiling.

"Her husband owns the hotel," Michael said stiffly.

"I know that. That isn't what I sensed. I sensed romance."

"You'd sense romance in an ad for surgical trusses. The lady is not romantic. I'm her hired help. I'm her ski guide."

"There is guidance and guidance." Susan laughed good-naturedly. "I'm waiting for something."

"We're having lunch in a little while."

"That's not what I'm waiting for." She approached him, playing at being extravagantly coquettish and batting her eyelashes. She had her sports, Susan, skiing outdoors and flirting within.

"I kissed you at the door," Michael said.

"Like a brother," Susan said, close to him. "Not good enough. I came miles and miles through the night, through sleet and snow . . ." She held out her arms.

He embraced her, kissed her lightly on the mouth, uneasily conscious that he was naked under the robe, broke away. "That good enough?"

"Fair," Susan said. "Anyway, better. Are you going to invite me to sit down?"

"By all means make yourself at home."

She flopped into a chair. "My legs are spaghetti. It's terrible how you age from the end of one ski season to the beginning of the next."

"Susan," Michael said, standing over her, "I have to talk to you. Seriously."

Susan sighed with mock despair. "I prefer it when men talk to me frivolously."

Michael ignored this. "It was my understanding that you and Antoine are just friends."

"That's everybody's understanding. What else is new?"

"He just told me he was demented about you."

"Demented. He's just trying out his English vocabulary."

"He wasn't trying out anything," Michael said. "He was sending me a message."

Susan shrugged. "Let him put it in a bottle and send it out to sea. I'm not demented about him."

"When I decoded the message," Michael said, "do you know what I heard?"

"I'm not particularly interested." Susan yawned.

"I heard, 'I love her,'" Michael persisted. "'Please don't do anything that will prevent her from loving me.'"

"I got a message today, too," Susan said. "Just now. In this very room. The message was from the mistress of the house: 'Mr. Michael Storrs is bespoke. Hands off.'"

"Nonsense," Michael said.

"I never heard a man say 'Nonsense' less convincingly. Haven't you realized yet you're catnip to the ladies?" Susan said lightly. "Or have you become so blasé about your beauty and charm that you don't even notice when the net's out for you?"

"I won't argue with you. You'd better go. I've got to dress for lunch."

She sank deeper into her chair and lit a cigarette. "Don't worry about me. I've seen men dress before."

"I'm sure you have, but . . ."

There was a loud knock on the door.

"You have quite a busy social life in the morning, don't you?" Susan said, grinning up at him. "Are you sure you don't need a secretary?"

Michael went to open the door, pulling the robe tightly around him. Antoine was standing there, holding a bottle of champagne and two glasses. Michael noted the champagne with displeasure. When he had said that he was going to finance Antoine until Christmas he hadn't thought it was going to include champagne in the mornings.

Antoine stepped gaily into the room, then stopped abruptly when he saw Susan. "Oh," he said, "back so soon? I thought we'd have a little reunion celebration, Mike. I see I'm missing a glass." He started back toward the door. "I'll go get another one . . ."

"No need," Michael said. "There's a glass in the bathroom."

He heard Antoine say accusingly, "Susan, you said you wouldn't be back until dark. What're you doing here?"

"What do you think I'm doing?" Susan said airily. "I was learning how to make parallel turns."

"Yeah," Antoine said, wretchedly. He was trying to open the bottle of champagne without success when Michael came out of the bathroom carrying a tumbler. "Here," he said, taking the bottle out of Antoine's hands. "Let me have that." He opened the bottle easily, the cork popping and the foam fizzing over.

"His strength is as the strength of ten," Susan said mockingly, standing, "because his heart is pure."

Michael poured for the three of them and lifted his glass. "To deep snow and sunny days," he said. Then he looked squarely at Susan. "And to messages," he added.

Susan looked demurely at him and held the glass with two hands to her lips, like a small girl innocently drinking her morning milk.

After lunch, Michael took Antoine down to town to outfit him, while Susan went upstairs to take what she called her beauty nap.

"Well, now," Michael said as Antoine came down the stairs from his room, dressed in his new outfit, with the high plastic boots clumping, "at least you *look* like a skier." He took Antoine up a small footpath that ran to a knoll behind the hotel. From the top of the knoll there was a gentle slope, well covered with snow, that could not be seen from the hotel and that ended in a copse of trees about seventy-five yards away. They put on their skis and Michael said, "Okay, start down."

Antoine started down shakily. Michael could see that he hadn't been lying—he *had* been on skis before. But not often. He was completely stiff, as though he had just been taken out of a deep-freeze compartment, his skis were far apart and wobbling, his arms were immobile, like those of a statue. After ten yards he fell. Michael skied down to him and looked pityingly at him, sprawled in the snow.

"Good God, man. Can't you even *stand?*"

"These things *slide,*" Antoine said pathetically.

"I'm afraid that's the whole idea." He helped Antoine up. Antoine was sweating already.

"Now watch me," Michael said and skied slowly, making two turns, calling back, "Loose, loose, skis together," then said, "Oh, Christ," as Antoine fell again.

"Remember," Antoine said, struggling once more to his feet, "this is only my first day."

"In how many years?" Michael said. "Forty?"

"I had a sergeant in the French Army," Antoine complained, "who was like a mother to me, compared to you." With a look of concentrated determination on his face he started downwards again. He teetered, his arms made wild circles in the air, one ski got out of control and he nearly split in half and he wound up in the snow again in a kneeling position, just as a little boy, aged perhaps nine, skiing without poles, sped down from the knoll and stopped and looked at Antoine, kneeling as if in church. The little boy grinned widely.

"Get out of here, you," Michael yelled at him. The boy, grinning even more widely, sped off and into the woods.

"Hopeless," Michael said, not bothering to help Antoine up this time.

"If I'd had a gun I'd've shot that little bastard."

"Hopeless," Michael repeated.

"Remember," Antoine said, "I have two weeks."

"You won't make it in two years."

"You're undermining my confidence," Antoine said aggrievedly.

"It's the least I can do for you." Michael scratched his head thoughtfully.

"Listen, Mike . . ." Antoine began.

"Keep quiet," Michael said. "I'm thinking. I'm trying to see if there's anything I can do for you aside from shipping you back to France. If Cully doesn't wait two weeks to see how you ski and looks you over tomorrow, as he's very likely to do, it's farewell in ten seconds."

"Don't sound so pessimistic, Mike."

"I said, be quiet, I'm thinking." Michael made a little circle in the snow with the tip of his pole. "I've never done anything like this before, Antoine," he said, "but I am now going to plan to aid and abet a felony or at least a misdemeanor. I'll tell you what you're going to do. Now, listen carefully. Tonight, we're going to go to the most crowded bar in town. Ski teachers, the hotshot kids of the town. I'm going to introduce you as the French bullet . . ."

"There is no need to exaggerate," Antoine said uneasily.

"Shut up. The bar is on the ground floor, but there's a kind of balcony on one side and there's a flight of stairs going up to it and the men's room is off it. At a certain point, when I give the signal, you're going to go up the steps. Then, after the men's room, when you start coming down, you're going to slip . . ."

"Mike, don't let your imagination run away with you, I beg you," Antoine said plaintively.

"Do you want to get a job or don't you?"

"I am in your hands," Antoine said, surrendering. "I am going to slip."

"You fall all the way down the flight of stairs."

"If I hurt my hands I will never earn a living for the rest of my life."

"Keep your hands out of the way. When you reach the bottom, you're going to moan heartrendingly with pain. You're going to grab your ankle. You're going to gasp that you think you've broken your leg. I'm going to say that I'll take you to a doctor. Only we don't go to a doctor . . ."

"You are enjoying this scenario," Antoine said reproachfully. "You are devoid of human feeling."

Implacably, Michael went on. "I'll take you to the hotel, where I'll have bandages ready and I'll tape your ankle. I'll put so much tape on it it'll look like a balloon. Susan will have to play along with us. Tell her you'll strangle her if she laughs. Every night, for two weeks, I'll take you out and give you lessons. If necessary, finally, I'll let Cully in on it. In two weeks you should look as though you can at least teach children, although you'll have to be prepared to unzip their pants when they have to pee and zip them up again when they're finished."

"I don't like the way you're smiling, Michael," Antoine said.

"Cully's a friend and maybe he has a sense of humor," Michael said, "and he needs instructors. If you perfect your act, he'll probably go along with you. If you don't pass inspection after the two weeks, unless you get a job playing the piano, you let it be known that you have a job waiting for you in New York and you get out of town? *Compris?*"

"You're a bastard, Mike, you know that?"

"On the contrary, I'm your friend. I'm trying to keep you from being arrested for taking money under false pretenses. Now, climb up this insignificant little pimple of a slope and try to come down in one piece."

"I'm exhausted."

"Wait till you see how you feel after an hour more," Michael said grimly. "Remember, this was your idea."

Antoine groaned and started laboriously climbing the little hill.

The Chimney Corner was the name of the bar. It was an easygoing place where everybody talked to everybody else. Michael had liked hanging around there when he had spent the winter in the town during his post-college holiday. The wood beams of the ceiling and the paneling on the walls were darker from the smoke of the intervening years and the photographs of famous skiers of the past hanging above the great fireplace now looked like mementos of a much earlier America. The people at the bar and lounging around at the tables all looked terribly young to Michael and he guessed that he was older by at least a decade than anybody else in the room. There was a jukebox in a corner which was blessedly silent and a battered upright paino to one side of the fireplace. As Michael and Antoine and Susan sat down at a table, Antoine stared apprehensively at the flight of stairs leading up to the balcony.

Jimmy Davis, the owner of the bar, with whom Michael had drunk on many a long winter evening, came over and Michael made the introductions. "How's your skiing?" Michael asked. They had often skied together. Davis was fat but very nimble and even under the worst conditions of snow and weather was unfailingly cheerful.

"My skiing?" Davis said. "It's just about nonexistent. My wife talked me into opening for lunch and even though I wonder why anybody pays to eat the food I serve, I'm working on my first million. So it keeps me tied down here. But I'll sneak away an afternoon or two if you can't find anybody else crazy enough to follow you. What'll it be, ladies and gentlemen, the first round is on the house."

They ordered whiskeys and Davis himself brought them over. "That piano in tune?" Michael asked.

"I wouldn't know," Davis said. "Nobody's played on it yet this year. Why? You want to give us a concert?"

"My friend, Antoine here, might play us a tune. He's a famous pianist from France."

"Be my guest," Davis said to Antoine. "A famous French pianist might just be what we need to tone up the joint."

The room was filling now and Michael said, "Jimmy—have you instituted a new rule here—nobody over the age of twenty allowed in after ten o'clock?"

Davis chuckled, but a little sadly. "It's true, they get younger and younger. Or at least that's what it looks like to old cocks like us. Somehow, they fight more than they used to. I have to keep a sawed-off baseball bat under the bar to preserve decorum." He moved off to go behind the bar and help the boy there serving drinks.

"Those steps look awfully steep, Mike," Antoine said.

"They'll look less steep after you've had a couple of drinks. Be confident."

"I don't even like the taste of whiskey," Antoine complained.

"Go play something," Michael said. "It'll settle your nerves." He waved to Annabel Fenstock, who was coming through the door with a boy who looked as though he couldn't have been more than eighteen years old.

Rita and a boy who, Michael guessed rightly, was her older brother came into the room and Michael gestured to them to come over. Rita introduced her brother, Eliot, and rather shyly greeted Susan and Antoine, whom she had served with Michael at dinner.

"Sit down, sit down," Michael said and moved his chair a little, so that Rita and her brother could squeeze in. "You've come just in time. The famous French pianist is going to give his first performance above sea level."

"I am not yet in the mood," Antoine said. He was not enjoying the evening and made a face when he sipped at his whiskey.

A waitress came over to the table and Rita ordered a Coke and her brother ordered a beer. Eliot was a husky boy and his face bore an unmistakable resemblance to that of his sister, with large, clear eyes and a straight nose with flaring nostrils and a wide, determined mouth. His hair, like hers, was close cropped, and he looked, Michael thought, like the youthful pictures of Muhammad Ali, when Muhammad Ali was known as Cassius Clay. He was wearing a leather jacket and it bulged with muscle at his shoulders. Under it he was wearing a sweater with a varsity letter from the town high school on it. Michael guessed that he had won it in football.

"Have you talked to Swanson yet about coaching you?" Michael asked Rita.

"We have a date for tomorrow morning," Rita said.

Michael turned to Eliot. "Your sister's quite a skier," he said. "But she says you're better than she is."

"I'm older, that's all," Eliot said.

"Why don't you sign up for the races, too?"

Eliot shook his head. "My legs're too precious," he said. "I've got a track scholarship to Dartmouth starting in September. You race, you're bound to get hurt. Anyway, like my father says, the hills won't be ready for black racers for fifty years and I like to stick to things where the brothers are welcome." He spoke directly, without embarrassment. "If you want to know the truth, Mr. Storrs, I advised Rita against going in for it."

"Oh, Eliot . . ." Rita said, "I thought we had it all out."

"I've seen too many old racers around this town," Eliot went on, ignoring his sister, "men and women, still looking for ways to show that they still have it, still looking for the old speed kick. Like that fella over there." He pointed to the bar, where Williams, the sole proprietor of the Green Hollow Hang-Gliding School, was drinking a beer. "He had half a good season on the junior circuit in the downhill and he cracked up his back, he was damn near paralyzed, so now he preaches hang-gliding. I heard you've done some of that yourself, Mr. Storrs, and I can see there must be some real kicks in floating down over a town, and Williams asked me if I wanted to give it a try, but I told him it's not for me. Being a black in America is enough of a kick for me, thank you."

"Eliot," Rita said, "I thought we were coming here to have a good time."

"I'm having a fine time," Eliot said, calmly, finishing his beer and waving to the waitress for another.

"If I drink any more of this stuff, I'll be sick as a dog," Antoine said, pushing his glass away. He stood up and went over to the piano and played a few chords. "What do you know," he said, "it's actually in tune." Then he began to play, softly at first, then more loudly as the hubbub in the room began to dwindle and people stopped talking to listen to him.

He played "Stormy Weather" because he knew that Michael liked the song and Michael called the waitress and said, "Give the pianist a lemonade," to show his appreciation.

Rita began to rock slowly in her chair in rhythm with the music and picked up the song, crooning softly. She had a clear, true voice and Michael and Susan listened with pleasure. "Rita," Michael said, "get up and sing along with him."

"Do you think I really . . . ?" Rita said doubtfully. "Won't your friend object?"

"He'll love it. Go ahead, go ahead."

"Well, if you think it's all right . . ." She stood up and went over to the piano and began to sing. Antoine looked up at her dubiously for a moment, then nodded affirmatively and shifted the key to accommodate her contralto. After a few slightly hesitant bars, Rita gained confidence and sang out boldly, with Antoine, in a kind of French Virginian accent, joining her in the last chorus. When they finished, there was loud applause all over the room and Antoine rose from the piano and gravely shook Rita's hand. She came back to the table with him, her hands shaking, but a big schoolgirlish smile lighting up her face.

"My dear young lady," Antoine said, "you're a real singer, do you know that? We'll have to work together. We'll astonish the natives with our combined brilliance."

"Don't make fun of me, please."

"I'm dead serious," Antoine said. "You've got a delicious voice. Should we try another one? What would you like to sing?"

Rita looked questioningly over at Eliot. He had not applauded and he was frowning. It was plain that he didn't approve of his little sister making a show of herself in bars. "Maybe some other night, Antoine," Rita said. "When we'd have time to practice a little."

Jimmy Davis came over, beaming. "Say," he said, "that was something. You do that a couple of more nights and I'm going to have a big poster printed up to put outside saying, Live Entertainment, the Best in Town. The Chimney Corner, The Hot Piano Bar."

"Ella Fitzgerald isn't having any sleepless nights yet, worrying about me," Rita said, giggling. She ducked her head, sipping at her Coke.

Michael nudged Antoine with his knee under the table. "Now," he whispered.

"Maybe I'll just play one more . . ." Antoine said uncomfortably.

"Now," Michael whispered.

"Excuse me for a minute, folks," Antoine said. He walked toward the staircase, slowly, then climbed up, stopping at every other step.

Michael watched as Antoine disappeared into the men's room. It was almost five minutes before Antoine reappeared at the top of the stairs and Michael was almost ready to go up and rout him out. He saw Antoine take a long, deep breath, then start down. Antoine gripped the banister, then twisted and let himself go. He made a surprising amount of noise as he tumbled all the way down and a sudden hush came over the room.

Antoine came to a halt on the last step, crumpled and screaming, with what Michael thought was admirable artistry. "My leg," Antoine screamed. "I've broken my leg."

Michael jumped up, along with Susan, and knelt beside the writhing Antoine. "Great," he whispered, as he put his hand on Antoine's calf, pretending to search for the break. "Congratulations. That was what I call a real authentic fall, kid."

"Authentic!" Antoine said, writhing. "It's broken, you bastard."

Michael ran his hand down Antoine's leg. Just above the ankle, he could feel the break.

"Holy man," Michael said, "you did! Idiot! Rita," he said to the girl, who had run over to the staircase behind him. "Call an ambulance. Antoine, now just lie still and . . ."

But Antoine didn't hear him. He had fainted dead away.

CHAPTER
SEVENTEEN

Antoine was in bed, half-lying, half-sitting, his leg in a cast, propped up on pillows, when Michael went into his room to see how he was doing. After the doctor had put the cast on his leg, he had refused to stay overnight in the hospital. "People die in hospitals," he said and Michael and Eliot, who had driven with Susan in her car to the hospital, had had to carry him to the car and up the stairs of the hotel at three o'clock in the morning, with Antoine being Gallically brave and not making a sound, although the unavoidable jostling must have been excruciating, even with the injection the doctor had given him.

Now he was being fed his breakfast spoonful by spoonful by Susan, who was sitting on the bed, looking dewy and fresh, despite not having slept more than four hours that night. Antoine did not look fresh. His face was greenish and his eyes were dull and glazed over, but he greeted Michael with a cheery wave. "This is the closest I've ever managed to get Susan into bed. Maybe in the long run it was worth it."

"Well," Michael said, "finally you look like a skier."

"Anyway," Antoine said, "I've got to give you credit. The idea worked. Now Mr. Cully will never find out what kind of skier I am. If any other problems develop, it's good to know I have you to depend on."

"Ready and willing," Michael said. "Count on me at all times."

"I did one intelligent thing, though," Antoine said. "Yesterday when I went into the ski school and talked to the charming girl there

I took out accident insurance for the whole season. I'm not French for nothing. I may not be able to walk, but I am a man of means now. Susan, in your long and varied experience, have you ever made love to a man in a cast?"

"Eat your eggs," Susan said.

"I see you're dressed for skiing, Mike," Antoine said. "Don't you think that's a bit callous, with me lying here just barely snatched from the jaws of death?"

"I'll give it a minute of silence when I get to the top of the hill," Michael said.

Antoine sighed. "It was such a nice evening, too, until you drove me up those beastly stairs. That little girl singing like an angel and all. And the piano in tune."

Although the door to the room was open, Eva Heggener rapped politely before she came in. She was carrying a vase with a small bouquet of jonquils in it from the hotel hothouse. "Ah, my poor dear guest," Eva said to Antoine. "Not here even for twenty-four hours and already *hors de combat*. You may be interested to know, though, that you have eclipsed all previous records for speed in leg breaking in this hotel. I hope these little flowers will help cheer you on your bed of pain."

"It is very good of you, madam," Antoine said.

"If there's anything you want to make you more comfortable, please don't hesitate to let me know."

"I am being very well taken care of by my dear friends," Antoine said.

"I can see that," said Eva, looking without affection at Susan. "We have a wheelchair in the basement in case you wish to move around. I'll get two of the boys to carry you down. They have a lot of practice at that sort of thing."

"Maybe tomorrow," Antoine said. "I'm not particularly anxious to move around today."

"I understand. Michael," she said, "may I have a word with you?"

Michael nodded. "Antoine, the doctor told me you had a nice, clean break."

"Thank the doctor for me for the good news," Antoine said. "I would be ashamed if he found my break unsanitary."

Susan was putting another spoonful of egg to Antoine's lips as Michael followed Eva out of the room and along the corridor.

"Andreas is waiting for you downstairs to take him skiing," Eva said, stopping when they were out of earshot from Antoine's room. "In spite of everything I had to say on the subject." She spoke bitterly, "I don't suppose I can change your mind, either."

"I'm afraid not," Michael said.

"There will be more than one sickroom in this hotel tonight," Eva said. "I won't be skiing this afternoon. I'm going to start moving in the things from here to the house. Your place is ready, too. Perhaps you'd like to move today, too."

"I think while my friend is immobilized, I'd better stick around, in case he needs me."

"He has that girl."

"She came up here for a holiday."

"And what did you come up here for?"

"For you, my dear," Michael said, annoyed by the antagonism in Eva's voice. "And for the general tranquillity of the neighborhood."

"Don't make me wish that I had never set eyes on you," she said in a low, tense voice, then turned and went up the steps toward the floor above, her heels beating an angry tattoo on the staircase.

Heggener was standing in the sunshine in front of the hotel, holding his skis and poles. He was dressed in smartly cut navy blue ski pants and a gray loden jacket and a blue balaclava wool cap, which was folded up now but could be pulled down to cover the throat and the lower part of the face if it got cold.

"Ah, Michael," he said. "It's such a lovely morning I wanted to get all the sun I could. I'm terribly sorry about your poor friend. He won't get in much skiing this winter, I'm afraid."

"No, he won't," Michael said, picking up his skis and poles, which were leaning against the wall. "Maybe it's for the best."

They drove to the bottom of the lift in the Porsche. "Eva wanted me to buy one of these," Heggener said, "but I told her I'm too old for anything as gaudy as this. It always saddens me to see elderly gentlemen, their white hair blowing, trying to look as though they were dashing young blades. One must learn, no matter how painful it is, that there is an age for everything, especially the trappings of youth."

"I'll turn it in for a black Volkswagen four-door sedan when I reach forty," Michael said.

Heggener laughed. "I don't think you have anything to worry about—yet."

Once on top, Michael slowly and carefully led Heggener down the easiest of the runs. Heggener skied easily and stylishly, fully controlled. He breathed normally when Michael stopped to let him rest and there was no sign of effort on his face. It was hard to believe that this elegantly dressed and graceful man had been declared doomed by the doctors and had not been on skis for two years.

"Michael," Heggener said, "I would like you to do me a favor. Dave Cully tells me you used to be the best trick skier in town. Somersaults, hot-dogging, things like that. They add a welcome note of gaiety that was lacking when I learned the sport. Would you mind putting on a little private performance for me?"

There was nobody else on the slope for the moment and nobody, Michael thought, could accuse him of showboating for an audience this particular morning. He was feeling fit and hard from the skiing he had done and the snow was perfect and harmless. He gave his poles to Heggener and started down the hill, skating backwards, tumbling and jumping up, and raced toward a bench that was set on the pedestrian path below and somersaulted over it, his arms out and his back arched, as though he were doing a swan dive and whirled over and came down solidly in a flurry of snow and stopped, smiling with pleasure. Heggener skied down to him.

"My Lord," Heggener said, "what a performance! You could have broken your neck. I see now that one has to be very careful before asking you to do anything . . . ah . . . strenuous. But I must say, it added just the right note of derring-do to the morning and I thank you for it."

They made only one more descent. Michael didn't want to bring Heggener back to his wife exhausted. Heggener agreed immediately when Michael said he thought the two runs were enough for the first time out. But he seemed pleased with himself and there was good color in his cheeks, and when they were standing at the bottom of the slope, he looked up wistfully at some young people dashing down the steep incline of the Black Knight, and said, "When I first came here I did all the runs—including that one. In fact, it was my favorite slope."

"Maybe later in the season," Michael said diplomatically.

"How do you feel?" Michael asked as they were driving back to the hotel.

"Tingling," Heggener said gaily.

Michael felt a sudden surge of admiration and something more than admiration for the courageous and complex man sitting erect, his fears secret, beside him.

Jimmy Davis was in Antoine's room when Michael went up to see how he had weathered the morning. Davis was apologizing to Antoine. "I've been telling my wife," he was saying, "that we ought to put a bigger light on that damn staircase. She said it would spoil the atmosphere. As though anything could spoil the atmosphere of that beat-up old saloon."

"Do not trouble yourself, Mr. Davis," Antoine said magnanimously. "I never look where I am going and I am unusually prone to accidents." He touched the long scar on his cheek. "As you can see."

"You're a gentleman, Antoine," said Davis. "Almost anybody else took a fall like that he'd slap a suit on me for a hundred thousand bucks, minimum."

"Do not tempt me, Mr. Davis," Antoine said. "Mike, how did it go this morning, you and Mr. Heggener?"

"It was beautiful."

"How I regret not being able to join you," Antoine said.

"We missed you," Michael said gravely.

"Listen," Davis said to Antoine, "maybe I can do something for you. For both of us. After you . . . uh . . . left last night a lot of people came up to me and my wife and said how much they liked the way you played and sang. I wonder if maybe you'd consider doing it as a job—say six nights a week, ten o'clock till about one in the morning . . ."

"I might consider it," Antoine said, as though he were reflecting. He looked significantly at Michael. "Perhaps my acrobatics were a blessing in disguise."

"The money wouldn't be much," Davis said hastily, "but you'd get your grub free in the saloon. It might give you an ulcer but it'd be on the house. And there's a little annex out in back we use for a storeroom that we could fix up for you to live in. All for—" He seemed to be making some rapid mental calculations. "Let's say, seventy-five bucks. I bet you pay a hell of a lot more for this palace here."

"I do indeed," Antoine said. He did not refer to the fact that it was Michael who was footing the bill at the hotel.

"You can play with one leg, can't you?" Davis asked.

"Superbly," Antoine said.

"Should we call it a deal?" Davis said.

"Michael?" Antoine looked inquiringly at Michael.

"There are pros and cons," Michael said, teasing Antoine. "But if Jimmy doesn't ask you to lower your standards . . ."

"As long as he doesn't drive my clientele down the street to the Monadnock," Davis said, "he can play anything he pleases. And if you can get the kid—Rita—to sing a few songs on the weekends there'd be some loose change in it for her, too."

"Well," Antoine said, as though he were reluctant to decide, "if the sight of the pianist making his way across the floor on crutches won't distress your clients . . ."

"They're used to crutches," Davis said. "If they didn't see them they'd think Green Hollow was going down in class. When do you think you can start?"

"Tomorrow night all right with you, Mr. Davis?"

"You're in, Antoine." Davis put out his hand and Antoine shook it. "I'll see about getting your room in shape this afternoon," he said, as he was leaving, with a pleased smile on his face, as though he had succeeded in a highly profitable piece of business.

"Well, Mike," Antoine said after Davis had left, "I seem to have found a home. Thanks to you. I may even be able to pay back some of the money you have advanced for me. Although," he added hurriedly, "that is definitely not a promise. And for once, *merci à Dieu,* no questions asked, where is your work permit, where is your union card, what is your Social Security number, that kind of fascist harassment. Though maybe I made a mistake in using my real name when I came here. I could easily have invented another name."

"Nobody'll bother you. Jimmy Davis is in with everybody. And he knows he's got something dirt cheap. He'll keep everybody off your back, well, at least until the season is over in April."

"Please do not remind me of April," Antoine said gloomily. "You are beginning to sound like Susan. She learned the fable about the grasshopper and the ant in French class in high school and whenever she thinks I am doing something extravagant, like buying tickets from a speculator at grotesque prices to take her to the theatre or inviting her to dine at a French restaurant where they charge like bank robbers for a bowl of soup, she is likely to recite, *'La cigale, ayant chanté tout l'été, se trouva fort dépourvu quand la bise fut venu.'* In pure English that means, the grasshopper—that's me—having sung all summer, found himself in the shit when winter came. I cannot change my character just because a girl learned a foolish little poem in high school. And her accent, besides, is abominable."

Michael laughed. "By the way, where is she?"

"Skiing. Left me in my agony with a careless wave of her beautiful hand. If that girl was as fond of sex as she is of skiing, she would be known as one of the greatest courtesans since Madame Pompadour. Anyway, she said she'd be back for lunch. Now that I am immobilized, she will take advantage of my condition to make time with you."

"Trust me, *mon vieux*."

"A man with a broken leg cannot afford the luxury of trusting anybody. Especially someone who looks like you. Older women may love invalids but young women despise them."

"Is that another French saying?"

"That is the saying of an experienced man of the world, namely myself. I plead with you, do not let her catch you in a weak moment."

"Antoine, I never know whether you're serious or you're joking."

"Half and half. It is part of my charm. I have no looks so I have to depend upon other attributes. Do you think a glass of wine would keep my bones from knitting?"

"I'll send up a bottle when we go in for lunch."

"Remember," Antoine said, "I was kind to you when you were out of action in the hospital, although out of friendship I hid my revulsion when I saw what they had done to your face."

"I will remember," Michael said. "Forever."

"If they have a decent Beaujolais," Antoine called after Michael as Michael was going out the door, "that would be nice."

◇◇◇◇◇

After lunch that afternoon he skied with Susan. She was fun to ski with, zestful and daring and constantly delighted with the speed and glowing weather and the changing shapes of the mountains with their low-hanging flecks of clouds. When they finished they stopped off at the Monadnock bar and had tea with black rum in it. "Sometimes I wonder," she said thoughtfully, "if I could ski every day of my life, would I be happy. I guess not." She answered her own question. "When I see people whose life is one long holiday, they seem pitiful to me. If you don't work, your holidays seem like drudgery."

"You like your work, don't you?"

"I love it. The result isn't all that valuable—making foolish women think that I can mix a magic powder or prepare an elixir that will make them beautiful or at least acceptable, but I do it well and there's always the element of surprise—maybe one day we will find something that *will* turn ugly ducklings into swans. That would be worthwhile, wouldn't it?"

"I suppose so," Michael said. He looked at her closely. In the city she was always a walking advertisement for the products she worked on, but today he saw that she was wearing no makeup and even her nails were natural colored.

"I see you're noticing that I'm just plain Jane today," she said, laughing. "That's because I don't want to insult the mountains." Then she became sober. "You're not going to stay up here forever, are you?"

"When I ski, I'm not on holiday, I'm working," Michael said. "I get paid for it."

"Oh, come on now," she said impatiently.

"In my office, there were quite a few men who felt like you about their work. Even if they knew it wasn't of world-shaking importance and maybe even guessed that it was harmful in the overall scheme of things, they gloried in the challenge, and it wasn't only in making the money. When he got drunk my boss used to boast that in the morning he couldn't wait to get to his desk, that it was like the Super Bowl every day for him. And he had enough money to do whatever he wanted to do for the rest of his life, without worrying about a thing."

"You can't tell me that you believe escorting ladies down little hills is a challenge to you."

"No," Michael admitted. "I'm just waiting and seeing."

"For what?"

"For waiting and seeing." Michael grinned. "Naturally, if I were a great artist, a painter or a poet or a great athlete, or even just thought so, I'd think what I was doing was valuable and I guess I'd be like my boss when he sat down at his desk. Or even like Antoine, doing something that gives him and other people so much pleasure. . . . But I'm none of those things. I'm a manipulator of numbers for profit, other peoples' profit, although that isn't what really bothers me. After twelve years I felt I was living in a void. And stuck in the void with me were maybe eight million other souls, whirling around, making believe the void didn't exist. Here, at least for the moment, maybe for a couple of weeks, maybe for a couple of seasons, I'm out of the void. Susan," he said, a little plaintively, "this isn't the sort of conversation we should be having after an afternoon like the one we just had."

"No, it isn't," she said. "You should be telling me how marvelously I ski and how beautiful I am and how you can't live without me."

"Yes, I should," Michael said good-humoredly, "and it is a flaw in my character that I can't."

"You know, you're the one man I've ever set my cap for—what a nice old-fashioned expression to cover my essential lewdness—" She giggled. "The only one I haven't made even a dent in." She sighed melodramatically. "Well, win some, lose some. Still, if it's some weird notion you have about Antoine and me . . ."

"Antoine may have something to do with it," Michael said, "but not all that much. Our schedules and destinations, yours and mine, just didn't happen to mesh. Maybe five years ago—before I got married. . . ."

"God save me from honorable men. Oh, that's another thing I wanted to talk to you about. Honorable men. Antoine isn't one of them." She was speaking very seriously now. "I thought you should know. I know he's amusing and talented and you think of him as a kind of darling clown and I've gone along with the clowning. Clowns are okay in a circus, Michael. In the home, their tricks can be nasty."

"Antoine?" Michael said incredulously. "He wouldn't hurt a fly."

"Little you know," Susan said. "I'll tell you a little story about poor dear amusing Antoine, who wouldn't hurt a fly. He was introduced to me by a girlfriend of mine, who was married, with a child. She fell in love with him, she told her husband, she was preparing to get a divorce because Antoine said he was going to marry her. She loaned him some money. A considerable amount. She wasn't all that rich, either, and she couldn't afford it. And, naturally, he didn't give any of it back. The night he met me, he called me after he had taken her home and tried to get me to invite him to my place. And then two weeks later he went chasing after another woman to Paris. How do you like that for a prankish bit of clowning?"

"Not terribly amusing," Michael said quietly.

"And the first day he got back from Paris," Susan went on, "he called me—this was after two years—and asked me to marry him. If you want to know what I really think—it wasn't because he was so wildly infatuated with my beauty, as he keeps telling me—it was because he could then become an American citizen."

"I'm sorry you told me all this, Susan," Michael said.

"Let him amuse you," she said, "but don't ever vouch for him—for anything. You've already gone too far for him in this town. And don't ever depend upon him."

"You've ruined a perfectly fine afternoon, Susan," Michael sighed. "People ought to have tags on them, describing the contents of the package. I must talk to someone at the Pure Food and Drug Administration in Washington about it."

"Do you now want me to say something on the subject of you and the formidable Madam Heggener?" she said challengingly.

"I do not."

"I didn't think you would," she said.

CHAPTER EIGHTEEN

Using the excuse that he didn't want to leave the hotel until Antoine was mobile enough to get around well enough on his crutches so that he didn't need any help, Michael postponed moving into the cottage for another week. During that time, when the weather was fine, he skied every morning with Andreas Heggener. He was surprised to see how much pleasure it gave him to see the man get stronger and stronger. While they still stayed away from the Black Knight, they ran all the other slopes, doing three, then four a morning, with Heggener moving more swiftly and with greater assurance every day.

On a clear, sunny morning, when they had done four runs and Michael had suggested that it was enough, Heggener had shaken his head and had said, "I'd like to do one more."

Michael hesitated, then said, "If you feel up to it . . ."

"No problem," Heggener said.

So they went up in the chair lift again. As they soared above the trees, Heggener said, "Have you noticed something?"

"I've noticed that you're really skiing," Michael said.

"Not that," said Heggener. "Haven't you noticed that not once today have I coughed? Last night I threw all my medicines away. It may be meaningless. But then again, it may not. And I've put on two pounds this week. That, too, may be meaningless and it may not."

They rode in silence. Michael was so moved that he didn't trust himself to say anything for a full minute. Then he said, softly, "Andreas, how do you say 'We are blessed' in German?"

"Why in German?" Heggener looked over at him, puzzled.

"It might mean more to you in your first language."

Heggener touched his arm lightly, in what might have been a gesture of appreciation or amusement. Then he said, quietly, *"Wir sind gesegnet."*

"Wir sind gesegnet," Michael repeated. He glanced across at Heggener. A single tear was running down the man's cheek.

"You are a delicate man," Heggener said. "Forgive me. I am growing old before my time. Old men weep."

Somehow, Michael thought, by luck, I have come to the right place at the right time.

⬦⬦⬦⬦⬦

A week later, Antoine was hopping around on his crutches with great agility and moved into the annex behind The Chimney Corner. Michael waited for a day when rain and a thaw made skiing impossible to move his own belongings into the cottage on the Heggener estate. Unluckily, it was the Saturday on which the first hang-gliding exhibition and the race for which Rita was entered were scheduled and both events had to be postponed. "I don't know whether to laugh or cry," Rita said when she heard the news about the race. "All week long I've had two different kinds of dreams. One about winning it and drinking champagne out of a big silver trophy cup. The other about falling at the first gate and hearing everybody in town laughing and laughing."

"Dreams're always extreme," Michael said. "The next time you dream, try to settle for something more moderate, like coming in fifth and having a Coke after it."

"It's funny you used that word," Rita said, soberly. "My father keeps saying that I don't know how to be moderate in anything. He thinks you're a bad influence on me."

"He does?" Michael said, surprised.

"Don't get me wrong," Rita said hastily. "He likes you, he thinks what you're doing for Mr. Heggener shows you have a big heart. But he says anybody who goes in for hang-gliding is a dangerous example for the young." She giggled. "You know, if Daddy ever took a vacation, I'd try it myself. There're a couple of houses in town where people I know live that I'd like to fly over and bombard."

"I know what you mean," Michael said, laughing.

"He's against my singing at The Chimney Corner, too. He says if I have a success, it'll turn my head, because I'm so young. My mother's for it, though. I get my voice from her and in church we sometimes sing duets together. My father grumbles, but he doesn't argue with my mother. Nobody does, not even Daddy. But he wants me to go to college in the autumn, like my brother, and study to become a lawyer. He says in this world you have to know your rights and being a lawyer you know how to get them. Even so, my mother's got him to agree to come to The Chimney Corner the first night I sing there."

"When will that be?"

"Next Saturday night. Antoine and I're working up a program. He sure knows his music, that one-legged Frenchman. You'd never guess it from talking to him, but he has an awful temper when you work with him and you don't do what he says."

"Is Mr. Davis paying you well?"

"I don't know what well is," Rita said. "They don't pay me *anything* at the church. Ten dollars a night, three nights a week. That's pretty good, isn't it?"

"Pretty good," Michael said, thinking, I'm going to have a little talk with that miserly saloonkeeper.

"I hate to see you leave, Michael," Rita said, as she walked with him to where the Porsche was standing, fully packed. "It won't be the same without you here. You treat everybody like a human being. A lot of the people we get never took human being lessons. You ought to hear what some of the help here have to say about some of the guests, people with their name in the paper all the time, leaders of society, as they say in the articles. It would turn your hair." She giggled again and waved as he started off.

Michael drove directly to the big house to announce his arrival. The house was built in a style that the architect must have imagined was like a Southern mansion, with tall white pillars going up to the second floor. It looked comfortable, but out of place in the harsh Vermont landscape. It was the first time Michael had gone there and he rang the front doorbell and waited. The door was opened by Andreas Heggener. Michael had called earlier to say that skiing was out of the question that morning and that he was moving to the cottage around eleven and Heggener had asked him to stop by the house and have a drink for luck with him.

"Come in, come in, neighbor," Heggener said. As usual, he was impeccably groomed and dressed, his white hair and beard carefully brushed, his face, which was now tanned, freshly shaved. He was wearing a collar and tie and a loose corduroy suit and his brown shoes were polished to a high, rich gleam. The seventy-year-old maid might be deaf and unable to understand any language but German, but she certainly knew how to polish shoes.

Heggener led Michael into the large living room, where one long wall from the floor to the high ceiling was devoted to books, with a librarian's ladder standing in front of the cases. A splendid faded old Persian carpet covered most of the floor and among the paintings on the walls there was a Kandinsky and a Kokoschka. Michael's trips to the galleries and museums with Tracy enabled him to recognize the painters, but all he said was "What a nice room," because he didn't want Heggener to think that he had any pretenses as a connoisseur of art.

There was a table set up for backgammon, with two high-backed wooden chairs on each side of it, in front of the French windows that gave onto the red-bricked porch and the row of white pillars. The room was uncluttered and sparingly furnished and gave evidence of Eva's meticulous sense of order.

When I am his age, Michael thought, I would like to live in a room like this. But not now.

"Eleven o'clock," Heggener said. "What should our pleasure be at this time of the morning? Would you object to a Bloody Mary?"

"Not strenuously," Michael said. Heggener went over to a sideboard, where there were bottles and glasses, an ice bucket and a silver pitcher filled with tomato juice. Michael watched as Heggener poured the vodka over ice cubes in a glass shaker, then added the rest of the ingredients. His movements were deft and precise and he obviously enjoyed bartending. He fixed a silver cap over the shaker and shook the mixture briefly, then poured the drinks into two large-bowled wine glasses. He gave one to Michael and lifted his own. *"Prost,"* he said, "my German-speaking friend."

"Prost," Michael said.

"Ah," Heggener said, after the first sip. "The perfect thing for eleven o'clock. Eva thinks it is a barbaric drink, but I have begun to grow a bit tired of her Austrian wine."

It was the first time Heggener had said even one mild word of criticism of his wife to Michael. "She's in town, at the veterinary's," Heggener said. "Bruno needs some sort of shot. But this is a little gift from both of us, to keep you company in case you get lonely in your little cottage." He picked a box with a quart bottle of Johnnie Walker Black Label in it off the sideboard and handed it ceremoniously to Michael.

"Thanks," Michael said, putting the box down on a library table behind one of the sofas. "It might just come in handy on a cold night."

"Sit down, sit down," Heggener said and went over to the backgammon table. He sat in one of the wooden chairs and motioned to Michael to seat himself in the other. "I like to sit here and look out," Heggener said. "The view is pleasant, even on a nasty morning like this." He cleared his throat, as though preparing to make an announcement. "I understand," he said formally, "that Eva has been trying to prevail upon you to stop our skiing together."

"She has mentioned it once or twice."

"So she tells me." Heggener sipped at his drink. "I trust that our— ah—divergence of opinion—has not made you uncomfortable."

"If I thought it was doing you any harm, I'd tell you so," Michael said.

"She is a determined woman," Heggener said, "and is used to having her way. But she has an absurd faith in doctors. A faith that I have given up for some years now. I doubt even that Bruno needs the shot that the veterinary is inflicting upon him at this moment." He chuckled. "Oh, I almost forgot to give you the key to the cottage." He fumbled briefly in the side pocket of his coat and took out a heavy iron key. He weighed it in his hand and smiled. "It must be at least a hundred years old. In an emergency you might even use it as a weapon." He gave it to Michael. "Will one key do you?"

"Until I lose it," Michael said. He was sure that another key existed and that Eva had it.

"I may not be able to ski with you next week, Michael."

"I'll miss our mornings together."

"It's polite of you to say so. Eva is insisting that I go to New York to the Columbia Presbyterian Hospital for a series of tests. There is a doctor there that she has heard of . . ." He shrugged. "There is always a doctor she has heard of," he said, and there was a note of weariness in his voice. "We had the worst scene of our marriage the night I threw away all my medicines. She accused me—and I'm afraid, you—of shortening my life. I tell you this because I don't want you to be surprised if she turns on you."

"Thank you," Michael said. He didn't say that nothing that Eva would do or say could surprise him.

"I have not yet given in. But in the end—for the sake of peace . . ." He left the sentence unfinished. "But, on the brighter side, it will give you more time to ski with that beautiful Miss Hartley. It's amazing that she isn't married. A young lady as pretty and delightful as that."

"She prizes her freedom."

Heggener nodded. "It is a state that one can overvalue. It is the old saying—giving up the good in the search of the best. You, I understand, are still married. I'm not prying, am I?" he said hastily.

"Of course not. As far as I know," Michael said, "my marriage is public knowledge. We've been separated for quite some time."

"Am I wrong in feeling that you miss her?"

"No," Michael said slowly, "you're not wrong."

"If it's painful for you to speak about it, we can talk of other things."

"She demanded that I give up something it was impossible for me to give up," Michael said. He knew so much about the man opposite him who was now his friend and his responsibility that it seemed to him only justice that Heggener should know more about him. "Somewhat as your wife thinks about you, she thought that I was shortening my life. It all started on our honeymoon, when I took a bad fall in a ski race because I was skiing above my talent, taking risks . . ." It was coming out in a gush now, in a relief from pressure that had been building up ever since he had left Tracy. "And she had the bad luck to be on the spot when I was doing some skydiving with friends and two of them were killed. I don't blame her and I suppose you don't blame Eva, but she was asking me to give up just those moments that made me feel that life was worth living. If I had given in and had stayed with her our marriage eventually would have been worse than any divorce."

"Everyone to his own destructive necessary passions," Heggener said. "Yours, mine, Eva's, your wife's. We live by them, we die by them. We are understood and misunderstood by them. When we believe we are shouting, we are screaming soundlessly, as we do in dreams. My dream is a young wife, whom I can no longer serve, except as a refuge. In our day, we like to believe that we can explain all behavior—sane, insane, almost sane. In the case of the gay and high-spirited young woman I married, there were explanations—although it was years before I learned them. But after the first manifestation—she left me and disappeared entirely for two months—I consulted with her father, who by the way is an old rascal and not to be trusted at any time. He told me Eva's mother had committed suicide, as had her brother. That much, at least, I found to be true. The father also told me that as a child, when Eva was denied anything, no matter how trivial or impossible, she would fall into convulsions or merely run away from home until she was brought back by the police. Genes, I'm afraid, play their role in all this, but it is difficult to know what the role actually is or the moment when a particular gene is triggered into disastrous action. There are long periods when Eva is serene—over-controlled, the pressure building up silently and secretly. They are periods of peace and beauty. But she is always poised for flight, as she was as a child. And if she escapes, I know she will be destroyed and I fear I will be destroyed along with her. If I were an honest man I would have counseled you to leave the first night I talked to you. Eva is again on the verge of madness. Verge is the wrong word. She slips across the border, slips back. I use what measures I can to hold her. Psychiatrists, clinics that are too expensive to be called by their correct name—asylums. You are this year's measure, my poor friend. I am selfish. I should tell you to get into your car, which is neatly packed and standing outside the door, and drive off once and for all. But I will not. Perhaps you cannot save her, but I feel you are saving me. I did not summon you here, I cannot blame myself for that. But, providentially, you came. And for your own reasons, again providentially, you have elected to stay. So be it." He put down his glass on the backgammon board with a sharp, decisive click and stood up. "I would be most grateful if next week, when I will have to go to the hospital in New York, you would be good enough to drive me down."

"Of course," Michael said, standing.

"Oh," Heggener said matter-of-factly, "I nearly forgot. I told you I would show you where I keep my pistol." He went over to a fragile inlaid little writing desk near the door of the living room and pushed a small button that was almost undetectable on the side. A drawer slid out. He picked up the pistol from where it was lying on a soft piece of flannel. "Notice where the button is," he said. He held the pistol loosely in his hand. "It has no safety—the revolver—and it is fully loaded, so be most careful if by any chance you feel you must display it." He flipped the chambers and they revolved smoothly, oiled. "I am happy to say that it has never been fired. Eva, I must tell you, does not know of its existence." He put the weapon carefully into the drawer and snapped the drawer back into place. "It is the only weapon in the house," he said. "I am not an advocate of accidental duels by members of the same household. Oh, I almost forgot—knowing where the gun was wouldn't do you any good if you could not get into the house to use it. Come with me, please."

Michael followed him into the small library that adjoined the living room and watched while Heggener removed a small painting to uncover a wall safe. He twirled the combination and reached in and brought out another, smaller key. "The key to the front door," Heggener said, giving it to Michael. "Eva is uncharacteristically careless with keys, so I have taken to locking a spare one away." He closed the safe and put the painting back in place.

They went back into the living room and Heggener said, "Now don't forget your whiskey. And I hope our hospitality this winter will not prove to be too onerous." He made a little stiff bow and went out of the room, leaving Michael to find his way to the front door alone.

Michael was unpacking his bags in the cottage when the door opened and Eva came in without knocking. He had left the door open, with the key in the lock. He could hear the dog whining in the car outside. It was raining now and the rain was beating at the windows. Eva was wearing a red cape, with the hood up. She looked demure and rustically sensual, like a Watteau shepherdess, and certainly not mad. It occurred to him that perhaps Eva was not the mad one in the family, that it was the elegant, soft-spoken aging man, the confessed murderer in the white-pillared mansion with the concealed, loaded revolver, who was involving him in some cunning lunatic scheme and was even now chuckling to himself about how he had taken in a credulous and easily deceived stranger.

"I see you left the key in the lock," Eva said. "Were you expecting company?"

"You."

"I am under instructions from my husband to see to it that you have everything you need," Eva said, smiling. "Do you?"

"Yes, thank you."

"Aren't you missing something?"

"What could that be?"

"This, for example." She came up to him and kissed him, her mouth open, her tongue sliding over his. For a moment he stood rigidly, trying not to respond, remembering what Heggener had just told him, but the touch of her lips, the feel of her body against his made him forget or not care about anything else and he held her hard and ran his hands over her, under the cape, on the thin silk fabric of her blouse.

When she pulled away from him she was smiling, victorious. "You see, you did need something."

"Damn it, Eva," he said, shaken, "we shouldn't do this."

"Why not?" She took off her cape and threw it carelessly over the Victorian silk couch.

"Your husband is why not. If I had met him before I met you I'd never have . . ."

"You say that now. Anyway, my luck, you met me first."

"I like him," Michael said. "More than that. I admire him. His courage, his gentleness . . ."

"I admire him, too. But that's another department. You'll remember that, I hope. Another department. We have some very well-defined conditions in our marriage. You fit one of those conditions admirably. Shall I go in and see that the bed is made properly?" she asked, mischievously.

"Can't we wait for tonight?"

"There's nothing wrong with tonight. And nothing wrong with right now. Don't try my patience, Michael. I really should be offended at your lack of gallantry."

"There's nothing gallant about us," Michael said bitterly. "We fall on each other like two wild animals. We're not lovers, we're antagonists."

"Whatever you wish to call it, my dear," she said sweetly. She started toward the bedroom, but stopped, because there was a knock on the door.

Michael opened the door. Susan was standing there, carrying a big bowl with a large red-blossomed azalea plant in it. "I brought you a housewarming gift," she said as she came into the room and Michael closed the door behind her. "Although," she said, nodding politely and greeting Eva, "the house seems to be pretty warm already."

"Good morning, Miss Hartley," Eva said coldly. "That's a very pretty plant. Although in general I dislike azaleas. They hang on so long. One grows tired of looking at them."

"When Michael gets tired of looking at this one he has my permission to throw it out. I won't know—I'm leaving tomorrow."

"Yes," Eva said, "the manager told me. It's too bad you have such unpleasant weather for your last day here."

"Oh, I've done enough skiing and I'll be back."

"You will?" Eva said. "You must remember to call in time for reservations. We need ample warning. We're almost solidly booked until March."

"I'll remember, thank you," Susan said. She looked around the room. "What a charming little house. You're lucky to have found it, Michael. Don't you think you might offer the ladies a drink of welcome?"

"Sorry," Michael said. "Of course." He took the bottle of Johnnie Walker out of its box and opened it.

Susan sat down gracefully on the little sofa, pushing Eva's cape gently to one side to make room for herself. "No ice, please. Just a little water."

"I don't like whiskey," Eva said. "Don't you have some wine in the house, Michael?"

"I'm afraid not."

"I must tell the boys at the hotel to bring you a case," Eva said. The implication behind the remark was clear and the little smile that played around Susan's mouth told Michael she had caught it.

He went into the kitchen with the bottle of whiskey and poured a drink for Susan and one for himself and ran some water into them. When he returned to the living room, Eva was twisting the dial of the little radio on the desk. The room was filled with the crackling of static and the voice of an announcer over it, rising and then falling away. "It's almost impossible to get good reception in the mountains," she said and turned it off. "We have to make do with country amusements."

Eva's use of the English language often surprised Michael, as it did now, but he didn't show it as he gave Susan her drink and she touched glasses with him. "Michael," she said as she drank, "Antoine is giving me a farewell dinner tonight at The Chimney Corner. And of course you're invited. And you and your husband, too, madam."

"I'm afraid we're busy tonight, Miss Hartley," Eva said. "Please convey my thanks to Monsieur Ferré."

Susan finished her drink quickly. "Well, I must be pushing off. Congratulations again, Michael, on your cozy little nest. See you around eight. Good-bye, Mrs. Heggener. And thank you for how beautifully everybody at the hotel treated me. I look forward to coming back."

"I'm sure all the help will be pleased to see you again, Miss Hartley." There was just the slightest emphasis on the word "help."

Susan went out, supple and springy, and neither Michael nor Eva spoke until they heard the sound of her car driving off. Then Eva said, "There is only one rule in this house. You are not to entertain that lady here."

"In that case, thank you for everything and I'll find someplace else to live. I'm peculiar—I like to make my own rules." He began to throw the things he had just unpacked back into the open suitcase.

Eva watched him for a moment, then went over and held his arm. "All right, you bastard," she said. "No rules."

CHAPTER NINETEEN

The dinner at The Chimney Corner had been surprisingly good, refuting Jimmy Davis's low estimate of the food he served, and Susan was in high spirits, just a little tipsy and preparing for the city with green eye shadow, little circles of rouge on her cheekbones that made her look like a child's doll and a new streak of blond in her hair. The room was full and Antoine was playing marvelously, his eyes half-closed against his cigarette smoke so that he looked, bent over the keyboard and swaying with his music, as though he were in a religious trance. Just behind Michael's chair, Annabel Fenstock was sitting at the next table with a big young man by the name of Barlow, whom she had introduced to Michael the weekend before and who had not endeared himself to Michael when he had said, "You another member of the harem?" and had laughed loudly. Annabel's taste must be deteriorating, Michael had thought, or she's getting desperate, and had moved off.

With Antoine's playing and the hum of conversation in the room, Michael could not hear what Annabel and Barlow were saying, but he could tell by the tone that they were engaged in some sort of argument. Suddenly both of them stood up, Annabel's chair rapping against Michael's, and they started out. Michael could see that Barlow was gripping Annabel's arm, hard, and that she was in pain, but she made no sound as they went out of the restaurant together. Michael gave it a few seconds, then said to Susan, "Excuse me for a moment, I need a little fresh air." Then, as quickly as he could without getting attention, he followed the couple. As he went out of the door into the snowy night, he saw them standing a few feet away, Barlow still gripping Annabel's arm and Annabel squirming, trying to pull away. "What's the matter with me," the man was saying loudly, almost shouting. "You put out for everybody else in this bullshit town, you little cock-teasing whore, why not me?" Then he hit her with his fist and released her and she fell to her knees on the snow-covered pavement.

"You son of a bitch," Michael said quietly. "Get out of here and stay out of here." He moved to help Annabel, who by now was unsteadily trying to stand.

"Who's going to make me get out of here?" Barlow said, his face livid and contorted in the light of a street lamp.

"I am," Michael said, as he helped Annabel to her feet.

"You and who else?" Barlow said. "You come near me and this is waiting for you, brother." He put his hand to his breast pocket and half-drew a knife from it, just enough so that it caught the gleam from the street lamp.

Without thinking, exultantly, as Annabel screamed, Michael leapt at Barlow, swinging his right hand with all his power at the hateful, leering face, feeling the beautiful shock go up from his fist through his arm and entire body as the punch landed on the man's jaw. Barlow swayed and went down face first, blood spurting all over the snow. Michael turned him over, as he groaned wordlessly, and took the knife from his pocket. He threw it as far as he could, over the roof of The Chimney Corner. Then he put his arm comfortingly around Annabel and said, "That's all right, darling. He won't bother you anymore. I've just scored the first and only knockout of my career. Come on, I'll take you home."

He led her to his car and drove her home. She seemed to have recovered completely and insisted that he needn't come in and promised to telephone him at The Chimney Corner if Barlow made any further trouble.

But an hour later, Norman Brewster, in uniform and with a worried look on his face, came into the restaurant and over to the table and said, in a low voice, "Mr. Storrs, can I talk to you for a minute outside? And better take your coat. This place'll probably be closed by the time you can come back."

"I have to go, Susan," Michael said. "See you before you leave in the morning."

"Is anything wrong, Michael?" Susan asked worriedly.

"Probably a parking ticket I forgot to pay," Michael said, taking his coat off the rack and following Norman Brewster through the crowd of tables, conscious that people were looking curiously at the two of them.

Outside, Michael said, "Wait a minute, Norman. What's up?"

"Man came in about an hour ago," Brewster said. "I drew night duty this week—he could hardly talk, a mouth full of loose teeth and bleeding like a stuck pig and said you'd assaulted him. Fred took him to Doctor Baines and he just called in to say that the guy's jaw is broken in four places and he's going to lose at least five front teeth."

"For Christ's sake, Norman," Michael said, "I only hit him once."

"That musta been some once. I didn't know you were a fighter, along with everything else," Brewster said, admiration plain in his voice. "But I better get a report from you, too. The guy kept saying, 'The sonofabitch—' he meant you—'the sonofabitch is in for a load of trouble.'"

Michael followed the policeman to the station, which was just around the corner. The rain had turned to heavy snow at dusk and Brewster said, "Ought to be pretty good skiing tomorrow." Having lived all his life in a place that depended upon snow for its livelihood he would probably make the same remark to a murderer he was conducting to the gallows in a snowstorm.

In the station, Michael said hello to Henry, who seemed drunker than ever behind the high desk and who smiled when he saw Michael and said, "Assault and battery. Naughty, naughty."

Norman Brewster sat at a desk with an old typewriter on it and slowly pecked out his report as he listened to Michael's account of the incident. "Okay," Brewster said, "you say he hit the lady and he says it was unprovoked and you say he had a knife—Godalmighty, are you crazy enough to go after a man with a knife on him? Where's the knife now?"

"I threw it over the roof of The Chimney Corner."

Brewster shook his head. "You ought to know better than to destroy evidence. You'd a done better if you'd a come right down here with the lady and the knife right off."

"Good God, Norman," Michael said. "It was just an ordinary little Saturday night fight outside a bar. It's not a massacre, for heaven's sake."

"Even if we find the knife, and there's a good chance we won't,"

Brewster said, "there's no real way we can pin it on him. Knives aren't registered or anything like that although it might be a good idea if they were. And you say the lady was down on the ground and maybe she didn't see it and even if she did she was in a dazed condition according to you and she's your friend and you could influence her . . ."

"Norman," Michael said, irritated, "you should have been a lawyer, not a cop."

"I'm too dumb to be a lawyer," Brewster said honestly. "I'm lucky to've passed the exam to be a cop. And I'm just trying to help you in case the guy really wants to start trouble." He pushed the typewriter away from him a little, as though the sight of it hurt him. "Anyway—I'm releasing you on your own recognizance."

"You mean to say you were thinking of arresting me?" Michael asked angrily.

"If I didn't know you and where you lived and all that, I'd have to, Mr. Storrs. Don't be sore at *me,* for Christ's sake, *I* didn't bust anybody's jaw tonight."

As Michael went out through the front door, Henry, who had been dozing, opened one eye and said, "Thug, mugger, speeder, breaker of the peace, unwelcome element," and cackled.

By the following Wednesday, Michael had almost forgotten the incident. He had made a desultory search for the knife behind The Chimney Corner, but the snow was piled high there, with new snow coming down, and Davis used the yard for old crates and cartons and broken bottles and it would have taken a platoon of Army Engineers to find anything there. He called Annabel on Sunday morning to find out if she was all right and she sounded cheerful and relaxed and said she had had a good night's sleep. She, at least, was taking what had happened lightly. A good deal more lightly, Michael thought resentfully, than Norman Brewster.

By Monday morning, the weather had cleared and turned cold and he skied with Heggener, with both of them avoiding speaking of their conversation over the Bloody Marys on Saturday morning. Heggener skied so well in the new powder and enjoyed it so much that he said, come what may, he was going to get Eva to permit him to postpone the visit to the hospital in New York until the weather turned bad again.

In the afternoons, Michael skied with Eva, and she, too, seemed to be enjoying the sport so much that when she spoke to him he thought he detected a new note of almost affection in her voice. He spoke neither to them nor to Antoine about what had happened on Saturday night.

But on Wednesday morning, as he was about to leave the cottage, there was a loud rapping of the iron knocker on the door. When he opened it, a man dressed in city clothes asked him politely, "Are you Mr. Michael Storrs?"

"I am."

"I have something for you, sir," the man said. He produced a folded set of white papers and thrust them into Michael's hand.

"What is this?" Michael said, staring stupidly down at the papers in his hand.

"A summons. Good day, sir." The man about-faced and walked smartly away.

Michael looked through the papers. It was a summons to appear before a judge in Montpelier in a civil suit for damages of fifty thousand dollars brought by one Clyde Barlow, the victim of unprovoked and dangerous assault by the aforesaid Michael Storrs, causing grievous bodily harm to the plaintiff.

Michael called Heggener at the big house and told him that he was sorry but he had business to attend to and there wouldn't be any skiing today. He asked him to tell that to Eva, too, then called Herb Ellsworth and asked to see him in his office.

"I guess I need a lawyer," Michael said, after he had told Ellsworth the whole story.

"I guess you do," Ellsworth said. "Fifty thousand dollars! Just for a sock on the jaw! People don't care what they ask for these days." He examined the summons that Michael had given him with repugnance. "You wonder what we pay the cops for. They still haven't found my truck. Well, for *my* money, the best guy for you in town is old Harry Lancaster. He's honest and he doesn't charge an arm and a leg like some of these smart aleck young guys. I don't know this law firm in Montpelier." He tapped the summons gingerly, as though it might jump up and bite him. "Four names. I hate to do business with a law firm with four names. I got to warn you, Mike, the lady's reputation isn't going to do you much good in court."

"What's that got to do with a man hitting her and pulling a knife on me?"

"What's anything got to do with anything once the lawyers start on you? You want me to call old Harry for you?"

"Please."

Ellsworth put in the call, chatted in a neighborly way for a minute or two, then told the lawyer that a good friend of his, Michael Storrs, was in a bit of trouble and might need some help. He nodded at the man's reply and put down the phone. "He's waiting for you. His office is over the bank."

"Thanks." Michael stood up.

"I'll have two or three of my men go looking for that knife," Ellsworth said. "Though probably some kid has picked it up by now and is practicing the art of mugging with it in the schoolyard." He looked up quizzically at Michael. "By the way, if it's not too personal a question, do you *have* fifty thousand dollars?"

"Just about," Michael said.

"Hang onto it," Ellsworth said and stood up and shook Michael's hand.

Harry Lancaster looked to be about seventy years old. He had a babyish rosy complexion and bushy white eyebrows that loomed over his bifocal glasses and only a few wisps of hair stretched over his balding pink skull and he was fat and worked in suspenders and shirt-sleeves at a desk that was piled every which way with papers. He also smoked cigars, and the small room over the bank, with framed diplomas that looked as though they had been earned sometime in the middle of the eighteenth century, was blue with smoke.

He did not fill Michael with optimism. All he said was "This firm representing the plaintiff is aggressive, very aggressive." He said it as though he thought being aggressive was a major virtue for a law firm. He sighed, smoke pouring from him. "You made certain mistakes, of course," he said.

"That's what the police told me."

"It says in the complaint that you stomped the man while he was lying on the ground."

"I never stomped anybody in my life."

The lawyer sighed again. "You have no marks, bruises of any

kind, to bear evidence that it was in fact a fight and not a one-sided assault?"

"I hit him before he could use the knife on me," Michael said, exasperated. "What should I have done—waited until he'd stabbed me?"

"It is always advisable to have witnesses . . ."

"Next time," Michael said sarcastically, "I'll hire Madison Square Garden when somebody draws a knife on me."

The old man looked at him shrewdly through the cloud of tobacco smoke. "You will only hurt your case if you permit yourself to get angry, Mr. Storrs."

"Sorry," Michael said.

"Herb Ellsworth called me again after you had left him," the lawyer said. "He wanted to fill me in with some background matter on the lady who will have to serve as your only witness. Mr. Storrs, I'm afraid I must be frank. The opposing lawyers will delve into her past, accumulate data about her reputation in town, the estimate of her character by her neighbors. If what Mr. Ellsworth has told me is even partially true, an aggressive lawyer could make mincemeat of a judge's or jury's estimate of her reliability. It is sad, unjust perhaps, that while using violence to protect the honor of a virgin brings with it many intangible elements of extenuating circumstances, the same force applied to the protection of a—shall we say—a self-admitted modern woman of the world—against a perhaps too ardent suitor— You do get my drift, don't you, Mr. Storrs?"

"You mean it's going to cost me some money."

"Very likely, sir. Not fifty thousand. After all, this is Vermont, not New York or California. But some. In any event I would be on surer ground after I had a word or two with the lady. The sooner the better."

"I'll call on her and see if she wants to talk to you."

"That would be wise, sir, before we proceed any further. In the meantime I'll get in touch with the plaintiff's lawyers and let you know what the situation is."

"Thank you, Mr. Lancaster," Michael said.

The old man was shuffling papers back and forth across his desk as Michael went out, his eyes smarting from cigar smoke.

◇◇◇◇◇

"Oh, dear," Annabel said, as they sat in the living room of her house, drinking coffee, "what a mess I got you into. I'm terribly sorry. But the truth is I didn't see anything of what happened. I was practically unconscious and I couldn't honestly say I remember I ever saw a knife. . . . I would like to help, of course, in any way I can, but . . ."

"There's something else, I'm afraid," Michael said. "Something the lawyer brought up. Something rather ugly."

"About me?"

Michael nodded. "If you're a witness, my lawyer says the other side will go into your history, your reputation in the town . . ."

Annabel put up her hand. "Enough said. I can see it now. Town bang's honor defended by heroic ski teacher. Columns of names of gentlemen who have enjoyed the lady's favor, select list of eminent gentlemen, nationally known politicians, Olympic skiers, movie actors, children in high school . . ."

"That's enough. Don't torture yourself."

"To say nothing," Annabel went on, "of the epidemic of divorce actions, ranging from Quebec to Palm Beach, as irate and alimony-conscious wives learn of mates' dalliances in the frozen North."

"Forget it," Michael said, standing up. "We'll get along without you."

"I'm sorry, Michael." Annabel stood, too. "I just couldn't go through with it."

"I understand." He kissed her cheek.

"Boy, oh, boy," she said, "have the chickens ever come home to roost! You know, Michael, I think the time has come for me to move. I've had enough of this town and the town has had enough of me." She smiled wanly. "Maybe I'll be taking up Eastern religions a little sooner than I had planned."

He stopped in front of The Chimney Corner, which was just opening for lunch. On a chance, he went through the restaurant and out the back door to the yard, to see if he could find the knife he had thrown over the roof. Jimmy Davis and two men from Ellsworth's company were digging with shovels and sorting through the piled junk. For once Davis didn't look cheerful. "Herb Ellsworth called and told me what happened Saturday night," Davis said, "and that you have a law case on your hands. We haven't found the knife yet and we probably never will, but even if we did I don't think it'd help you all that much, anyway. But I've got another angle. You got a minute?"

"All day," Michael said.

"Come on inside." Davis led him into the little office off the kitchen and closed the door. Davis produced a bottle of bourbon and they each took a shot, neat. "I know something about that guy Barlow," Davis said, "that might come in handy, if it gets too sticky in Montpelier. The guy's a pusher . . ."

"A what?"

"He peddles dope. Marijuana, heroin, cocaine. You name it, he supplies it. We put the narcs on his trail and they nail him, he won't look like a little innocent lamb when he has to stand up in court."

"Give me a little more booze," Michael said. He wanted time to think and he drank slowly. "If he finds out who turned him in," he said quietly, "and most cases they do, he and his friends'd be coming after you."

"Possibly."

"Those fellas play rough."

"I know."

"I don't think they'd have any trouble finding another knife, Jimmy."

Davis shrugged. "I'll play that by ear."

"I don't want them to find you dead in an alley just because of me."

"When you keep a saloon," Davis said, "there are certain little risks you have to take. You say the word and I'll go over to the Feds in Montpelier and tell all. In fact, come to think of it, whether you say the word or not, I'm going over to Montpelier when the time is ripe." He said this defiantly, almost angrily, as though Michael were trying to deprive him of a project dear to his heart.

"You know, Jimmy," Michael said gently, "you're a pretty sturdy friend."

"Opinions vary," Davis said offhandedly.

"What's on the menu for lunch?"

"Lamb stew."

"That's just what I want for lunch today," Michael said, "lamb stew. Bland and simple."

"You need any dough?"

"Maybe something in the neighborhood of fifty thousand."

Davis grinned. "Put me down for five hundred," he said.

Antoine was at the piano at the far end of the bar, near the chimney, fooling idly with sad, long, disconnected chords. When he saw Michael come in, he got up from the piano and hobbled over on his walking cast and sat down opposite him. He didn't look as melancholy as he usually did. "I didn't know that you'd turned into a daytime drinker," he said.

"I came for lunch. Join me?"

Antoine made a face. "I just got up a half-hour ago. I'd still be asleep if those guys weren't making such a racket in the backyard. What're they looking for—buried treasure?"

"Something of the kind. I'll have the lunch, miss," he said to the waitress.

"Coffee, please," Antoine said. "Black."

"How's it going?"

Antoine's face brightened. "Things're looking up. I bared my heart to Davis and he's been talking to people and he says he's pretty sure he'll get the Immigration to give me a green card and a work permit in a couple of weeks. He's got connections everywhere, Jimmy. He's not much on paying, but he's great on connections."

"That's the best news I've heard in a long time," Michael said as he began on the soup the waitress put before him.

"Soon as I get the card, I'm off and running," Antoine said, blowing on his steaming black coffee. "I don't mind playing here, although the bunch of kids you get in here isn't what you'd call an ideal audience for a man of my caliber. And I'm getting itchy. I'm not a small-town boy. I'm a big-city man. And Green Hollow isn't even any Mégève, by a long, long shot."

"You owe a lot to Davis," Michael said, disappointed in his friend. "You might at least last out the season."

"I've got to think of my future, Mike," Antoine said. "The cast'll be off in two weeks or so and then it's New York, here I come. There was a *mec* in here last night, diamond rings on his fingers and wearing a cashmere jacket that must have cost him eight hundred dollars and it turns out he owns a classy *boîte* on the East Side and he gave me his card and told me to come and see him soon, he likes my style, and he says he'll give me an engagement."

"Congratulations," Michael said sourly, remembering what Susan had told him about Antoine. "It's too bad," he said, "that rascals are more likely to be fun than honest burghers."

"What are you talking about, *mon vieux?*" Antoine asked defensively.

"You," Michael said.

"I warned you once I had a deplorable character, didn't I?"

"You certainly did," Michael said, starting in on the lamb stew as Antoine got another cup of coffee.

"You thought I was joking," Antoine said, "I wasn't joking."

"I see you weren't."

"Good people find it hard to understand bad ones," Antoine said gently. "And strong people have no patience with weak ones. You must remember not to confuse talent with virtue, my friend."

"I'll remember," Michael said.

"Now on to more pleasant things," Antoine said. "You coming on Saturday night? The kid—Rita—is making her debut."

"How is she coming?"

Antoine scowled into his coffee. "She's awfully stiff and shy," he said. "Then I had a brainstorm. I gave her a joint and she loosened up like a cloudburst. She sang like a forest full of birds. They'll eat her up on Saturday night."

"You mean to say you made that kid high on marijuana?"

"High as a kite. She was wonderful."

"If her father finds out he'll kill you," Michael said. "And if he doesn't, I will, or at least break all your fingers."

"Michael," Antoine said plaintively, "you're talking to your old friend, Antoine. Every jazz musician you've ever liked has used the stuff, if not a lot worse things. How many times have you and I smoked a joint together, *mon Dieu!*"

"I'm not a sixteen-year-old child. I'm not kidding. I'll break your own piano stool over your head if you do anything like that again."

"Okay, okay," Antoine said gloomily. "She'll be a total bust, I warn you."

"Then she'll be a total bust. Though I don't think so."

"New England has gotten to you," Antoine said despondently. "You've turned Puritan."

"A little streak of Puritan wouldn't do you irreparable harm, either," Michael said. He pushed away from the table, although he had eaten only half his lamb stew. "I'm getting out of here."

He left Antoine shaking his head disbelievingly at the table.

What a day, Michael thought as he got into his car, what a miserable, fucking day.

He drove to the cottage and put on his ski clothes. There was still time to take Eva out, but today he wanted to ski alone. What he needed today was the mountains and speed and solitude.

When he got to the top of the lift, he traversed over to the top of the Black Knight. He stopped and looked down it. It fell away, steep, slick, with big moguls, to the line of trees where the sharp turn to the left led to the trail through the woods. There was nobody on the slope. He would have it to himself. He adjusted his goggles, took a deep breath, and skated off with his skis glued together, gathered speed, flew over the bumps in a straight line, the wind tearing at his cap and goggles. His legs began to ache halfway down and he had to remember to make himself breathe, but he schussed the whole slope, nearly being hurled backward on a big icy bump just a few yards from the line of trees, righted himself triumphantly, his muscles screaming, and swung, with a bone-wrenching effort, at the turn and shot into the trail between the trees. Out of control, he just managed by inches to sweep past the big boulder in the middle of the trail. Coming full blast onto the open field, he nearly slammed into a class that was lined up diagonally across the slope. He swerved, dug in his edges and came to a stop just above Dave Cully, who was teaching the class.

Gasping, he grinned down at Cully.

"Good God, Mike," Cully said, recognizing him. "You could have killed somebody. Especially yourself."

"I needed to blow the body out," Michael said. "As they say at the track."

"This isn't the track," Cully growled. Then in a loud voice, he addressed his class. "Ladies and gentlemen, you have just had an educational experience, put on by one of the less sensible of our sterling band of instructors, on how *not* to take this run."

There was a little titter from the line of skiers and Michael waved good-naturedly at them. "I was letting a little light into my soul, Dave," he said.

"Next time you have to let a little light into your soul, let me know. I'll clear every slope. You take this class. I want to get back to the office. And I expect you to make one thousand slow, absolutely controlled turns with them between here and the bottom of the lift."

"Yes, sir," Michael said cheerfully.

Cully skied off, ostentatiously careful.

"You heard what the man said, ladies and gentlemen," Michael said loudly. "We are to make one thousand slow, absolutely controlled turns. Let us make one in single file and stop. Then we will only have nine hundred and ninety-nine others to make before dark."

And it was almost dark by the time they got to the bottom and Michael was humming cheerily as he took off his skis and carried them to his car.

CHAPTER
TWENTY

The next morning he was still in a good mood when he took Heggener up the mountain. On the way up Heggener said, "Eva has kindly agreed to let me wait until next Wednesday before going to New York. Do you think you can take me down? I don't like to drive alone and I find driving tiring. Eva has offered to go with me, but it would mean a long argument on medical matters all the way, which tires me even more than driving."

"Of course," Michael said.

The skiing was good and Heggener seemed inexhaustible, his color high, a small, pleased smile on his lips when he stopped. It seemed foolish to Michael that a man who looked so formidably hale should have to go into a hospital, but he said nothing to Heggener.

"Ah, that was a nice morning," Heggener said, as they drove up to the big house. "It will help to get me through all those doctors' hands —at least for a day or two."

Eva was waiting for Michael and said she wanted to skip lunch and take advantage of the good snow and the sunlight, so Michael and she went right off, leaving Heggener standing between two of the white pillars, waving amiably at them.

They spoke very little while they were on the hill, but concentrated on whipping around other, slower skiers and working on technique. If it were always like this, Michael thought, I'd stay on here forever.

In the middle of the afternoon Eva said she'd like something to eat and they went into the lodge and had a sandwich and tea.

"Michael," Eva said, pouring her tea, "I heard you got yourself into trouble Saturday night."

"Who told you?"

She shrugged. "It's a small town. News gets around. I must say, your taste in the ladies you choose to do battle for is—shall we say—somewhat curious?"

"She's an old friend."

"So I've heard. She has many old friends. The town bang."

"Don't be a bitch, Eva," Michael said, his voice low so that the young people at the next table couldn't overhear him.

"Andreas is an old friend, too," Eva said sweetly. "Did you know that?"

"I don't believe you."

"Ask him," Eva said. "I imagine it is a pleasant memory for him. It was his last old friend. He had already announced he could no longer sleep with me. His disease must have already hit him, although we didn't know it at the time. The lady was not the sort that I would have thought attracted him, but as I said, it's a small town and the choices are limited. And perhaps he wanted to prove something that he no longer could prove to me. That for one last time he could tell himself he was potent. In a way, I don't blame the poor man."

Michael remembered the two nights, one with the physiotherapist he had met at The Golden Hoop and the other with the old, nice girl, when he, too, had tried to prove something and had failed, and pitied his friend Andreas Heggener and hated Andreas Heggener's wife for knowing so much about men.

"Let's not talk about it, if you don't mind," he said. "I'm not interested in what went on here before I came on the scene."

"And what are you interested in now, may I ask?" Eva said, crunching healthily into her sandwich.

"Your husband," he said. "At the risk of boring you or making you angry at me, I think I must tell you once more that I think you're wrong in insisting that Andreas go into the hospital."

"I hope you haven't told him that."

"I haven't. But he looks so well—and he skis like a boy of twenty."

"Michael," Eva said sharply, "you don't know the harm you're doing."

"Harm?" he said incredulously. "He's getting stronger every day."

"He *thinks* he's getting stronger. And you're encouraging him. He's beginning to hope again."

"What's wrong with that?"

"The hope is false," Eva said dogmatically. "When he has a relapse, which can be any time now, it will shatter him. And you'll be responsible."

"What do you want me to do—tell a man who's just beginning to reach out to life again that he's living a dream, that he must just sit wrapped up in blankets and wait to die?"

"Obviously," Eva said ironically, "you know better than all the doctors."

"Maybe I do," Michael said stubbornly.

"If you won't do it for him, do it for me."

She was exasperating him with her tenaciousness, her serene belief that only she could possibly be in the right.

"We have a certain arrangement," Michael said, brutally. "I ski with you for pay and make love to you for pleasure. There's nothing else in the contract."

"You know," she said thoughtfully, refusing to be insulted, "I believe you have an ulterior motive."

"What ulterior motive?"

"You're deliberately trying to shorten his life."

"Oh, my God! Why would I want to do that?"

"To reap the rewards," she said calmly.

"What rewards?"

"Me," she said. "The rich widow, who is passionately attached to you, or at least to your useful body, and who would, after a decent interval, be delighted to marry you."

"Is that what you think?" he asked, controlling his fury.

"I think that it is a possibility," she said flatly. "If not a probability."

He stood up. "The fun is over for the day. Come. I'll drive you home."

"No need," she said. "I'm enjoying the afternoon. I'll continue skiing. Don't worry about me, I'll find somebody to drive me home."

He strode out of the room. Demented, he thought, demented. The man is right. I should leave this town right now. But the thought of never having that soft, practiced Viennese body in his arms again was intolerable and he knew he would not leave. I was happier when

I was impotent, he thought and laughed bitterly, aloud, as he hurled his poles and gloves into the back of the Porsche.

◇◇◇◇◇

The Saturday of the race was raw and windy, but the visibility was good and the course in perfect condition. Andreas Heggener was there to see the race, although, as he told Michael as they drove to the bottom of the course, Eva had objected strenuously, on the grounds that standing around for an hour or so in the cold would be bad for him. But he was bundled up in his black mink-collared coat and had on a fur hat and a long wool scarf and fleece-lined after-ski boots and warm gloves. "The little girl—Rita," he said, "was so excited about it yesterday evening and about singing tonight, I had to tell her I was coming to cheer her on in both events. And I gave her a little Austrian locket on a gold chain that used to belong to my mother and she's going to wear it around her neck as a good luck charm."

"She'll calm down once she gets going in the race," Michael said. "She should be able to handle that course easily. Cully told me he wasn't going to make it too demanding and they've been working on it and flattening the bumps."

There was quite a crowd of gaily dressed onlookers, the ones, like Michael and Heggener, who were not on skis, at the finish line, and people on skis lining the course. Michael kept looking up at the scudding clouds. He was entered in the hang-gliding exhibition that afternoon and the wind would make it dicey, if it didn't have to be canceled completely.

The forerunner came down, a young ski instructor, moving easily through the gates and there was a hush of expectation and then shouts of encouragement from up the hill as the first racer started down.

Michael looked at the mimeographed program. Rita was listed as the tenth racer to start, a good position, with the course just nicely marked by the preceding skiers and not too rutted, as it would be for the thirty-five skiers behind her.

"She told me," Heggener said, "that she had forbidden any of her family to watch the race, she was nervous enough as it is. By the way, Michael, how good were you when you raced?"

"I never raced seriously," Michael said, "just town things like this.

And I never came in better than fifth. These kids are born with skis on their feet. I started when I was twelve and already that's too late. Or maybe," he laughed, "that's the excuse I gave myself for my lack of talent." He watched intently as the girls came down. "She's going to have to take some chances to beat at least three of the first seven," he said and he began to worry, then was amused with himself that he was taking it so seriously.

The ninth girl finished in very good time and smiled happily when it was announced over the loud speaker system. Then there were the shouts and cheers as Rita started from the top of the hill, which could not be seen from where Michael and Heggener were standing.

She burst into view, skiing very well, her time, Michael guessed, among the best for that particular point. She looked graceful and sure of herself and gave an incongruous impression of strength, with her long slender legs and flat skinny torso. Michael found himself coaching her under his breath. Then, at the next to the last gate, she caught her ski on the outside pole and flipped and rolled and landed in an explosion of snow, one of her skis coming off, at the feet of the spectators on the side of the course. She shook off the people who tried to help her up, to indicate that she wasn't hurt, and picked up the ski that had come off and came down on one ski to where Michael and Heggener were standing. As she approached, Michael saw that she was crying.

"There, there," he said and put his arms around her, so that she could hide her tears against his shoulder. "There never has been a racer who hasn't fallen from time to time."

"I'm so *clumsy,*" she sobbed. "Eliot was right. He said I'd make a fool of myself."

"It's only the first time. And you didn't make a fool of yourself."

"My first and last time," the girl said. She pulled away from him and brushed the tears from her eyes. She tried to smile bravely at Heggener. "I'm sorry, Mr. Heggener. I didn't bring much honor to your locket."

"You were doing very well until you . . ." Heggener said.

"Until I did very badly," Rita said. "If you see Antoine, Michael, tell him I'm not going to sing tonight, either."

"Nonsense," Michael said sharply.

"Everybody'll laugh when I stand up at the piano. They'll wait for me to fall on my bottom there, too."

"Listen, Rita," Michael said seriously, "you can't quit *anything* at the age of sixteen. And Antoine is sure you're going to be wonderful," he lied, "and you will be."

"He told you that?" she said doubtfully.

"Absolutely. And he's a real pro."

"Mr. Swanson said I'd do great in the race, too," Rita said, "and he's a real pro, also."

"There are no gates at The Chimney Corner," Michael said.

Rita giggled. "I guess you're right. I can't go all my life being a scaredy little baby. My mother says, Just pretend you're in church and you'll have no trouble."

"I guess," Heggener said, "the locket does not really work out in the open, Rita. But it is magic in bars."

"We'll see how magic it is," Rita said. "I hate to disappoint people who've been so nice to me. If I flop tonight too I want to die."

"You won't flop and you don't want to die," Michael said. "Don't talk like that."

Just then, at the same gate at which Rita had fallen, the fifteenth girl fell ingloriously.

"Ah," Rita said, with satisfaction, "that makes me feel better."

"Spoken like a true sportswoman," Heggener said.

She giggled again and said, "Aren't I terrible?"

"Michael," Heggener said, "I am beginning to feel a little cold. Would you mind driving me home?"

"Of course not." He blew a kiss to Rita, who was taking off her other ski, and went to the car with Heggener.

After lunch, Michael drove to the hang-gliding school in the valley. The wind was still bad but had abated somewhat, and Michael decided it was manageable. There were about twelve young men, all very much of the same mold and manner as Jerry Williams, the proprietor of the school, and all of them, aside from Michael, with their own gliders. There were about a hundred people milling around as Michael stepped out of his car.

"Hi, Mike," Jerry Williams said as Michael came up to the shed. "I was afraid you weren't coming, either."

"What do you mean, either?"

"There were supposed to be twelve more fellas, but they dropped out. Too much wind, they said. And these guys here just took a vote and they decided nine to three not to go up. There goes my big event," he said bitterly. "It'll take me all season to pay off what I owe around town. How about you?"

Michael looked up at the sky again. "I've come down in worse. If the other three guys will come up, too, I'll go first."

"You're a pal, Mike," Williams said gratefully and went to talk to the others as Michael got into his jump boots.

"Okay," Williams said, when he came back. "You got three customers. I got the kite for you tuned like a watch." He was lending Michael his own machine. They put it in its bag in the back of the pickup truck, and with two caravan trucks following them with hanggliders strapped to the roofs, they started up the steep, bumpy road to the plateau on top of the hill from which they would have to take off. The wind was whistling up there, first from one direction, then changing abruptly to another, and the other men moved around nervously and one of them said loudly, "We're crazy to take off in this."

Michael helped Williams assemble the glider, then methodically got into the harness, felt the controls, and without hesitating made his run off. There was the old wonderful, weightless sensation, and he grinned as he felt the air buoy him up, but then the turbulence began and he side-slipped, recovered, felt himself being dragged down fast, fought it, saw the ground coming up at him with alarming speed, side-slipped again and saw he was going into a stand of bare-limbed trees. Oh, Christ, he thought, what luck Tracy isn't here to see this. He crashed into the tree to the sound of metal being crushed and the tearing of fabric. When he came to, he found that he was hanging on a gnarled branch. He moved his arms and legs cautiously. No broken bones. But his face was wet and warm and he knew it was blood. Under him he saw Williams making a loop in a long rope. Williams threw him the rope and Michael secured it around the branch. Then he freed himself from the wreckage and slid to the ground.

"You owe me for one kite," Williams said.

"Worth it," Michael said. "It was a nice ride."

"You *are* a cool son of a bitch," Williams said. "But the show's over for the day. Everybody else is driving down."

◇◇◇◇◇

When he looked at his face before getting dressed for dinner, he saw that the encounter with the tree had not improved his appearance.

There were scratches all over his face and a big disreputable lump over his right eye. Nothing serious, but he looked as though he had been in a battle with a crazed cat and there was no question of his being able to shave.

The phone rang and he picked it up. It was Eva. She had invited him to have dinner at the house that evening with her and Heggener, but Andreas had gotten a chill and was running a fever and she had put him to bed. "So much for the medical opinions of both of you," she said tartly and hung up.

He decided to go without dinner himself and gave himself a drink instead and lay down for a little nap before going off to attend Rita's debut as a public singer. Every muscle in his body felt as though he had been beaten by a baseball bat and movement of any kind had to be considered carefully before he made it.

He had invited Rita's parents and her brother Eliot and he made sure to get to The Chimney Corner before they did and secure a table not too close to where she would be standing, so she wouldn't be distracted by their presence as she performed.

The family all came in together, carefully dressed for the occasion, the two men with jackets and ties and Rita's mother in a neat navy blue dress.

Rita had on a white dress that Michael guessed she had worn at her graduation from high school the June before. She looked pretty and happy, but nervous, and if she hadn't been with her family, Michael would have smuggled her one tot of rum in a cup of tea to calm her down. Grandly, he ordered a bottle of champagne for them all when Jimmy Davis came over to the table to welcome them. Rita didn't touch her glass, but her mother drank her wine with appreciation and nodded her head approvingly along with Antoine's music, which was now soft and unobtrusive, as the room filled up. Michael explained that the Heggeners hadn't come because Mr. Heggener wasn't feeling up to snuff and Mrs. Heggener was taking care of him.

"I been watching you and that man," Rita's father said, "the last week or so, Mike, and I got to give you credit. Beginning of the season I would have laid odds he wouldn't see the first buds of spring, the way he looked. Yesterday, he looked twenty years younger. Maybe you ought to take me skiing a few mornings a week, too." He laughed jovially, then took the untouched glass of champagne that was standing in front of Rita and drank it. "Might as well use this stuff since nobody else is," he said to his wife, who had glared at him. "I hear Rita didn't do all that good this morning in the race," he said to Michael.

"She was doing fine," Michael said. "I figured she was in the first five when she hit the gate."

"Good for her," Jones said. "Lesson in humility. She can use it. Her teachers're always telling her how smart she is and all, if we didn't put her down now and then, she'd be putting on all sorts of airs. I believe in occasional defeats. At least for the young. You had a little comeuppance yourself today, too, from the way your face looks. If it was harvest time I'd say you got caught in a reaper." He laughed heartily. He was used to accidents and didn't take them too seriously. "When I was a kid I got stung by a hive full of bees and I didn't look much worse than you do tonight. I know all about the ills that the flesh is heir to, but I don't go looking for them, like some folks."

"He was trying to help Jerry Williams, Daddy," Rita said, defending Michael. "Everyone else was finking out on him."

"Jerry Williams better get onto the idea that if folks want to fly they ought to buy a ticket on TWA," Jones said.

"Hush, Harold," Mrs. Jones said authoritatively, "the man is going to make an announcement."

Antoine had played three thunderous chords on the piano and the room fell quiet. "Ladies and gentlemen," Antoine said loudly, "we have a special treat in store for us tonight—one of our own home-grown beauties, the lovely Rita Jones, *chanteuse extraordinaire,* has, by special arrangement with our beloved boniface, Jimmy Davis, consented to sing for us. Rita Jones . . ." He nodded toward the table and waved to the girl to come toward the piano.

Rita stood, with an erratic smile on her face, looking, Michael thought, about ten years old, and walked, on very high heels, rather unsteadily, toward the piano, where Antoine took her hand and kissed it, to a burst of applause.

"What's that man say about the girl?" Jones asked suspiciously.

"That she's an extraordinary singer," Mrs. Jones said. "In French. Hush, Harold."

The room fell silent as Antoine vamped for a few bars, then nodded to Rita as he started into "Oh, What a Beautiful Morning," and Rita began to sing. She wasn't stiff and wasn't shy, as Antoine had predicted she would be, but sure and true and loud and her voice was full of gaiety and celebration and filled the room with confident youthful melody. When she had finished, there was a roar of applause, led loudly by Harold Jones. She sang three more songs, all old favorites, shrewdly picked by Antoine to show off her variety and all familiar to the listeners, so that there was nothing new or strange for them to puzzle over.

At the end, the applause was deafening and there were cries for more, but Antoine shook his head, intelligently, Michael thought, getting Rita off on a triumphant note for her first time out. Rita came over to the table, grinning, saying, "Ain't this something?" and her mother kissed her and said, "You did real well, honey," and Harold Jones kept on applauding, beaming, until all the other applause finally died out and even Eliot looked pleased.

Jimmy Davis came over with a bottle of champagne and said, "For the first star ever to be born in Green Hollow." He did the pouring with a flourish, filling Rita's glass first. Michael saw Mr. Jones begin to frown as Rita started excitedly to pick up her glass. "Honey," he said, "there's a law against drinking for minors in Vermont," but Mrs. Jones said, "Hush," to her husband, "just this once," and they all lifted their glasses in honor of the singer.

"You didn't miss a gate tonight," Michael said and Rita laughed uncontrollably, as though he had told the greatest of jokes.

It was almost midnight before the party broke up, the Joneses going off together in an old station wagon and Michael driving off under a clearing sky, with a bit of moon dipping in and out of racing clouds and the mountains outlined in the distance.

When he reached the cottage, it was dark, but when he went in and turned on a lamp he saw Eva sitting on the sofa, wearing her lynx coat.

"Good evening," he said. "Why didn't you turn on the light?"

"I wanted to give you a happy surprise," Eva said. She did not sound happy. "How did it go?"

"Beautifully. It was a wonderful evening. How was it at the house?"

"Not wonderful. Not wonderful at all. His fever is up to nearly a hundred and two." She said it accusingly. "But he's asleep now. It will be a miracle if he's well enough to go to the hospital without hiring an ambulance."

Michael sighed.

"Don't sigh as though you wished I was a thousand miles away. Aren't you going to kiss me?" She stood up.

"Eva," Michael said wearily, "I nearly got killed this afternoon and I can hardly move . . ."

"You don't care whom you kill, do you, yourself, my husband . . ."

"Please," he said, taking off his coat and throwing it on a chair. "I'm dead tired and I want to go to sleep."

"Your face is a mess," she said, without sympathy.

"I know."

"You're not taking proper care of the property."

"I'm going to sleep."

"I didn't come down here to watch you sleep," she said.

"I'm sorry," he said. "I can't do anything . . ."

She began to pace up and down the small room, the coat open and swirling around her, making her look like a giant, ferocious cat. "I'm getting tired of being rejected. By you. By my husband. You want to kill yourself—fine. He wants to kill himself—fine. Maybe the sooner the better for everybody. Maybe I won't even wait. You're not the only two men in the world. Just for your information, and you can pass it on to your beloved, perverted friend, my husband, if you wish, there's a man who's come over from Austria three times in the past year to ask me to marry him."

"Good for you, I wish you every happiness."

"I'm tired of this miserable little town and these piddling mountains," she said, pacing wildly. "Of these dull, heavy American peasants. Of drunken brawlers with their mangled faces . . ."

"Be reasonable, please . . ."

"I want to live among civilized human beings. I thought maybe you'd help pass the season . . ." She was almost snarling as she spoke. "But I'm afraid I made a mistake. You're a little more intelligent than the rest, perhaps, and better educated, but you're like them all. After the first fine careless rapture"—she threw out the phrase mockingly—"the same old middle-class, timid censoriousness, the same hypocritical cowardly morality. So, you're too tired to go to bed with me. Other nights, other excuses. Go to bed with my husband. I'm sure he'd be pleased and so would you and maybe when he dies next week or next month he'll die happy and leave you his fortune in his will."

Michael slapped her. She stood stock-still, her lips drawn back, and laughed. "So, you're too tired to go to bed with a woman, but you're not too tired to hit one. You're going to regret that slap, Mr. Storrs." She swept out of the cottage, leaving the door open behind her. The wind blew in, cold and raw, and Michael shivered. He walked slowly over to the door and closed and locked it, then took off his jacket. He was too tired to get undressed and fell on the big bed with all his clothes on.

CHAPTER
TWENTY-ONE

The ringing of the telephone awoke him. He groaned as he got off the bed to go into the living room to answer it. His muscles had stiffened even more during the night and the wind had blown open a window and chilled him as he lay on top of the covers, and he wished he had awakened in a warmer climate.

Bright sunlight streamed in through the windows as he limped toward the telephone. The clock on the mantelpiece showed that it was a quarter to ten. He hadn't slept that late in years. He had a vague memory of involved, disturbing dreams, luggage lost in airports, dark passages leading to the wrong exits.

"Hello," he said into the phone.

"Michael . . ." It was Andreas Heggener.

"Good morning." Michael tried to sound cheerful and wide-awake.

"I hope I didn't awaken you."

"I've been up since seven," Michael said, lying to conform with what he hoped was the public image of himself as an energetic, principled, hard-working citizen. "How are you feeling today?"

"Fine. No fever and no cough. I was just wondering if you could manage to take me down to New York tomorrow instead of waiting. I'd like to get the whole foolish business over with as soon as possible."

Michael ran his hand over his face and scraped the stubble of beard and felt the scabs of the scratches from the branches of the tree he had crashed into. He would have liked to be more present-able for New York, but he said, "Fine. What time in the morning?"

"Nine okay?"

"Nine it is. I'll get it squared away with Cully."

"Oh . . ." Heggener said. "Eva says she's not in the mood for ski-ing today."

"Neither am I," Michael said. He wasn't in the mood for Eva, ei-ther. "See you tomorrow morning." He hung up, wondering if the imprint of the slap he had given her the night before was still visible on her cheek and if Heggener had noticed it.

He went into the bathroom, glanced at himself hastily in the mir-ror for a moment, was not pleased with what he saw, then patted some cold water gingerly on his face, which made very little difference in the way he looked or felt.

He put on fresh clothes, and, too lazy to make his own breakfast, drove down to the café across from the ski school. Dave Cully was sitting, scowling as usual, over what might have been his fifth cup of coffee. Cully waved to him to sit down and scowled some more when he heard Michael order a large glass of orange juice, waffles with bacon and eggs and coffee.

"People like you drive me crazy," Cully said. "I eat one bran muffin I put on two pounds and you eat like that and I bet you don't weigh an ounce more than when you were twenty years old."

"Two pounds less," Michael said smugly.

"It should be against the law," Cully said. "Your face sure is a mess." He said it as though it made up, at least in a small way, for Michael's metabolic processes. "The way I heard it you're lucky to be alive."

Michael shrugged. He didn't want to discuss his hobbies with Cully. "The way I hear it," he said, "we're all lucky to be alive."

When his meal came, he buttered the waffles generously and poured maple syrup over them. He ate hungrily, remembering that he had skipped dinner the night before. Cully watched him with a look of sour longing and ordered another cup of coffee, black.

"If you'd been killed," Cully said, relishing the theme, "most of the folk here would have been real sorry, but've said, Well, the stu-pid sonofabitch was asking for it, and it'd be forgotten in two days. If one of the local boys'd crashed, they'd have lynched Jerry Williams. And I'd've held the rope. Going in for any more crap like that?"

"Depends upon what comes up," Michael said.

"One day, Mike," Cully said soberly, "your luck is going to run out."

"The crowds will cheer."

"No, they won't," Cully said. "I know *I* won't and neither will most of the people in this town. I don't know whether you know it or not, but you're well-liked here. Except for the goddamn Porsche, you haven't put on the dog and everybody's admired the way you've brought Heggener around. Except maybe the doctors." He grinned.

"And Madam Heggener," Michael said.

"Oh."

"The franchise has just about run out, Dave," Michael said. "You better look around for another victim."

"Well," Cully said, "you had a longer run than most. We've got a good racing class here and they're fun to ski with. I could switch you and . . ."

Michael shook his head. "Thanks, but I've decided I'm not cut out for the life of a ski teacher. I'm resigning my commission, Dave. I'll give you back my jacket during the week."

"No hurry. You going to leave town?"

"Only for a couple of days. I want to make sure I'm not kidding myself and that Heggener is really on his feet before I go. And I certainly don't want to be paid for skiing with *him*." What he didn't say was that for some good reasons, like feeling that he was rescuing a valuable man from despair and death, and some bad reasons, like proving Eva Heggener was wrong, no place on the face of the earth that Sunday morning held more interest for him, bound him more securely, than Green Hollow. "Still, Dave," he said, "whenever you get overloaded and need someone to fill in for a couple of days, you can always call on me."

"Thanks," Cully said. "I'll remember that. Oh, I have some news for you—Norma's having another baby."

"Congratulations," Michael said.

"Wait till we see if I can raise the money to send the kid to college before you congratulate me," Cully said, but Michael could see he was pleased at the prospect of a third child. "This time we're aiming for a girl. Norma's mother says girls're more trouble than boys, but they sweeten the atmosphere around the house. While we're talking about it . . ." He hesitated and gulped at his coffee, and Michael could see that he was approaching a difficult subject. "I never believed that stuff about you and Norma before we were married. I guess I should've told you sooner, but I was a little chicken. I *knew* nothing'd gone on between you. She was a virgin the night we were married." He grinned sheepishly, as though admitting to a youthful peccadillo that he had gotten away with, unpunished, a long time ago.

"Did you tell the Ellsworths?"

"No." Cully smiled again. "I didn't want to destroy my wife's reputation in the eyes of her family."

Michael laughed. "Dave," he said, "you've done a lot for me here when it would've been just as easy to run me out of town and I want to thank you for it."

"Horseshit," Cully said gruffly. "I hired a competent ski instructor. That's what they pay me for. Now, get out of this restaurant. I can't stand the sight of you eating like that."

He was ordering more coffee when Michael left the café, smiling.

❖❖❖❖❖

Exactly at nine the next morning he drove up to the Heggener house. He saw the door to the garage was open. Heggener's Ford was there but Eva's Mercedes was gone. There wasn't any barking, so he guessed the dog was gone, too. Heggener was waiting for him, dressed warmly. For his trip to the city, he had given up the Tyrolean hat and was wearing a soft black felt hat, which sat squarely on his head. As Michael carried Heggener's bag to the Porsche, Heggener said, "This is hospital day. Bruno coughed all night and Eva's taken him to Burlington. She doesn't trust the local veterinarian and she's heard of a wonder animal doctor in Burlington. She should be given a yearly retainer by the American Medical Association for her devotion to disease." He smiled forgivingly, as though his wife's hypochondria in respect to husbands and dogs was a charming little quirk of character. There was no hint in his manner that he knew anything of what had passed between Eva and Michael two nights before.

The Porsche ate up the miles of highway smoothly. Heggener said he liked to go fast so Michael held the car at eighty-five, while keeping a careful watch in the rear-view mirror for police cars.

"In the old days when I returned to Europe as a young man," Heggener said, "there was no speed limit and I had a beautiful Alfa with a custom built body and if I went slower than a hundred and twenty miles an hour I felt I was dawdling. Driving was a sport then, but I suppose we must always expect civilization finally to interfere with our pleasures."

He sat in silence for a while, erect, the black hat nearly touching the roof of the little car. Then he said, "Michael, I've been thinking about you. You're not going to spend your life teaching skiing, are you?"

"No," Michael said. "In fact, I'm not even going to spend another day teaching skiing. I told Cully I quit yesterday."

"You did?" Heggener said flatly. "Are you leaving Green Hollow?"

"Probably not until the end of the season—if then," Michael said. "When I leave more or less depends upon you."

"Does it?" Heggener sounded surprised. "In what way?"

"If, when you get out of the hospital, you still want to ski every day with me," Michael said, "I'll hang on."

"That is most kind of you. And Eva?"

"I imagine she'll be looking for another instructor."

"I see." Heggener nodded. "She does have a reputation for being difficult to please."

"Well-earned." Michael couldn't hold back from saying it.

Heggener smiled again, the same smile as when he had spoken about Eva's predilection for hospitals. Then the smile vanished. "I feel sorry for her," he said. "She didn't know what she was getting into when she married me. The atmosphere of sick rooms, a small town, America. . . . She feels out of place here, it is not congenial to her. She is bored. She has kept her Austrian passport, you know, although she is married to an American. She is constantly warning me that she is only in passage here, she is not rooted. When I die, she will be on the plane for Europe within a week."

"You're not going to die."

"We shall see," Heggener said calmly.

Again he was silent for about ten miles, looking out at the countryside. "Winter shows the bare bones of a country," he said. "And the bones here are magnificent. I admire many things about Europe, but I am rooted here. I am not divided." He was quiet for a while, as though reflecting about roots and divisions. "About you," he said. "After the season . . . what do you intend to do?"

"I have no plans."

"For a man your age, with your abilities," Heggener said, "to have no plans is a little sad, wouldn't you say, if not downright un-American . . ." He smiled, to take the sting out of his pronouncement.

"Both," Michael admitted.

"If I were to say that perhaps I have a plan for you, Michael, would you consider it an unwarranted intrusion on your privacy?"

"Of course not."

"My manager, Mr. Lennart, is leaving in April," Heggener said, "with no regrets on either side. He has been offered a much better job in a big hotel in Chicago and I have begun to have some doubts about his complete honesty. What I have been considering offering you is the position of manager."

In the rear-view mirror, Michael saw a white car that might be the police coming fast over a hill. Until the car swept down and past him, he didn't speak. Then he said, "It's very thoughtful of you, Andreas, but I don't know the first thing about running a hotel."

"It's not as complicated as people think," Heggener said. "I have a good staff and one of the boys who has been with me three years is ready to move up to the position of assistant manager and would be of great help. You like Green Hollow and the town likes you. The duties would leave you a great deal of time to ski. In fact, you would attract guests by being available to ski with them, which Mr. Lennart is not. You are easy with people and as you showed with Rita, who, by the way I am sorry you did not get to sing in *our* bar instead of Mr. Davis's, you have an idea of what might please our clientele that would help us considerably. I would be prepared to offer you a decent salary plus a percentage of the profits, which are also, I am happy to say, considerable. As part of your training I would finance trips to Europe to see how other hotels I admire are run and in any case, your vacations would be quite long, since the hotel is a seasonable business. Of course, I don't expect you to give me an immediate answer. You have all the time you want to tell me yes or no."

"Have you spoken to Eva about this?" Michael asked. One thing was certain—if Eva Heggener was to be in a position to tell him what to do and what not to do he would decline with thanks.

"No, I haven't spoken to her," Heggener said. "From our discussions, it would seem that she will be gone from now on for longer and longer periods. In any case, where the business is concerned, it is I who make all the decisions. It would be understood that she would leave you severely alone."

Michael could imagine what those discussions must have been like. They would be more likely to drive a man into a hospital than any bouts of coughing, with or without blood.

"Let's talk about it," Michael said, "when you get back."

"Of course," Heggener said and put his chin down on his chest and dozed until they reached the hospital.

Michael felt a twinge of pity as he saw Heggener put into a wheel-chair, already somehow diminished, with a no-nonsense nurse pushing him swiftly and efficiently out of sight to God knew what pain, what tests, what probing and predictions.

◇◇◇◇◇

He checked into the Hotel Westbury, because it was on Madison Avenue near where he had lived and he had often dropped into the bar for a drink. It was the cocktail hour and the bar was crowded with couples, released and joyful after the day's work and he felt a pang of self-pity because he was alone and there was nobody in the city to welcome him and feel the evening was improved because he had arrived in town. On an impulse that he didn't examine, he called Tracy's number. The phone rang and rang and he was about to hang up, not knowing whether he was relieved or sorry that she was not at home, when the phone was picked up at the other end and he heard her voice, a little breathless, saying, "Hello."

"Hello, Tracy," he said. "I was just about to hang up."

"I just came in," she said. "I was coming up the steps when I heard the phone ringing and I ran, as you can tell by the way I'm breathing." She laughed. "Where are you?"

"Around the corner. At the Westbury."

"Oh." Suddenly she sounded cautious.

"Am I too close for comfort?"

"Don't start in like that," she said warningly.

"Sorry."

"Are you all right?"

"Why shouldn't I be all right?"

"I mean calling me like this—out of the blue. And in the city. *Are* you all right? All in one piece?"

"I'm fine," he said. "I'd be better, though, if you joined me for a drink."

There was a long silence. "Are you sure you know what you're doing, Michael?"

"No," he said.

She laughed. "In that case, give me a half hour."

He hung up and took the elevator to his room and shaved, not very well, being careful to avoid opening up the scratches on his face, but well enough so that he wouldn't look as though he had been sleeping out in the wilderness since she had seen him last. He showered and put on some clean clothes and remembered to wear a tie she had given him for Christmas some years ago, which was a color she said she liked on him.

Then he went down to the bar, no longer feeling any self-pity, and found a small table and said with satisfaction to the waiter, "We'll be two," and ordered a martini.

When she came into the room, the men turning their heads, as usual, to watch her and the women looking secretly damaged, he rose to greet her. He kissed her cheek, which was cold from the walk from her apartment and fragrant of only slightly scented soap. There was no sign on her face or in her clothes that she had spent a whole day in an office and that she had probably made a hundred decisions that might conceivably change the course of her life or the lives of the people who depended upon her.

She frowned as she looked across the table at him. "What in the world happened to your face?"

"I ran into a tree," he said. "Hang-gliding."

"Oh, Michael," she said sadly. "Still?"

"I was careless," he said. "For once."

"For once," she said, her voice dead. "As usual. Do people know where to find me to tell me when you've been killed? After all, I'm still your wife."

"I'll have a dog tag made up and hang it around my neck," Michael said, displeased, "saying, 'Please call my wife, in case of decease,' with the telephone number. I may not make *The New York Times*."

From then on the evening was all downhill. He tried to entertain her, told her about Antoine falling down the stairs, but she was not amused and said, "That's not like you, being involved in a con game," as though without her at his side he had allowed himself to become corrupt.

He could not tell her about Andreas Heggener or Annabel, the town bang, or the suit against him for breaking the jaw of a man who had pulled a knife on him. He could not describe his feelings when he had schussed the Black Knight or the ecstasy he had felt in bed with Eva Heggener and his complicated emotions about her or about David Cully revealing to him that Norma Ellsworth Cully had been a virgin on her marriage night. It was impossible to ask her advice about whether or not to take up Heggener's offer of a job or what he felt about Green Hollow or about Antoine's persuading an innocent black girl to smoke marijuana to help her singing or about Jimmy Davis risking his life to inform the Feds about Clyde Barlow, or about the cigar smoking old lawyer, Mr. Lancaster, or the dotty old drunken cop saying, "Thug, speeder, mugger, breaker of the peace, unwelcome element." He could not tell her that he was as committed to saving a man's life as he had ever been committed to her, or of being accused of being homosexual and a fortune hunter by the man's wife. There was no way of letting her know how he felt when he looked out his window at dawn and saw the glow of sunrise on the tops of the mountains or sat at the table with Harold Jones allowing his sixteen-year-old daughter to drink a glass of champagne because she had had her first triumph in a shabby little hill-town bar. He could not tell her of his moments of peace and his moments of turmoil, of the gun in the secret drawer and the man who had as much as threatened to kill him if he treated the man's wife, who was his mistress, badly. Marriage was an ongoing, continuous, intimate, confiding, interlocking history; separation was sealed vaults, crammed with classified, nonrevealable documents. When he asked her if she had found any men who interested her, she said, coldly, "You know I won't say anything on that subject."

Even her drinking habits had changed. When they were together and she found him drinking a martini she would always say, "The same, please." Now she was drinking straight vodka on the rocks. At just what moment in the time between had she changed? Never to know.

And he longed for her, achingly, overpoweringly, but no word he could say that night could please her. And the truth was, no word she said to him pleased him.

They went to a restaurant on Sixty-first Street where they had dined well in the past and where they had been warmly welcomed by the whole staff. But now the management had changed and nobody recognized them and the meal was awful.

And still he longed for her. The strangeness between them, the sense of their being two new persons facing each other, only intensified the longing. And that, above all, he could not tell her.

When he walked her home and asked if he could go upstairs with her, she said coldly, "I don't go in for one-night stands," and they didn't kiss goodnight and neither of them inquired when they could see each other again.

After he had left her he went back to the hotel and had a whiskey. He knew that he couldn't sleep, although he had awakened early and had driven more than three hundred miles that day. The desire she had aroused in him had now become general, vengeful. But the city he had known before Tracy, the city teeming with lovely, pliant girls, had vanished as completely as Troy, telephone numbers buried in the ashes of Pompeii. Suddenly he remembered the number of Susan Hartley. She had written it large on a piece of paper and mailed it to him after she had left, with only the words "Use it, Susan" on the sheet of paper.

He was not good at remembering telephone numbers, but now, late at night, after the lethal evening with his wife, it came to him clearly and he called it and she was home and she sounded unsurprised and pleased and gave him her address, which he could walk to, which was convenient. He walked to it and spent most of the night with her and he enjoyed it, if that was the right word, and she was a delicious girl, and it served Antoine right, but he kept seeing his wife's face as she said, at her front door, "I don't go in for one-night stands," and he couldn't make himself be a gentleman and stay in Susan's bed until morning, but said he had to get up early to drive back to Green Hollow and she didn't seem to mind, but said, "It was bound to happen," but didn't explain why she said it and he dressed and went back to his hotel without knowing what Susan had meant. Either she had meant that it had been inevitable that they would go to bed together or that he would leave when he shouldn't have left. In either case, it didn't matter at the time.

Feeling drained, he got into his own bed and slept fitfully and dreamt of his mother, which he had not done for many years.

◇◇◇◇◇

He awoke late, with a huge and senseless erection, feeling bruised and as though he had a hangover, although he hadn't drunk all that much the night before. He called the hospital, but Mr. Heggener, he was told, was in X-Ray and could not be reached. He left a message saying that he would call again to find out when Mr. Heggener would be discharged and that he would come to fetch him.

Dave Cully would have been more tolerant this morning if he had sat across from him at breakfast, because he had only one slice of toast and three cups of black coffee. He dressed slowly and paid his bill and got his car out of the garage and saw that he would arrive back at Green Hollow long after dark and got caught in a traffic jam in the Bronx and cursed New York as he left the city, under a pall of winter smog, behind him.

It was nearly midnight when he arrived in Green Hollow and he hadn't eaten all day and was hungry, but he was too tired to stop at The Chimney Corner for a sandwich. He drove straight through the town to the cottage. When he got there, he saw a car parked, without lights, near the gate, pointing toward the town. He did not recognize the car. He drove on a little farther and parked the Porsche deep in the shadow of an embankment and walked quickly back to the gate. He hesitated only a moment at the gate, then he went up toward the mansion, staying on the soft, wet side of the road so that his footsteps were noiseless. Almost instinctively, as he came to the big house, he bent over to make himself as invisible as possible. There was no barking and he remembered that Eva had taken Bruno to the animal hospital. He could see a light in the big bedroom at the front of the house and then the beam of a flashlight in the little library that led off the living room. The light was enough for him to see two dark figures moving around in the library, where, he knew, there was the small wall safe where the Heggeners kept their valuables. The front door was slightly ajar, so he didn't have to use his key. He slipped into the dark hallway and then into the living room and started feeling his way between the familiar pieces of furniture to the desk where the pistol was kept. There were footsteps on the staircase that led down to the hallway and then a sudden flare of light as the hallway chandelier was switched on. He heard something being knocked over in the library and the crash of glass, then saw two figures running past the French windows that gave on to the porch.

"Stop!" he shouted, "or I'll shoot." He ran toward the desk and was feeling for the spring to open the drawer when a shot rang out from the hallway and he heard the whistle of the bullet as it passed over his head and smashed a windowpane. He dropped to the floor and screamed, "Stop! Stop!" Eva Heggener was standing outlined in the doorway against the hall light. She fired again. He crawled behind a couch, yelling, "It's me, Eva, Michael." She fired again and again, wildly, the bullets thudding into furniture and ricocheting off the walls. In a minute, she had used up all six cartridges in the revolver. He heard the click of the hammer on the empty chamber and stood up and turned on a lamp. "For the love of God," he shouted, "what do you think you're doing?"

She wavered unsteadily on her feet, looked down at the pistol in her hand, then dropped it on the floor. "I heard noises . . ."

"You let them get away," Michael said angrily. "And you damn near killed me."

"I heard noises," Eva repeated dully.

"It's okay," he said. "They're gone now." He went over to her and put his arms around her. She was in a nightgown and shivering. "There, there . . ." He tried to comfort her.

"This damned house," she moaned. "Stuck away in the woods. I'm always alone when I need anybody . . ." But she didn't cry and she didn't sound frightened, only angry.

"Listen, Eva, why don't you go upstairs and get dressed and I'll take you to the hotel for the night."

"I'm not going to be driven from my own house by you or anybody else," she said. She pulled away from him. "I'm going to sleep in my own bed."

"Whatever you say," Michael said soothingly. "I'll stay on down here if you need me for anything."

"I don't need anything," she said and turned and went steadily up the staircase.

When he heard the door of her room slam he bent and picked up the pistol. It was a small, pearl-handled revolver. Despite what Heggener believed, there was more than one weapon in the house and there easily could have been a death because of it. He pocketed the gun. Eva might have a dozen boxes of shells secreted upstairs.

He left the hallway chandelier lights on and went through the living room into the library and turned on the light. Except for the broken window through which the men had escaped and a table that they had knocked over in their flight, nothing seemed to have been touched. The painting hiding the wall safe was neatly in place.

Michael went back into the living room and inspected the damage Eva's fusillade had caused. It was considerable. For a moment he considered phoning the police, but that would mean keeping Eva up all night answering embarrassing questions about whom exactly she was shooting at and having to endure Norman Brewster's lectures on the criminal folly of the indiscriminate use of firearms. He decided not to call the police, but settled in an easy chair, with the lamp still on, and tried to sleep.

He was sure he hadn't slept at all, but he was awakened by Eva, shaking him. He blinked up at her from the chair. The morning sunlight streamed in through the windows. Eva was dressed and her face was calm. "I have to leave now for Burlington," she said. "I have to pick up Bruno. Thank you for being so vigilant in guarding my safety." Her tone was ironic, because she had had to shake him to wake him.

He stood up, still groggy. "Before you go," he said, "I have to have a word with you about what happened."

"It was very simple," she said calmly. "Criminals broke into my house and I routed them."

"What I want to say is, I don't think you ought to let the police in on it," Michael said. "Criminals or no criminals, they won't take a kindly view of all that shooting. They'll badger you for weeks."

She nodded, as though she were a teacher and he was a student who had come out with a surprisingly intelligent suggestion. "Perhaps you're right. I'm sure they'd never catch the men, anyway. When the house was looted last year they never even arrested anyone. They're useless."

"I looked into the library after you went to bed," Michael said, "and as far as I could tell, nothing had been taken."

"I frightened them away before they could get their hands on whatever it was they were looking for. Whatever else I am," she said proudly, "I am not a coward."

"No, you're not. But," he added drily, "one shot into the air would have done the job just as well."

"I would gladly have killed them," she said calmly.

"You damn near killed me."

"I thought you were still in New York," she said. "It was stupid of you not to let me know you were coming. If you had been hurt, it would have been your own fault."

"I yelled my name ten times."

"I didn't hear you," she said, staring hard into his eyes. "There was so much noise." She looked around the room. "This mess will have to be cleared up."

"If you agree," Michael said, "I'll ask Herb Ellsworth to come and mend everything he can. He's a handyman and he's dependable and he won't talk if I ask him not to."

"Tell him to come tomorrow when I'll be back with Bruno," Eva said. "Now I have to go and explain to the cook what happened so she won't run screaming from the house when she sees the state of this room, and then I have to go to Burlington. You ought to get some sleep. You look perfectly dreadful."

She left the living room and he could hear her shouting in the kitchen in German to the seventy-year-old deaf cook.

Before he left the house he put the front door key on the library table back of the sofa. He was not going to have any further use for it. As he walked slowly down the graveled path toward the cottage, he wondered if, despite the noise, she hadn't heard him calling his name after all. And he remembered that she hadn't asked him anything about his trip or how her husband had taken it. He went out the gate and got his car. It had not been touched. He drove it up to the cottage door. For a moment, out of habit, he reached in to take out his bag. He had his hand on the grip and was raising it, when he let it drop back. Then he went into the cottage and packed the remainder of his belongings and put them in the car. If Eva Heggener was to be protected she would have to find someone else to do the job.

He drove to Ellsworth's office and explained what had happened. "The lady was hysterical," he said, "and just fired all over the place at random. There's some patching and mending to do and she'd rather not let the police get wind of it."

"I can understand that," Ellsworth said. "They still haven't found my truck and whenever they have nothing else to do they come around bothering me asking me questions about people who worked for me ten years ago, as if I remembered. I'll do what I can, Mike, and keep my mouth shut."

"Thanks, Herb. You're a good man to have in a town."

"They're asking me to run for mayor," Ellsworth said. "Fuck them."

Michael laughed and said, "By the way, I've moved from the cottage."

"Where you going to be? The hotel?" If Ellsworth thought Michael's moving had anything to do with the shooting, he kept his suspicions to himself.

"No. I'm just going to mosey around the countryside for a week or two and settle my nerves. I'll be back when I get Heggener out of the hospital."

"About this time of year," Ellsworth said, "I get mountain fever, too, and feel like taking off. Only *I* can't. Some people're born lucky and some have to work. Have a good time. See you."

"See you," Michael said and went out and got into his car and drove slowly through town and out along the sunny road.

CHAPTER TWENTY-TWO

He went from one ski village to another, always alone, going up when the lifts opened in the morning and ending the day when they closed in the late afternoon. He skied in a snowstorm, in sleet, in powder, on ice, always at full speed, then when night fell got into the car and drove on to the next village, where he would take a room at a motel, gulp dinner and fall into bed, exhausted. He avoided talking to anyone and lived in his ski clothes and only took them off when he went to bed. He slept without dreams, woke early, barely looked to see what the weather was, went grimly to the mountain to ski as though the mountain were his enemy, to be defeated only by speed and relentless onslaught. He didn't fall once in the whole week he spent on this purgative downhill voyage and when the week ended and he knew from calling the hospital that Mr. Heggener was expecting him to come and drive him back home the next day, his body, at least, was singing and his face was so burned and whipped by sun and wind that he looked like a lean and dangerous Indian brave after a long and hazardous raid.

He drove all night so that he could pick up Heggener early the next morning. Heggener was waiting for him just inside the hospital entrance, not looking as well as when he had gone in just the week before; not ill, but a little pale because his tan had gone from his face in the seven days.

"My God, Michael," Heggener said when he saw him, "what have you done to yourself? You look absolutely gaunt."

"I took a little skiing holiday," Michael said, as he stuffed Heggener's overnight bag in beside his own piled luggage.

"How was the snow in Green Hollow?"

"I don't know," Michael said. "I've been in Stowe, Sugarbush, Mad River, Big Bromley, other places."

They got into the car and started off.

"How was it?" Michael asked. "In there, I mean."

"Not so bad," said Heggener. "They believe I'm well on the road to recovery." He smiled. "Although one of the older men said there must have been some faults in the tests and he's going to go over the data again. They want to see me again in a month." He made a sound of distaste. "Enough of illness. How about you? Have you come to a decision about the hotel yet?"

"I'm afraid not, Andreas. I'll need some more time, if you don't mind. If you can't wait, please make other plans."

"I can wait," Heggener said.

They were on the big open highway winding north when Michael asked, "Did Eva tell you what happened?"

"I haven't spoken to her," Heggener said quietly.

"She didn't call?"

"No. I imagine she was busy," Heggener said. "With Bruno coughing and all." He permitted himself a small smile. "And I decided to give her a rest for a few days from thinking about me. We may be on better terms because of it when we see each other again. What *did* happen?"

For a moment, Michael was tempted to tell the man that nothing in particular had happened or make up some harmless little lie of village gossip. But no matter how skillfully Ellsworth had worked at patching up the damage to the living room, he couldn't have done enough to hide all evidence of the shooting. Heggener would know soon enough and it was better that he be prepared before he went into the house.

"All right," Michael said. "There was a burglary. Or rather an attempted burglary." Then he told Heggener the whole story, the car parked with no lights, his own scouting expedition, the two figures and the flashlight beam in the library, his moving toward the desk to get the pistol, then Eva's sudden appearance and the wild shooting and the men's flight.

"Good God," Heggener said, "Eva handling a gun! Where did she get it?"

"I don't know," Michael said. "It's a little pearl-handled thing. I have it in my bag. Didn't you know she had it?"

"Certainly not." Heggener sounded angry. "Didn't I tell you that the Smith and Wesson was the only weapon in the house?"

"I thought you might have forgotten," Michael said tactfully.

"You may think I'm an old man with a failing memory," Heggener said, "but I would remember if my wife had a gun."

"I didn't call the police," Michael said. "No real harm was done and Eva was in no condition to answer questions by policemen."

"That was considerate of you, Michael," Heggener said softly. "In fact, your whole performance makes me rather ashamed of myself. I wonder if I would have done as much."

"I didn't do anything much," Michael said. "I was curious about the parked car and I went to investigate. That was one of the reasons you gave me the cottage, remember."

"Yes, I know. But it didn't include getting killed."

"Sneak thieves in a place like Green Hollow weren't likely to be carrying guns," Michael said, although he remembered that the year before Bruno's predecessor had been shot. "In fact, they went out the window so fast when they heard footsteps a greyhound wouldn't have caught them. All I did was duck."

"All I can say is that there won't be more than one gun in that house from now on," Heggener said grimly. "Not if I have to go through every drawer and look under every carpet and bed and behind every book in the house to make sure."

"I'm positive Eva must have learned her lesson by now."

"*I* am not so positive," Heggener said.

"Anyway, to avoid any further target practice," Michael said, "I've moved out of the cottage."

"I don't blame you," Heggener said. "Are you staying at the hotel?"

"I'm not staying anywhere at the moment."

"Oh."

"If you want me to hang around and ski with you, I'll check in at the Monadnock."

Heggener considered this for a long time. "Yes, I believe that would be better," he said quietly. "The less Eva sees of you after what's happened the better for all concerned. And I *do* want you to hang around and ski with me. I want it very much. I'm going to say thank you now and then not say it again." His voice trembled as he talked and Michael made a point of keeping his eyes steadily on the road.

When they reached Green Hollow, Heggener surprised Michael by saying, "Why don't we have dinner at The Chimney Corner to celebrate our homecoming? Do you know—I've never been there—in all the time I've been in this town—and I'd like to hear Rita sing."

"She only sings on weekends."

"Even so," Heggener said. "I'll call the house and tell Eva that we stopped at a roadside restaurant somewhere and I'll be home around ten. I'd like to enjoy a little quiet dinner with you, and since Eva doesn't know I'm coming, there won't be anything to eat in the house."

"Whatever you say. I'm starving," Michael said and drove up to The Chimney Corner and parked. He did not relish the idea of a surprise confrontation with Eva Heggener and postponement, although he felt it was cowardly, had undeniable merits.

It was early and the restaurant was almost empty and Antoine had not yet come in. Davis, the headwaiter told Michael, was out of town for the day, but it had been a banner weekend, with full houses to hear Rita sing. "That kid isn't going to stay in Green Hollow for long," the headwaiter said. "You mark my words. She'll be in New York or Hollywood before the season is over. That is, if her old man doesn't chain her to the front porch." He grinned. He was a young man and obviously his career hadn't included the joys of parenthood.

Michael had a drink at the bar while Heggener went to telephone. The telephone was on the balcony, up the stairs down which Antoine had made his historic descent. Michael remembered how Tracy had rebuked him for thinking up the plot of the faked fall. It was the first time in more than a week that he had thought of her and he wished he hadn't.

When Heggener came back to the bar, he looked grave.

"Anything wrong?" Michael asked.

"Not really," Heggener said. He ordered a whiskey. "I talked to the maid. Miraculously, she heard the ring of the telephone. Trouble must have improved her hearing."

"What trouble?"

Heggener sipped at his whiskey before answering. "Eva's gone," he said quietly.

"What do you mean—gone?"

"Packed and gone. With Bruno. Well, it's her dog. A gift from me."

"Gone where?"

"Hulda doesn't know. She says there's an envelope for me."

"Well, then, the hell with dinner." Michael got off the bar stool he was sitting on. "I'll drive you . . ."

Heggener put a restraining hand on his arm. "No hurry," he said. "I invited you to dinner and I was looking forward to it. I insist. Sit down, Michael. You know this place. What is the best dish they have? And if you can prevail upon the headwaiter to bring the wine list, I'd like to order the best bottle of Bordeaux they have in their cellar."

The dinner was good and Heggener pronounced the wine excellent and said, "I must come here more often. It's a welcome change from Hulda's cooking—which bears the full weight of centuries of Mitteleuropa on every dish. And our cook at the Alpina, I'm afraid, has exhausted his repertoire." He ate slowly and everything on his plate and then ordered coffee and brandy for both of them and a cigar for himself. He dawdled over the brandy and lit the cigar with loving care. Looking at Andreas, sniffing his brandy and lolling comfortably back in his chair, no one, Michael thought, could possibly think that here was a man who knew he had a message waiting for him just fifteen minutes away that might, conceivably, alter the entire course of his life.

When he finally paid the bill, Andreas said to the headwaiter, who was helping him on with his coat, "Thank you very much for a fine dinner. Will you tell Mr. Davis for me that his success here is fully deserved."

"Thank you, Mr. Heggener," the headwaiter said, pocketing the five dollar bill that Heggener had slipped into his hand, "I'm sure Mr. Davis will be pleased to have your opinion of his restaurant. And he'll be sorry that he wasn't here to welcome you himself."

"Now that I've found the way," Heggener said, "tell him I'll be back often."

Outside, he looked up at the starry sky, where a high moon made pale outlines of the crests of the hills. He breathed deeply. "Ah," he said, "it's good to be back in the mountains."

They drove in silence, which held as they swung through the gate and past the dark cottage and up to the big house, its pillars gleaming ghostly in the moonlight. Before Heggener could get out his key to open the door, the door opened and the stooped, bulky figure of the maid, sobbing convulsively, stood in the glow of the hallway chandelier.

"There's no need for you to come in, Michael," Heggener said, taking his overnight bag from Michael's hand. "I'll have to spend at least fifteen minutes comforting Hulda. In German. Unless," he said, smiling slightly, "you are in the mood for a lesson in that lovely language. And I enjoyed the day." He spoke soothingly to Hulda, saying, "*Aber, aber, Hulda, weinen hilft auch nicht.*"

"Call me if you want anything," Michael said. "I'll be at the Monadnock."

"It looks as though it's going to be a fine day tomorrow," Heggener said. "I would like to get back on skis."

"At whatever time you say."

"I'll call you in the morning." Heggener went into the house, closing the door behind him, stifling the sound of Hulda's sobs.

He called the Monadnock at nine in the morning. "Michael," he said, his voice calm, "it *is* a fine day, as I thought it would be. The skiing should be perfect. Is ten o'clock too early for you?"

"I'll come and get you."

"No need. The Ford is in the garage. I'll meet you at the lift at ten."

Michael was there ahead of time. Promptly on the hour, he saw the Ford drive up to the parking lot. Heggener got out and took his skis off the rack and carried them over his shoulder, swinging his poles jauntily as he came to the bottom of the lift. He looked fit and straight, and as if he had spent a peaceful and comfortable night. "Punctuality is the courtesy of princes," he said, "or is it kings? I never can remember. I've never known a king, but I've known some very unpunctual princes, though. One of the things I found immediately endearing about America was the absence of both kings and princes."

On the chair lift going up, Heggener breathed deeply, with evident relish. "I am finally getting the hospital smell out of my lungs," he said. "Oh, Eva's Mercedes arrived this morning. She kindly arranged to have it driven by a chauffeur from Kennedy."

"Kennedy?" Michael said.

"Yes, she has flown to Austria." Heggener spoke offhandedly as though reporting that his wife had gone to Saks Fifth Avenue on a shopping expedition. "In the note she left me, she said she is not coming back here. If I want to see her I must come to Austria."

"Are you going?"

Heggener shrugged. "Perhaps when the season is over. Wives endure, snow melts."

But much later in the day, when after hours of hard skiing they were sitting in the lodge having tea, he said, "If I go back to Austria I am sure I will die. I know that it must sound foolish to you, but I'm a superstitious man and when I am dying in my dreams it is always somewhere in Austria."

It was the last thing he said on the subject. They continued to ski every day when the weather was good and they played backgammon in the evenings, for small stakes, with first one of them and then the other winning a little. Hulda had stopped crying and they dined together in the house two or three evenings a week, where Michael found Hulda's cooking most satisfying, and other nights went to The Chimney Corner, where Heggener expressed great admiration for Rita's singing and Antoine's playing.

Antoine looked sallower than ever and was in a dour mood because the doctor had told him it would be at least another month before the cast could come off his leg and he was sure Jimmy Davis had bribed the doctor so that Antoine would have to stay on playing the piano in this accursed backwater, unchic village for what Antoine described as a meager crust of bread. Gratitude was not high on Antoine's list of virtues and Michael decided that he was not as fond of the Frenchman as he had once been. Also, late one night, just before closing, when Antoine and Michael were alone at the bar, Antoine said accusingly, "So. When you were in New York, you saw Susan."

"How do you know?"

"I called her and she told me. And you did more than see her. The doorman at her apartment house is a friend of mine and I called him. He remembered you when I described you. You stayed almost a whole night. I hope you had a good time."

"I had a very good time," Michael said angrily. "And it's none of your business."

"You are a disloyal friend and dangerous to introduce to anyone," said Antoine and got up from the bar and hobbled out.

After that, whenever Michael came into the bar, he and Antoine merely nodded coldly to each other.

The weeks passed and the end of the season approached and Heggener's face turned a skier's deep tan and he seemed to glory, to Michael's profound relief, in his regained health. It was a good time, Michael felt, for himself as well as Heggener, peaceful and relaxed, with all problems held in abeyance and neither of them asking any questions about the future, not even the question of whether or not Michael would accept the manager's job at the hotel. If Heggener was grieving about his wife's absence, he made a perfect show of hiding it.

Michael's feeling that he was entering a halcyon season was increased considerably when his lawyer, old Mr. Lancaster, called him into his office to say that Barlow's suit against him had been dropped. Barlow, Lancaster told him through a cloud of cigar smoke, had been caught by two undercover federal agents posing as dealers, who had bought some heroin from Barlow and had arrested him, and found a switchblade knife on him and two guns in his home. After due consideration of all the facts, the law firm with four names in Montpelier had closed the case.

"That will be one hundred dollars for my trouble, Mr. Storrs," Lancaster said and Michael happily wrote out the check, saying, "I guess it's worth it, saving forty-nine thousand and nine hundred dollars."

He got drunk with Jimmy Davis that night and in the morning awoke clearheaded, with no flicker of a hangover. Automatically, as soon as he got out of bed, he looked to see what the weather was. It was snowing hard, the snow driven in sheets by a northwest wind. He telephoned Heggener and said, "No skiing today. Build a big fire and sit near it and read a good book. I'll do the same." He had borrowed a copy of *The Pickwick Papers* from Heggener's library and it was just the sort of weather for *The Pickwick Papers*.

When he went down for breakfast, Jerry Williams was in the lobby. "Hi, Jerry," Michael said. "You come over here to tell me what a great day it is for hang-gliding?"

Jerry grinned. "If I said yes, you'd be just damn fool enough to believe me. No, it's something else this time. There's a guy I know, over at Newburg, does some free-falling. He's organizing a jump for Saturday afternoon. It's for some advertising concern that's got an account for sports watches. He wants to get five guys and do a star.

He'll jump and he's got a friend. He wants five bodies altogether. I already have Swanson and myself and you'd be the fifth. I get a three-hundred-buck watch if we do it."

"What do *I* get?" Michael asked.

Williams grinned again, his long drooping blond moustache giving him an evil appearance. "You get a free airplane ride and the thanks of the Green Hollow Hang-Gliding School."

"I'd do anything for the Green Hollow Hang-Gliding School, you know that," Michael said.

"You damn near did," Williams said.

Michael thought for a moment. He felt the familiar electric tingle, even just thinking about it. "What time Saturday?"

"Noon," Williams said. "High noon. At the Newbury airfield. If it ever stops snowing."

"I'll see you there," Michael said.

"Don't get drunk on Friday night," Williams said and slouched out of the hotel front door, hunching into his coat and pushing up his collar against the whip of the snow.

After breakfast, Michael read all morning, lying on his bed and feeling deliciously lazy, chuckling from time to time. He had two drinks before lunch and a half bottle of wine as he ate, with the book propped up on the table in front of him. He had read *The Pickwick Papers* in English class at preparatory school, but it had just been another assignment then. Now he read with great enjoyment, marveling at how alive and vigorous the book remained after so many years.

The drinks and the wine and the food made him sleepy and he gave himself the luxury of a nap after lunch. When he awoke it was dark and still snowing. He turned on the light and picked up the book and was about to begin reading when the phone rang. It was Dave Cully. "Mike," Cully said, "is Mr. Heggener with you?"

"No," Michael said. "Why?"

"Harold Jones just called me. Heggener's Ford is still in the parking lot. And Jones saw him go up at three-thirty this afternoon."

"Holy God! Alone?"

"Alone. I'm organizing a search party," Cully said. "Flashlights, a sled, two guys from the patrol, Dr. Baines. I imagine you'll want to come along."

"Of course. Wait for me. I'll go out to his house. Maybe he got a lift home and forgot his car."

"I already called his house," Cully said. "There was no answer."

"The maid's deaf. She probably didn't hear the phone. I won't be long. See you at the lift."

He got into his ski clothes and boots swiftly and put on his heaviest anarac over a thick sweater, cursing under his breath. He hurried downstairs and got the Porsche out from the shed where it was parked to keep it out of the snow. He sped out of town, the snow hitting like thick white flour at the windshield, making it almost impossible to see the curves in the road. He skidded through the gate past the cottage and up to the house. He left the motor running and ran to the front door. It was locked and he knew it would be useless to ring. He ran around to the back of the house and saw that the kitchen was brightly lit. Through the window, he saw Hulda bending over the stove. He knocked on the windowpane and finally got her attention. She looked frightened until she recognized him and hurried to the back door and fumbled for what seemed minutes at the lock. Finally, she opened it. "Herr Heggener?" Michael shouted.

She shook her head. *"Nicht hier,"* she said. *"Skifahren."*

Michael turned and ran back to the Porsche and jumped in and wrenched it around and gunned the motor. He nearly hit a car as he sped out of the gate, but it wasn't the Ford.

When he got to the lift, Cully and the others were there waiting for him. Harold Jones went into the control room and started the lift. The chairs swung dizzyingly in the wind as they went up in the darkness.

"The damn fool," Michael said to Cully, who was riding with him.

"It'd just about stopped snowing at three o'clock," Cully said. "I guess he thought the storm was over."

"Did anybody see what run he took?"

Cully shook his head. "There was hardly anybody else on the mountain. Jones closed down the lift at four because it began to really come down again and the wind was beginning to blow up hard."

At the top they divided up, the two boys of the ski patrol with the sled going down one run, and Cully, Michael and Dr. Baines going down another. They skied slowly, their big flashlights searching the storm. It took them an hour and a half to get down the first run and the ski patrol boys reached the bottom of the lift the same time they did. Neither party had seen any sign of Heggener. They went up again and again divided up, this time going down two different runs, stopping every minute or two to call out Heggener's name. From the other run, Michael could hear the voices of the ski patrol boys, faint through the trees. The shouts echoed in the darkness, but there were no answering cries.

More than an hour later, they were all down at the bottom of the lift again. The storm was getting worse, the wind rising, and Jones told them that he'd have to slow the lift down to a crawl and even then he wasn't sure a cable might not swing off a tower wheel.

It was torture, bitterly cold, going up now, inch by slow inch, and Cully and Michael sat hunched in grim silence, their gloved hands under their armpits to keep them from freezing. There was only one more slope they had not covered and when they got to the top, Cully asked Michael, "Did he ever do the Black Knight with you?"

"Never," Michael said. "But this might just be the time he . . ." He didn't finish the sentence. A man who admitted he had killed a friend might be mad enough to do anything.

Now they all went down the Black Knight together, painfully slowly. Michael pitied Dr. Baines, who was a portly man of fifty and not all that good a skier. Baines was tiring badly now and fell twice on the steep slope and had to be helped back to his feet and brushed off. The snow had frozen on his cheeks and the others took turns rubbing them to keep them from being frostbitten.

They worked their way down to the turn in the forest and followed the trail past the boulder and then all the way down to the lift. Jones had a big pot of coffee on a hot plate in the lift house and to keep Baines from collapsing they had to go in and pour the coffee into him and sit him down in front of the wood stove that Jones had piled high with split logs. It was fifteen minutes before Baines could get on his feet again and Michael said, "Listen, Doctor, I don't think you ought to go up on this one."

Baines didn't say anything, but merely looked icily at him, then put on his gloves and went out and started putting on his skis.

Harold Jones went out of the lift house with them, scowling, looking uphill as the wind howled through the cables. "I'm sorry, fellas," he said. "You can't go up again. I can't run the goddamn chairs in this wind. Either a chair'd hit a tower or the cable would fly off a wheel and you'd just drop off and like as not somebody'd be killed."

"Harold," Michael said, "there's a man up there somewhere . . ."

"I'm sorry, Mike," Jones said.

"Don't argue with him, Mike," Cully said. "He's right. We just have to sit inside and wait until the wind dies down."

Silently, they watched Baines take off his skis and carefully stand them up against the side of the lift house. Then they went in and took off their gloves and parkas and boots and sat on the floor in the steamy warmth, because there was only one chair and they had a hard time getting Baines to take it. Nobody said anything and the only sound was the loud ticking of a battered alarm clock. Michael stared at it wearily. It was ten past one in the morning and Heggener had been out in the cold since four o'clock the afternoon before.

Outside the wind rose higher and higher, shaking the windows in their frames.

Baines fell asleep sitting in the chair and his snores were added to the ticking of the clock.

The wind began falling at dawn, the light the color of steel coming in through the lift house windows. "Okay, boys," Jones said. "You can go up now. But it's still going to be slow."

They woke Baines, who groaned and stood up stiffly, and they all put on their boots, which had been warming in front of the stove. They put on their parkas and gloves and went out into the suddenly still, steel-cold air, where they stepped into their skis, none of them saying anything, their faces grave. There was a thermometer on the outside wall of the lift house, but Michael refused to look at it.

Jones started the lift and Michael and Cully took the first chair up. It had stopped snowing and the trees of the forest below them made a cemetery of pale symmetrical monuments.

"My guess," Michael said to Cully, "is that our best bet is to try the Black Knight again. I skied all the other runs with him and he never had any trouble with them. But I kept him off the Knight because I didn't want him to get hurt . . ." He left the sentence unfinished.

"Okay," Cully said. "If you have a hunch, it's as good as anything else. Though if we do find anything I'm afraid it's going to be dead."

Cully was the one who saw the handle of the ski pole, just barely sticking out of the piled snow and moving in a little circle. It was about ten yards into the forest, on a line with the big boulder in the middle of the trail.

"This way," Cully shouted, and traversed swiftly between the trees and knelt beside the snow drift above which the pole was making its slow little circles. He was digging frantically with his hands as the others came up to him. In a moment he had uncovered a gloved hand gripping the pole and moving. Michael was digging, too, and felt something hard under the snow. Carefully, he removed handfuls of snow from whatever it was. It was the top of Heggener's head, the blue wool balaclava helmet frozen stiff. A second later, as through a thin white veil, Heggener's face appeared. His lips moved, but there was no sound.

"That's all right, Andreas," Michael kept saying as he held Heggener's head while the others cleared the piled snow off the stiff body, "everything's all right, all right."

Now the others had the snow off him and Cully was feeding him little sips of hot coffee from the thermos bottle he had in his pack and Michael could see by the position of Heggener's right foot that the leg was broken. Somehow Heggener had managed to get his skis off and to dig himself a hole in the snow.

Roughly, tearing at Heggener's cement-stiff clothes, Baines bared a patch of Heggener's skin and injected a shot of camphor, for the heart. Heggener groaned and shut his eyes, which had been staring, unblinkingly, up into the limbs of the tree which had sheltered him. He groaned again as they put him on the sled, his leg in first-aid splints, and covered him with blankets. Then the ski patrol boys took off down the slope with the sled, going straight down without making any turns, one in front between the shafts, the second boy behind holding the ropes to brake the sled.

Michael waited behind while Baines put on his skis. "Unbelievable." Baines kept shaking his head. "He's still alive."

Michael skied behind the doctor. Baines was wobbling and each turn he made looked as though it might be his last, and if he fell and got hurt, Michael wanted to be sure he would not be left alone on the hill.

At the bottom, Cully and the two boys and Harold Jones were putting Heggener into the back of Cully's station wagon. When he saw Michael, Heggener tried to smile and raised his hand a few inches and waved his fingers weakly. "Sorry, Michael," he whispered. "Terribly sorry."

"Don't try to talk, Andreas," Michael said.

Baines got into the back of the station wagon and said to Cully, who was at the wheel, "My place, Dave. And quick."

Michael stood in the parking lot with the ski patrol boys watching the station wagon speed off. Then he turned to the two boys. They were about twenty years old, with childish, innocent faces. Michael had seen them around for months now, but he had never really noticed them before. He didn't know their names, had perhaps said "Hi" only once or twice to them when he had passed them, local boys who made their living at odd jobs when the season was over, American peasants, as Eva would describe them. But now, looking at the youthful faces, grim with the exhaustion of the night's deadly search for a stranger they had probably never even met, Michael wanted to put his arms around both of them, weep with them, tell them that he loved them. But all he said was, "God, it's a good thing you two guys were born."

Then he went over to the Porsche and wearily put his skis on the rack and got behind the wheel and sat there for a minute in silence, too tired to move, as the motor coughed, caught on. Then, maneuvering very carefully, he drove to Dr. Baines's office.

Baines and his nurse and Cully had gotten Heggener's clothes off and Heggener was lying on a white operating table covered with a sheet and Baines had given him a shot of morphine and was gently moving his ankle. Heggener was almost out, but when Michael came into the room he smiled at him drowsily and murmured, "You were right, Michael, that run was not for me." Then he dropped off to sleep.

"He'll live," Baines said. "Fifteen minutes more . . ." He shook his head and did not finish the sentence. "I don't know how or why, but he'll live."

⬦⬦⬦⬦⬦

When Michael and Cully came out of the doctor's office after waiting until the cast was plastered on Heggener's leg and Heggener was in a drugged sleep and the nurse had called for the ambulance from Newburg, the sun was high over the mountains and the sky was blue and the wind had shifted to the south and was soft against the skin, and there was the splash of running water as the snow melted. Cully squinted up at the sky, took a deep breath. "Winter's over," he said. "One more winter. I never know whether to mourn or celebrate."

"Celebrate, Dave," Michael said. "Celebrate."

⬦⬦⬦⬦⬦

"They were very kind to me this morning," Heggener was saying, his right leg, in its cast, propped up over a wire frame at the bottom of the hospital bed. "They took me off the critical list."

He had been on the list for three days, but now the pain had almost disappeared in the injured leg and all his vital signs, Dr. Baines had assured Michael, were back to normal. Michael had only been allowed in to see Heggener for a minute or so a day and Heggener had been warned by Baines not to waste his strength trying to talk. Now his color had returned and he seemed comfortable, breathing deeply in the soft warm wind, with its smell of spring, that came into the cheerful, bright room through the wide-open window.

It was Saturday morning and Michael had his jump suit and boots in the car ready for the skydiving at noon.

"You look especially fine this morning," Heggener said. "As though you're looking forward to a pleasant afternoon."

"I am," Michael said. "I'm going to have a good lunch and then take a long walk through the woods." Somehow, he felt that it would be unwise to tell the man in the bed about the skydiving. Perhaps after it was over. "Dr. Baines is very pleased with you, too."

"For what?"

"For being alive."

Heggener chuckled. "Many people seem to manage it."

"He said it was touch and go there for a while," Michael said seriously. "If you had fallen asleep . . ."

"I made a point of not falling asleep," Heggener said. "I haven't been in the mountains all these many years for nothing. When I found that I was able to crawl to the shelter of that tree and could dig a hole for myself, I knew I had a chance. I discovered once and for all I had no wish to die. So I took the necessary steps to avoid doing so, like moving at all times and keeping my eyes open. You know, I heard you calling my name some time in the middle of the night and tried to call out to you, but the wind was making such a noise and I was covered in snow and I heard your voices fade away down the hill. I must admit, for a while after that, it was difficult for me to keep my eyes open."

"What made you do it, Andreas? Go out alone, in bad weather, down that particular slope? You knew how dangerous it was, didn't you?"

"I knew it was dangerous," Heggener admitted. "But just how dangerous it was going to turn out to be—no. I had received a cable that afternoon. From Eva. In it she said that if I didn't come to Austria immediately, she was going to sue for divorce and marry someone she was seeing there." He sighed. "I couldn't stand staying in that big house alone that afternoon and felt like doing something physical—testing. Some ultimate test. Putting some final, live-or-die questions to myself. You know I've wanted to do that run just one last time and that afternoon seemed like the most fitting time to do it."

"Are you going to Austria?"

"Perhaps if nothing had happened on the mountain I would have skied down and gone home and packed my things and flown to Europe the next day," Heggener said, his voice just above a whisper, "but lying there, helpless, with the snow drifting over me, I made my decision. There are some things in life—like life itself—that you must make enormous, heartbreaking sacrifices to preserve. In this case, what I was preserving was myself. I will be desolate, perhaps, for a long time, without Eva, but I will be my own man and in the long run I will be free of her and my obsession with her." He paused. "And with death. So," he said, smiling faintly, "a night out in the snow can help clear the mind and set things in their proper perspective. We must make use of the facts as they are presented to us. Well, I've talked enough. I know how boring visits to a sick room can be. Go and enjoy your lunch and your long walk in the woods."

Michael leaned over the bed and kissed Heggener's forehead.

"What was that for?" Heggener asked, smiling. "Farewell?"

"No," said Michael, "it was a salute."

He left the hospital feeling invigorated, young and glad to be alive in the fresh spring breeze. All his vital signs, he thought, were sparkling like diamonds.

He drove to the airfield. There were about a thousand people who had assembled to watch the exhibition. He saw that Williams and the other men he was going to jump with were already talking in a little group out on the runway where the plane was standing. He reached back for his jump suit and boots, then let them drop onto the back seat. He got out of the car and walked through the crowd at the edge of the field toward the plane.

"Hey," Williams said as he approached, "you're going to make us late. Where's your suit and boots?"

"I have to talk to you, Jerry," Michael said. "Alone."

He walked away a few paces from the group and Williams followed him.

"What's up, Mike?" Williams asked.

"I'm not jumping," Michael said quietly.

"Oh, Christ," Williams said. "You don't mean to say you're chickening out."

"That's exactly what I mean to say," Michael said. "I'm chickening out. I've given up jumping. Among other things."

"There goes my three-hundred-dollar watch," Williams said. "Shit."

"I'll buy you the watch. It's the least I can do," Michael said. "Make my excuses to the others."

"Mike, you're the last man in the world I'd've thought would do something like this."

"Until a few minutes ago," Michael said, "I'd have thought the same thing. I learned a lesson this morning. It took some time to sink in, but I learned it. If you ask me, I may tell you what it is. It might help you, too." He waved to the men around the plane and walked back through the crowd to the Porsche. He got in and drove back to the hospital.

Heggener was having his lunch and looked up in surprise when he saw Michael enter the room. "Is anything wrong?" he asked, looking anxious.

"Nothing at all."

"I thought you were going to have lunch and go for a long walk."

"That's exactly what I'm going to do," Michael said. "But I have a question to ask you first."

"What is it?"

"Is that job still open?"

"Of course."

"I want it."

"You've got it," Heggener said soberly.

"On one condition."

"What's that?"

"If you promise to be around to help me."

Heggener smiled. "I promise," he said. "I've learned something. Marriage bonds do not a prison make . . ." He picked up the edge of his blanket. "Nor hospital beds a tomb."

"Good," Michael said. "Now go back to your lunch."

He went out of the room and downstairs to the telephone booth at the entrance and called Tracy's number collect because he didn't have any change on him. He smiled when he heard Tracy's voice and heard the operator ask if she would take a collect call from a Mr. Storrs in Vermont.

"Certainly," he heard Tracy say.

"Go ahead, sir," the operator said. "You're connected."

Connected was the word for the morning, Michael thought, as he said, "Hello, Tracy, how are you?"

"I'm fine." Then she said, worriedly, "Are *you* all right?"

"Never better," he said. "I want you to do something for me. I want you to drive up to Green Hollow as soon as you can. I'm planning to build a house here and since you'll be using it, at least on weekends and holidays, I think you ought to be in on choosing the site."

"Oh, Michael." He heard her gasp. "Is it going to work?"

"If it doesn't," he said, "it will be one tremendous try."

"What do I need up there?"

"A warm and forgiving heart."

"Idiot." He heard her laugh. "I mean clothes."

"Whatever you have on at the moment will be perfect," he said. "And thank you for paying for the call. I'll make it up to you somehow."

Then he went and had the lunch and the long walk in the sunny woods he had promised himself.